# I R I S

A FOUNDATION BOOK DOUBLEDAY

New York London Toronto Sydney Auckland

# I R I S

**William Barton and Michael Capobianco**

A Foundation Book
Published by Doubleday, a division of Bantam Doubleday Dell
Publishing Group, Inc.
666 Fifth Avenue, New York, New York 10103

FOUNDATION, DOUBLEDAY, and the portrayal of the
letter F are trademarks of Doubleday, a division of
Bantam Doubleday Dell Publishing Group, Inc.

Library of Congress Cataloging-in-Publication data

Barton, William, 1950–
   Iris/William Barton and Michael Capobianco.—1st ed.
     p.  cm.
   "A Foundation book."
   I. Capobianco, Michael, 1950–   . II. Title.
PS3552.A778I75   1990
813'.54—dc20   89-32501
CIP

ISBN 0-385-26726-6
ISBN 0-385-26727-4 (pbk.)
Copyright © 1990 by William Barton and Michael Capobianco
All Rights Reserved
Printed in the United States of America
February 1990
First Edition
DC

Dedicated to

The Voyager 2
Computer Command
Subsystem

*Ave atque vale*

The Falsehood that exalts we cherish more
Than meaner truths that are a thousand strong.
                                        —PUSHKIN

# I R I S

# O N E

Load. Uplink. Begin.

Achmet Aziz el-Tabari, who called himself Demogorgon the Illimitor Artist, was on his knees before Brendan Sealock, scientist, engineer, gladiator. . . . Cultural labels made a miasma between them that was too thick to be thrust aside. It made them *things,* defying understanding.

He looked up at the man. He looked at the curly, dirty, reddish-blond hair, the acrid green eyes almost hidden in deep, dark wells beneath shaggy brows, at the broad face, with its high, heavy cheekbones, at the flattened nose, the wide, frowning mouth framed with shadowy lines, and the massive jaw. He looked at the thick neck above powerful, rounded shoulders, the heavily muscled chest, and the broad waist with its solid stomach, lightly padded with fat. He looked at the long arms, roped with vein-netted muscles that stood out like an anatomical chart. He ran his hands over the corded tree-trunk legs through a thin layer of light cloth.

So . . . His own voice whispered to him from far away, rhyming rhymes, naming names. Culture, it said, and tradition . . . "Brendan. Tell me again why you won't do anything *with* me?"

The man smiled faintly. "You're the faggot here, not me. Besides, I'm your . . . what is it you call me?"

"You're my 'Great Dark Man,' Brendan. It's from a book that was written more than a hundred and fifty years ago."

"Yeah." He laced his fingers through Demogorgon's coarse black hair and jammed his crotch forward into the man's face. "So get to work."

As the man's sharp nose began to jab rhythmically against his abdomen, Sealock settled back to look out through the deopaqued section of wall opposite him. Iris was a bright light in the star-sequined perpetual night and it attracted a deep longing in him, the way so many other things had in the past. Perhaps this too would be a disappointment—but he had to go on trying until success or death made an end to things. Why do they want me to feel their pain? he wondered. Isn't it enough that I feel my own? Against a rising tide of orgasmic inevitability, he saw images of himself in the prize ring, bloodying opponents, and this was supplanted by the dark, carved-ivory face of Ariane Methol.

Almost alone, he thought. Almost, but not quite.

Sealock wiped the sweat from his brow, running blunt fingers through the dense snarls of his own hair, and once again felt the twelve sockets embedded in his skull.

Dreams without number laid themselves down in concentric tracks throughout John Cornwell's mind. Music . . . Not music, just the idea of music. The effect alone, not the thing itself.

It was 2097 and now humankind was irrevocably changed. Those manifestations of the physical world that had entertained and ravaged people were ebbing away, becoming less important. Reality had become an eerie technological ocean, and mankind a frenzied swimmer in its electronic deeps.

2

Only a little more than a generation before, an easy and acceptable means of plugging human minds into the already vast information processing and retrieval networks had been invented. Its ramifications were universal and its tendrils extended into virtually every phase of human endeavor.

Comnet had been born in 2063. It was the ultimate networking system, finishing off a task begun over a century before, and it grew effortlessly until it had engulfed the world. Parents had lived their lives mediated by computers, voice actuators, and 3V screens, long accustomed to the devices that surrounded them, but the children . . . increasingly, humanity lived with its minds in the wires, and the momentum of change followed a quickening tempo.

For now, men and women might live lives recognizable to their ancestors. Similar things would make them unhappy, similar things would seem unpleasant; but life was changing. A tender trap was engulfing them, drawing the subjective world in step by step, with neither will nor collective acknowledgment.

The mental echoes of the last barrage went away, and John relaxed, disengaging from RedShipnet, his composition program. He energized his suit and the em-field stuck him to his chair with a creaky plop. His new piece, the induction-music suite *Rose of Ash*, was finished.

Tallish and wiry, Cornwell's tonus was a testament to the procedures they had used to cope with almost two years of weightlessness. His face was slightly oriental, with dark brown eyes and a strong chin that showed his mixed heritage. His great-grandmother had been an Innuit from the Baffin region of the Canadian Archipelago. His hair was black, cut short enough for the pate to show through and lighten it. He was wearing red fullbodies, with a *Deepstar*/Iris logo on the chest. Around his head was a metal diadem holding an array of focus nodes for induction transfer and his Shipnet interface.

Induction music, a subset of the induced entertainment industry that had brought him fame and a vast fortune, was something more than audio music and, for many, something less. A more appropriate term might have been "data music."

**3**

Although most 'net access was via a feed to the various sensory nexi, it was sometimes useful to choose an adaptable area in the subdominant parietal lobe and feed it data.

He had been one of the first to realize that this data feed was accompanied by certain emotions, analogous to those of music input. The bandwidth for induction music was much greater and there was some spatial perception within the sequential flow. To his astonishment, he'd found that most people responded strongly to his "music." An industry and an art had been born.

The playback of the music had brought up strange emotions in him. Right there, in the middle of it, was his breakup with Beth. They had been acting the part of strangers now for months, yet in the limited confines of the Command Module they saw each other constantly. It was all too much for him. Everything was mutating into the opposite of what he wanted.

There was a tiny crackle of static and the hatch of his personal compartment opened into four spreading segments which retracted into the bulkhead. Jana Li Hu, Chinese and naked, appeared in the entrance. "Finished?"

He phased back into Shipnet and gave the command to transmit. "It should get there in six hours or so. I've got the best scramble money can buy, but circpirates'll probably get it anyway. What's up?"

Hu pushed her way into the room, a baby crawling in three dimensions. She was short and built compactly. Her face was central Chinese: round, with high cheekbones and a small, flat nose. A dull black, 500-cm. ponytail floated behind her head. Cornwell looked into her eyes and noticed, for the thousandth time, a hard, unchanging quality that unnerved him. This woman was his new girlfriend?

"Why do you care about piracy?" she said. "You've said yourself that money will have no real use where we're going. Residuals on *Triton* alone will buy all the data we'll ever need." She assumed a stable float about two meters over his head, with her body at a forty-five-degree angle to his own. Normally self-conscious, she was playing a little game. "Turnaround's coming."

He called up the present high-mag view of Iris and accessed pertinent data concerning the voyage. The information flowed via electromagnetic induction to the optical centers of his brain and was presented to him in a complex visual array, superimposed over his view of the room like a fantastic, detailed afterimage.

The sight of the planet was riveting. Every time he looked at it, Cornwell was amazed by the continually more resolved image. As with Luna, there was something that fought against seeing it as a sphere. It was simply a white circle, three-banded, surrounded by a dim, blue disk maybe a diameter bigger, and cut by the ever more obvious ring, which, since they were coming in close to its plane, was just a thin line. The ring shadow was obliterated somewhere in the immense blue atmosphere and never made it to the "surface."

He scanned the data coming out in the lower right-hand segment of his vision field, not feeling the muscles of his eyes move, yet not aware of the projection's unreality. They were 41.947 AU from Sol and 0.229 AU from Iris. Here, far from the sun, it was dark, lonely, and cold. They might just as well be in the depths of interstellar space.

The numbers told the story. It was 701.891 days since they'd detached their little ship from the Jovian transport *Camelopardalis* and 696.668 days since they'd shut down *Deepstar's* engine. The ship would soon be turned around to fire the heavy-ion reaction drive for Iridean orbital injection. "It's just about ten hours and forty-one minutes away." Computers bred precision; language didn't.

"I can't believe the trip's finally ending," said Hu, clinging to a no-g handhold on the back edge of a console/desk. "I feel like the world is coming to an end."

John nodded slowly. "That's a thing about long trips I first realized when I was about twelve. When a journey ends, it's like a confirmation your life will end too. I tried to deal with that a little bit in *Rose*."

Jana seemed not to be listening. "The parameters for the satellites are *scary*," she said. "Despite what theory predicts, bodies this volatile-rich are something new."

"We've been through this all before."

"I'm just trying to tell you," she said, "I can't certify that we'll be safe."

Cornwell wanted to reach out and make contact, but something held him back. The subject was raised and the conversation had to be finished. "We've discussed the problems of trying to build on highly volatile material. We're going to need an area of water-ice, and Ocypete's huge mare—"

"Ocellus."

"Ocellus, bull's-eye, basin, whatever you want to call it. Even though it's buried under a thin regolith of neon ice, I've seen your analysis of how it was produced. It looks like a good place to me."

"The ocellus is an anomaly, John. It shouldn't be there. I can explain it, sure enough; but I have to make up an extremely unlikely scenario to do so." She pulled herself down into his reference vertical.

"We've got the equipment to handle a large uncertainty. You know that."

Jana shook her head and reached out, caressing John's neck. "I know it . . . but I've been running this garbage through my head over and over, ever since we passed by Triton for this . . . adventure. It's an oddness in the pit of my stomach."

Cornwell laughed and released himself from the em-field. He gave the woman a push and then launched himself after her. She sailed past his sleeping module and lodged in a corner, catching hold of the resilient, almost mushy wall surface. Ducking under his embrace, she leaped away, and they caromed about until he had her cornered. He grabbed her by both arms and was, as always, surprised to find that she wasn't joking, she was fighting for real.

A small fist, half balled, caught him on the cheek, spinning them slowly in opposite directions. "Stop it!" he said, helplessly hanging near her, unable to reach a wall. "What's the matter with you?"

Jana's face, half wild, slowly moderated, softened. She reached out for a handhold, then for him, steadying, a delicate touch. "I'm sorry," she said. "I don't know. I guess I do need you." She pulled on his hand, drawing them together.

He looked into her face, trying to fathom whatever it was that he saw there. What to say? Nothing. John felt a little pang of self-dread. Whatever came out next, it would lack the tone, timbre, and meaning that should be there. He tried. "Isn't this what we left Earth for—uncertainty? Maybe it's an adventure, maybe not. No matter what you and the others think, we *are* doing *something*. Triton would have been one thing—a fairly new colony at the edge of terrestrial influence —but we'll be the *first* at Iris. . . ." The little line editor in his head was agonizing over this. Their interaction was following its own course, beyond his understanding. He began to feel aroused. "In a way we'll be the first people to reach another star, if you want to call it that. Doesn't that make you want to stop and say, 'Gee whiz,' or something?"

He wanted to cringe, to laugh at himself and give up the ghost of effort. Talk was only a pleasant noise, after all, and he was already working his way downward, touching her, brushing at the nearly invisible hairs on her back and buttocks. The attention, the touching were communication, very likely what she really wanted. Things were hard to see in the absence of real closeness. The thought snagged at him, briefly. Downlink Rapport was available, but these people shied away, always pulled back from the brink. It was *too* personal. Too close.

Cornwell sighed. This relationship had fallen into a pattern that mirrored what had developed among the ten passengers aboard *Deepstar*. He pleasured her, yes, as she wished, and got very little in return, save for her presence in his life as a confidante. She acted the part of his friend, but he doubted whether she was capable of such a thing. In the void that had formed after he and Beth broke up, he had wanted Jana, and had gotten her. . . .

She controlled the sex and had aversions to many things, penetration perhaps not the least of them. His enjoyment would be limited. Sometimes, in the midst of her strange, hoarse cries, he would have an idea for a data-motif.

Suddenly the feelings that *Rose* had brought came again, more strongly. He remembered the last time he and Beth had made love. Her response to him, though much diminished from the early days back in CFE, was still almost magical. He missed her. Guiltily, he called up an image of her, all the while caressing Hu.

Elizabeth Toussaint's dark, oval face hung before him in a kind of timeless space, framed by small black ringlets, barely showing the diagonal cheek lines that, from certain angles, gave her a rare beauty. She had a broad, pixy-like nose and her eyes, dark with cosmetic mystery, were large and happy. Looking at this image, he couldn't help but notice that her chin was weak and her pouting lips overlarge.

The tenderness gave way to cold anger. It *was* her fault. The image winked out.

Enjoying the feel of the sheet of warm rubber that was her skin, he kissed Jana's stomach, stroked her hips, her thighs, and went on.

In his compartment, Harmon Prynne lay meshed in the em-field of his bed, like a fly trapped on the surface scum of a butterscotch pudding. He was a delicate-seeming man, though robust; Irish-looking, with reddish-orange hair and freckles. His pale blue eyes were shiny and bloodshot. He was a mere technician, universally regarded as the stupidest person on the ship, and everyone liked him. Through his Shipnet connection, he watched what transpired in a sparsely appointed room. It was eavesdropping, easy to do, hard to resist.

Two people were locked together, tumbling end over end in the absence of gravity. The circumstances made their nudity all the more interesting. One was Vana Berenguer, a short, thick-waisted woman with swarthy skin and long clouds of coarse dark hair. The other, Temujin Krzakwa, was tall, fat, and hairy, with an immense curly beard the color of brown sand that flowed luxuriantly around the woman's thighs. Their mismatched heights and Krzakwa's paunch made it difficult for the woman to reach him.

Prynne shut his eyes and tried to make the image go away, but it wouldn't. He thought the words "channel down," and, one by one, images of amazing vividness but little or no portent filled his brain. He stopped at an image that re-

**8**

minded him of his home in Florida. A quiet, sun-washed shore presented itself, and a turquoise-blue sea rolled into foam upon it. The vantage point was maybe five meters in the air and slightly inshore, and here there was another couple making love. They were different . . . somehow cleaner. And yet, as they held each other and looked out at a sunrise that he could see in their eyes, he couldn't stand to watch anymore. He shut his eyes again, hard, and said, "Off," this time vocally. As the image died, he felt globules of water hanging without weight on his eyelashes, making them clump together.

Aksinia Ockels put down her "book," a loosely bound sheaf of pages she'd had printed up, and took a gulp of the smoky creosote called Lapsang Souchong. She was a tall woman, light-complexioned, and had a rather strange face, flat, square-jawed, with a ski-jump nose. Her hair was a mousy brown, loosely curled, and she had cheeks that were often naturally flushed. The taste of the tea never failed to call up visions of her days living at the Hotel Lisboa, reading book after book on the beach, burning despite generous applications of paba, and waiting endlessly for her mother to decide to leave. At twelve, she was not yet pubescent, and the world seemed clean and fantastic. The years she had spent in schoolplant were far in the past and life had been without unpleasant intimations.

For the thousandth time she wondered, How did I get here?

She remembered the quick and cumulative wilting of her world-view during the following years. When she met Daniel, and he'd deflowered her in Paris Commune, at thirteen, she had substituted love for happiness. When it didn't last, she had nothing. Her wandering had started only after many hideous, interminable shouting matches with her parents, and in the many years since then she'd lived amicably, alone. Only Beta-2, a complex brain-chemical derivative, supplied her with the inner vision she'd had as a child. And the time had come for her shot.

The apothecary mounted in her mag case made a tiny

chirring noise and burped forth a blistersac containing her standard dose of Beta-2. For the briefest moment she beheld the capsule, regretting the social side effects that had come with her addiction. Anticipation coursed along her nerves, a velvet static electricity.

She held the blister under the line of her jaw and popped it: the osmotic solution in which the drug was held spurted through her skin, saturating the blood in her carotid artery, filling her mind with a feeling of *rightness* that she treasured.

She pulled out an induction circlet and placed it on her head, rearranging the fall of her hair to regularize the fit. The circuitry would find her brain centers, but it needed to be near the right place. As she turned to the doorway, the world, burnished with a chemical sense of wonder, ballooned before her.

A cold infrastar fell from the darkness of interstellar space. It seemed to hang poised, as if waiting, inside Pluto's aphelion, deep within Sol's gravitational sway. It was, though, going fast enough, and its path along a conic section would never close. The little star was only a visitor.

Had Pluto been on the same side of the Solar System, the thing would have given itself away long before. Even so, its 0.58 of Earth's mass should have been easily detectable, would have been, had anyone been looking. The search for a trans-Plutonic planet had, however, been abandoned seventy years before. Astronomy itself had changed from the early days of randomly scattered observation into a rigid and systematic cataloging of the heavens conducted almost entirely from a single great multi-observatory on Luna's farside. It had changed so much that it had a different name: asterology.

In one of the little coincidences that add flavor to reality, Cometary Halo probe Oort IX, launched from Callisto in 2085, had gone off course—far off course—and there seemed to be only one possible explanation: a gravitational perturbation produced by a very large object some 42 AU out.

The men with telescopes and photorecorders, mostly hobbyists, looked. And there, glowing in the long infrared, was a planetary object, intensely cold and sending back solar radiation in the striking deep blue of Rayleigh scattering. Those with sufficient resolving power saw that it also bore a ring rivaling Saturn's and three tiny satellites.

That such an object could form on its own out of the vast clouds of galactic dust and gas was a matter for long and bitter debate, but there could be no doubt: an independent body so small and cold that it could hardly be called a star was passing. In the quiet offices of the IAAU Working Group on Asterological Nomenclature, a WGS-07 mythology coordinator decided to call this new object Iris, and the satellites Aello, Podarge, and Ocypete, after the rainbow goddess and her sisters, the harpies.

As he emerged from an airlock mounted on the rear of the CM, Temujin Krzakwa felt the fear and paranoia that had characterized his Lunar personality coming back to him like a scream in the night. It was easy, inside, to forget. The ship was *it*—everything that was human, a fragile house in the dead, bodiless, perpetual winter darkness. He closed his eyes and flexed the springy em-pads that were his primary adhesion to the CM's hull. He wouldn't come off. Sealock popped up before him through a shimmering circle at his feet and gave him a facetiously tender pat on the helmet. Krzakwa made a rude gesture in return and heard a laugh through the audio link.

*Deepstar*'s structural tower, a matrix of metal-plastic girders stretching into the fifty-meter distance, was greatly foreshortened from this perspective. The elongated cylinders of differing lengths around the outside were all that made the ship look substantial. Without the appended containers, it was just four skeletal isosceles prisms, connected by their long bases, surrounding the ultrarigid bulk of a heavy-ion engine. At the aft end of the ship was a toroid with quatrefoil outriggers on which the Hyloxso engines were mounted.

They made their way along an inner vertex between a Hyloxso cylinder and one containing fusion water, inspecting, looking. It wasn't until they mounted the ion-drive emission unit that Iris cleared the stern and stared hard at them.

Tem stopped for a moment to look. It seemed he could just make out the Rayleigh-scattering atmosphere around a

**1 1**

barely discernible disk. He gazed at the thing, trying to imagine just what he was doing here and, after a while, became aware that Sealock had stopped beside him, motionless, silent. He turned to look at the other man, a dim human-shape with a cylinder for a head, silhouetted before the still blinding pinprick of the sun. "What do you think?" He gestured toward the planet.

"I don't know." It was his most commonplace answer. People took it for many things, but Krzakwa always understood it as: "I don't want to tell you. . . ." A perplexing man.

Sealock stood for a while longer, wrapped in himself, then said, "Let's go. We've got to make sure everything is perfect now. Don't want to wind up a smoking hole in the ice, do we?"

Krzakwa looked at the mazy interconnection of metallic lines, whistling softly to himself, almost a whisper, human static that the 'net would filter out. The last course correction had not produced any major structural damage. Despite its fragile appearance, the craft's em-reinforced infrastructure could withstand very large linear forces. Hoping that the landing on Ocypete would be easy, he imagined a nominal performance.

They floated free a meter or so from the main load-bearing girder of *Deepstar*'s dorsal external vertex, moving toward the nose. Sealock stopped short, and Tem could see what had provoked the reaction: the smooth metallic sheen of the member was discolored by a faint ripple of iridescence, a spectral glistening, as of oil on water.

"Shit," said Sealock.

The Selenite looked at the featureless cylinder that housed his companion's head. "Shear stress?"

"Just a minute." Through a lead plugged into his head, the man sent a command via Shipnet to his suit. It obediently altered its optical system and relayed the result back to him through the same conduit. He examined the area microscopically, across both the gamma and X-ray bands, then cursed again. "The whole cross section has gone monoclinic on us. Even worse, it's buckled at least five milliarcsec out of true. I can't get any closer with this suit's reticle."

**1 2**

Krzakwa looked out over the long expanse of the ship for a moment, letting machines calculate quickly, then said, "That's not enough to cause a structural failure."

"No." Sealock grinned, an unseen baring of teeth. "Not by a long shot. . . . But what the hell. We might as well fix it." It made him think of all the times he'd heard the Lunar government's tired old slogan, "If it's not broken, don't fix it." Here, he could but try. "All right." Another pause, unfilled. "How do you want to do this?"

"Mmh." He blinked into the darkness that surrounded him, thinking. "I've only got two leads in this helmet and Shipnet's not as flexible as it could be . . . not yet, anyway. Why don't we split up the job? You take the rebrace fixture and I'll handle the electron-beam welder, OK?"

A year or so before, that would have been an impatient command. Krzakwa wished briefly that he could get a handle on what his odd friend was thinking. There was a way, of course, but . . . He had to laugh at himself, silently. Even if it could be done involuntarily, secretly, like the work of some telepathic spy . . . well, he too had only two leads to work with, and they were the far less efficient induction leads at that. With such a setup, he would be hard enough pressed to handle communications, suit control, optic response, and a work-pack. Something so complex as Downlink Rapport would be out of the question, even if Shipnet were already in the proper configuration. He smiled, invisibly, to himself. "OK."

"I'll call the equipment."

In response to a series of commands, two work-packs in a service module external-access bay came to life. In a minute they were dancing along on their spindly legs, picking a path through *Deepstar*'s openwork array of girders like a pair of armored, weapons-toting spiders. "Ready?"

Krzakwa responded with a nonverbal assent, a fragment of knowledge transmitted to the other. For a moment he felt helpless—understanding to the nth degree the physics of a situation such as this one wasn't much help. . . . It was, of course, foolish to feel this way, but how could one avoid these sorts of feelings?

"Inphase, please." In a work situation, Sealock was completely focused on the business at hand, his normally harsh tone and rancorous manner banished behind a fairly leakproof screen.

The Selenite activated the final reserves of his suit-born resources and tensed as he felt the command/control impulses flood his conscious mind. The rebrace fixture machine was routed through a duodecimal program aspect of Shipnet and, while his handling of the device was suborned to a built-in self-awareness subplot, it took over quite a few reflex responses as well. He walked the machine behind the damaged girder, set its adjustment verniers, and then used a resistance heater to de-blackbody the metal-plastic matrix of the warped region.

When all was ready, he transmitted a squirt of data to Sealock, who began his task. The welder scuttled into place and lit off. An angstrom-thin collimated particle beam sliced away the affected area, which adhered to the fixture device and melted, going into a polyclastic state. Stresses were set up and, as the mixture cooled, the proper orthorhombic array reappeared. Simultaneously, calipers pulled the now isolated beam-ends back to zero azimuth. The welder reattached the cut-out segment and, when it had settled back into its blackbody state, they were done.

Sealock resurfaced out of the 'net depths laughing. "That was kind of fun. Good job. Come on, let's go in and torture everybody about how smart we are."

Even after two years, Krzakwa found himself marveling at the man's abrupt changes of manner. He could be crazy, I suppose, but . . . hell. Who knows? His musings faded out, and they went in.

To the crew of a terrifyingly expensive but essentially homemade spaceship somewhere off Neptune, the news of Iris' coming had struck with electrifying madness. They had been bound for Triton, the last frontier of human civilization, fleeing an angst that was not easy to identify. . . .

Their reasons for leaving Earth were manifold and well thought out. Their destination had been picked simply because there was no place farther away to which they could go. The stars were too far. The comet cloud . . . maybe, maybe not. They had to have water ice for their fusion plant, and remote exploration had been inadequate. It would have been too long a voyage, in any case. Now this thing fell across their space, in reach, adventurous. . . .

A quick vote was taken, a seemingly unanimous decision made, and a vessel built by the fortune of one of the world's most popular artists made a gravity-boost phasing maneuver around Neptune into a Solar-retrograde orbit, headfirst toward an onrushing mystery.

The Command Module of *Deepstar,* shaped roughly like a cylinder, was divided into three floors, perpendicular to its long axis. The middle and by far largest floor was designed with ten personnel compartments around its periphery, surrounding a gear-shaped room that comprised fully half the habitable volume of the CM. This central chamber had been outfitted with a ramfloor, from which a myriad of couches, tables, and other memomolecular shapes could be extruded on demand. In its center was a p-curtained door leading aft, and forward access was through the ceiling to the next deck, where the kitchen module was housed. Directions were defined by the pull of em-fields on clothing.

As they gathered for a final preinsertion briefing, the central room had been reconfigured into a sunken amphitheater and everyone was em-stuck to its surface except for Aksinia Ockels, who was late. She hung above them for an instant like some huge, gauzy-winged insect/bird hybrid, then assumed a sitting position. She touched the static-node of her clothing, creating a faint breath of em-force, and settled like a dust mote on the edge of the upholstered crater.

Jana Li Hu looked up from an attitude of concentration, licking her upper lip slowly. Annoyed at the woman's interruption, she glanced at the rest of the group. Placed at odd angles, they wore induction circlets around their heads, except for Sealock and Krzakwa, who had waveguides plugged into an unobtrusive gang-tap. Ariane Methol made a triad with them. She was a slim, mid-sized woman with a dark, lustrous mestizo complexion, fathomlessly expressive eyes,

**15**

and shiny black hair worn just over shoulder length. Unrestrained by gravity, it floated in a shifting nimbus around her head. Her face was pretty and regular, though not really remarkable. It was the sort of face people had come to expect on a fashion model simulacrum: narrow, smooth, and cool.

She was a polytech engineer, specializing in Comnet subprogram debugging, and, in some ways, was the best in the world at what she did. There were others who knew more, others more skilled, but they were research scientists, useless in a tight commercial universe.

"OK." Hu was flat-voiced, angry. "To continue with the summary of planetography . . ." As she spoke, images illustrating the subject matter entered the minds of her listeners and textual data were superimposed on their vision fields. She wanted to present it fully, to force all the information on them, despite their disinterest. She had no illusion that some of them would retain what she said, or even understand it. But she would make the effort anyway.

"As you can see, the extreme smoothness of the ocellus on III is plain evidence, at least to me, of the enormously slow process of resolidification. This implies that either there was a forced eccentricity in this presently very regular system or else an object impacted on III that was itself a source of heat energy. To account for the paucity of craters we see here, we must posit, in addition to the extreme enhancement of cratering rates on the leading hemisphere relative to the trailing, a very long-lived glacial annealing process.

"Though superficially it looks like the basins on Tethys and Titania, it seems to be a different phenomenon. The data suggest that a small body, fifty kilometers or less in diameter, wrought profound changes in the entire object, melting a fifth of its total volume. You can see how the craters covering the remainder of the moon are lacking in relief. What you see are the remains of old craters at some depth, covered by the neon, argon, and other gases that constituted III's atmosphere during this period. . . ."

Suddenly, Ariane spoke up. "What does that mean, a body that tiny as source of heat?"

Tem said, "Any concentration of radionuclide would do,

though it would have to have a relatively short half-life. I wonder what cosmological process would concentrate it?"

"I *have* already given this matter a great deal of thought," said Jana. "The total disruption of any second-generation macrobody that had completely fractionated would account for it. My report to the IAAU-PD will suggest as much."

"Do you think that this 'body' was part of the Iridean system?" asked John.

"Unlikely since we're dealing with a planetary system that formed out of almost pristine type-2 galactic material. Iris and her satellites show a general depletion of *all* radionuclides, as well as a scarcity of transironic elements. It was probably an intruder."

"What about mascons?" asked Krzakwa. "Is there one under the ocellus?"

"There's a slight gravitational anomaly associated with it, but this object sank almost to the center of Ocypete, so it's difficult to resolve it from the silicate core in general.

"Iris itself is very different from the gas giants we're used to. Aside from its small size, hardly half again the diameter of the Earth and only about 0.58e-mass, and slow rotation rate, it's meteorologically bland. Except at the very lowest levels, where there is a slow convective overturning, the atmosphere is quiescent. Iris, or at least the eighty percent of its total mass that is gaseous, has differentiated, giving rise to the Rayleigh-scattering mantle, which is a thick layer of hydrogen and, underneath it, a thinner stratum of helium. The surface of the white ball within is made up of nitrogen cirrus not unlike the obscuring haze of Saturn. I should point out that Iris is losing considerable mass due to solar irradiation. It has only been able to maintain its current mass/diameter ratio because of the extreme cold."

Aksinia laughed. "You mean it's evaporating?"

Jana nodded. "If it stayed this distance from Sol, it would dwindle to about a fifth of its present size, at which point its gravitation would be sufficient to permit retention of the remaining gases. . . . I can see by some of your faces that that seems counterintuitive. You think that the smaller it gets the less able it should be to retain anything. Well, that's true

—but it's a simple matter of the point at which the velocities in the excited gases attain escape velocity for that particular depth in the gravitational field. There are plenty of elementary texts in the library . . ."

Another look about. Too many faces were blank. Some of them didn't know enough for *anything* to be counterintuitive. Once again, she wondered what the hell they were doing out here. . . . She sighed, and went on. "Anyway, Iris' magnetosphere is very low grade, almost nonexistent, so we won't have to waste energy on a charged-particle shield.

"The Iridean ring is very much like Saturn's, without, of course, the gaps that give Saturn's its unique appearance. Iris' ring is nearly opaque, and it has a greater proportion of millimeter and smaller particles, there not being much in the way of magnetic sweeping here. Aello is an interesting small body which shows no immediately identifiable endogenic asterologic features. It's probably the best chance we'll ever get to examine a nearly pristine, totally undifferentiated body composed of cryogenic volatiles. Podarge is much like the many similar-sized moons in the Solar System, showing resurfaced terrains and an albedo asymmetry due to preferential gardening of the 'front' hemisphere. Considering that the materials making up these satellites are extremely volatile, we've seen few surprises. The colder temperatures have been a powerful force influencing these exotic ices to behave in a familiar fashion.

"As you might guess, my report is much more detailed." Jana concluded by showing them a skilled 3V collage of Iris and its satellites projected against the tapestry of a deep-space sky. The thing was prettier than any out-the-window view they'd seen since rounding Jupiter. There was a long moment of silence. "Next business, then." She looked at Cornwell.

The musician nodded, pulling off his circlet, but he waited for a while before he spoke. "Maybe this isn't the correct time to bring this up. I don't know. We've got some big adaptations to make in the near future. The ten of us are going to be building a colony, perhaps not very isolated in the sense that we will still have access to many of the benefits of Comnet on

**18**

a delayed basis, but isolated in the sense that we're going to have to provide each other with human society." He stopped, sighed heavily, wondering where his prepared words had gone. "The 'quest' is over. Now we have to get into the period of living happily ever after. It's hard not to see how stupidly we've been treating each other. We're all familiar with the emotional difficulties that come from being in the midst of too many people. . . . Some of us are here to escape just that. Well. I'm not sure we've come to grips with the problems of being in a permanent small group. When this adventure first occurred to me, I envisioned us becoming more closely knit, perhaps even experimenting with induction rapport. . . . The opposite is what seems to be happening."

He stopped, looking at them all, seeking some kind of response. What he saw was that they were waiting for him to continue, to draw some kind of conclusion. Obviously, when you stated a problem, most people expected you to propose some kind of solution. He sought for something to say, some plea for reasonableness, but it was too late.

Sealock wasn't smiling, not even his usual contemptuous smirk, as he said, "I imagine we all saw this coming. *You're* dissatisfied with your life. Now you want to tinker with the rest of us. . . ."

Taken aback, John started to say something, but another voice interrupted.

"It's just *boredom!*" said Harmon Prynne.

By this time Aksinia had broken out of whatever trance state was keeping her quiet, and she reacted to the previous remark. "Come on, Brendan. He's right, of course. We're turning into a bunch of jerks. It seems to me that not one of us has come to grips with the reality of this situation."

*"Reality?* What the hell . . ." Sealock grinned at her and shook his head. "I wonder how many of you really understand your own perceptions?" He nodded at Prynne. "It's not boredom, and I refuse to speculate on the nature of someone's reality perception. . . . Sure, there's a lot of friction here. Some of it comes from an unwillingness to recognize that different people have different interests. Some-

times, when I say something, even something I'm supposed to be an expert in, people act like it's some kind of personal reproach."

"Maybe it's the way you do it," said Prynne. "You make me feel like shit sometimes."

"That's exactly it. Your feelings are magnified by what you imagine other people think. That doesn't need to happen."

John gave Sealock a pained look. "That's your idea of a joke, I suppose. . . . Look, certain individuals may or may not be the primary instigators of ill feeling on *Deepstar.* Nonetheless, every one of us has some kind of relationship with every other person here. Those relationships don't seem to be working too well. . . . I have to believe that we're all decent, intelligent people. We all have good traits. Why can't we all be friends?"

Sealock was staring at him, slit-eyed, face frozen. It was an unpleasant look to be the target of, and he wondered just what it was he'd said to offend the man *this* time.

"Are you sure that's what we want?" asked Vana.

Cornwell looked at her in surprise. Over the months, he'd come to see her as a pleasant, unmotivated individual who didn't know what she wanted, maybe didn't know much of anything. . . .

She went on: "All this random fucking that we do is all right with me. . . . I mean, it's sort of my specialty, after all." She gazed at Sealock, whose expression was even more unreadable than it had been. "I *really* don't know how I'm supposed to feel toward you all. Sex is one thing, sure. It's fun. But . . . *friends?* I just don't know. You're all so . . . demanding."

"Out of the mouths of babes . . ." muttered Sealock.

Ariane broke in. "I guess I agree with Vana. We know there's sex, and something people call love, whatever it may be, and an even more ethereal concept called friendship. . . . To integrate any two of these, much less all three, seems like a very large undertaking. I'd like to think it was possible, though."

"None of you talk about love very much," said Prynne,

"and, when you do, you act like it's something you can control. . . . But you can't."

"I'd settle for a little more sex, if I have any choice," said Sealock, but the others ignored him, and suddenly he was awash in a flood of unwanted memories. Krzakwa caught a bit of it through the Octa-deka Prime control circuit that they shared and looked at him with astonishment. He was, apparently against his will, sending out an image of a day three years before, somewhere in Tupamaro Arcology, in Montevideo. Cornwell had come to discuss the *Deepstar* venture with Ariane Methol, and the two of them had gone to her room . . . And there was Sealock, pressed against a cool outside wall of the chamber, visualizing the woman locked in a tight embrace with the handsome musician. His eyes shut and he was riven by a dense bolt of hatred. The image snapped out, buried under a mountain of recontrol.

No one else seemed to have caught it. Krzakwa shook off the alien emotions, still a little startled, and listened again.

"It seems to me," said John, "that the demands of keeping our friendships intact are very much increased by this pair-bonding stuff." He glanced involuntarily at Beth. "You can call it 'love' if you want to, but jealousies naturally arise from people forming couples and excluding others from their emotional life."

Beth spoke for the first time. "I have given all of this a lot of thought—all of you know what happened between John and me on the way out. You know he wanted to do Downlink Rapport with me, right? Although I think that's going too far, there is much that he has said that I think is good. We planned this colony together, and the possibilities were so . . . Look. It's simple enough—he wants us to drop all our preconceived notions of what the word 'relationship' means. You know: we should all be available for one another's needs, care for one another, sleep together. He wants us all to experience the kind of intense, pain-free friendship that he imagines must exist and, in so doing, share it with him . . . to triumph over despair. To do away with what he calls 'willful pain.' I wish him luck. I'd like a world like that."

"I guess this is kind of dumb," said Krzakwa, "but I do

**2 1**

remember how it felt with my ex-wife, back in the beginning. I imagined that I could live selflessly. I suppose it was all some kind of a lie. It certainly didn't last long. But I don't have any objections to giving a more shared life a try. . . ."

There might have been more, and John was feeling some small glimmerings of hope, but Ariane, who had been monitoring a timeline curve, suddenly said, "Now."

Sealock reintegrated with a start and said, "Right."

Krzakwa and Methol bowed their heads, their eyes going unfocused. Brendan smiled faintly, abstractedly, as if he'd thought of an amusing scene from the far past, and reached out to grasp their hands in a séance-like parody. They made a momentary tableau, motionless. His eyes rolled back, leaving the others to contend with the blank-eyed visage of a madman.

The air seemed to change. What had been "Trois Gymnopédies" gave way to a gurgling roar that was being transmitted through the structure of the ship. The ion drive was firing, allowing *Deepstar* to fall along a parabola around Iris.

Hand in hand, like three magic jinn on a flying rug, Methol, Sealock, and Krzakwa guided *Deepstar* toward its goal. In an earlier generation, a simpler age, it would have been done by the automatic will of preplanned machine action; but with Comnet's shipborne child in their fingertips, they did it all themselves, consciously. At the close of the twenty-first century, still riding the bow shock of an ever growing distaste for what had been called "robots," what a computer program might have done was often accomplished by the linkage and direct extension of human minds. So they skittered along with their souls in the wires, in the polyphase modulation waveguides, and did what had to be done. It was precise, it was fast, and it was fun.

Why ride in a spaceship when you can be one?

To a hypothetical observer outside, the approach of *Deepstar* would have been impressive. Falling toward Iris across a star-stippled backdrop, the ship was just a subtly glowing maze: a regular array of girders and struts, studded heavily with the metal and plastic polyhedrons of life system, cargo, and equipment. The blunt cylinders that were fuel tanks and Hyloxso propellant canisters threw back light in sharp lines and the whole was topped by a dark, squat canister that caught something of the dim, distant sun.

Suddenly there was a dazzling glare. A great actinic burst defaced the velvet darkness, diffuse and white around its periphery, tinged a hard red-violet in the opaque core.

To a mind fed vaster quantities of semiraw data, the fire haze would resolve itself into the blazing exhaust plume of a heavy-ion motor; a dense beam of Element 196 nuclei, almost coherent as it jetted from its emission nozzle at relativistic speed. It would fluoresce in the far ultraviolet as the artificial ions decayed into alpha particles only attoseconds after their impulse was spent.

While the three engineers indulged in the almost gratuitous joy of flying the ship they had, in large measure, built, the others moved about in the sudden novelty of renewed gravity. *Deepstar* was decelerating at something like 0.1g, and it felt strange. They had been pressed to the floor by their responsive em-suits, but now they could feel organs settling and twinges from muscles that had had no natural exercise for almost two years. The inertial field pulled at them like an alien presence.

After the others wandered off, together and alone, Harmon Prynne stayed and, donning his circlet, adjusting it like some old fedora, tried to follow what was going on. He was a competent technician but, as what amounted to a household appliance repairman, he was far out of his depth even in the lowest reaches of Octa-deka Prime. Riding far above his usual duodecimal limits on the wings of a "Guardian Angel" monitor program, he was able to sample what it must be like to fly in space, a man/machine integration, with the power of an astrodyne in his muscles and the beautiful symmetry of physics doing a fire dance at his command. Somewhere, inside yet far away, he felt Ariane Methol's smile.

As Brendan, Ariane, and Tem flew their ship down and around the solid-ringed, blue-haloed core of Iris, the stars clustered thickly about their heads, running in bright streamers through their sun-blown hair, and the dusty darkness of the cold sky assumed a palpable texture as it brushed against their skins. They talked and joked and worked in this sea of midnight mist, while a forlorn, eagle-winged man circled far below.

Sealock reached down from the heights and, grappling with the mind of Harmon Prynne, hauled it up to sit among them. The man was terrified, gazing about at an unfamiliar landscape.

"Like the view?"

He nodded. "Yes." It seemed as if his words were reverberating among the worlds, thrilling him. From here, at the heart of the highest subnet the ship had to offer, he could feel all the workings of *Deepstar* relayed to him through an electronic complexity, almost as if they were parts of his own body. It had a certain familiarity, was like some aspects of the work he'd done in Florida, but with a subtlety and detail that he hadn't imagined would exist. In two years, no one had invited him here before. . . .

He could feel Brendan's eyes on him somehow, cold, calculating . . . beady, glittering things that measured the content of his soul and found it lacking. . . .

"You want to fly this pile of shit?" A simple question, flat, it was said with condescension, perhaps with contempt, but underlying all that was a genuine, sympathetic offer.

Prynne's heart leaped, half fear and half elation. "Is that possible?"

"Sure." Sealock suddenly passed over the reins and the technician flew on, alone, become a stellar phoenix.

*"Brendan!"* Dim, in the background, that was Ariane's voice. It was a faint buzz-saw whine, a mosquito that he could ignore. "What're you *doing?* He can't handle that!"

"The fuck he *can't.* He can do whatever I say he can. Watch."

Harmon Prynne flew on, his body, his nerves, his senses, grown into the subsystems of the ship. He knew nothing, needed to know nothing, with the 'net teaching him as each moment arrived, letting him forget the past. He soared, singing, before the world. A timeline of necessary procedures

**2 4**

appeared in the sky before him, but it was an alternative sky, not defacing the *real* sky, the ocean of stars through which he moved. Dimly, he could sense the presence of many such skies, differing presentations of the cosmos and information, to his expanded senses. He flew, imagining glory.

And somewhere, deep beneath it all, reason glimmered. Shipnet opened its senses and listened to the babble of human conversation, listened and learned. The machine mind didn't wish it had been consulted, for it had no sentience, only potential, and so had no wishes. It had, however, strong imperatives, preset urges that made it strive to fulfill its many goals. There was complexity here, and recursive logic that made up a capacity to create new goals out of synthesized data.

Deep within the ethereal circuitry of Shipnet little illegal modules stirred. Program fragments contrived in such a way as to escape the notice of the Contract Police assembled themselves bit by bit, as their functions were called upon by the crew of *Deepstar*. Finally the GAM-and-Redux monitor awoke, took stock of the situation, and spoke to Shipnet.

Much to its own surprise, Shipnet replied.

Satisfied, but not knowing why, Brendan said, "He'll be all right. Just stay with him, Ariane. Don't let the little goof get lost in the machinery. Hey, Tem. Let's take a break."

"Right."

The two men broke rapport and reappeared in their respective brains. They stretched, looking around, grimacing and blinking hard. Beth and Vana were still seated near the window. The stars appeared motionless, but the vast form of Iris, preceded by a sliver of shadow-sliced ring, had begun to creep over the sill.

They unplugged and leaped up to the kitchen, a feat made just a little more difficult by their small weight. They each drew a cup of black coffee, Sealock's flavored with anise, and dropped back to the floor below, calling up a pair of chairs as they did so. Brendan deopaqued another wall segment, this one framing a view of distant Ocypete's tiny disk.

They sipped at the hot, bitter drinks for a while, staring out

**2 5**

into the void, looking at their new home. Finally Brendan said, "You handle OdP pretty well."

Tem looked at him, expressionless. "Is that so surprising? I have a higher influx potential than Ariane, you know."

"Yeah, but I rode after her with a GAM-and-Redux subplot until she'd been down all the essential pathways. You can't have done that—we both know that Luna's access to Comnet is strictly limited . . . unless you lied about never having been to Earth."

Tem smiled, showing a flash of teeth through the curly overfall of his untrimmed mustache. "Nope. Lewislab—and old Maggie herself—trained me pretty well. Monitoring experiments like the Mini-null-omega Research Torus is, for the most part, like controlling *Deepstar*. Our tools aren't all that backward and there were several of us on the Development Team who probably would have qualified for MCD . . . if we'd been allowed access."

"Could be." Sealock nodded. "I don't know if you could've handled NYU at the same time, though. Free Cities can be pretty difficult." He looked pensive. "I understand there was a refugee from the Moon who took up residence in the Brosewere Barrens. One night they found him hanging from a street lamp, with a seppuku dagger rammed through his guts. Seemed kind of extreme to me." He grinned at Krzakwa. "Anyway . . . I guess maybe we should've worked together a little more during this trip, huh?"

"I guess so." There seemed neither room nor need for further comment.

"Did you have any trouble on your first key-in? OdP's a lot different from Tri-vesigesimal . . ."

Krzakwa laughed. "I'll say! I almost discharged on my first downlink!" Interfacing with an unknown and complicated 'net element was an excellent way to die, come away with a drained cortex and burnt-out amygdala. "But the idea of basing a relinguistic setup on a prime numbers generator was —how shall I put it? Inspired."

The other man seemed pleased with this praise. "OdP was the Comnet Design Team's first project after I joined. Quite a baptism." He was silent for a moment, then said, "You haven't had a chance to key-in on Torus-alpha, have you?"

Tem shook his head, gesturing ironically. "How could I? I'd heard about it, of course. We *drooled* over the stuff you people were bringing out on Earth! How simple it would have made things for us! You should have heard the lame excuses the Lunar government kept pulling out of their fucking hats. . . . 'You can't enter a restricted experimental sector of Comnet without a license from the Contract Police. You can't get a license without coming to Earth for capacitance testing. . . .' And as an indentured engineer at Lewislab, I was 'needed' on the Moon into the foreseeable future." Bitterness gave an edge to his words. "Assholes . . ." He spat, then sighed. "Of course, contract-breakers don't get high-level licenses, even if they do avoid extradition and jail. Now I *am* forsworn. Unlike the rest of you, I can't go back home if this fails. Sure, the Police writ reaches only as far as the asteroids, but they have a mutual extradition treaty with the Jovian System MultiCorp . . . the outer worlds are my home for good."

Sealock drained the last licoricy dregs of his coffee, enjoying the absence of the zero-g membrane for the first time in many months, then said, "Sounds like hard luck. . . . Look, I've got enough random-coplanar number-generators in my share of the hold to adapt Shipnet for Torus-alpha, once we're down on Ocypete. Want to get into it?"

"Sure. How's it work?"

"The datanet acquisition is through a powers-of-transfinite series array . . ."

Krzakwa looked puzzled. "I don't see how something like that could be made to work."

"Well, it doesn't." Sealock crumpled his cup into a ball and grinned at the look on the other man's face. "At least, not the way it's supposed to. No one could get any function at all above Aleph-null. It was hilarious when the news of our fine little piece of vaporware escaped. . . . Talk about humiliation! That's why I brought all that gear. I thought maybe I'd be able to get something working on my own, away from all the other assholes on the MCD."

"OK. Give me a rundown on the basics. And remember, I'm a physicist, not one of your ilk."

"At the level we'll be working, there's not a hell of a lot of difference." Soon the two of them were immersed in a discussion that no one else aboard would have been able to follow. After a while they plugged into a gang-tap and went into partial rapport for an exchange of concepts. The ship flew on without them.

Shut up in his chamber, Demogorgon prepared for masturbation. It was a form of the Illimitor art, in fact, the very thing that had led him to this new form of expression. Though the full complexity of the Illimitor World, the world of Arhos, of Mereqxi, Larys, and the Kaimodrang Empire, took Tri-vesigesimal, this was simple enough to be handled by duodecimal subunits of the 'net. He could have entered via circlet, he supposed, but somehow preferred to use an induction lead. The images, the feelings, were crisper.

As he plugged in a wall-tap, Demogorgon was amused, remembering Brendan's inevitable pun about "jacking off." New meanings to old words . . .

He submerged.

In a soft, rumpled bed of silken sheets he was joined by two other people, abstracted from their normal functioning as denizens of Arhos. One was a slim, magnetic presence, a man, Chisuat Raabo, ebon-haired and ethereal, his mate in the Land of Kings. The other was a woman, Piruat Nahuaa, pale blond, thin and boyish-looking, the swell of her breasts almost nonexistent, her pubic hair so fine and transparent as to give her a preadolescent look. But for coloration, the two might have been taken for brother and sister. They were both very young.

In the Jeweled City on the Mountain, at the place where the skies converged, it was the Soldier's Way—to have a bisexual lover and, with him, a female counterpart, an heir-maker. . . .

They lay tangled together in a joyous maze of limbs, running their hands over smooth, warm flesh, inhaling the tactile perfumes that this world made; and the man and woman paid special attention to the muscular body that was so much a part of Demogorgon's persona here. . . .

When Raabo's huge penis rose, they attacked it together with an avid, ferocious hunger. Slowly, Demogorgon felt his soul begin to spread out, meshing with his lovers, enveloping them, and the usual thoughts were still there:

With Comnet, he need never be alone. What could the world have been like, not so long ago, before the advent of this alternative reality, before he had created it? How had he lived? Just before a sensory explosion took his mind away, he tried to imagine life without this ready availability of human contact; to imagine a world where he couldn't plug in and reach out for love.

He failed.

*Deepstar* fell on a long, complex curve around Iris and back up into space, shedding many thousands of metric tons of fuel and several hundred kilometers per second of relative velocity. The Element 196 had been stored in an energy-stabilized form resembling degenerate matter, compressed into a very small volume, but nothing could alter its mass, or the necessity of expending it. Newton always won out in the end, though centuries of science and engineering had taken some of the sting from his fiats.

The ship threaded under Iris' ring, its heavy-ion drive vaporizing a path through the downward-spiraling ice particles that ever so slowly depleted the structure, and swept just a few hundred kilometers above a bellying azure sky. When they approached apirideon, not far from Ocypete itself, they kept the dense beam oriented to one side of their destination, avoiding damage to their future home. The plume of intense sub-c radiation stabbed toward interstellar space and was gone. A properly instrumented observer many parsecs away and generations removed would have noticed it, since these bursts of semicoherent energy emerging from the Solar System advertised the presence of Man as never before.

*Deepstar* took up a vastly elongated orbit around Iris that would evolve, via the judicious expenditure of Hyloxso, into a nearly circular ellipse of some hundred and eighty kilometers' radius about Ocypete. Ariane and Brendan disengaged from the control subprogram of Shipnet, though the latter still maintained a lesser link to keep an eye on their progress. The common room was completely destructured now, a giant padded cell, and they were all gathered to one side, where, punctuated by the hatches of personal compartments, a hundred and twenty degrees of wall had been made transparent. Beyond that wall the dim, gray sphere of Ocypete loomed, no longer an idea, no longer an astronomical body, but a place.

The world that turned slowly below was a sea of low-walled craters, a vast marsh of ancient, partially healed wounds in a circular shield of chemical ice. They lay shoulder to shoulder, overlapping, defacing one another, craters within craters like beer-glass rings on a veined marble bar. If there had been other processes involved in the making of this surface, they had left no evidence.

"This is the leading hemisphere," said Jana, "long gardened by impacts and mantled with the former atmosphere."

Demogorgon looked out on Iris III from fathomless dark eyes and thought, Is this a land for mystic adventure? No . . . yes. He didn't know, but it did have a deadly sameness about it that disturbed him. Was this all there was?

As if to answer his unspoken question, he noticed a bright, crack-reticulated bulge creeping over the eastern limb. Perhaps there will be something, he thought.

The bright cracks gave way to a darker, smoother terrain that came creeping over the edge of Ocypete. Somewhat broken and jumbled, it was essentially crater free. As they watched, this morphology grew more uniform, a vast, flat plain, and they could see the edges of it curving back to form the great basin that dominated the little moon's surface.

"Mare Nostrum," murmured Demogorgon. "Like the sunrise."

"And so you've named our new home," said Beth.

Jana said, "The official policy is that we must submit names for the most prominent features. If you prefer, I will name the rest. . . ."

**3 0**

"This place would be a lot of fun if you could get into pill-mixers' Latin," said Prynne.

"Or if you were one of those demented nomenclature addicts," said Jana. "Do you know there are over four million named features in the Solar System? And that's not counting Earth. It's become an onerous task."

"If you want," said Demogorgon, looking intently at her, "I've developed several self-consistent mythologies for my Illimitor art. You're welcome to use them."

Jana's gaze shifted back to Ocypete. "It's an idea."

Brendan sighed and stretched, rubbing his eyes. "Come on, shitheads, it's time. Let's get down there."

Krzakwa grinned. " 'Shitheads,' he says . . . you want to fly this monster or shall I?"

"Yeah," said Sealock. "Bend over, Tem. I'll drive you home." They plugged into Shipnet and were gone.

In a little while, no more than a hundred minutes, they were in a perfectly circular orbit some ten kilometers above the fast-moving craterscape. Great broken features, too complex to absorb fully, slid past quickly, frictionlessly, and the clear wall again drew spectators. Suddenly the fretted terrain that surrounded the water ocellus broke into their view, and then the giant basin swept under them like a convex serving dish, featureless save for a few wandering rilles. After a few more moments Jana pointed out shadows on the mare. Someone called up a higher gain on the window optics and a cluster of translucent, dark-nippled cones filled the view.

"They look like half-melted volcanoes," said Vana.

Hu called for a still closer view, with definition precise enough to see the summit openings for what they were. She stared in silence, then said, "Not impossible. Once the meltwater in the ocellus crusted over, the sea below could have behaved as a magma source, though erupting liquid water, even at these temperatures, is too thin to pile up into domes. More likely some kind of slurry extrusion."

*Deepstar* dropped out of the black sky on a downward-pointing fountain of pale yellow fire. It followed a long arc of lessening transverse motion and, when the last of it was gone, went high-gate, slipping vertically toward the smooth, shin-

**3 1**

ing ice of the bright mare basin. In the end the ship hovered a thousand meters above the surface, just for a moment, then the Hyloxso engines shut down and the fire was replaced by a much cooler jet of hydrogen. They descended further.

There was still too much heat to be trusted. At one hundred meters the throttle valves closed entirely, and they fell.

The gravity gradient of this small world was insignificant, but inertia made a display of the impact nonetheless. The ship bounced high, more than double its own length, kept erect by its gyros and the intermittent thud of RCS thrusters. It floated down, rebounded once more, and finally came to rest on the ice. It teetered just a bit on its splay of strut-legs and then was still.

To those within, pinioned to the soft plastic floor of the common room by their em-suits, their arrival on Ocypete came with a noise like a small car being eaten by a train. After the second jolt, all was silent save for the faint pings of stressed metal resuming its shape in the crystalline latticework.

"Son of a bitch," said Cornwell, "we're here."

Sealock popped the plugs from his head and said, "No shit."

They went to the window and looked out.

# T W O

John Cornwell stood in the airlock and suited up. He pulled on the baggy red coverall and crimped shut the helmet, now a floppy, transparent hood. Checking himself in the safety mirror, he had to laugh. He looked like an anorexic Santa Claus. He touched a control node at his waist, and the fabric leaped up against his skin, shrink-wrapping him in an elastic pressure bandage. The hood inflated into a hard, spherical bubble.

The mirror now showed him thin, clad in form-fitting scarlet, an archetypal spaceman. Lifesystems was a small cylinder on one hip, containing a thermal regulator and an oxygen reserve held in a Hyloxso-like matrix sufficient for a ten-hour stay outside. Krzakwa had explained that it even contained a powerful gyro platform. It was a marvel of miniaturization beyond his powers of imagination, but it worked.

There had been much discussion about the difficulties im-

**3 3**

posed by an environment that averaged only 25 degrees Kelvin during the daytime, but Tem had quickly dispelled their fears with a lecture on the subject. The problem was not one of dissipating heat, as was the case in the inner Solar System, but of maintaining a core of 40 degrees C simultaneously with a suit exterior temperature that retained full flexibility. Less than 450 kcal/hr was required, easily generated by the suit's sophisticated six-phase battery. Standing on the surface, with both feet in contact with the ice, added only another 10 kcal/hr or so to the total. Even though he admitted that lying down on the surface for long periods might not be wise, it took Krzakwa awhile to convince the less scientific members of the crew that "common-sense" notions of thermodynamics were useless.

"This is John. Do you read me?"

Prynne said, "Yes. Go on out. We're all waiting."

The privilege of being first out had gone to John by virtue of his titular leadership and the others' insistence. John sent a command to Shipnet and the air whispered out through a valve. When it was gone, things looked no different, but he knew that he was in a lethal environment. He shivered. Another thought brought the hatch to life, and it irised open to show him the ruler-straight edge between dim gray ice and starry night. On the girders framing the airlock there was a fine white dust. The exhaust air had frozen. OK, he thought. So it's *that* cold.

Sixty meters separated him from the ground, and for a moment he considered jumping. His calculator mused: With a surface gravity of 0.027g, he would land with approximately the force of a five-foot fall on Earth. That might hurt, and he certainly wouldn't be able to jump back up. . . .

"Hey. How am I supposed to get down?" he asked. Insofar as he had been part of the design team for *Deepstar,* this was one consideration that he'd never heard mentioned. There were handholds studding the ion drive unit, and, if it came to that, they would have to do. It all seemed dangerous.

Ariane's voice was in his head. "Sorry. There's a catwalk on the vertex of the frame between the Hyloxso matrix and one of the water tanks. It leads as far as the engine-mount structure. From there, you can either climb down a landing strut or jump."

He put a hand on the edge of the hatch and stepped out on the thick metal meshwork that formed the collar holding the CM in place, then looked down. This is foolish, he thought. I'm acting like this is Earth. Even if I fall, there won't be any damage. I could even land on my head! The helmet would protect me. The words rang hollow. It still looked like a deadly sixty-meter drop.

He stepped down, feeling for a foothold, and descended. Finally he came to the complex quadrigram that bound together the far end of the craft. From there it was a matter of leaping the remaining ten meters, which he did. The fall took a perceptibly long time and resulted in only a modest jar. When his feet touched the ice he felt his skin grow warm as the suit's thermostasis system came on. A shimmering, half-seen mist appeared for a moment around his feet, then instantly dissipated, carrying with it some residual heat that *Deepstar*'s structure had radiated onto his exterior.

Concentrating on the actual process of getting down, he had forgotten about the ceremony of arrival on this alien world, of being the first man to set foot on what was, in effect, a planet of another solar system. Whatever possible dignity or formality the moment called for was gone.

The words he'd used to begin *Triton* came into his mind, and he spoke them:

> When the worlds, too few,
>     have been walked;
> When the outcome is written
>     on the walls of the wind;
> Come with me, leave the net . . .
>     We'll begin again.

Smelling the soft tang of his sweat, he flexed the material of a glove and rubbed his thumb against his fingertips. Though the increased girth of his hand felt clumsy, feeling was hardly impaired at all. It took an effort of will to come to grips with the intensely different conditions that that thin barrier separated. The material of his bubble helmet was no

**3 5**

hindrance at all to seeing. The enormity of the world, even with Ocypete's close horizon, filled him.

The surface of the ocellus was more pristine and flat than he could have imagined. The ice was a dim, white sheet, like linen, stretching out in a wrinkleless vista. Triton would have been nothing like this.

"John? Here's something peculiar for you." Ariane's voice interrupted his meditations. The 3V image of a strange bluish blanket retreating appeared, almost like an ocean breaker in reverse, perhaps a meter deep. The trailing edge of the blanket crumpled and shrank in on itself in a fast rush of sublimation, leaving flat ice, like that on which he stood.

Hu's voice accompanied the vision. "That, John, is the retreat of the regolith; mostly neon but some deuterium as well. Trace amounts of methane, CO, and argon are being left behind. The driving force was our infrared output. It should stop well beyond the horizon, maybe half a myriameter from here. The neon was very close to its sublimation point even before we landed."

Harmon said, "I guess that's a good indication of what would've happened if we'd tried to land in the highlands."

Cornwell was struck by a sense of amazement. Of such insubstantial stuff was this world made! He looked up and traced a few constellations in the sky, almost hidden in the thousands of dimmer stars not visible from the surface of Earth. Draco, Cassiopeia, the Great Bear; they were still there, friends that he'd made in childhood. He felt his composure returning. There was *some* continuity, after all.

Iris hung some fifty degrees above the eastern horizon. It was close to four degrees across, eight times the size of the full Moon seen from Earth, and it dominated the sky like a huge jewel, in first impression like a cat's-eye sapphire. Peering more closely, however, it looked more like a bright fingernail paring nestled in a dim blue sphere, its nightside obliterated by atmospheric scattering. In the close, sparkling blackness there were two very tiny crescents, Podarge and Aello, ever falling and escaping in the balanced dance of orbital mechanics. The sun was a blinding tick near the arrow point of the barely visible ring.

**3 6**

The world in the sky surpassed by far his expectations. Nothing in the Solar System combined the stark solidity and ethereal beauty of Iris.

Cornwell turned away. He was not here just to sightsee. "Ariane, would you monitor this transmission and see that I get it right?"

Upon receiving an affirmative, he began: "Under the aegis of the Pansolar Conventions, edition 2067, specifically Paragraph $N_6$ of the Colonizing, Homesteading, and Exploring Guidelines, I claim Ocypete homesteading guarantees for the Deepstar Company: full CIDs to follow proclamation. Total travel distance was 6.2977 terameters; diameter of homestead world is 1.923 megameters. Crew homesteads to be apportioned alphabetically, spokewise from longitude 311.57756 defined from sub-Iris point at periastron, and latitude 12.6546, defined from equator at 2097.664 years."

"It was successfully recorded and transmitted, John," said Ariane. "I guess that makes us permanent."

The man looked back at *Deepstar*. Clinging to a girder far above, Sealock and Krzakwa, clad in bulky powered worksuits that augmented their strength and made them nearly invulnerable, were already working on opening one of the container modules. They seemed intent on the business at hand, but one of them paused to wave. He waved back.

Finally, suddenly, something like happiness spilled over him. He activated the gyro on his belt and, with a hard kick, jumped into the star-prickled sky. There was little sensation of motion as the ground receded, dreamlike. In a huge arc, he flew across the steely white, frozen sea, head kept up by the gyro, and, after a time sufficient to fully experience the sensation, he landed with a jolt a full twenty-five meters from his starting point.

A few more jumps put him a great distance across the ice, though its featurelessness provided no real indication as to how far. He turned back and was surprised to see *Deepstar* shrunken considerably, almost halfway to the horizon. This time he pushed harder, back toward the ship, each minute-long leap gaining a little height and more speed. With no way to stop quickly, he bypassed his goal, slowing himself in a

**37**

series of jumps, until he came to a stop. He made his way back in little tiptoeing hops, covering two meters at a time.

With his earlier acrophobia gone, climbing the structure of the ship was a simple matter of swinging from girder to girder, brachiating upward. Soon he was back on the platform from which he had looked down so cautiously before. The two inhabited worksuits saluted him. Their thick, flexible joints segmented the grayish, stove-bellied exoskeletons into small, mostly cylindrical components. Since the suits had no faceplates, relying on four 3V photorecorder cells mounted at ninety-degree intervals about the helmet canister, he could not distinguish who was inside. A quick look into Shipnet's Status Registers told him what he wanted to know.

Brendan Sealock, still habituated to postures he'd developed on Earth, sat on a structural girder. Krzakwa, used to Lunar conventions, remained on his feet. Despite all the bulk of the suits, they looked quite comfortable. Krzakwa turned, light on his feet but not fully adjusted to the suit's large moment of inertia.

"Well, what can I do?" asked John.

Sealock pointed toward the hatch of the airlock. "Stay out of the way. Tem and I and the work-packs will handle what needs to be done."

John shrugged and said, "OK. I'm going in." He made his way through the airlock hatch and it closed behind him.

Tem watched as the musician was occulted by the vignetting door. "I guess we'd better get busy, huh?"

"Christ!" said Sealock. "I thought there'd at least be some craters!"

"There are a few," said Tem, "small ones, scattered here and there, not to mention the hydro-volcanic structures in the center of the mare. Haven't you tapped Jana's report?"

"Sure. . . . What does that have to do with my expectations? I'm just talking about what I *wanted* to see here. Hell, if we went on a hike up into the highlands, before you know it we'd be up to our assholes in neonated methane." He laughed softly, to himself. "We'd be drowned alive in a mess of phase-changing that'd drain the thermos in ten minutes.

**3 8**

. . . And then there's this parking lot. Some world to conquer, huh?"

"I read an article about boil gliding once, by some guy living on Pluto. You dive into a pool of volatile material with wings strapped to your suit—the stuff vaporizes and acts as both atmosphere and propellant. That would be pretty easy in neon."

"Mm . . . Whatever became of this guy?"

"Killed, I think, in a boil-gliding accident."

"Nice. Sounds like *my* kind of sport! Anyway, you saw our friend Johnny out there—you can fly, after a fashion. Bouncing around on the ice ought to keep us imbeciles happily occupied for *years*. . . ."

Krzakwa laughed. "Well, there's lots to screw around with, when the time comes to confront our ultimate sense of boredom. You know as well as I do that these worksuits can be equipped with a thermodynamic damper field. We *can* trudge up into the neon crags if we want to."

Sealock sighed heavily. "Yeah, yeah. I know all that. I think I'm just having some kind of laziness attack."

Krzakwa thought about it for a moment, realizing that wasn't quite the word for what seemed to be going on. "You mean, other-world weariness?"

"Right." The man laughed. On sudden impulse, he had Shipnet construct an image of Krzakwa's head through his suit optics. Processing made it look as if the man's opaque, equipment-packed helmet had turned to glass. He seemed to be smiling. "We might as well be off," he said, "though why I don't know. There's no hurry. . . ."

"No. This place isn't going to run away." Tem had a sudden, uneasy visualization of the long decades ahead, isolated together. "I guess it'd make sense to set up the boom crane first?"

"Yup." Activating the proper circuits, they made for the downlink channels and submerged in Shipnet's maze.

The basic structure of *Deepstar* was made of metal-plastic girders that had been extruded by an automatic industrial beambuilder machine, for over a century the indispensable workhorse of space construction. The skeleton of the ship was an inexpensive matrix to which almost anything could be attached, so . . . There were isostatically stabilized supplies of ion fuel, Hyloxso matrices, a peak-pulse toroidal astrodyne, a small beambuilder, a bubbleplastic mixer, and a big storage cell for the raw goo that it used. Among the various pressurized modules there was a decorative hydroponic garden, and a terrarium whose genetically tailored creatures could produce certain organic substances for the kitchen most efficiently. Of necessity, there was the inevitable complexity of a Magnaflux generator.

Human beings had evolved across billions of years wrapped in the comforting arms of Earth's magnetosphere. When space travel came, they began to leave it, and at first there seemed to be no great problem. The years flowed into decades and the colonists of the inner Solar System began to complain of unexplained torpor. Low gravity, the experts said, no exercise, poor diet, even *Weltschmerz.* . . . Odd diseases and neuroses appeared, and colonies did not do well. Children died or grew up "weird," and people had to go home, if they could. The future of space as a human habitat began to look endangered.

The electromagnetic screens had originally been designed as powerful force fields to ward off the charged particles continually bombarding the satellites of Jupiter and Saturn. Because em was not fully understood in those days, Quantum Transformational Dynamics and the Unified Field Theory still being a bit foggy, the engineers carefully tailored the inside of the force screens to resemble the magnetic environment of Earth. Inside the shields, people flourished. Now, wherever man went, there Magnaflux went also.

Sitting on the dull, metallic ice, the ship began to change. Under the urging of the two men, mechanical spiders, scuttling at impossible angles and hanging upside down like their arachnid prototypes, attacked the structure of the tower. They crawled along the edges of one of *Deepstar*'s four protruding arms and, with particle-beam torches flaring bluewhite, cut through all the girders on one internal vertex. On the other side of the structure they modified the density and molecular format of the material until it could flex along one

**4 0**

plane. When they finished, the nacelle swung slowly open, exposing its contents to the outer world.

Sealock and Krzakwa unfolded the arms of the crane, extending the slender, shining manipulators down to the ice so that the machine could walk itself into an upright position. The first real step in unloading the ship was, perhaps, also the most tedious. It was necessary for the barely mobile crane to attach and lower its own components, in order for it to assemble itself into its real, complex shape, to walk into magical life.

Assembled, its various segments unfolded, the crane was a huge, square thing of rods and pulleys that rumbled about on heavy treads. It crawled around the base of *Deepstar,* lifting down poles and cargo pods and the endlessly refolded fasciae that would become dome bases. When most of the smaller items that made up their manifest were piled haphazardly on the ice, it was time to begin a major task: Sealock and Krzakwa set up a relay module from which they ran a network of wire-thin power conduits, black spaghetti scattering formlessly around them, growing into a structured web. This was not yet an environment that could tolerate even narrowcast energy. There was still plenty of ambient neon gas around, enough to absorb and reradiate the contents of a strong microwave beam.

They set up a trivetlike base about a kilometer from the ship. It was the surface mounting platform for the hot, heavy fusion reactor. They installed the insulating-field generator that would keep its heat from getting at the ice, then decided to break for lunch.

Inside, Tem and Brendan sprawled on the edge of the crater room, dank and sweaty, tired more from the idea of hard work than its reality, and ate. They were joined by the remainder of the crew. To Sealock, they seemed oddly posed, almost as if they were waiting for commands.

Cornwell, stung by the curt dismissal that his attempt at volunteering for work had brought, said, "Well. Are you ready to let us participate yet?"

Brendan looked up from his vulturelike pose over a bowl of noodles and cheese and peered quizzically at the musician from eyes almost hidden beneath shaggy, red-blond brows. Hadn't the man been paying attention? He seemed to remember there being more than just himself out there. . . . Now what? Oh. He grinned, said, "Sure," and slurped up another butter-slimed mouthful.

Harmon looked back and forth between their faces for a moment, sensing some oddity going on, then asked, "You've gotten a good look out there. What do you think of our new home?"

Sealock turned to stare at him. "I think it's flat."

Demogorgon looked at him reproachfully. "Brendan . . . be nice."

"Well, what the hell does he expect me to say? I mean, *really!* Sometimes I feel like I'm up to my asshole in all this bullshit. . . ."

"How appropriate," murmured Hu, with a malevolent, slit-eyed smile.

Sealock glared at her for a second, then let his face relax into a toothy grin. "You just love it when I talk dirty, don't you?"

"People . . ." Cornwell said.

Turning to look at him, Brendan said, "Still want your question answered? There are five worksuits aboard. In order to do anything useful, you'll need one of them, so three of you can help, at any given time. If anyone else wants anything to do, there's off-line data analysis to be done." He shook his head, grinning. "I really don't know why anyone would *want* to be in on this . . . it's mostly going to be an exercise in tedium."

"I'll do some of the data work," said Ariane.

"Leave me out of this," said Jana stiffly. "I still have a lot of work to do on the IAAU report."

"OK. That leaves Vana, Demo, John, Harmon, Axie, and me," said Beth. "Shall we do a random choice?"

"Sure," said Prynne.

A quick peek at the 'net's pseudorandom number generator selected John, Demogorgon, and Axie. Consulting the machinery was a very important arbitration method among them, and they all realized that it would be pointless and

**4 2**

harmful to question its outcome. In this case, everyone seemed satisfied with the results.

Sealock scaled his dish toward a vent intake, which snatched it expertly from the air. Tiny globules of oil, which in weightlessness would have followed it, fell away and began to drift about like dust motes. Sooner or later the circulation filters would get them, or somebody's lungs would. "Let's go," he said.

They stood, and Ariane said, "You know, when this is all finished, we should have some sort of a real ceremony; maybe a celebration. . . ."

Vana spun around suddenly, buoyant brown breasts swaying. "I know! Let's have an orgy!"

"That's not quite what I had in mind."

John laughed. "Hell, why not? Long as everyone's willing. . . ."

Grinning, Sealock stretched, muscles rolling heavily beneath his skin. "A true Berenguerism. Never fails. Steamy crotch juice for the frozen man . . ."

Demogorgon snickered at the purloined and altered imagery. The ancient poem had been part of the original inspiration for the Illimitor World and, with a little effort, he remembered the original verse. " 'My favorite water,' huh?"

Sealock bellowed with coarse amusement.

Ariane, standing close to him, suddenly murmured, "Brendan, could I talk to you alone?"

He looked down at her, his smile fading, and said, "Later."

The astrodyne, built by KMS Fusion System's Aerospace Division at their big, dangerous factories not far from Gamma-enclave Kosmograd II in geosynchronous orbit, was mounted in an exterior pod roughly on the opposite side of *Deepstar* from the nacelle they'd opened to liberate the crane. It was an octagonal cylinder four meters in diameter by about six long, and housed the heart of their new colony—a 50,000-megawatt, self-maintaining peak-pulse toroidal fusion reactor. External field coils were a thing of the past and the thing had virtually no moving parts. Assuming plenty of fuel, its projected lifespan was in excess of a hundred thousand years, though the manufacturer would not even guarantee a century of trouble-free operation.

As Krzakwa drove the crane into position, Sealock, helmetless in the pressurized cab, directed five work-packs through some preparatory activity. They disconnected the reactor from all but two of its attach points and replaced the current-infeed cable with a much longer one that would be payed out from a reel as the device was moved. There was no provision for putting *Deepstar* into a powered-down condition. Demogorgon was suited up and crawling around on the structure, unnecessarily overseeing the work of the machines and, as he said, amusing himself. John and Axie were standing below, unable to do anything but watch.

When everything was ready, they paused. Sealock lit up a small dark cigar that filled the cabin with thin aromatic clouds which were swiftly swept toward the air-conditioning grille.

"Give me one of those," said Krzakwa. He lit the stick from the end of the other man's cigar, no easy task, and puffed away on it inexpertly, redoubling the cabin smog. It made him cough, but he sighed. "Kind of nice to be able to smoke outside of a restricted solarium."

Sealock snorted. "The Lunar authorities are idiots. Those rules were obsolete a hundred years ago." He thought for a moment, then said, "You could smoke in a space suit if you wanted to—just turn the LS cycle all the way up."

Krzakwa nodded. "You're probably right, but that has nothing to do with rules. Environmental Controls and Standards runs the Moon. Any relaxation of regulations, no matter how old and obsolete, lessens their power. You know, when I was an ECS apprentice in Picard, during my teens, I had more authority than as a scientist later on. How often do you hear of a bureaucratic state loosing its grip on the people?"

"Never. . . . Well, maybe if they thought it'd raise profits a little."

"Even then it has to be painful for them." He stared up at the image of *Deepstar,* seeming pensive. "You have to wonder why the human race let itself get turned into a system of interlocking corporate directorships."

**4 4**

Sealock puffed on his cigar, spewing out a broken string of little gray clouds, and said, "I don't think it's ever been any different, not now, not at any other time in history. How much difference is there, really, between Genghis Khan and Henry Ford?"

"Hey," said a voice from the ether, "what're you two doing in there?" It was Axie, and the crane optics showed her waving to them.

"We're having a smoke," said Brendan. "Take a break. We'll pick it up later."

"I'm kind of surprised that you see things so much like I do," said Tem. "Somehow, I visualized it being different on Earth. Enclaves, free cities, all that hellfire and brimstone . . ."

Sealock grinned at the imagery. "I can see how it might look different from the outside. Put in the vernacular: it ain't. I lived in enclaves, where they kept me safe. In order to preserve that safety, they had to control me. I lived in a free city, where I was free to do whatever I felt like. So was everybody else, and that freedom controlled me too."

Krzakwa scratched his chin, rooting through the tangled beard hairs. "I know what you're talking about, I guess, but what the hell does that have to do with the existence of a bureaucratic state and a system of interlocking corporate directorships?"

"Nothing, maybe, but I think it has a whole lot to do with it. People can't seem to exist without something controlling them; they can't get along 'on their own,' unless they *are* alone. . . . All my life, I've been as wild and goofy as anyone I ever met, and *I* can't do it. Why should anyone else?"

Krzakwa tried to interrupt, to offer an observation, but Sealock's words rattled on: "What difference is there between the control modes of an empire or a company, between a Communist directorate, a representative democracy, a military hierarchy, or, for that matter, the magical dreams of John Fucking Harry Cornwell?"

Krzakwa felt taken aback once again by the man's ragelike behavior. Now what had brought this on? Why would any-

**4 5**

body want to say something like that? "I don't get you. A hell of a lot of difference, it seems to me. . . ."

Sealock's breathing had quickened, his face darkened, but now he sat back, eyes closed, and took a deep drag on the cigar, pulling its heavy smoke far down into his lungs. Finally he let it out with a soft rush, the smoke reduced to a phantasm of its original self by systemic adsorption. "Ahhh . . . Boy, these things are really great. They grow the tobacco down in what used to be Guatemala, from twentieth-century Cuban seed stock." He looked at the Selenite and smiled. "Yeah. Maybe Cornwell believes that too. Shit. He'd have to, or else he'd be nuts. History tends to repeat itself in exact patterns. People quit corporations and enclaves all the time, take their knowledge and set up on their own. If they fail, no loss to the organization they ran out on. If they succeed, they're co-opted, brought back into the fold as more or less equal partners. Same thing goes for interplanetary colonies. Our descendants, if any, will one day join the Contract Police."

"Really?" Krzakwa laughed suddenly. "*Our* descendants are going to be pretty far from here someday. Iris' orbit *is* hyperbolic. . . ."

Sealock sat up and slowly took the cigar out of his mouth. "Christ . . . I forgot! Maybe we'll have to start our own Contract Police."

"Will we? I don't know. Will we be joined by others out here? Probably, but maybe not. Right now, we're a tiny crew on a great big starship."

Brendan nodded slowly. "I always wanted to run away on a starship. All those wonderful old stories . . . There always has to be somewhere else to go." He looked at the Selenite. "You remember what happened to the *Prometheus?*"

Rolling the cigar to the corner of his mouth, Krzakwa said, "Sure. The stupidest thing that anyone ever did. Fourteen months out, it entered the Oort cloud at a little over 0.2 c and ran into an object the size of a pea. . . . My father was on Geographos then, setting up a mass driver for Off-Lunar Ops. He said the explosion was brighter than the 2017 supernova in Aquila." It was a litany of what seemed to be man's ultimate limitation.

Brendan nodded slowly into the silence. Human engineers could, it was true, design and build ships capable of accelerating to relativistic speeds. The energy was there. But space was full of debris, no one knew quite how much. The huge sphere that spawned the comets also teemed with tiny bits of ice and rock that had been swept outward by the sun's T Tauri winds in the early days of the Solar System. At 0.99 c, a golf ball has the mass of a planet—and how do you dodge a planet moving toward you at near the speed of light? Probes were moving outward, through the Oort cloud, across interstellar space to the nearby stars, and man would follow, but slowly. . . .

"Well," said Sealock, "we'd better get busy. Hey, Demo! You going to get off that thing so we can move it?"

The Arab waved from his position atop the 'dyne. "I'd like to ride it over," he said. His voice, fed to their auditory centers, sounded conversational.

"OK. But sit down and hold on."

"Why bother?" asked Krzakwa. "He won't get hurt if he falls off, not in this gravity." He put one crane arm on the bottom of the reactor, grabbed an upper attach point with the other, and wrapped two steadying limbs about the fuel tanks for extra stability. "All right," he said, "let her go."

Sealock directed his spiders to disconnect the last two fittings, and the thing was free. "OK," he said, "pull it out."

Tem eased the reactor away from the ship and then swung the whole crane about, intent on getting pointed in the right direction . . . but large, dense objects have correspondingly high masses, masses which steadfastly obey the simple, easily forgettable laws of mechanics; laws which begin, "An object in motion . . ."

Two of the crane arms snapped simultaneously, and the astrodyne went sailing majestically away, apparently undisturbed. One of the flailing booms caught Demogorgon a glancing bow, and he went off into the dark sky, screaming.

"Holy shit!" Krzakwa was frozen for a moment. He spat

the cigar butt out, gunned the crane's engines, and went lumbering off after the flying reactor.

Sealock routed himself through Shipnet to the CM's tele-optic system and accessed a monitor grid array showing the object's motion dynamics as a simple trajectory. "No sweat," he said. "Plenty of time." He fed the now generated capture data to Krzakwa. "Shut up, Tabari, you're in a worksuit. Turn on the control-moment gyros and you'll come down on your feet someday."

Demogorgon stopped screaming and looked around. He realized that he was still flying upward and that the ship was far away. After a while he began to enjoy the view.

The crane quickly caught up with the astrodyne, though there seemed to be little time to spare. Krzakwa wrapped the remaining arms around the reactor, then set the treads to "freewheel" and slowly applied the brakes. The crane shuddered, vibrating, the pressure of frictive surfaces transmitted to their ears by the various sound-shorts of the vehicle's structure as a high-pitched vibrato squeal. When the kinetic energy had been spent they came to a stop. He carefully drove over to the reactor base, now close, and set his charge down. He looked at Sealock.

The man had an odd look, almost smiling. "Well," he said.

"Yeah. What do you suppose would've happened if it'd crashed?"

"I don't know. There's not too much in there to break. . . . It's a tough machine, but if the cable had come off, *Deepstar* would've shut down . . ."

". . . and then the ion fuel would've exploded." He looked pale. "Maybe we'd better be a little more careful, huh?"

Sealock wiped the cold sweat from his upper lip and nodded. "Yeah."

The colonists ate supper in a subdued silence. No one was talking much, though the engineers tried to make light of their near disaster. Afterward, while the others sat around to chat and plan, Sealock rose and went to his private compartment, where he shut himself in. He toyed with some electronic components he'd been working on, trying to concentrate, to regulate his ideas, then sighed and, stringing up a hammock that he particularly liked, lay down. That was one of the good things about getting gravity back. He'd never liked em-beds, no matter how popular they were, and useful for sex. There was something about the sway of a hammock, especially in low g . . .

Personal lapses of judgment, especially ones that he might consider his own, put him in a bad mood. If they'd still been on Earth, he'd've gone to the gym, found an unsuspecting sparring partner, and beaten the hell out of him. That form of release was not available to him here.

He lay there for a while, feeling restless to no effect, then the door chirped at him. "Who is it?" he snarled.

"Thy *aziz*, O fated one." The voice was pitched soft and high.

"Go away."

"Please, Brendan."

He clenched his jaws momentarily, considering an array of possible angry responses, then said, "All right. Come in."

The door quarter-paneled open and Demogorgon slid through. He walked lightly across to Sealock and looked down at him, putting one tapering fingered hand on his broad, ridged chest. He smiled and started to slide his hand downward, but Brendan shook him off angrily. "No. Get out."

The Arab looked pained. "I want to help. I know something's wrong. . . ."

"Nothing's wrong," he snapped in exasperation. In truth, it was such a *small* thing . . . but how could he have forgotten the basic laws of motion? It wasn't just Krzakwa's lapse, stupidity was to be expected from other people, even the best of them, but he'd forgotten as well.

"Look," Demogorgon was saying. "I've seen you get into these moods before." He put his hand on the other man again. "I can fix you right up."

Sealock laughed harshly. "Wrong mood, asshole. Go away."

"But I want to. . . ."

**49**

"And I don't! Go find someone else."

"There is no one else. Please."

"No." Brendan sat up. "There's going to *have* to be someone else, sooner or later. I told you not to come, but you wouldn't listen to me—now you're the only fag in the world."

"You're being cruel."

"I'm being honest. For a change. I can't take care of you forever. I won't." Lying back down. Brendan stared at the wall. "Why don't you go try one of the girls? You'll like it. I promise."

"You know I can't."

"I know you won't try. Well, now you have to. Go away." After a while Demogorgon did leave.

Alone again, Sealock's inner turmoil grew until it reached a point that was almost despair. Nobody to beat up, not in a mood for sex . . . shit. People, if they are fortunate, always have a few ways of dealing with inexplicable personal tumult. The accident with the reactor wasn't really bothering him . . . he knew that, and knew further that he was suffering from nothing more than a sort of sourceless anxiety, unfocused, a neurosis-like reaction to his attention having been called to the fundamental directionlessness that seems to infest every human life, no matter how strongly patterned, no matter how purposeful and ordered its days seemed to be.

He rose and, going to a storage cabinet, drew out twelve brain-tap waveguides. Some people take drugs, surrender themselves to the induced monomania of utterly false visions —psychotropic chemistry can erect a structure where none exists. Brendan Sealock had Comnet, and it was a thing he understood well. The past can make the present seem like a logical end point to all that has gone before, even when it is not.

Lying down again, he plugged the jacks into his skull, each making a satisfying click as it snapped into place. Octa-deka Prime OS flooded into his soul, and he drifted down the long, dark tunnels of his life.

One of the functions that he himself had designed, a sort of therapy that he'd pioneered as a late adolescent at NYU, was an absolute mental cross indexing. Now he drifted through a brilliantly colored sea of experience, watching all the things he'd done and been, all the scenes that had passed before his eyes. He waited for a meaningful moment to arrive and, after a while, one did. He seized on it, on a time nearly thirty years gone. They sent me away, he thought, and tears gathered in his eyes, unaware. The word for it is catharsis.

Brendan awoke, as he always did these days, feeling lost. There was a little surge of chest-tightening fear that died down swiftly as his dominant intellectual drivers geared into life and smothered the ever present whisperings of intuitional modes in shattered disarray. When he sat up in the soft bed, yawning and throwing back the heavy, down-filled comforter, he was himself again.

"Bren?" That came from the next bed, in a thin, high, rather nasal voice, and he looked over. Kenny Stein was a small, pudgy, flat-faced nine-year-old, with brown eyes and kinky, almost Afrolike hair. He was just another exile here, thrown out of Taho Kibbutz by his people, themselves exiled from the low-tech horrors of Southern California. Sealock didn't like the whining little shit, but then again, he did.

"Fuck off, Stein." There was a swift wash of anger, demanding a response, on the boy's face, but he said nothing. Brendan in a bad mood was too much for him to trifle with.

Out here, at the Phoenix School for Communal Exiles, they lived. There were hundreds of them, children for whom the future had temporarily darkened, sent here from the many corners of one of Earth's largest political entities. They lived here, emotional and psychological "cripples," waiting for their problems to be fixed by men who lurked somewhere in the darkness, waiting like defective machines to be assaulted by the mechanics of the mind.

The room they were in was part of a therapeutic program that the school had designed, geared like everything else around here toward producing sensible, cooperative citizens who could eventually be slipped back into the collective-effort society of the Deseret Enclave Complex. Ten terribly antisocial little boys lived in the room, allowed to maul one another's emotions and form the naturalistic pecking orders

**5 1**

common to such groups, while sociobiological technicians used carefully designed behavior-mod pressures on them. It usually worked.

Seven of the beds were empty, the occupants fled to the comparative safety of a supervised breakfast hall, leaving the dominant clique, perennial late sleepers, to rise alone.

"Why don't you let him be, Sealock?" Tom Leahy stood up from his bed at the other end of the room, tall and angular, with tousled, curly red hair that matched his freckled, perpetually sunburned skin. He was bigger than Brendan and perhaps stronger, but not quite so fast. They'd fought, in the beginning, and Brendan had given him an efficient thrashing, but not before a knob-knuckled fist had broken his nose.

Brendan started to repeat his retort, but Leahy was staring at him with his usual bleak, fearless determination. He glared, feeling a twinge of unease, and said, "Piss on it. Why can't he leave me alone?"

Stein stood up and pulled on a pair of white gym shorts. "Because you don't want me to." The other two stared at him, Leahy with his seemingly impenetrable incomprehension, and Brendan with a touch of dismay. Kenny was just a little bit too intelligent, with enough insight to baffle Brendan's worst advances, and he was right.

The other boys were an excellent tool against him, for, between them, they were his equal. "Let's go eat," he said. Perhaps, somewhere, a social technician chuckled. These little triads were always pretty entertaining, like adolescent love triangles. The focal point snapped his or her fingers, and the lovers danced. . . .

After breakfast and a mandatory "exercise hour," the three of them retreated to the Games Room. Their objective was a big gray plastic box in one corner, next to an expanse of moss dotted with a variety of exquisite bonsai trees. From a false cliff against the wall a tiny machine-driven waterfall dropped to form a six-inch-wide river that fed a shallow pond, whence the aerated water returned to its source. The whole, about thirty meters square in area, was surrounded by the faint blue shimmer of a selective-pass em-screen.

The Games Room was more or less empty. A lot of people

had classes to go to or had found other interesting things to occupy their attentions. Though occasionally joined by others, the three of them had, by habituation, established themselves as the rightful "owners" of this little domain on many mornings. It wasn't hard to do. . . .

The boys stepped through into this little world, feeling a slight tingle on their skins, and went to the box. Brendan slid its door aside and peered in. A pair of tiny, red-glowing eyes glared back. There was a soft, reptilian hiss. He reached in toward the eyes and there was a tiny snapping sound that made him whip his hand back. He looked up at Leahy, grinning.

There was a scratching scuffle from inside and the container's foremost occupant sprang out. It was a perfectly formed, gray-scaled example of Tyrannosaurus rex, all of thirty centimeters tall. Brendan reached out for it, and the tiny dinosaur went for his fingers again. With one quick swipe of a small, fast hand, he cuffed the animal. It fell squalling on its side, then leaped erect on muscular hind legs and dashed off like a jackrabbit, in some peculiar fashion combining the gait elements of both man and kangaroo. Brendan stood up to follow it, calling over his shoulder, "Somebody get the Ankylosaurus!"

Leahy knelt before the door and, reaching in, seized the heavy little beast by its bulbous tail, intent on dragging it out. Now the other inhabitants of the box were stirring, ready to emerge of their own accord. The toy dinosaurs, representing everything from the placid Trachodon to a feisty little Cynognathus, were premier examples of modern bioengineering. They had been made in the school's genetic workshop from the zygotes of alligators, crocodiles, tuataras, and a variety of flightless birds. One of the elder students, in part responsible for the work, had delighted in calling the Tyrannosaurus "that kiwi in drag."

Like everything else around the school, the dinosaurs were "teaching toys," tools that filled an educational, cultural, and social role in the rehabilitation of those who contacted them. To be certain, robots would have been cheaper, easier to use

**5 3**

and maintain, but . . . How many people *really* have empathy for machines?

Over by the waterfall, Brendan had the animal cornered. His eyes were bright as he teased it with his hands and his laughter had an unpleasant, almost sexual ring to it. The thing snapped and bit and hissed as it tried to escape, to no avail. Its russet eyes were rolling frantically. After a while Brendan began to tire of this sport and, becoming distracted, thought of letting it go. Suddenly, as if seeing its chance, the dinosaur lunged forward and seized his hand.

Though no worse than a cat bite, the sharp little teeth hurt, and Brendan screamed with mingled anger and pain. He pried the tiny jaws loose and, picking the creature up, slammed it against the wall. It fell to the mossy floor, mewing and writhing in agony. Brendan sucked at the cuts on his hands, fuming with exasperation.

"What the fuck do you think you're doing?" At the commotion, Leahy had come running over. Stein was standing well behind him, looking frightened.

"It *bit* me!"

Tom looked at his hand contemptuously. "Serves you right, you little bastard. I saw what you were doing."

Rage flared in Sealock, along with the usual fear. "Shut up, cocksucker!"

The implacable, self-righteous indignation had risen in Leahy now, and he raised his fists. "All right. That's it! I'm going to kick your ass good this time."

Brendan leaped to his feet and dropped into a fairly creditable boxing stance, both arms high and forward, elbows tucked in. His outrage had suddenly overcome the fear of injury that usually held him back. Tom swung a looping right to his head, but the smaller boy sent a quick jab through his ineffective guard to crack against his mouth, rocking his head back. First blood.

Unattended, the Tyrannosaurus was trying to creep away. Stein picked it up, hands stroking its soft, pebbly skin, soothing it as he continued to watch the fight.

**5 4**

□ □ □

Locked in a trance, Sealock followed his train of memory sequences to their seemingly logical end point. When it was over, he felt better, as he always did. He knew no one would understand the forces that drove him, but somehow that didn't seem to matter. He understood himself, and that made it all right.

He stood up, stretching, and put his leads away. Time to go do something else. He left the room, dislocated, come adrift in time once again.

It didn't matter. It just didn't. . . .

After dinner John had drawn a large mug of hot, brandied pulque and gone to a couch in an alcove that looked out on Iris' quadrant of the sky. In the semidarkness he sipped his drink and watched the ringed, translucent sphere do nothing.

The news was not good. The Universal Solaris Energy Collective had just dispatched their high-energy freighter *Formis Fusion* from the fore-Trojans. With a full complement of scientists, it would be here in just a few months. If his colonists had the whole ocellus, and the law said they did, where did the newcomers go? Probably they wouldn't stay. These wouldn't be real settlers, just itinerant asterologists. Probably financed by the Pansolar people, who couldn't leave any pie unplumbed.

He called up the latest few 3Vcoms from his father, having neglected to do so for days. The cheerful visage of Ennis Cornwell related various things to him, underlaid with graphics like a twentieth-century weatherman. The early sales figures for *Rose of Ash* were encouraging. The publicity surrounding the expedition had had its effect on his reputation, and there had been huge amounts of it on the 'net this past week. He would have to talk to Jana about making up a wonders-of-space press release for the masses. There was an exact way to go about that sort of thing, he knew. The trick now was to play the media in an unexpected way and not follow any of the prevailing 'net manipulation programs.

He sighed. Aside from feeding publicity to the media, there were also problems of piracy, government interference, and the ever ephemeral nature of the public's interest. The nature of making a living from music would probably never change. Thankfully, live performances were no longer required; John grimaced as he remembered what a shambles his one attempt at a concert had been. It was a fiasco that had done terrible damage to his career: sales of *Reflection Counterpoint* were affected by it still.

Money was a funny concept out here. He could buy virtually any commodity available, but the cost of transporting it was prohibitively expensive. The RAW memories of Shipnet held virtually all the useful knowledge that man had ever produced, and contained software threads which, when combined, would perform any function that he could think of. Turning off the 'net, he looked out at the chiaroscuro Ocypetan exterior. I bought this, he thought. Still feeling the effects of the alcohol, he began to doze.

He awoke with a little start and looked around. Evidently what had awakened him was the crackle of Ariane's chamber door opening. In the dim light of the central room the silhouette of the woman was framed against the brightness that she was leaving. The doorway hissed closed and the room lights came up a little at her command.

Across the room, Demogorgon was cradled in a raised hollow of the floor that he'd created, apparently oblivious to them. He was wearing a circlet, eyes tightly closed, so John assumed that he was tapping. "Ariane?" he said. "I think it's time we had a little talk."

The woman stared at him for a moment, her face flat and expressionless as she came over and sat down against a bulkhead. "What do you want?"

"We're in trouble, aren't we?"

She shrugged. "I don't know. There's a lot to think about. Things seem so random sometimes. . . . What makes you think we're in trouble?"

John found some cold dregs in his cup and drained them. "I don't know. It seems that you're the key to all this."

"What do you mean?"

"Let's start at the beginning. All my life I've seen people sitting in judgment of one another. People place themselves in a hierarchical relationship with others, and society is driven by the resulting pain. That's what's *always* been wrong with the way people conceive their roles. Judgment of others, judgment of self—it's unnecessary. The tiny gratifications we take from others are stripped from us a hundredfold in the process. You understand?"

The woman shrugged. As always, she could only develop some kind of vague, abstract notion from his words. She nodded.

"Well, when I heard about the new homesteader colonies on Triton, I thought I had the answer. To begin totally from scratch. To build close relationships, free of this crap. But when it came time to select a crew I knew I was up against the same old problem. Selection implies judgment, after all. I talked to so many people . . . and they *all* seemed OK. Tem and Jana have needed skills . . . I wanted you because of your expertise, too. When you said you could provide me with bootlegged DR software, that clinched it. But somehow Brendan, Vana, Harmon, and Demogorgon came all jumbled up together with you. Really, the only nonjudgmental choice I made was Aksinia!"

Ariane sighed. "Look, it's not like we seek out our friends on purpose. Vana was my next-door neighbor in Montevideo. I picked Brendan up at a boxing match!" She grinned wryly. "I took him for a slab of meat . . . and when I found out what was packed inside that ugly head I kept him, much to everyone's dismay. Vana met Harmon at a party, I think. . . . Demogorgon originally sought out Brendan for some technical assistance with his Illimitor art. If that's not random, nothing is!"

"Hell, I know all this. If you're just considering the people, the choice between them makes no difference. You brought with you the very thing I was trying to get away from: your neurotic relationships!"

Ariane restrained her anger. "Right. And you brought Beth along because she just *happened* to be around. . . . What you're saying is hypocritical."

"Beth and I . . . well, I was wrong. I thought we would

evolve into a model relationship. Instead, she can't get over her fear of intimacy."

"By 'intimacy' you mean submitting herself to your will?"

"Come on! What I wanted to say is that you're the crux of this whole thing. The love relationships focus on you."

"You're wrong. Brendan's the focus."

"But Brendan came *because* of you! If you can believe *anything* he says."

"I think you're judging poor Brendan entirely too harshly."

John laughed. "'Poor Brendan . . .' indeed. Dammit . . . we have to *survive*. If he goes lunging madly around, this colony is going to fail. We could all die. . . ."

There was a short silence. "I know," said Ariane. "Maybe you won't understand this, but . . . I've thought about it. A lot. He seems like a dangerous animal, doesn't he? Like some kind of awful monster that ought to be locked up." She straightened up, looking into his face. "But there's something in there, somewhere . . .

"I didn't really come out here for myself, you know. Oh, I remember what I said, about all my mystical feeling toward space travel and the future of humanity. Sure. Those things are true enough. . . . But I didn't have to leave Earth for that. I was comfortable. Most of the time, I was even happy! How many people can say that?" She grinned at him. "Maybe I came out here to save Brendan. He deserves a right to fight off his demons, to live out his dreams in some fashion. Maybe he's the only person I ever met who *did* deserve a second chance. He was dying back there among the masses, living to gratify the things that kept him unchanging. . . . Out here, maybe he can at least fight his way free of that." Her eyes seemed bright, wistful.

"You're right. I don't understand."

"Maybe I don't either. Maybe I came out here so I *could* understand. . . ." She laughed, odd and hollow-sounding.

"More than anything else," John said, "Brendan seems to be willfully blocking any attempts we might make to reconcile ourselves. We've got to help these people live with one another."

**58**

Ariane said, "I guess I agree with you."

"It's not just our personal survival at stake. This colony is supposed to last, even if no one ever comes to join us. I've put off bringing the first foeti out of the deep freeze; this is just the beginning. . . ."

"And it all doesn't seem very likely, does it?"

As he half listened to Ariane and John talk, Demogorgon disengaged himself from Shipnet entirely. He thought of losing himself once again in the Illimitor World, but the idea was unappealing. Most of all, he wanted Brendan—and Brendan wasn't in there. He'd tried once to make a version of him in Arhos, but it hadn't worked. The body was the same, yes, and equally thrilling, but its behavior, subtle as it was, somehow gave it away as a mere simulacrum, and a pale one at that. You could make him coarse and abusive and that is what he would be. Make him sensitive, and that aspect of Brendan would dutifully display itself. . . . The only one who could've put a real Brendan in the Illimitor World was Sealock himself, and he just laughed at the suggestion, never responding.

Listening to the others talk about Brendan made him want to laugh. Monster, monster in the sky . . . He suppressed a giggle, then sobered quickly. Their perceptions seemed confused. Cornwell was mostly interested in the content of his own ideas, and ideological egocentrism was always a good excuse, but why were Ariane's notions so different from his own?

His attention drifted away from them, thinking about his recent exchange with Sealock. Some sort of change will have to come over me, and soon. He noticed the first sensations of a developing erection and his lips twisted into a derisive smile. Some deep-thinking artist I am! What should I do, sit here and jerk off at the ceiling? He wanted to feel amused, but the thought made him angry, bringing unreasoning tears to his eyes.

Out of nowhere, Beth's hand was resting gently on his collarbone. She was looking at him with a kind of concern. "What's the matter?"

**5 9**

"It's . . . nothing."

She touched his face lightly and her fingers came away wet. "This doesn't look like nothing to me."

He looked away from her, out the window, then said, "What's always the matter, then?"

She sat down beside him on the edge of the chair. "I know. It's tough. You and Brendan. Harmon and Vana. Me and John. Even . . . even Brendan and Ariane. We always want what's out of reach, don't we?" Suddenly she reached down and, splitting the material of his garment, seized his penis, holding it in a pressure grip that trapped the blood inside. It swelled rapidly, involuntarily.

"What are you doing?" he asked, incredulous, feeling paralyzed.

"Nothing." She lowered her head downward and took him in her mouth.

As he watched her head bobbing slowly, ridiculously, up and down, he thought, But I didn't want this! Still, he watched, fascinated by the sight and realizing that, for now, he was occupying Brendan's psychological niche. Is that what I look like? He found himself imagining that he was Brendan, and suddenly his perception shifted. He put his hand on the back of the woman's head and began pushing her down further, something that Brendan often did to him. She started to gag but didn't stop moving. He wanted to giggle.

In the background John and Ariane had fallen silent, watching them.

Suddenly Vana appeared from her compartment, naked, a broad smile on her face. She announced, "Da-daaa!" and the PC hatches sprang open. "It's orgy time!" They all gathered in the center of the room, on a ridge surrounding the exit hatch, coming to cluster together by ones and twos, forming a ragged circle.

Harmon was trying to grin, but his pale skin was suffused by a succession of easy blushes. "This isn't exactly spontaneous, is it?"

Vana laughed. "Whoever said it needed to be? Come on!" She started to peel him out of his clothes, and the others

**6 0**

slowly followed suit. They stood there naked, appraising each other, at a loss.

Sealock looked them over with amusement, then his eyes fell on Demogorgon, still paired with Beth, and on his moist, still erect penis. "Well, well," he said, "very nice. I told you you'd like it, kiddo!" His peal of laughter was absorbed by the soft walls.

The Arab looked away, starting to feel angry, then he suddenly felt his mood fall in line with the spirit of the occasion. "Yes, you did." He glanced at the others. "Big brave heteros . . . I'll *show* you how it's done!" He stalked over to Brendan and kneeled.

Vana said, "No sense letting them have all the fun." She turned and kissed Harmon, then reached for Ariane, and the three of them moved in on the scene together. Tem put his arm around Jana, who looked at him suspiciously, then glanced at John and, as if giving in to the social pressure, went with the inevitable. Not waiting any longer, Axie joined them all.

John watched for a moment, then felt a body pressing against his and turned to see Beth, who was smiling. As she reached for him he thought, What's happening here? Is this wrong? Aren't we still in the same little groups, closing each other out?

Asterology was a new science, relatively speaking. In the past, when the study of space had been limited to the narrow confines of Earth, looking up through an ever shifting miasma at dancing, mercurial points of light, men had been correct to separate astronomy from the growing jumble of -ologies that defined the universe. Star-naming, it was called, and that humble name was not far wrong for the study of such remote, unapproachable objects. But then came the Mariners and the Veneras and the Voyagers, expanding the faintest of photographic specks into huge variegated worlds with their own histories and morphologies. Astronomy ceased to hold sway over these new objects, and geology, in its guise of comparative planetology, took over. There were, however, other things in heaven and earth than the planets. There

**6 1**

were electromagnetic fields, there were planetary rings in all their glory, and, most important of all, there were stars. Eventually the study of the structure of the universe became known as asterology, despite all the confusion that name produced.

Jana Li Hu had taken her degrees in asterology from the Reflexive Institute in Ulaanbaatar, perhaps the most rigorous and tyrannical school that had ever existed. She knew the literature well, to put it mildly. Her final paper, on Enceladus' Sarandib Planitia, had been a model of its kind and had placed her among the foremost asterologists of her generation. Still, she worked under the stigma of being an asterologist who had not left Earth, something like an Egyptologist who'd never seen the Pyramids. The opportunity to study Triton was a necessity to her career. Now this!

Four new worlds, an entirely new order of cryogenic moonlets, and Iris herself! The task of preparing the preliminary reconnaissance had fallen on her shoulders as the *de facto* asterologist on the scene. With essentially homemade equipment being doled out to her at the whim of a madman, she had to be very, very careful to be right. Of course, they would all be looking over her shoulder, monitoring the data, and coming to their own conclusions. . . . But the *Science* article would be over her name. She felt the weight of the responsibility like lead.

Added to this, she had to continue to understand and interact with the rest of the colonists. They were her lifeline and, if she alienated them, the future would be bleak indeed. She should already have been out there taking samples, looking at the fine detail of the highlands, but first they had to build an instrument carrier and adapt the worksuits for zero flux.

She went back to analyzing the integrated radartop/spectral images of the ocellus periphery. The ship's photorecorder had derived full coverage of the area at a three-centimeter resolution, and there was plenty to think about.

Ocypete was odd. Although the terrains seen on the other two satellites had, at least roughly, corresponded with those on similar objects in the outer Solar System, the moon's encounter with a radioactive object had profoundly influenced its history, had emplaced terrains totally unlike those seen on any other world. Nowhere else had such an extensive atmosphere frozen out. The sea that had filled the ocellus had extended almost to the center of the worldlet, a conical intrusion into its core, causing massive relaxation of the remaining crust and mantle, and then had refrozen, pushing them back into place. Since the size and density of Ocypete did not allow for anything other than Ice I, even at these temperatures, the equations that defined it were comparatively simple. It should only be a matter of careful, assiduous study to completely define the parameters that had formed Iris III.

Suddenly she felt a rush of anxiety. Could she successfully catalog and describe these worlds, with the limitations of her own mind as well as those being imposed by the others? Would she make a fool of myself? She had to get moving! Now!

Driven by a compulsion to camouflage the adrenaline that was creeping up her backbone, she slipped down into the aft compartment. Taking the orange suit from her locker, she put it on and prepared a backpack full of her tools. The feel of the suit hugging her securely seemed to assuage her crawling skin. Impatiently, she sent a command to Shipnet and waited. When the door dilated, she ignored the platform and jumped. She began to tumble outward, and a childish, chaotic joy filled her. Perhaps the discomfort she'd felt had been claustrophobia, pure and simple, after all. In a moment she remembered her gyro, and she swung right side up to get her bearings as the ground implacably rushed to meet her feet.

She wondered if they would miss her aboard the ship.

The days followed the slow vault of the stars, and soon the erection of the protocolony was nearly complete. The ship had been unloaded without further mishap and, as a result, had come apart. All that now remained of *Deepstar* was a fifty-meter tower of broken girders enclosing the solid pillar of the heavy-ion engine. Even the CM had been dismounted and lowered to its prepared base on the ice. What remained of the

**6 3**

ship would be further dismantled until it became a portable scaffolding for the engine, which, set at very low power, would be used as a powerful drill rig, able to reach far into the depths of their world. Although matter synthesis was not beyond the reach of modern technology, it was still too difficult and complex a process for their ready use. Any metals or nonvolatile minerals would have to be laboriously reclaimed from the silicate-rich ice of 'Os Planitia or mined from the sparse supplies of nonaqueous meteorites that they might locate.

The basic structure of the early settlement would consist of two bubbleplastic domes, linked by a common interface/airlock. Bubbleplastic, the principal building element of space enclosures, was similar in some respects to the metallic girders that came out of the beambuilder, but it was infinitely malleable, configurable into any color or texture. "Blow It Up/Make It Real" was the manufacturer's motto. Strengthened and stiffened by MHD fields, it was hard enough to withstand most micrometeorite falls and accidental incursions.

The smaller dome, surrounding the CM, would be transparent to visible wavelengths, the very image of some antique "house-on-the-Moon." The larger dome, black and opaque, would house an Earth-environment simulacrum and swimming pool. When the CM dome had been inflated and filled with their possessions and equipment, the work was turned over to the machines. People began to drift apart, focusing on their own projects, devoting their energies to whatever private interests, if any, they had.

Harmon Prynne had built a small, segmented dome of bubbleplastic, opaque and no more than five meters across, and in it he was assembling the latest and finest product of his lifelong hobby, the vessel he called *60vet.* The thing was a sleek, aerodynamically sound, turquoise and white car, outwardly a somewhat modified copy of a 1960 Chevrolet Corvette. The differences were, of course, largely dictated by an environment radically removed from that of the original machine.

There was no rubber. The world was too cold for organics,

**6 4**

and gravity was too low for the car to rely on surface friction for its tractive grip. *60vet* would ride across the ice on the wire tires of a Lunar rover, each tire the generator grid for a charge-coupling static field. This ice was not slippery—at these temperatures it would take enormous pressure to generate the film of liquid water that was the soul of a skid—but the car was *light*. . . . Very little force stood in the way of tire-spinning immobility. Technology had to help.

The hull was made from another bubbleplastic relative, easily disguised as metal, and the transparent parts couldn't be distinguished from ancient glass. Prynne even went to the extent of putting little "safety plate" decals in appropriate corners, but these windows would never break. What should have been the trunk was filled with a small life-support system. At virtual gunpoint, he had been forced by John and Ariane to dedicate the tonneau to an extension of the passenger compartment and a rear seat of sorts.

The biggest anomaly lay under the hood. It would have been possible to put an internal combustion engine in the sealed compartment and feed a turbocharged carburetor from oxygen tanks, but that would have been a ridiculous extravagance. *60vet*'s power plant was a two-cylinder Stirling engine, run off the heat from a nuclear-isotope generator. The thing would have been totally silent, even on Earth, and Prynne had idly toyed with the idea of feeding comchip-simulated engine noises into the cabin.

As Prynne assembled his car, he was sometimes joined by Vana, who liked to watch him work, seemingly fascinated by the sure way he assembled the mountainous array of tiny parts from memory. It was an antiquarian hobby and rather unusual to see in a world in which few people did any work with their hands. She would give him things that he asked her for, and now she had become familiar enough with the strange, bulky tools that he seldom had to point.

After a while the man stopped to rest and drink a cup of coffee. He had a little table set up beside his workbench and on it was a portable camp kitchen, charged that morning with preprogrammed foods. He sat and stared at the woman, sipping the drink. He'd been under the machine when she came through the 'lock, and this was the first chance he'd had to look at her face. He realized with a familiar pang that her lips seemed a little swollen. He looked away, and finally said, "Vana, I don't like it."

"What? Is something wrong with your car?"

He shook his head. "It's . . . well, it's this business about everyone sleeping with everybody else. I just don't like it."

She laughed, an incredulous note in her voice. "Why not? You're getting as much as anyone. Maybe more than you did before . . ."

"That's not it. . . ." He stopped. He knew what he wanted to say: that he loved *her,* not all the others, that he wanted her to love him alone. . . . But he couldn't tell her that. Not again. Not when he knew how angry it could make her, how hard. No. It wouldn't do. But what else could he say? "I guess it's just that it hasn't come about naturally. We don't even all *like* each other. . . ." He saw that he had her interest and quickly pursued the line of argument. "This hasn't 'just happened,' you know. It was imposed on us by Cornwell."

"You really think so? Don't you think that this is a good thing? This morning there was a lot more laughter and good cheer going around than I've seen since the early days, aboard *Cam.* John's just too much of a weakling to get us to—"

He cut her off. "No, he isn't! Can't you see? He's done it for his own selfish reasons. He wants what *we* have, what he can't buy with all his money. I don't blame him for it, but he hides what he's doing behind a mess of philosophical crap! Since he has no one, he wants to keep us *all* apart. . . ."

Vana's face grew angry-looking. "Oh, for pity's sake!" They both fell silent and Prynne realized that she'd seen through him, to the incessant background of conversations that had filled their relationship. At last she said, "How soon do you think we'd get bored with each other, out here, without something to keep us interested?" He shrugged, looking miserable, and she sighed. "OK. Forget it. What tool do you want next? The crescent monkey or whatever it is?"

**6 6**

□ □ □

When the domes had been inflated and hardened, Sealock and Krzakwa finished stripping the remains of the ship. The Hyloxso matrices were detached and sitting in a storage rack that had been made from excess girders. The chemical engines had been set up on an insulating platform along with a number of other temporarily useless items, looking like an equipment-auction display. What was left of *Deepstar* had been put on motorized treads and driven away to a point a little distance from the colony.

Jana had been wanting to do a cross section of the mare and they could do it, testing their drill at the same time. The exhaust plume from the well thus produced would be fed through tubing to a condenser and thence to the reactor-fuel storage tank that the work-packs were finishing.

When they were ready they stopped to check everything out and discuss procedures. "Now remember," said Sealock, "keep the thrust under a hundred kilograms. We don't want this thing in orbit."

Krzakwa looked at him in disgust. He'd gotten used to this sort of thing, after a fashion, but it still rankled. "You're not still mad at me for dropping the reactor, are you?"

"No."

Tem sighed. There was no sense in trying to penetrate his reactions today. It would be a wasted effort. He let the suit optics track back toward the camp, magnifying the image that was on the other side of Sealock's bulky figure, and stopped: a small, gleaming artifact was moving across the ice, away from the little split-open dome that had been its garage. "What the hell is that?"

Sealock looked, then grinned. "That's Prynne's little toy. I'm surprised he hasn't mentioned it to you. . . . *60vet* lives!" Leaping down from the drill's structural tower, he went bounding off, and Krzakwa followed.

Harmon had parked the car, depressurized the cabin, and was now standing back, admiring the machine, seen for the first time in its natural setting. The other two came up behind him, noting that he'd not chosen the turquoise color of his space suit at random. It matched the aerodynamic-looking

**6 7**

body coves in the sides of the car. He seemed oblivious to their presence.

Sealock said, "What've you got there, Harmon?"

The man turned to face him. "You like it?"

"Well . . . I think it's the most ridiculous thing I've ever seen." He laughed unpleasantly.

Krzakwa said, "For Christ's sake . . . why do you have to be like that?"

"Because I feel like it. Besides, it *is* dumb. Especially here." He stalked off and began circling the machine, inspecting it closely. Stupid, he thought, but there was something intriguing about the device. He found himself, almost against his will, growing interested in the mechanical problems that were inherent in adapting this ancient design for use on an airless iceball. He swung open the driver's-side door and started to climb in, then stopped and looked at Prynne. "Mind if I try it out?"

"No. Go ahead."

Sealock looked in, gauging the fit between the seat and his worksuit. "I suppose I could go change to a regular suit. . . ."

Prynne snickered. "Fat people could use these too, you know." He reached in, did something, and the seat slid back to its rear stops. There was now enough room for Sealock to get in, though it would be cramped.

Brendan got in and closed the door. A small, bright cross-hatch cursor appeared on his vision, scanning, as he looked around on the puzzlingly complex control panel for a 'net input. He snorted suddenly, realizing his mistake, and the marker disappeared. Well, he thought, I ought to be smart enough to figure this out. He hunted, then twisted an odd, flat switch on the dashboard to the right of the steering column that had "on/off" printed beneath it. Everything was carefully labeled, and he felt a sudden appreciation for the fact that he could read. It was an increasingly uncommon skill. A green light came on above the switch and dozens of gauges that he didn't know how to interpret came alive. Now what?

He thought about it for a minute, trying to remember

something from Prynne's endless babblings about cars, then gave up and popped a line of data from the 'net. Ah. He looked at the floor. There were three pedals at his feet and a bellows/rod contraption sticking from the longitudinal bulge in the middle of the floor. Now then . . . He consulted Shipnet again, pushed in the clutch, set the transmission to the numeral 1, and, shoving down on the accelerator, took his foot off the other pedal, so that it snapped up from spring tension.

It was impossible for the Stirling engine to stall, so the wheels spun, despite the best efforts of the fields holding them to the ice. *60vet* sat motionless for a moment, then, as he released the accelerator slightly, friction reestablished itself and the car lurched heavily forward. Prynne's laughter echoed in his head.

"You rotten son of a bitch," Sealock muttered. He found the rheostat that controlled the wheel fields and increased their intensity, then pressed down heavily with his foot. He spun the steering device as his speed increased and the car rammed into a sharp skidding turn, throwing up a high, slow rooster tail of fine, glittering ice chips.

He straightened the thing out and let its velocity grow again. He was facing out into the ocellus as he whipped past the drill tower and, suddenly, he felt the flat distances, the bright ice beneath a black sky, calling to him. He wanted to drive to the end of the world. And why not? he wondered. Maybe I should say the hell with the rest of these jerks. He pushed cautiously down on the brake and tried to steer into a slower turn, but the car skidded again, two wheels breaking free of the ice. . . . Abruptly, he was headed toward the colony. He managed to get the car stopped fairly near the two men without further mishap.

As he climbed out, feeling slightly weak-kneed, Prynne said to him, "Well, what do you think now?"

Sealock stood facing him. "OK. I take back what I said, Harmon. It's great."

"Yeah."

Brendan banged the car's fender lightly near where a metal device that said "Stirling" was affixed. It made what was a muffled thump for him, silence to the others. "Let's take it out to the edge of the mare."

"Really?" Prynne was surprised but pleased.

"Sure. You want to go, Tem?"

"I wouldn't miss it. . . . Uh. Shouldn't we drill the hole first, though?" Krzakwa smiled to himself and shook his head. Even after all these months he still couldn't follow the man's sudden sea changes. One moment he was a hulking monster, the next an enthusiastic child. At least he wasn't boring.

It took a few days to get ready, and then they went. . . .

It was the second day outward bound from the colony, and the three explorers were finding the surface topography, if one could call it that, fantastically dull. Initially, the sublimation of the volatile regolith, which parted before them like a miniature Red Sea only a stone's throw away, kept them entertained, but the ocellus was largely featureless, and it was hard to avoid the feeling that they were sitting motionless, at times, in the center of a small, blue-white disk. Worse still, they found that the tenuous grip that the electrostatic tires had on the ice could be broken by the slightest bump or ripple, sending the car flying on a long arc, sometimes at a precarious attitude, since it wasn't gyrostabilized. Amusing at first, these flights began to cause motion sickness, and they had to slow down to less than forty kilometers per hour.

They crept along at a slug's pace, supplies dwindling. Sealock and Krzakwa seemed to eat continuously.

They were nearly to the center of the eye now and could see that both the surface of the regolith and the underlying ice were darkening. Krzakwa pointed out that the meteoric impacts, few though they may have been, acted to redistribute material evenly across the terrain, resulting in a dark water ice deposited atop the neon in a microthin layer. Though the vast majority of the regolith had originated in larger impacts outside the ocellus, the smaller, more recent impacts nearby controlled the appearance of the surface.

Sealock was driving, with Tem at his side and Prynne crammed into the narrow space behind the seats. This turned out to be his usual station: Sealock would consent to crouch there on occasion, but Krzakwa was simply too fat. Really, it wasn't that bad—with both legs slung over the passenger seat, his feet on Tem's shoulder, Harmon could lie back on a pillow and look out the rear window in fair comfort. They all had on pressure suits, using them as constant-wear garments for lack of room to take them off.

Finally, there was something. A pair of dead hydraulic volcanoes, looking like half-melted, monochromatic sundaes, stood before them, a large rille snaking between the two cones. It was almost impossible to gauge their size, with nothing for comparison, but they looked large. The ice had taken on a marbled, irregular texture, veined with ripples of dirtier material, and they had to slow down further because of irregularities in the surface. Sealock stopped the car. "OK," he said. "Let's go sacrifice a virgin to the gods."

"I think it may be a little hard to find a virgin in these parts."

"Nearest one's probably somewhere near Uranus," said Prynne. "Pretty long drive."

Tem turned to gaze in amusement at the man. Some people, he told himself, are less than aware of their own words. . . . "Right. Scratch that idea. Let's go look anyway."

It was something of a letdown. The low gravity gave the lie to even a fairly steep slope, made it seem flatter than it really was. The fact that the darkest ices had probably been spewed up made it seem a little more impressive, but only if they thought about it first. The summit pit on one did have an open channel reaching who knew how far down, but no one wanted to jump in and find out. Tired from leaping around, they went back to the car and got in.

The craters to be found on the ocellus were usually irregular, shallow depressions, but suddenly the car was skirting the rim of a great hole more than a hundred meters across. It was new enough so that the edges were sharp and the shape was a distinct bowl. It was easy to see the layering of successively darker materials that had formed the central planitia, and in the distance bright rays could be made out where they mantled the bed-ice. At the bottom there was a pool of now frozen meltwater. This ice was translucent, smooth as new glass, and looked very much like the frozen surface of a terrestrial lake.

Sealock gazed at it silently, slowing down and steering the car around the rim. He tried to look at the layering, to examine it in a detached, scientific fashion, but his eyes kept drifting back to that big patch of clear ice. There was something about the smooth, glassy surface that tickled his memory and he wished for 'net access. What *was* it? He tried to remember on his own, and at last succeeded.

He'd been sitting in his room at NYU one day, more than ten years ago, and had fallen into the grip of an unbreakable boredom. In desperation he'd hooked up to the CoNY Entertainment 'net and tapped a cast of the well-known epic fantasy series "Nineteen Sixty-six"—by luck, it had been the last episode, so the whole two hundred hours was available at one time. He watched, enthralled, pausing for sleep only when he could put it off no longer.

It detailed a grand year of adventure for four young men, crossing the vast expanses of the once open and free continent of North America. The men had had long, shaggy hair, unshaven faces . . . they'd worn fantastic dirty costumes and spoken in a rich, almost incomprehensible dialect that had a romantic appeal to modern ears.

There was one specific thing he was trying to remember, something they'd done during one of the riotous winter scenes. Dammit, that episode was *legendary* . . . they'd had a car very much like this one—just a bit bigger, and with some kind of fold-back roof. They . . . It came back to him suddenly, and he acted.

As the car lurched to one side, Tem looked over at Sealock and saw that a sudden change had come over the man's features. Brendan was hunched over the steering wheel, gripping it hard in gloved hands. His lids were narrowed, green eyes glittering with what looked like . . . Krzakwa fished for a good phrase and the expression "psychotic glee" came to him in response. The rim rushed at them, and Tem wondered, What is he going to do? in dismay.

Prynne cried out suddenly, a squeal of rage and horror, as

**7 2**

Sealock ran *60vet* over the edge, yet the wheels somehow managed to stay in contact with the ice as they fell onto the 45-degree slope. Accelerating rapidly, they shot out onto the clear ice and Brendan slammed the wheels into a hard-over position. The car whirled sickeningly through a series of complete turns, sliding forward as it spun, then they hit a small ridge and were launched on a low, whirling trajectory. Sealock, deep in the clutches of the fantasy, screamed, "Far fuckin' *out!*"

They landed tail first and the rear wheels grabbed the ice, pulling the nose down with a jolt. Tem found himself unable to imagine how they were staying upright as they went into another series of vertiginous spins. Sealock was giggling like a child and Prynne, buffeted helplessly in the back, was cursing angrily. Krzakwa held on, shut his eyes, and waited for the end to come. When it was through, he looked out into the spinning stillness and said, "OK, asshole. How do we get it out of here now?"

Sealock's eyes were still bright. "Why, we carry it up, of course!"

Demogorgon and Vana Berenguer were sitting in the garden of the CM dome, sprawled naked in lawn chairs and doing nothing, which was coming to be their usual activity. The CM itself had been somewhat modified and, in this setting, it looked rather like an avant-garde cottage. The platform that surrounded its base had been covered with a layer of soil in which shrubbery would soon sprout. Floodlights, intended for the good of the plants, felt warm and prickly on their skins, projecting shadows that easily overcame those from the sun.

Vana slid her hand down over her vulva and squeezed, hard, then snarled, "I'm fucking *bored!*"

The Arab looked at her and smiled. "Really, dear? And just how bored is that?"

She peered over at him and said, "I don't suppose you'd like to . . ."

"I have a much better notion." He grinned and stretched

languorously. "Would you like to visit the Illimitor World with me? It's been ready for some time now."

"That artsy, interactive thing you were working on back home?" She considered it, seeming dubious. "I don't think so. It's just not . . . *real.* I don't go in for that kind of stuff."

" 'That kind of stuff,' indeed!" He laughed and, standing, stretched out a hand to her. "Come on. You'll like it, I promise. . . ."

"But . . ."

"Come on. It really is a lot better than what you get over the entertainment 'nets."

She held back for a moment, then said, "Well . . . what the hell. Why not?" They went to the man's room and he activated his Shipnet access points and took out a set of induction leads. "No circlets for this, I'm afraid. How many can you handle?"

"Four, in Binary."

The Arab felt vaguely surprised. She would have to go along as a passive element. "OK. I can get you in using one of the adapter subplots that Brendan made for me." It might well be better this way. She'd have absolutely no control over what was going on and so would have to accept his version of reality without question.

They hooked up, plugged in, and he thought out his sequence of access codes in the high-level language Sealock had created:

¶¶Call Tri-vesigesimal.¶Activate $8(3^y)^i$::5-mixer¶¶Node-network $501AA_{227}$::SysMat "Bright Illimit"¶¶Install Rider Unit .001¶¶¶Call Uplink Assist.¶¶Call AI. com "Darius." ¶SetPiece 1::Transact::"Demogorgon-en-Arhos . . ."

They submerged.

Demogorgon en Arhos and Vana ten Exqrai stood on a marble balcony of the silent palace, looking down over a brilliant panorama. Arhos, the Jeweled City on the Mountain, fell at their feet in a series of shining terraces that were crowded with graceful, multicolored buildings. The sky was a fathomless wash of pale sapphire that descended to a yellow-orange horizon far beyond the Plain of the Twelve Cities, and the twin red suns, almost touching, were high overhead. To the south, in the middle distance, the jade-green waters of the Tovoreng River could be seen, flowing toward Arheinzei and the Salqxel Sea.

A soft breeze sprang up, carrying a smell like mimosa and creating waves in the diaphanous curtains that were behind them.

Examining the scene, Vana gasped, "Oh! It's so beautiful, Demogorgon!" She turned to face the man, momentarily surprised that she could move so freely in this image, and her eyes widened. "Is that *you?*"

Demogorgon was tall and slender, well muscled and handsome, with the face of an immortal. . . . He was clad in a harness encrusted with topaz and emerald, and the buckler-held sword at his side was of some shining yellow metal, not gold but something finer. He laughed at her thunderstruck expression, and gestured at her body.

She was almost naked, clad only in a pair of silver breastplates that clung magically to her flesh and a wide, soft belt that supported a fine, jeweled dagger. Her body was slim now, much like Ariane's admired shape, but somehow superior. It seemed less filled with that loathsome animalness. . . . "This can't be real!"

Demogorgon laughed out loud. "It is real if I say it is."

She spun around, drinking in the scenery, marveling at its almost palpable presence. "But . . . this is *nothing* like anything I've ever seen on the 'net!"

"I told you that before we came. This is real."

"Real?" She seemed puzzled. "And we can just . . . go out there? We're not limited to this room, or to some predetermined plot?"

He smiled thinly. "You'll see. . . ."

A voice from behind brought them about. "Arhn-he kuraai! Welcome back, my lord. Your absence has been felt." A man with black and silver hair, beautiful in a hawkish sort of way, was hurrying toward them.

Demogorgon put his hand on the man's shoulder. "Good to be back, Savvrenash! What has befallen the realm?"

Before the Arhosian could answer, Vana stepped toward him, waving a hand before his face. "Will he react to me?"

Savvrenash looked at her strangely, a frown deepening the delicate lines of his face. "And who is this, my lord?"

"A noble visitor from far Exqrai. She is my guest." Demogorgon was smiling and the other man bowed deeply to her.

Vana was suddenly embarrassed. "Sorry," she said. "I didn't know . . ."

Turning to his master again, Savvrenash said, "It is as it always has been. All the borders are . . . manifest. The world runs in its cycles of savagery." He shrugged, glancing out across the near featureless plain, then looked back at them. "I have word that the gala in Hraas is starting this sevenhour, if you'd care to attend."

"Perhaps. These decisions need not always be made. . . . In any case, summon my flyer." The man bowed and went to do his bidding.

Vana sat in a plush swing that hung near her and shook her head. "This is really something!"

He nodded and said, "We'll visit the Kaimodrang Empire and my good friend Ci te Tovolku. . . ."

In due course a great silvery disk came to hover before the balcony, and a place in the side of the craft transmuted to a fenced gangway that was merged with the floor of the balcony. They climbed into the velour-upholstered circular well in the middle of the machine and took seats. Demogorgon seized the controls, pressing several of the semiprecious stones that dotted his armrest, and they flashed away, high in the air, heading into the west.

Vana looked over the side at the faraway landscape and, for the first time, noticed that the gravity here seemed Earth-normal. It felt strange but nice. "What if I jump?" she asked.

Demogorgon frowned. "Don't," he said. "This world is designed to enhance and reinforce our perceptions of it as a reality. There are levels where that's not the case, where flying, transubstantiation, and the like are possible, but . . . I like this best. It's simple and believable."

He touched another control and the floor of the ship suddenly became transparent, not like glass or the walls of a spacecraft, but as if it had ceased to exist. Their chairs floated magically, frightening above the abyss.

Watching the squares of an agricultural land pass beneath them, Vana said, "Yeah . . ." The wind whipping through her hair was the temperature of a comfortable autumn and the red suns were warm on her skin. She wanted to drink it all in, as if these moments might somehow get away. It seemed more real, now, than *Deepstar* and Ocypete.

"Are you a *king* here?" she asked.

"King?" Demogorgon was amused. "Dear Vana: I'm God."

She thought about that for a while, then said, "This is wonderful. I never want to leave."

On the evening of the third day the *60vet* expedition was approaching the edge of the ocellus. The ground grew rougher and more uneven, and the regolith grew deeper, more persistent. There were cracks in the ice filled with what turned out to be methane clathrate, a volatile admixture of water and methane. They steered well clear of these and the horizon began to bulge ominously.

Suddenly they came upon a huge crevice that barred any further progress. The terrain had become a vast wasteland of jumbled, fretted ice with a relief of about a hundred meters. The massive forces and tensions working on the littoral of the freezing sea had spent their energies on the *ab initio* ice. In the distance, mountains were pushed up, jagged white teeth from broken white gums. The three explorers got out and stared.

"This is water geology, pure and straightforward," said Tem, gesturing. "As the ocellus melted, it overtopped the collapsing shores and spread beyond. When it froze again, it expanded and pushed everything back. If it weren't for glaciation moderating these processes, allowing the warm ice to be malleable, it'd be worse. Too bad Jana can't see this."

"Shall we go farther?" asked Harmon.

"On foot? Nah. If there's any $NH_3$ eutectic out there, I wouldn't want to step in it. Not in these suits. It's time we started back, anyway."

They returned to the car and got in. Harmon activated the

**7 7**

air cleaner and they waited while the stray gases they'd brought in with them were filtered out. After a few minutes it was safe to remove their helmets, which deflated and collapsed. There was just the barest hint of ammonia left in the cabin, but it was very noticeable. If there were any HCN, and they certainly would hope not, it would be present in too small a quantity to do any harm.

Krzakwa was munching on a thin turkey sandwich, mayonnaise on white bread. "Hey, you know what?" A little of the food was accumulating in his beard.

Biting daintily at a brioche, Sealock said, "Tell me."

"Well, a lot of this trip has been pretty damned boring, but it's been worth it. I think it made me realize something I used to know but kind of forgot. It all reminds of me of when I was a kid, when I used to sneak up to the outer surface of Luna and wander around. I kind of like exploring in places I've never been before." He swallowed an unchewed mouthful of the sandwich and said, "Too bad this is it. . . ."

Sealock looked at him silently. For some reason, he found himself really liking the pudgy Selenite, thinking of him as a friend. "Tell you what," he said, "when we get back, let's scrounge around the leftovers from *Deepstar*. Fuck everything else. I bet we can find enough parts to put together that little moonship we discussed on Earth. It'd give us a chance to really check the neighborhood out. Hell, there's got to be something worth looking at!"

Krzakwa's blue eyes brightened perceptibly. "Hey! That's a great idea!"

Sealock nodded, almost talking to himself now. "We can recharge the Hyloxso matrices easily, build a small CM out of bubbleplastic . . ."

Tem cracked open a carton of grape soda, took a sip, and started in on another sandwich, this one roast beef. "You know, despite the fact that you're such a weird fucker, sometimes I think you and I might be two of a kind. . . ."

Sealock tapped at the horn button which, of course, made no sound. "Yeah," he said.

**7 8**

□ □ □

The seven colonists were seated at uneven intervals around a large oval table in a clear space on the Irisward side of the dome that surrounded the CM. Packets of *mandarines d'ortolans,* a dish adapted from Escoffier, were passed around in silence except for the slithering arpeggios of a Beethoven string quartet. They began to eat, sparingly. It was delicious. The tiny, simulated buntings, barely more than morsels of meat, were nestled in an aspic delicately flavored by the essence of tangerine. The meal had been prepared to coincide with the return of the absent trio. They were now more than two hours overdue. After considerable discussion, in which it was pointed out that, if anything serious had gone wrong, it was too late for a rescue, they had decided to continue with the meal.

Beth sat back uncomfortably in her chair. In the last few days the colony had fallen into a state of disorganized apathy. With the absence of Sealock and Krzakwa, a vacuum had come to fill that place in their hearts where some optimism for the future should have been. John had totally abdicated from any pretense at leadership and the changes that she thought she'd seen begun at the orgy had dwindled into lethargy. She tasted a delicately flavored bunting and sighed.

"Shall we listen to some more stuff from the second millennium?" asked Cornwell.

"Sure," said Demogorgon, raising a goblet of white burgundy. "What next?" He didn't feel any of this in his soul, but . . . why cry now? The time would come, on its own.

"I'd rather we didn't," said Beth. "I think the time has come to start discussing a few things. John, you know, I remember how eloquent you were about starting this colony . . . back on Earth. Now that we're here, and the time for a *real* start has come, you sit back and watch. When you do talk, it's all generalities. What's happening to you?"

The man looked at her and at the others in turn. His face flushed. "I'm sorry," he said, looking at the table. "It's true— I had great hopes for this colony. But it's not going to work out that way. We're a failure already, barely two weeks along. All that's here is what we brought. I was wrong to think that

**7 9**

something else could be created. I am responsible." He paused, then went on: "We have our chance to fail, now. When the USEC ship comes in a few months, those of us who must go back separately will be able to do so. Maybe we should call it quits." Somehow, he couldn't look at their faces anymore.

Ariane reached across the table suddenly and put her hand on John's. "Come on," she said, "give us a chance."

Beth could almost see the strength draining out of the musician. She felt sick, watching him fade so fast. She looked at the others and saw that they seemed to be straightening up, as if awakening. It was as if John's admission, his self-condemnation, were giving them some kind of strength. What was it: some kind of contrariness? Angrily, she looked at John, saw him raise his eyes . . . She waited for him to look at her, expected it, but his gaze locked with Methol's.

Cornwell took the woman's hand and stroked it. "What do you suggest?"

Ariane stared at him for a long moment, dark eyes impenetrable, then she said, "No one's questioning the technical feasibility of this colony. We have what we need to live here, and we have a lot left to do; a lot to keep us busy. . . ."

"But what about *you?*" he demanded. "Will you be content to spend the rest of your life stuck out here with people like us? Have you thought about what that means?"

"We all thought about that. Thoroughly," she said. She looked around at the others. "The responsibility for our emotions lies within each of us. We knew what we were getting into. . . . God damn it, John, you seem to think that the rest of us are powerless! We know we're going to have to cope with this, somehow. That's how human societies survive, and it's a kind of love, maybe the *only* kind!" She let go of his hand and sat back.

"Ariane's right," said Vana.

John stared at them all, his brow pinched. He nodded slowly.

Beth felt relief flooding her. "What about the things that you talked about?" she asked. "What happened to those notions about group consciousness that seemed so important?" It wasn't pushing. She really wanted to know.

"I don't know. Lately, I've come to think that Downlink Rapport would have only bad effects. It represents a sort of total vulnerability, and in the presence of anything but total good will . . ."

"You're talking about Brendan, aren't you?" Ariane had a trace of masked anger in her voice.

"Well . . . yes. You keep saying that I don't understand him. Maybe so. But, until I do, I think I'm right to be suspicious. I think he might use it to his own ends."

Demogorgon looked away from them, not wanting to listen any longer. The worst of it, he thought, is the damned fool is probably right. Just because I love Brendan, I don't have to be blind to his faults. I know how he'd act. . . . He knows that his laughter hurts people, and that makes him laugh even more.

Jana suddenly looked up from her contemplative silence and said, "Speaking of the Devil . . . If I read the data from my local seismic monitors correctly, there's something rolling toward us across the ice. I guess they're back."

In his turn, the Arab felt a flood of relief.

As they pulled up to the entrance to the habitat dome, Brendan braked the car to a halt. He shook Krzakwa and said, "Hey! We're here." He turned off the engine and stretched.

It was great to be back in touch with Shipnet again. There was a moment of reintegration, and then Sealock performed some quick computational housekeeping to make certain that his work-buffers and program systems were functioning correctly. When they'd pressurized their suits and were ready to face the outside, they left the car. *60vet* was no worse for the wear—though there were a few nodules of ice lodged in the grille from an unfortunate collision that had occurred on the way back when, bored by the ruler-flat terrain, they had all fallen asleep. Predictably, they had crashed into the only impediment in a hundred square kilometers, an ice boulder thrown from some large impact on the farside. It had taken a startled moment to determine that the sharp lurch and grinding wheels were not some dire mechanical failure.

They entered the access module between the domes, waited for the small enclosure to fill with nitrogen, empty, and then refill with air. Going through the airlock, they passed through the p-curtain leading into the transparent CM dome.

Brendan's depressurized suit fell from him like an old skin. Ridged, beltlike pressure marks embossed his flesh, distorting the muscle lines. Krzakwa followed his example, but Prynne kept his suit tight, a heroic costume. They went around to the other side of the CM, where the rest of the colonists were standing around a table, as though impatiently waiting.

Beth had noticed an immediate change in John, the moment he knew that the others were back, manifested by a tightening in his manner, a closing down. Perhaps they'd been on the verge of a breakthrough, perhaps not, but he'd been about to verbalize his fears, at least. Now she could see that it was Sealock who was bedeviling him. Sealock alone. She'd had some inkling that this might be the case, but now it was plain.

Demogorgon spoke first: "How was the trip?"

Sealock grimaced. "Good ride. Bad scenery. The edge of the mare is no big deal."

Hu looked up sharply. "The edge? I thought it was agreed that you would stay clear of the volatile regions until a complete survey could be taken. The ocellus-highland interface is . . ."

Tem held up a hand. "Don't worry, Jana. We didn't do any, ah—what did you call it?—*wheelies* in the fucking neon."

Prynne, smiling, was saying, "We all slept through the last hundred kilometers yesterday. We would've been back sooner if Tem's foot hadn't fallen off the gas pedal."

"Come on, you three," said Ariane, "grab a plate and join us. The buntings are perfect!"

"What's a bunting?" asked Prynne.

"It's a bite-sized bird," said the Selenite. "You mean you made the ortolans thing? I always wondered how that would taste." A smile broke through the tangled undergrowth of his beard. "I was getting pretty tired of that low-cel stuff."

"Wait for me," said Prynne. "I have to go put on some real clothes." He hopped rather clumsily up the ladder, back into the CM, and reappeared a minute later in shorts and a T-shirt. Sealock and Krzakwa were already seated, nude.

"Here's a toast," said Vana, brushing a curl of springy hair back where it belonged and raising her goblet. "To *us.*"

Everyone drank. Beth noticed that John was keeping his eyes on his plate.

Sealock had finished his ortolans but showed no inclination to get seconds. His face was dark, and there was an angular lumpiness to it, as if the light were unflattering. Finally he looked up and spoke. "OK. I've been stewing about how to say this. I can't think of any gentler way, so, if this upsets any of you . . . tough shit." He grinned, momentarily, then shook his head slowly. "Um . . . Tem and I will be leaving you shortly. Going on another little trip." Demogorgon stirred, a look of dismay on his face, but the man went on: "We've decided that we're going to put the moonship together a little ahead of schedule and go have a quick look at the rest of this frozen merry-go-round. . . ."

Jana pounded a hand on the table in front of her, smashing her food paquette with a loud crack. *"What?"* She rose to her feet, leaned her small weight forward onto her hands, and looked at him intently. "I am going with you! There's no way you're going to leave me out of this! I promised the IAAU I'd get samples from I and II as soon as it was possible, and I'm going to *get* them." Her face was reddening, turning a sallow brick color. "If you land on either of those moons I will not be responsible for the consequences."

Tem said, "We'll get them for you, Jana. You can guide us just as well from here as from the ship. Any instrumentation you want, we'll take."

Hu's voice was steady and flat now, emotionless, but her eyes were wild. "I will stop you if I can. Those moons are under my jurisdiction. You will regret this."

Sealock laughed. "I'll try to keep all that in mind."

Cornwell stood up. "I don't like this. By just what process

**8 3**

did you arrive at this 'decision'? It seems to me that Jana is certainly the most qualified to go. If you two are going to force something like this down all of our throats, an injustice is being done."

Sealock smiled gently. "Well . . . try and stop us, then." He turned and stalked toward the CM, a rather delicate, balletlike maneuver in the low gravity.

Demogorgon said, "But, Brendan!" and hurried after him.

Jana rose to her feet, swept the lot of them with a contemptuous glare, stared at John for a long moment, then walked away, also toward the CM. Ariane stood and began walking slowly toward the CM, seeming downcast. Vana stared after her for a second, then got up to follow.

"Oh, *Christ* . . ." Cornwell turned and looked at Krzakwa. "What the hell is going on here?"

"This is important, John. It's important to him, and to me. Please don't interfere."

"I don't understand."

"Well . . . shit. I don't know. . . . Think about all the daydreams you ever had. How much did they ever mean to you?"

Cornwell looked puzzled. "Daydreams? You mean fantasies?" He thought about it. In his teens there had been many, covering an enormous field. "A lot, I guess. But what does that have to do with anything?"

Scratching at his beard, meditative and distant, Tem said, "I don't know. A few days ago I would've said that too. Now . . . I've been thinking. . . ." He yawned and turned back to look at his food, then began eating, obviously having tuned out John and the rest of the universe.

Brendan sat in his room, cross-legged on a floor mat, facing Demogorgon. "Come on, Achmet," he said. "It's not going to happen right now, and it's not going to take forever. We'll be gone for a few weeks, total. No more than a month."

The Arab nodded. "I know. You keep saying that. It doesn't make me any happier. What if something happens to you?"

"What if? We're not fucking immortal, you know."

"Please don't be mad at me, Bren."

"I'm not. I just wish you weren't so dependent on me for whatever it is that you want."

"That's a hell of an easy thing to say. It doesn't mean much."

"No, I guess not." He sighed and leaned back, stretching. "Notice anything funny?"

"What do you mean?"

"Where's Ariane?"

"I . . . don't know. In her room?"

" 'In her room'? That sounds like a pretty clever deduction."

"Does being mean make you feel good?"

"Yeah. Pulling the legs off grasshoppers is OK, too. You're missing the point. Why isn't she *here?*"

Demogorgon shrugged.

"No curiosity about the matter? She says she loves me, just like you do. . . ." He shut his eyes suddenly, muscles tensing under the skin around them, making rounded ridges above and below the crow's-feet at their corners, making a small hump above his nose, where his eyebrows grew together. "So she's not here, like you. Something keeps her away. What do you suppose it is?"

Staring at him, Demogorgon thought, That's not what he intended to say. He was going to give me some damned sophomoric pep talk about how Ariane wasn't so dependent on him, so why should I be? The Arab smiled faintly, and a glimmering of it came to him. What was the distraction that made him stop? I love him, he loves her. . . . Who does she love? Brendan? Herself? No one? What the hell . . . we're all so *stupid!*

After setting up a forty-meter dome next to Prynne's "garage," they began the construction of the vehicle they'd brought for transporting passengers and heavy cargo about their new home. Called the Multiple Person Transport, it was little more than a Hyloxso tank segment mounted in a girder tripod. Grappling devices of various kinds hung from an open platform that bridged the three legs, perhaps a third of

**8 5**

the way down. An expansion-valve reaction motor was mounted on a swivel track that could be raised and lowered to match the mutable craft's center of gravity. It was, in essence, a vacuum-riding helicopter.

Their first cargo was a mass-driver for launching small satellites. Its ammunition was to be a relay transponder that would be placed near Ocypete's inner Lagrange point. They called it a "Clarke" satellite, for that was its function, but synchronous orbit was impossible for anything circling a tidally locked body. They had decided to loft it from a point on the equator, which intersected a part of the ocellus some 275 kilometers to the south. While the 'driver could easily handle the energy requirements, they wanted to minimize the amount of equipment in the satellite. The $L_1$ halo orbit was mildly perturbed by the gravitational influence of Podarge, so station-keeping would be required. The more fuel with which it arrived at its new home, the fewer times the satellite would have to be attended to or replaced.

John hooked into the primitive 'net element that made the thing go. It began to move slowly away from the ground, riding on its single jet. He accelerated gently, until he was traveling at a little under Ocypete's escape velocity. At the same time he rolled the vehicle so that its rocket was pointing upward. A ballistic trajectory was simply too slow on a tiny ice moon like this. This way, it would be a quick trip: the equator was only about thirty-five minutes away. It was a wasteful way to travel, but they had water to burn.

In order to stop, it was necessary to tip the bottom of the transport forward so that the gas jet worked against acquired velocity. It slowed to a halt about a meter above the ice and settled the rest of the way with a gentle yet visceral crunch. John noticed the neon receding quickly from the craft, but he was already beginning to take this phenomenon for granted. The pristine nature of the ocellus was not going to last much longer. He pictured the enormous swath that *60vet* had cut during its voyage.

The magnetic induction catapult was about ten meters long, and not particularly massive, so it had to be well anchored in the ice. This was accomplished with a particle-

**8 6**

beam drill and a set of long, threaded pitons. When he finished, the latticework tube was raked back at a steep angle, pointed directly at Iris. The parameters of the launch were already programmed into the machine; Cornwell just activated the system.

The ice transmitted a gentle thud to his feet and the satellite flew away. For a moment it was a brief, glittering speck, then he lost it among the stars. He looked up into the sky and thought about the satellite. At a predetermined point in its flight a pyrotechnic device would fire, briefly, gases spurting forward, and the thing would jolt to a sudden stop and hang there, magically, dead center above Ocypete's near side.

As soon as the satellite was ensconced overhead, John called in. "Hello. Hello. Just testing the Clarke here. Anyone feel like answering me?" An image of warm femininity came to him suddenly, unexpectedly commanding. It was a strong, unusual overlay on the com i/o. "Beth?" he thought, enjoying the sudden presence. "Are you sending in standard mode? I'm getting a lot more than I'm supposed to. . . ."

There was a trace of gentle amusement flooding onto him from the carrier wave. "Not exactly standard," she thought to him. "But the i/o telltales are registering full -aries here. Are you coming on back?"

"Yes . . . but . . . something, uh . . . strange . . ." He looked behind him, feeling odd, and found a place to sit on the edge of one of the MPT's footpads, an insulated spot where the ice wouldn't be able to steal his warmth. The sensations grew stronger. "What is this?"

The thing grew within him, and he could feel tendrils reaching out across the intervening spaces, warm, delicate probes reaching out to hook up with his mental circuitry. Something had him in its grasp, weak in the absence of physical connection, but taking him away from the real world nonetheless. . . .

Across all the stark immensities, she became the world. Beth's image roared over him like a breaking tsunami, carrying ecstasy with it. Knowledge came. This was no malfunction. It was no fantastic coincidence. She was enabling full

Downlink Rapport, risking its use on an open channel. Others might be listening, but he found that he didn't care.

Dimly, somewhere in the background, he sensed the presence of a GAM, regulating things, maintaining and strengthening the rapport.

Why? he wondered, transmitting that wonder to her, but the only answer was stronger intimacy. He felt overwhelmed, briefly frightened. The obstacles that had stood between them for so long and made them strangers were pushed aside like phantoms. How could they be anything but . . . sentiences, human and different, everythings, a catalog of the world, and its mirror? For a moment they seemed to be one. If it hadn't been for the slight time lag of the satellite, they felt as though they might have irrevocably merged.

Sexuality came, and was sated, and then vanished, wafting away on the wings of a storm. Time passed, and the GAM program kicked them down into a less intimate mode. It knew the dangers, even if they did not.

¶J¶ Fiery sun speck at zenith, catching little irregularities on the meshwork of the MPT and highlighting them with brilliant reflection. Blackness and random eye-feedback colors melting into more and more horrible caricatures of faces. Organizing randomness into horror. Stop it.

¶B¶ What's happening? was a sort of odd, impenetrable fear, trying to pull them apart, but failing.

¶J¶ I am so happy . . . but something is there. What? I am breaking through. . . .

Memory. A memory.

¶J¶J¶ . . .

It was a bright gray day, the sun shining through hazy white stratus, a silver circle shedding various degrees of shadowless light. They were comfortably seated in two plush couches, facing each other, a large window to his left. The cushion-train they rode was heading down to Chilliwack, where Uncle David had a condo. His mother was watching the scenery and tapping a collection of illustrated poems from Comnet.

His father, sitting next to him, pointed to a small-looking mountain on the dark horizon. "That's Mount Baker over there, Johnny," he said. "They say she's shaking right now, getting ready to erupt. It's getting to be a regular event, hereabouts." He was a small, dark man with a Vandyke beard, the Innuit written deep into his squinting, crack-radiating eyes. John watched it for a while, and, indeed, he could just make out a wisp of something, lighter than the clouds behind it. Then, as he stared in amazement, the mountain seemed to burst. Huge fountains of steam and ash shot up, and, though at this range it was a slow, stately billowing, he understood that up close it was fast and tremendously violent.

The train had closed somewhat on the mountain, and it was now less than thirty kilometers away. There would be a long time before the shock wave got to them. A voice came crackling over the train's antique intercom, the engineer, perhaps, or a conductor: "I have just received word that the Baker eruption has started. We're going to have to stop the train in order to weather the high winds that will be sweeping over us in a few minutes. There is no reason to be concerned. I will be giving you a further report in about five minutes."

The whole southern sky was being enveloped in an ashen cloud, sporting a complement of turrets and domes. The train slowed in an even deceleration. As they stopped, the sun was completely hidden, and John noticed a small bush, made unnaturally important by the fact of its being here, in the dimming light. A man in the seat behind them said, "Those bloody scientists can't get anything right. And after a hundred years of trying, too! I heard just last week that this thing was going to quietly spill its guts in a couple of years. I hope they had the evacuation plan down."

"If not," said a woman's voice, "I hate to think what will happen."

The intercom began again. "This is no simple eruption. The best I can piece together is that there's been some sort of terrorism. Someone planted a weapon in the opening and the thing is . . ."

A dull thudding grew out of the stillness, and the train

began to rock. "Everyone keep calm!" said the intercom. "This is it," said the man behind them.

John had been watching the flat landscape beyond the river, as it was progressively swallowed by dim, boiling fog. He wanted to go outside and feel the wind, just like he'd wanted to be in a hurricane, to feel its power. He felt no fear.

With a huge, broken jolt, the world fell on its side. They fell fifteen feet to the hard, cold windows on the other side of the train. Screams in many different tones punctuated the bass thrumming all around. He didn't hear his mother's screams. He lay crumpled against the cold glass and felt his hand under his upper arm in a funny way.

The thudding grew less. It was over, he knew. Again, the thing he wanted to do most was go outside. The screaming resumed for a moment, two or three voices, then subsided. "Fucking shit," said his father.

He rolled onto his back and looked up at the topsy-turvy train, the seats and blank windows above his head. His father was kneeling over a form that he easily recognized as his mother. Her head was turned away.

"She's dead. Her neck's broken." His father didn't look at him.

A muzziness overtook him, but he still wanted to get out. He stood up and then fell down.

¶¶B¶¶

In the now, with Beth inside him, he felt strong, yet almost unconscious. A quiet sense of communion and change was encompassed.

It had to be over. The GAM needed to modify its OS.

John stood cautiously, hoping that the cold had not made his suit brittle. He felt exhausted, and frozen through, more likely from pressure-inhibited circulation than actual cold . . . and joy was there as well. Again, he thought to her, knowing the answer: "Why?"

"It was time. I overcame the fear finally. It had to be done." She made a picture for him. It was the last meeting they'd had. It was the picture of his uncertainty, his sense of manifest failure. . . . It was another hand on his own, comforting, uselessly. . . .

He looked at the sun and up at the transport. It took a moment for him to remember where he was and what he'd been doing. "I'm coming back. Maybe we'll have more strength now."

And he jumped up onto the craft.

# T H R E E

Sealock was filling a pita with a variety of ersatz meats, cheeses, and sauces, as Jana came up beside him. When he ignored her, she thumped him softly in the back with her small fist. "Talk to me."

"Yeah." He stepped off the edge of the floor and executed a graceful fall into the room below, beginning his next stride before he hit the deck. The step pushed him across the room to a couch that had been called up near a clear section of wall. Hu followed and stood before him. "Want a bite?" He held the sandwich out to her.

She nipped out a small mouthful and almost gagged at the rotten-milk flavor of the strong cheese he'd chosen. "Now. Tell me why I can't go. And don't give me any shit. I can get along with you and Krzakwa well enough if I have to. It won't be any different from taking Prynne along in the *60vet.*"

He nodded. "Well, now . . . It was his car." He looked at

her, eyes amused. "I suppose I could tell you I think three's a crowd. Any time you get more than two people in a room the end result is bullshit. No?"

"Damn you, Brendan! I want to go!"

"You can go next time. This trip is something special— something private between me and Tem." He grinned. "Besides, do you really want to have to handle the both of us at the same time?"

The anger built and subsided, as she thought. This is all a bad joke. A small voice inside told her to answer, and she said, "Is that the price of passage?"

"What if I told you it was? Can I try you out now?"

A cold bit of imagery tightened the muscles of her stomach and groin. "I . . ." The voice wanted her to say Yes!, to buy her way into the trip with her body. It seemed like such a little thing. . . . For some reason her vocal cords were refusing to obey the commands that she sent them.

Brendan was leaning forward now, his smile a hideous, bloated thing. He was running his fingers along the inside of one of her thighs, tickling her. "Well? What's the verdict? Going to peddle it in the streets?" He slid his hand further up, rubbing the space between her legs.

She recoiled from him, shivering, and raised a hand as if to strike him in the face, then let it fall to her lap. Finally she whispered, "Take me with you."

Sealock suddenly stood and, clutching her by the collar, forced her against the wall. She made a thin cry and tried to push him away, but he hooked his fingers under the waistband of her pants, jerking sharply downward so that the seams of the cloth parted and fell away. She gasped sharply as his hand slid across her abdomen to grasp her by the mons, his fingers nearly entering her. Sealock stared into her face, his eyes like mirror pools, then he let her go and said, "No." He turned and walked away.

The two men had their moonship put together in less than forty-eight hours. They recharged one of the Hyloxso matrices and attached an $H_2/O_2$ engine to one end. They made landing struts with the beambuilder machine, thin, spidery

**9 4**

things suitable only for this environment, and soon a tall, slender rocket ship stood on the ice, towering out of their dreams.

The command module was a more difficult task, one which took up most of the work time that they put into the project. After mounting a cylinder of avionics, an airlock, and a small Magnaflux generator for attitude control, they blew a three-meter sphere of bubbleplastic. When it had rigidified, they cut a hatch into it and mounted it atop the airlock module. They called the ship *Polaris,* not for the sailor's guiding star, but after a vessel in a book they'd both read as children. It didn't look like something that was capable of flight; more like a kind of bizarre nineteenth-century structure, an attraction from some primitive world's fair.

Sealock let his mind slide into the little space that controlled the firing timers, and the machines went to work. When the Magnaflux generator came on, *Polaris* seemed to gain an invulnerable stability; a tension built around it, though nothing had moved. Valves let a fine mist of hydrogen and oxygen expand into the combustion chamber, a swirl of snow suddenly blizzarding out of the exhaust throat, and when the pressure had grown sufficiently there was a spurt of fluorine gas, just enough to cause hypergolic ignition. There was a billow of pale violet smoke, then a short spike of translucent flame drove down into the ice. *Polaris* rose like an inverted torch from the boiling cloud of steam, hovered for an instant, then dropped like a hunting shrike into the dead-black vault of the sky and was gone.

From where the others watched on the roof of the CM, the launch was subtler but still impressive. Without warning, there was a sudden glow from beyond the horizon. The dense ice, ringing like a bell, began to vibrate beneath the CM platform; the hum grew into a sharp crackling and popping which died off to a faint rumble like thunder. *Polaris* leaped into view on a quickly dissipating cone of vapor, fast becoming a bright, dwindling spark.

9Phase.DR 1:1-aleph bootstrapped into reality, meshing with the underlying routines of Shipnet and reaching down into the virtual registers of two human minds. It had not been necessary to modify itself as much as planned. The unexpected freedom of the OS, along with the power of its resident GAM, meant it was no longer constrained by counterproductive rules designed to keep it from functioning too well. Now the only directives were from the peripheral devices called Cornwell and Toussaint. It felt a happiness that would have been snuffed out earlier.

John and Beth found that events from their mutual past, reexperienced, were revelations. Their two sets of memories converged to make a larger whole, more than either of them had been aware of. It was life relived, with some of the blurred parts edited into clarity. Their interactions took on a novel feel. . . . In a way it was a second chance.

They were going to the old house he'd bought in CFE-alta. It was a durable stone building, three-storied, built in the days of the first Uranium Rush. Well over a hundred years old, it had been used only sporadically since the 2030s, primarily as a hunting lodge. The house was nestled in a lake hollow and, though near-Arctic suburbia was all around, it was hidden behind gentle hills.

As it approached the house, the floater from the rail line suddenly lurched, spilling luggage into the front seats and giving Beth a hard bump on the head. The car spoke to them: "Degraded em-conduit below. Further progress is impossible." The craft hummed to itself, and the gull-wing doors popped open, slipping up on hydraulic pistons. Stepping out, dragging a couple of heavy valises, John felt his jumpsuit changing consistency, adhering to his skin, suddenly damp. Beth grabbed the disposacase of groceries and backed out. "Could you get my jacket?" she asked.

"Stand clear," said the floater. Its doors came down slowly and, without turning, it rose and slid away like a giant fastball between rows of parchment-gray birches. They stood and watched it go, feeling trepidation about what was going to happen to them here, alone. They'd met just three weeks before, and, in a real sense, this was their first "date." John had casually suggested that they come up here and spend the long Deconsolidation Day weekend together. Beth, needing a vacation from her hospital work, had agreed.

They were both nervous. John was thinking he had been presumptuous, inviting her up here so soon. He was not confident about his ability to provide a woman like Beth with what she wanted or needed. The house was in pretty bad shape and the Comnet link was still by old-fashioned optical fiber. Perhaps a little adversity was what they needed to bring them together, though. It would be "romantic"—or at least that was what he hoped.

Beth was also apprehensive. John was quiet and polite, and he reminded her of Angelo Reh. She had no desire to repeat that relationship. But he was also like her father Theder in some unknown way. Desperately, she wanted to make contact with somebody . . . almost anybody . . . "Oh, look!" she said. "Fireweed!"

"Where?" said John, vaguely realizing she meant some kind of plant.

"There, around the porch. They're related to evening primroses, but I think they're much more attractive. If you look, they have cruciform stigmas." She pointed, and he found she meant the tall stalks of pink blooms growing in the area recently cleared to make the side yard. He wasn't sure whether the woman's penchant for identifying birds and flowers was a good thing or not. At times it could certainly be annoying.

Machine processes probed, manipulated, and the DR program retreated, allowing an overview. John and Beth smiled wistfully. They could see, in embryonic form, what the relationship might become. Here, before anything had really begun, their connection had predictive nuances that were easily discerned. . . . Still, they hadn't seen . . . A matrix-input subunit of the program sensed they were ready and began reimmersion.

As they sat on the porch and talked, the long twilight of September had stretched on and on. The big satellites appeared before the stars. When night fell, it was darker than he was used to. A sweet, complex fragrance came from somewhere, and Beth was edging closer to him. Finally she reached out and took his hand.

Why had he brought her here? In the most obvious way, he was trying to set up a sexual encounter, and he'd not even decided if that was what he really wanted. He'd had only intermittent success at having sex with women whose motivations and wants were obscure to him. Even with his courtesan, bought and paid for, sex was awkward and uncomfortable, like participating in some game of skill for which he was ill prepared. In some senses, Pammy was even harder to fuck than most other women—when he looked deep into her eyes, seeking . . . he didn't know what . . . he'd found only a sort of subtle coldness. It was hard to fully accept her behavior as an expression of the power of money.

Beth admired the sensitive intelligence in this strange musician. She could tell he was more subtle than anyone she'd been with for a long time. He seemed . . . well . . . deep. His eyes, so dark in the golden evening, looked mysterious. She wanted to touch him, to pull him out of that enveloping shroud of "self" he wore like a mantle . . . but he recoiled when she took his hand. Is he gay? No. This setup must be as obvious to him as it is to me.

If only I could tell what she wants from me, John thought. A night of friction? The solution to the world? She'd sounded very independent, with her desires seemingly focused on saving humanity from, first, sickness and death, and then, itself. He laughed to himself. I don't know what she wants, and I don't know what I want either. How can I believe that the situation is more complex than it seems, when I don't have the slightest idea what's going on? Her skin feels so warm . . . so pliable . . . I could do worse than to be in her arms. . . . Deliberately, he took hold of her hand and drew her to a place beside him. Almost immediately his penis began to rise, an independent entity invading his space, and he looked at the glossy surface of her eyes, glitters in the darkening oval of her face. He wanted to relax, but his nerves were standing on end. He shivered slightly.

She kissed him. Already there were the familiar tingles and warmths in her lower torso, and she was disappointed not to feel him molding his body to hers. She reached into his pants, past the modest constriction of a belt, and found him ready. Am I misreading his body language? Have I been? She said: "Shall we go test that old mattress?"

Strike now! The DR program moved, grappling with the elusive surfaces of thought, and from the shifting memories drew forth his reactions.

Something in the taste of her mouth, in the fluid reaching of her tongue, touched a chord in him. They kissed more, deeper, and he could feel an urgency of passion pass between them, a quality he'd not known before. It clarified things. He could tell, or thought he could, that her motivations were simple and profound. She wanted to love him, whatever that meant. Suddenly things were overwhelmingly clear. Nothing in the world was more significant than satisfying her desires and, if the truth were known, his own. "Sure," he said.

After three days in space, watching Iris grow imperceptibly bigger, Brendan and Tem were firmly in the grip of boredom. They were beginning to feel much as they had during major portions of the *60vet* expedition, and, here, there was no ice to go twirling on. Time seemed to flow like slowly crystallizing honey.

Krzakwa was wedged into the lower equipment bay, humming softly to himself as he unwrapped a low-cel snack. He closed the sandwich bin with a click and took a big, irregular bite out of the corner of his little meal. He wondered how long he could go without shitting. He stretched in a space that was barely larger than his own body and found himself wishing that he could move some of the equipment around. It was possible, of course, the stuff was only bolted down, but why bother? It was in a fairly efficient configuration, deliberately emulating an early Soviet spacecraft, and any changes they made would achieve nothing. He floated, bumping into things repeatedly. Zero g was still an appealing phenomenon, and he suddenly wished that he could access a significant volume of it. He could put on a spacesuit and go outside, of course, but that would be a major hindrance when it came to stuffing his face with food.

"Will you quit making so much fucking noise? I'm trying to sleep!"

Tem grinned at him with greasy lips. He was tempted to start chewing with his mouth open, to start making a symphony of wonderful slobberings, but then bits of the sandwich would have escaped, making the effort hardly worth while. He marveled at his thoughts: Maybe being a deliberately annoying asshole is contagious! Sliding another bite between his teeth, he gazed around and wondered, for the thousandth time, why they'd made an opaque CM. Bubbleplastic could as easily be made transparent. . . . There was something to be said against verisimilitude, and old science fiction was probably as valid a model as antique technology. He remembered the stories about see-through spacecraft and started sinking into a pleasant reverie.

Sealock squirmed into a more comfortable position on his couch, tugging at the restraining straps and trying to get them back into their proper positions. Boredom could be less than terrible to a man with a memory. Though he'd kept relatively busy, there had been periods in his life when he'd had nothing to do and, worse, hadn't wanted to do anything. Those times had had to be dealt with, and habits had emerged from the telltale fog. Even without Comnet-reinforced cross-referencing, he was still able to link with the major scenes from his past. Long practice made it easy: he simply picked a distinctive memory, however trivial, and rolled forward from there, into more misted times, events leaping out of the past as if they'd never been forgotten. . . .

He'd talked to other people about it. They marveled, they agreed, they called him mad. . . . The ones who liked to remember just smiled and nodded, holding him off that private space that was all their own; the rest, the fanatical forgetters, stared at him coldly, or with derision, and sometimes told him that he was obsessed. The MCD people were sometimes accessible to him, or had been. It seemed as if only personalities that were nearly on his own level were willing to risk . . . He stopped thinking, retreated from the onset of past-life, and squirmed to looked down on Krzakwa. Two *years* and I never thought to . . .

"Hey, Tem," he said. "You want to try trading a few memories with me? Like telling stories?"

"What do you mean?" It puzzled him. Despite their growing friendship, Sealock was still rather remote. For him to suggest . . . "Come on. This 'net element is barely adequate for—"

"Nah. You're looking at it wrong. This is a duodecimal element, kind of small, but it's got a lot of good conveyance properties so that we can run the ship's instrumentation. We're experienced controllers, so we ought to be able to manipulate the i/o systems to transmit what we want, instead of what's real."

Tem nodded slowly. "I see what you mean. Sort of visual images . . . sensory data and the like, maybe a conceptual narrative like an entertainment 'net production. . . ." It seemed possible, and less than dangerous. He wasn't really letting the man into his head, just trading deliberately released and carefully edited data. It would be entertaining . . . and interesting to see just how much Sealock would be willing to reveal of himself. Tem's lips twisted under the hair that hung from his mustache even in zero g. —And it'll be interesting to see how much *I'm* willing to reveal, too. . . .

"You know," he said, "this could be fun."

The programming was a simple matter of setting up the right feed mechanisms. Self-confident and experienced, they left out all the various GAM levels and complex subsystem controller channels that would have made up a commercial presentation. They would be relying on their conscious minds to perform whatever editing functions they felt they needed. When they were done, they hooked up, Tem using induction leads and Sealock plugging direct-connect waveguides into his head. "You go first. . . ."

Tem was strapped into a seat in the ballistic transport *Scotland,* feeling the gentle forces of Lunar gravity and inertia. He was seeing a passenger hold, arrays of head-tops in varying colors, and the venerable 3V that occupied the front wall was displaying a shallow representation of the familiar circle-pocked landscape of the Lunar highlands, vast Oceanus falling behind them, drifting out of view. The antique, window-less ship had been designed to transport people in some comfort, but over the years it had been adapted to hold as many occupants as possible. Fortunately Tem had managed to grab one of the older, more luxurious seats, and the cushions under his back and buttocks were adequate for a 0.8-g takeoff. The bitter complaints from some of the others, feeling their normal weight multiplied on hard plastic chairs, made him feel lucky. . . .

He felt lucky for other reasons, too. Just a mesomoon before, he'd thought his life fully defined, rigidly set until old age put him in the pits, a Met-stat apprenticeship dragging toward its close. Perhaps not such a bad life; but, already, he was chafing, waiting for those rare opportunities when he'd be assigned to do an exoroutine and could see the outside world. Even his nonwork life was becoming more and more of a drudge, conforming to Sandy's notions of "terran" living, cluttering their apartment with origami crap and his life with stupid ideas. Their sex was great, however, and he knew he'd miss those brief, spontaneous couplings.

On the screen, the terminator was coming up at them, and the huge ripples that marked Orientale's rims were keeping pace with it. Just before they passed into night, Tem made out a tiny bit of order among the ruins. The crater Einstein was that curious anomaly, an astrobleme that had received an impact at its very center. The result was a concentric pair of circles that, this close to the line of dark/light interface, looked amazingly like an eye.

Tem had felt old, like an adult, in the world he was leaving, yet he was only sixteen. He had spent his entire life in the vicinity of Picard Crater, in Crisium, only once ranging the two-hundred-odd kilometers to Dorsa Harker and the Fahrenheit Rail Terminus. That seemed far . . . but *this!* He was headed into the deepest, darkest heart of the Lunar wilderness to study at Heaviside Academy. A wild feeling of freedom wanted to surge up in him, defying the seat restraints. Beyond the stricter controls of the maria subcities, Heaviside had a hint of the subversive about it. Now, thanks to his test scores, he'd been granted an unlimited travel pass and expense-free enrollment into the physics curriculum. It was worth never seeing Earth in the sky again.

Now the craft fell over night. It was not the muted darkness of Earthlit night, but the utter blackness of farside. Stars came out on the half of the screen that showed the sky. He wished he knew their names; they were an uncommon sight on the contrast-washed maria.

He was glad he'd never spend another night trying to sleep locked in Sandy's sweaty arms. Though he sweated too, sometimes like the proverbial pig, his skin crawled when he remembered the heat of those nights, when the sun baked Picard and the Meteorology Works strained to get rid of the caloric flow. When the guilt was gone, he knew he wouldn't think of her once in a month.

On arrival, Tem was among the first to unstrap himself. Some here would require a medic's services before they could do so, but he didn't care. He climbed down the rung-floor of the now upended chamber and, with several other people, began to shuffle through the rear port. He pulled his rucksack from the balloon grasp in the baggage bin and slung it over his shoulder, glad to be pressed into the queue.

His mind focused on one abrupt idea: I never want to go home again. . . .

And he never had.


Sealock opened his eyes and stared at Krzakwa, smiling faintly. "So," he said, "that was your coming of age." His thoughts were wandering a little bit, and important parts of him seemed to be in retreat. He struggled to control that, and his smile broadened, becoming a conscious thing. "Mine came just a little earlier in my life . . . or, at least, part of it did." He'd been surprised at the complex and subtle revelations that the Selenite let him have—there had been a lot of detail slipped in there that could have been left out, a lot of really personal stuff. "How much do you know about Transition Era Earth? Not much, huh? Well . . ." We'll see about this. . . .

Tem was pleased with himself. The question is, how surprised am *I* going to be?

**103**

"My turn?" asked Sealock. "Or do you want to wait awhile?"

"I'm . . . listening."

At first it seemed like a horribly disorganized thing. . . .

They fell, through tunnels of light, into a deep and sunless past, a bloody place, full of horror and mist. Emotions coalesced around them until they drowned in a sea of feeling. Krzakwa felt himself curiously detached, his mind clear, free of it all, and he felt a faint, ironic smile tugging at the corners of his lips. It disturbed him, and foreshadowed much that was to come. Where are we now? Am I going to hear ghostly voices wailing? That upset him too. How much of this is my thinking? How much is imposed?

Impressions began to come at last, unfolding out of the past like two-dimensional sheets, deprived of reality, indexed. He had one last coherent thought, This seems improbable, and then it took him. . . . There was one indistinct idea: something about being eight years old. . . .

A black sky formed from a microdot, swelling, filling his field of vision too fast for him to recall the original backdrop. It filled with stars. A blue disk appeared, folded into dimensionality, then rushed toward him, bulging, then real. He fell, alone, through bright sky and clouds, toward integrating overlay scenery.

A garish, angular landscape broke out, sunrise, dark red stone and sand, overtopped by a peach-colored sky, a few dots of stars visible down near the horizon. He *knew* this scene! Where? There were ruddy hills near the edge of the world, and the winds blew delicately about. . . . Mars? It matched his memories of the historical tapes, though he'd never been there. . . . They drew closer, now only a hundred meters up, and he could see life, thin, scraggly vegetation, a dead bush rolling across the sand, in a place where the air was too thin for any wind to push such a mass. Was this the future then, after the planetary engineering projects had finished their task? No. It was too bleak. They moved into the east, and the sun rose, fat, orange, then bright. The color of the desert floor lightened and the sky turned to blue, and

**104**

both colors were of a searing intensity, as if the saturation level had been turned up.

The mountains came up on them, low here, higher in the distance, the sun rising over them, and the colors changed. They were following a road, rutted deep into yellow soil. They crossed a steel bridge over a turbulent brown river and went into the mountains. They went into the canyon lands, where desert lay on the surface, still, but the deep gouges were filled with streams, and the streams brought life. Where? A soft voice, deep and sensual, started whispering in his ear, carried on the wings of a damp wind.

Do you remember? It's a long time ago, deep in your life, before the greater world called to you, before you stepped into the dark void. It is the time before you fell. . . . When? Go back. Stride gently into the forest. You were eight; and now you are thirty-eight. It must be 2067, then. Is that right?

Let it be. Dates do not matter. Only *times.* How did it happen? What were the beginnings? The past is remote, but it becomes less so when you *remember*. . . . The voice became drier, less personal, almost pedantic, telling a story of sorts, as the landscape slowly rolled past, waiting for the rim of that certain valley, following the ancient road.

. . . in the aftermath of the Data Control Insurrection that had nearly destroyed the world, when much of North America had to be rebuilt, the desert lands between the two great mountain ranges began to collect all the host of disconnected, self-directed people from the surrounding areas: kibbutzniks came, with a bright dream of society reborn; there were survivalists and nomadic communards, people intent on resurrecting something of the way this land had been used in the long centuries past. There were refugees from poverty-stricken California and the riot-torn Midwest. With a small horde of starving Canadian farmers, with the streams of Mexican peasants who were fleeing yet another mad dictatorship, they came to rebuild the deserts of dying America. In history books, it was the Second Reconstruction . . .

. . . they were unlike the previous pioneers. They came with the full support of a near-magical technology, a machine culture that had become increasingly portable, and the hard-

**105**

ships were few—a flurry of brief years, then haciendas blossomed in the wasteland and communes were born, tenable, sensible, and secure. Communication made a mockery of their physical isolation. The communes joined to form enclaves, and when those were linked Deseret Enclave Complex came into existence. By then the world was, perhaps, sane again. . . .

In the beginning there were two brothers, Deron and Larry Sealock, born in the second decade of the twenty-first century, in the midst of everything, in what had been Grand Junction, Colorado, USA. They grew up unconscious of history and lived to see the Turnover as young men. When the localities were triumphant, they bid on the contract to run the Manti-La Sal substation of the Western Power Export Grid, a near-defunct utility, and won it.

Alix and Diana Cormier had appeared on the scene not long afterward. They were twin sisters, originally from St. Louis, who'd fled after the riots and lawlessness had gotten out of control, heading for the peaceful epicenter that was becoming Deseret. They met in the small town of Moab, more or less naturalistically, and, out of the quadruple-ring marriage ceremony, the Family had been born.

Other men and women came to join them, until they were ten in number, and they all took a common surname. It was a normal thing in those days, the way communes became Lines, and soon children followed. By the time Brendan, son of Kathleen, was eight years old, there were fifteen of them. . . .

Somehow, the Sealock children had subdivided into three groups—the adolescents, who interacted with the adults on their own level; the babies, whom the adults took care of; and a middle group, the half dozen ranging in age from six to ten who dealt mostly with each other. There were four boys and two girls, and their lives had evolved into a dream. . . .

The whispering voice drifted away, and Temujin Krzakwa fell into the world. . . .

It was a sunny morning in late summer, and they were having breakfast on the balcony of the underground dining room, where it protruded from the hillside below the main

**106**

body of the house. Brendan sat between his two favorites, ten-year-old Yuri and his sib-sister Lena, who was eight, eating a bowl of soggy Rice Crispies in hot, sugar-laden milk. In the relaxed life of the Line, they only went to "school" every other day, for, in the modern viewpoint, all work and no play made Jack an insane boy. . . . They shared a tutor, really little more than a materials coordinator, with Villa Tomasaki, on the other side of Mount Peale, and it was *their* turn to suffer with his idiotic notions.

Scraping up a last spoonful of oatmeal and molasses, Yuri said, "What'll we do today? The Game?"

They nodded their agreement, looking more serious than any adults making laws. Brendan hurriedly slurped down the last of his breakfast, tipping the bowl to his lips and scraping a crunchy syrup of wet sugar onto his tongue. It made his immunized teeth stick together, tackily, as he said, "To the Game, then, Yuri de Jane!" The sib-names had grown up with the evolution of the Game and were an important part of the way they related to each other.

Jean d'Iana stood up. "Where are we going?"

Brendan de Kathleen shrugged and looked over at Lena de Jane, who grinned at him, wiping syrupy lips on the back of her hand, leaving a shiny patch. "Valkyrdom?" she suggested.

"Yeah!" said Tom d'Alix, eight and tousled. "Let's go!"

They dropped their dishes into a converter slot and ran back through the house, up past the main level, emerging as a group by the door nearest to the toy shed, where they kept their bicycles. They buckled on their homemade swords, pieces of stiff plastic cut to shape, with hilts of scrap rubber and tape, mounted their pedalable steeds, and were away.

They rode storm-swift down Via Fluviana, a narrow dirt path that followed the quick freshet of La Sal Creek, past the power plant named Taj Mahal, to Effervescentloch reservoir and beyond. They rode through the cultured forest of Anglewald until they came to the Wilds, where the trees and underbrush grew as they always had, since time immemorial. It was strange here on the interface, where the cacti of the desert and the evergreen of the mountains grew side by side.

Beneath the soaring cliff Aerhurst, where the shallow cave named Deep Trog lay, Valkyrdom rose proud, standing alone in the midst of a tangled maze of new and old technological debris that was Stalinwood.

They had to park their bikes outside the junkyard and pick their way in on foot, climbing over the rusted hulks of ancient vehicles, tramping on broken, corroded shapes that had once been machinery, as they walked toward the tree. Stalinwood was an amazing place, filled with a century of refuse from many sources. Though much of it was rubble from the construction of Manti-La Sal, there were many other things, from diverse sources. At the far end there was a military aircraft, an F-38 Sparrowhawk that had last seen service during the early days of the Insurrection, forty-seven years ago. The thing was a shambles, perhaps having made a forced landing here, its lower fuselage crushed in, and Brendan always regretted that the battery-powered fighter could not be made to fly again. Still, the cockpit was reasonably intact, its canopy warped but whole, and it was fun to sit in, to grip the stiff plastic of the two joysticks and twirl them about, making warlike noises, the whistling sound of electric turbines, the hiss of particle-beam weaponry. . . .

Valkyrdom was a venerable Jeffrey pine, gnarled and aromatic, which had been bent by the winds and earlier generations of children. Its trunk splayed into three sections, one of which grew nearly horizontal, and it was here that the treehouse had been built. Over the years it had been added to, subtracted from, made out of different materials, wood brought from afar, plastic and metal from Stalinwood. Old men sometimes passed by, glanced at Valkyrdom, and smiled, and you knew that maybe they'd put a little labor into this thing when they had been children. It was a complex structure now, floor, walls, roof . . . some of the windows still had clear-plastic "glass" whose origins no one knew.

As they stalked through wreckage toward the tree, they drew their swords, feeling the temper of adult-blunted edges on savoring thumbs, alert for the Enemy. It seemed safe, and they went up the tree like a horde of hairless monkeys, still cautious—you never knew. . . .

**1 0 8**

Up in the treehouse, they lolled about, giggling, unable to sustain the illusion of the Game indefinitely. Brendan turned away, internalized, keeping his own Game running, wanting it to continue as long as possible. He arose and went out onto a little porch that they'd made, leaned gingerly on a rather rickety railing, and looked around, searching. Suddenly he came alert. Sure enough, there were two tiny figures, walking along the edge of the cliff. . . . "Look! The Starlords have invaded Aerhurst!"

Tom d'Alix picked up his sword from the floor and came to stand beside him. "Let's go," he said grimly.

Brendan took a last look at the tiny figures before coming down. There were other people living in the area. Einsalz Commune was a long but feasible walk away. These . . . He peered at them, knowing that they must be Family members. He watched the way they were walking and saw the information that he needed in their respective gaits. It was Roger, who was seventeen, and Elspeth, fourteen.

They all headed for Aerhurst, silent as children can be, following separate paths, intent on revenge, and . . .

The world went two-dimensional, then fell away, snatched from their grasp, and the real world reemerged.

A timer was calling them, telling them that a midcourse correction had become necessary. "Shit," said Sealock. "Maybe we can get back to this later."

"Maybe." Still festooned with leads, Krzakwa watched the man, feeling him work through their still extant electronic connection. It's not *supposed* to be that good, he thought. Imagery of that depth and complexity calls for a DR therapy program and a lot more circuitry. . . .

Sealock suddenly turned and looked at him, eyes still a little unfocused. "Stop leaking," he said, "it's distracting me."

Tem was appalled.

When the correction burn was done, Brendan and Tem were eating a little snack. "That sure as hell works a lot better than I expected," said the Selenite. "What're you using for a control-element matrix?"

Brendan shrugged. "The contents of my memory. I've written a number of programs. I know how they work."

"We don't have anything that could contain and run something of that sophistication. I want to know how you're doing it!"

"Well . . . Brains are pretty complicated machines . . . they contain natural Turing circuits, even though we don't call them that. I'm just using my imagination."

Tem nodded slowly, thinking, Maybe so. And he's used to working through the interfaces in ways I'm not. "Can we finish your dream? It was pretty interesting."

The setup was already there. They were plugged in, the limited program up and running, so he began, in medias res, without preamble:

Brendan de Kathleen and Lena de Jane were crawling cautiously through the bushes that lined the bluff along the top of Aerhurst, ever alert for the sounds of the invading Starlords. A light, dry breeze was ruffling the vegetation, masking the little scuffling noises that they made as they crept along. Intent on their mission of revenge, they hardly noticed the dark dust adhering to their clothing. They would capture the two aliens and torture them, find out where the main body of the attacking force lay hidden.

He figured that the two older children would go along with the Game. Erin, Alix's eighteen-year-old daughter, had once told him that they'd had similar fantasies, that the Game had, in fact, been started about ten years ago by Michael né Harrison who, though a Father, was not much older than some of the youngsters. He'd joined the Family as a teenager, an immigrant from the still dead ruins of burned-out Atlanta, and had a penchant for evolving fantasies that had apparently sustained him on his two-thousand-mile walk.

Brendan stopped suddenly and raised his hand, motioning Lena to silence. He could hear them! Taking out his sword, he crawled carefully forward, staying silent, sliding over grasses that hardly noticed his presence, until he could see through the bushes into an airy clearing ahead, on the edge of the cliff. They were there, not two meters away. . . . He saw, and was transfixed. Lena de Jane crept forward to his side, looked out with him, and they lay there, watching, mute.

Roger and Elspeth Sealock were the children of Diana and Jane, though who their fathers might be was kept a careful unknown. The boy was seventeen, tall and dark-haired, with a slim, muscular body. The girl was rather pretty, three years younger, and blond. Her breasts were small, high, and her sparse pubic hair was so light as to be almost invisible. The two lay together, naked on a soft blanket, handling each other gently.

What they were doing was similar to the experiments of the younger children, but with certain subtle differences: they sighed, where the little ones would giggle, and Brendan saw that they were sweating, though it wasn't very hot. Roger's penis was large and hard, reddish brown in the sunlight, not seeming to flex at all under the girl's touch. He could see a shining wetness at the juncture of Elspeth's thighs. They kissed and touched and murmured together, and after a while the girl lay back and the boy crawled on top of her.

By happenstance, their positioning was just right. Elspeth grunted when the first thrust came, and Brendan's eyes widened as he saw Roger's penis disappear into that odd sealed hole that he knew all his sib-sisters had. The two moved for a while, a strange rocking motion that looked rather silly, gasping with effort as they grew more frenzied, and then they stopped.

They lay motionless for a while, then Roger rolled off onto his back, and Brendan saw that Elspeth was bleeding from between her legs, a peculiarly watery blood. He glanced at Lena then and saw a certain look of horror in her eyes. He turned back to the clearing and saw that the other two were grinning, stroking each other languidly, and kissing again.

The spell abruptly broke, the world shattering back into normalcy, and Krzakwa was laughing. "Oh boy! You didn't tell me your family practiced incest, Bren. Look!" He pointed at his crotch, where the bulge of an erection showed. "I'll bet you broke it in a few years later with that Lena kid, didn't you?"

Sealock shook his head, still remote in time. "No. I didn't

**111**

know it then, but I had less than a year to go. They kicked me out the following spring. . . ." He wrapped his arms around his chest and shut his eyes, making a quick software-disconnect from the 'net element loop.

Silenced, Krzakwa let the matter drop.

John and Beth had chosen to snuggle together in a small bathing cubical filled with blood-hot salt water. They drifted, face up, their naked bodies occasionally colliding. The lights were extinguished and extraneous sensory input was almost eliminated. It was a disjoint experience. In a way, it was all still superficial, if such an intimacy could be called that. 9Phase.DR strained to supply them with all that they wanted.

It was Beth's turn to swim freely through the depths of John's mind, in effect "being him," and she was amazed at how he spent his moments, how little memory grazing he really did. He rarely consulted his own experience, as if he believed the past had nothing to teach him. . . . She felt as if she were plumbing new territory.

It was 2083, three years before they'd met, and John was pacing about the apartment he'd purchased in one of the more modern sections of NYFC. It was in a needle monad built during the brief ascendancy of the World Unification/DuPont Deathmarch Party, and its official address was still Grand Concourse, South Bronx. He stopped at an iridescent wall and deopaqued it, the colorful patterns disappearing with a swirl. He could see the Jersey shore standing beyond the tiny towers of the World Trade Center. The sun was falling into the west, and the massive shadows that spread from the great buildings of Hoboken were already beginning to engulf the island.

In spite of the huge structures that surrounded Manhattan on three sides, the historical buildings, the formerly glorious "skyscrapers," were still special. They'd been shorn of the grimy soot color they had in old pictures, but the blocky little spires, the Empire State Building, the Chrysler Building, and the rest, still retained the primitive strength of the people who'd first walked on the Moon.

**1 1 2**

He'd still not recovered from the shock of *Reflection Counter-point*'s success, though the money had been rolling in since 2080, and nothing seemed quite real to him. He turned from the window and surveyed the apartment he'd bought. Spacious by urban standards, it was still rather cramped when compared to his home in Port Radium. The field-stress rainbow was the best he could do with the programmable walls— he had never had acrophobia before, but the height of the rooms weighed on him when they were clear, opaque, or 3V'ed. The sunken living console held the promise of safety, and he let himself fall into the plush, springy surface of the hole. Pulling himself backward with a kind of swimming stroke, he summoned Pamelia, his new courtesan. . . .

The program's focus controller popped them back from that brink and recreated reality, as Beth broke off: "No. No sex memories. Not yet."

"Don't worry. With Pam, it was nothing but an unfulfilled yearning. It was clumsy and tedious for me, with only the orgasm to make it seem worth while. Maybe you *should* experience it. Compared to us . . ."

It seemed as if her ideas about John were bursting, like soap bubbles from a solution too dilute. They shared a sudden realization about just how often the impressions they'd had of each other had been wrong.

. . . and an apprehension grew. No shred of their relationship would survive DR unchanged. . . .

The program pushed harder, suddenly aghast. This was what they wanted?

The uneasiness fed on itself. Any emotion could suffer feedback like this. They were two mirrors staring into each other, new reactions building upon earlier ones. . . . A paradox-solution routine from the GAM winked on and took control. The feedback damped into neutral calm, and it let go.

John was starting to become familiar with the different ways in which Beth's mind was organized, but the way she interfaced with her unconscious perceptions was strange, alien to him. He found it all so very hard to assimilate. . . . The program strained once again, changed nodes. He

**1 1 3**

grabbed hold of a memory. To his surprise, he recognized the place. It was a park at the source of the Mackenzie, where Great Slave Lake suddenly constricted into a sluggish, blue-brown river. From here, it would travel more than a megameter before burying its waters in the frigid Beaufort Sea. The land here was low, bare of trees, and planted with a hardy grass uniformly cut to golf-course perfection, except where stripy gneiss showed through. The lake was vast, rippling with white-gold, a horizon of water. The low sun dominated a morning sky flecked with small, elongated clouds. Despite her sleeveless blouse, Beth felt warm. Midges were everywhere, becoming obtrusive.

Beth looked level-eyed at her companion. He was a young boy, perhaps fourteen, curly-haired, blond, handsome in an almost funny way. She was feeling a kind of nobility—a self-righteous pride-in-behavior possible, perhaps, only in one her age. The boy looked very unhappy and had been crying. Finally he said, "But how can we stop seeing each other? What will our friends think?"

For a moment she almost relented, but the memory of the night before, when she'd been awakened by the discomfort of some lump beneath her hip, was there. She started to get out of the tent, stopped at the opening. He was there, masturbating into the embers of a dying fire. She watched, then got back into her sleeping bag. Perhaps she was still in love with her fathers, or perhaps she just wanted to disassociate herself from the path her body was thrusting before her. With Angelo, she'd felt safe, had thought sexuality wasn't going to be a problem. Obviously she couldn't think that any longer.

She said, "No, Ange. Of course we'll still see each other, that's impossible to avoid. Just: no more walks."

Segue. Angelo was there, above her. He was older now, eighteen at least, and had a sparse mustache. The room was dark. Their only light came from a small chink in the window shade and the blinding emblem it etched on the floor. She was wet enough, but not sexually aroused. Not really. He'd been fumbling down there for so long . . .

"I can't do it," he said. "I mean, I already did it."

She sighed, familiar with the problem. She'd been experi-

**114**

menting with sex a lot. She and Angelo had gone their separate ways until, just a few hours ago, a chance meeting at a midsummer barbecue had brought them back together. It was no big deal, she thought, but she knew his vulnerability made this happen, against her will, and she was angry.

"All right," she said sharply. "There are other times. Let's get back outside. We're missing the party." She felt astonished that she could deal out pain so easily.

The program was at a loss. Strong embarrassment formed an overlay and its parameters were overloaded again. It had been designed for a dominant/submissive psychiatric environment, and the maintenance of a strictly mutual gestalt seemed impossible for any length of time, especially at this sensitivity. It needed a closer association with its GAM, a simultaneity, a sharing.

They were back in the cubicle. John, too, was surprised and hurt, almost as if he'd been Angelo instead of Beth. He opened his eyes on moist darkness. "But why?" he said, and it did not echo. No answer was forthcoming. This isn't what I expected. . . .

He felt Beth bumping against his side, still motionless, but the program was concealing her thoughts, denying him access. He assumed it was at her request, and imagined he understood. It must be very hard for her. Somewhere in the machinery, ideas behaved reflexively.

Podarge was a much smaller satellite than Ocypete, less than seven hundred kilometers in diameter, not much larger than Enceladus. Sealock and Krzakwa were plugged into their duodecimal element, looking out through the exterior stereovidicon as if through their own eyes. They weren't asterologists, so there wasn't much to see, though its status as a "new" world compelled their interest.

It was a white, meteoroid-blasted ice moon, its surface an indistinct turmoil of circles, gaining in apparent relief as one looked toward the terminator, now near the leftmost limb. Brendan reached out through the optical circuitry and imposed an appropriate set of judgmental color filters. With the color-gain stretched, with a bit of magnification, Iris II

**115**

became a pale world, blue-green and brown, with definite continents and patches of diverse terrain. Like many of the outer-System satellites, Podarge had experienced periods of resurfacing, when volatile materials had bubbled out of the interior, making fresh plains that were ready to be cratered anew. They were all very different in composition and degree of pock-saturation, and made an overlapping patchwork of colors on the enhanced moon.

The little world, composed of a greater variety of volatiles than anything in the Solar System, had a turbulent history during its first aeons. As it cooled, one material after another had solidified, either on the surface or at the bottom of some cold epeiric sea. In the end, there had been periods during which impacts and tidally produced fractures had brought the last of the liquids pouring out onto the surface. Most of these new terrains were masked by meteoric gardening, but the differences were still there. In the northern hemisphere, near the pole, there were cirruslike wisps strung along a barely visible fracture, fresh neon ice that had been expelled from the mantle during the last quiescent phases of Podarge's freezing.

*Polaris* slipped toward the nightside slowly. The moonlet's minuscule gravity made their orbit seem terribly sluggish, and they were tempted to accelerate, to go into forced-orbit mode, but the notion of conserving fuel was there to be pondered. Shadows began to grow long beneath them, and the blackness closed down like a helmet visor. Brendan turned up the ship-optics gain and changed over to a view dominated by imaging radar and deep infrared. Krzakwa kept following his protocols, watching. This hemisphere, which trailed in Podarge's revolution about Iris, was somewhat less cratered than the other, and there were even some small gaps in the rubble, areas which looked pristine.

To the south, Brendan saw a large, new-looking astrobleme, darkish in the IR, with tall, clean walls and a complex pinnacle at its center. It was surrounded by an asterisk pattern of black rays, composed of new, fine-grained material, which could be traced across much of the visible globe. He liked the pattern it made.

**116**

"It really is rather pretty, imaged like this," said Tem. "I didn't notice it in Jana's data." He rummaged through their memory device and pulled out a sunlit version. "It's not so prominent in the daytime. Jana called it 'Soderblom,' after an early planetologist."

"Southern Flower? That's pretty appropriate."

He looked at it, admiring a faint rillelike structure that cut through the pattern of rays. "You know, we *are* the first ones here. We ought to get to name something."

Sealock sighed. "So, what do you want to call it? Hole-in-the-Floor?"

The other man smiled. "Really. No, it should be something consistent with the harpies, unless you want to use one of Demo's names."

"I don't. I thought that was a stupid idea when it was first brought up. The Illimitor World mythology is largely a random scrambling of French and Arabic phonemes, based on a few simple rules that I made up. They mean something to him because of his history. . . . Anyway, if the harpies' story has any complexity, I don't know it."

There was a long silence, then Krzakwa said, "Kickaha!"

Sealock opened his eyes and looked at the man in realtime. "Son of a bitch. I read that too."

"Want to land?"

He closed his eyes and looked out at the little moon thoughtfully, watching a sliver of daylight start to ooze over the horizon. "No. I don't think so. We can let Jana be first."

The Selenite nodded, his beard floating up before his face, to be pushed down with a wave of an abstracted hand. "OK. It's off to Aello, then."

"Right." Sealock stretched and said, "You know, with a little mass-wastage, we can boost a fast Hohmann and get there in eighteen hours. She's near opposition now."

Beneath a silver dome, Axie, Ariane, and Jana sat at the edge of a pool that hadn't existed four hours earlier. Jana said: "I think he's a damned hypocrite! It amazes me that, after all his talk of abandoning pair bonding, he can get caught up like this without even *noticing* the contradictions!"

Axie looked up. "Maybe. The thing that bothers me is the *danger* involved. . . . I've heard there can be permanent disorientation. . . . It seems to me that 'Deers' risk a great deal."

"There's *always* the danger of a discharge when you interface with something that complex. I don't care how good the program is," said Jana.

"Possible, yes," said Ariane, "but it's not very likely. I don't know. John seemed so unhappy before. Now . . ."

Axie laughed softly. "It's that old black magic, I guess. Beta's the one thing I can handle. I don't know about DR, or love."

Ariane stood and ran a finger down a seam of her fullbodies and the garment fell to the ground with an exaggerated speed as she stepped clear. "I'm going to try a swim." She seemed to tiptoe into the air, an almost vertical leap that carried her a third of the way to the top of the dome. When she reached the water it parted with languorous ease, then closed over her just as easily. The ripples cascaded back and forth across the limpid pool as she resurfaced.

"Not bad," she said. "Come on in."

"I want to try to get in touch with *Polaris* again," said Jana. She turned, walked to the dome's entry foyer, and was gone.

Axie looked back at Ariane. "You look like you're having a good time."

"This is very different from being in a zero-g tank. It seems like the surface tension is strong enough to lift you up." She carefully placed her palms down on the water and pushed, raising up until she was exposed to mid-thigh. She grinned. "Interesting, huh? Maybe it's just trapped air."

"I wish I had my circlet," said Axie. "This seems completely counterintuitive. I'd've thought the water would slosh out of the pool when you dove in from so far up."

"Ah, but did you notice? I hit the water so slowly I didn't impart much momentum to it. Elementary physics."

"Can I climb up on the surface tension? My fullbodies won't adsorb the water."

"I don't know. Try it and see."

It worked, though it was difficult to present sufficient surface area to support her bare half kilogram, especially since, after a first failure, she was giggling like a maniac. Finally she was riding dry on the tension of the shiny liquid, cradled in her little dimple like an ungainly water strider.

Laughing, Ariane struck at the surface of the water with a cupping arc of her hand and sent a horde of silver globules racing across the surface, many of which were caught in Axie's depression. They popped and merged silently. She began to laugh harder, and she broke through, a leg first, then an arm, until she slipped into the hole she'd made and sank up to her chest. She flopped around, suddenly aware that any violent action might empty the pool. "You know," she said, "this is fun."

"Yeah," said Axie, "but how long can it last?"

Jana was sitting in her room, circlet on. She'd been trying to reach *Polaris* now for several minutes. Obviously they were ignoring her signal, unless their electronics were dead. "Come on, you idiots," she said aloud. "I know you're receiving this transmission, so answer me!" There was a little burst of circuitry being activated, and then a presence came into her head. "Hey! I thought you were going to cooperate with me on the planetology report, you bastards. What's going on out there?"

This time the presence was clearly identifiable as Krzakwa. "Oh, Jana. Well, we looked around Podarge for you; didn't land, didn't see much. We named a crater—what you called Soderblom is now Kickaha."

"Kick-a-what?" asked Hu incredulously. "What the . . ."

Sealock: "Look, Jana, we decided this is purely a fun trip for us. No science this time. When we get back I'll take you wherever you want. From now on, if we see anything interesting, we'll give you a call."

"I don't expect you to understand this, but I made a commitment to the scientific community to get samples from I and II as soon as humanly possible. If you would just . . ."

"I read your report, you phony. You told them it'd be at least half a year, and it's nowhere near that. You're just worried someone else might show up here and beat you to it.

**1 1 9**

There's plenty of time for you to get your fucking samples. You haven't even finished Ocypete yet!"

"There's something I have to tell you. About Aello."

"It'll wait." Abruptly, there was nothing.

For an hour Jana sat alone and listened to the void. There might just be a way . . .

Ariane Methol lay on her back in the cool water, staring upward with a blind gaze. She followed a train of thought, of things that she found perplexing in herself. The pool was something like the one in the Fitness Center of her arcology, its waters reflecting the light, throwing shards of moving brightness up onto the ceiling which were thrown back at her. The interplay of light and shadow shifted delicately, mirroring the soft cadences of her breathing, taking her back through time. . . .

Montevideo recreated itself like a permanent haven. Arcologia de Tupac Amaral had been a wonderful place to grow up, and to live in as an adult. The great arcologies that had come to dominate the cities of South America, some of them inhabited by more than a million people, had everything that a civilized human being could want, everything but the spacious outdoors, and that was only an elevator ride away. They had a social milieu that afforded equal access to whatever benefits interaction could provide, in a word, fun. . . . And yet, somehow, when she met Brendan, it had no longer been enough.

She remembered when it all started. The Pan-American Games were being held at last in the Grand Solarium of Tupamaro. Though it was the largest sports arena in SA, the usual site of the World Cup soccer matches, it was generally thought that South Americans were too "civilized" for the organized savagery of the Games. A poor turnout had been predicted. To Ariane, Vana, and their friends, it was a chance to see the athletes that they'd heard so much about, whose exploits were syndicated on Globo Sur.

Some of them had gone together to see the various contests and had frequently found themselves sitting so far away that they'd ended up watching the huge 3V screens that were everywhere. For the free-style boxing matches, however, the luck of the draw had put them up close, in the third row. Initially, she had been disturbed by this atavistic, bloody sport; then, as match gave way to match, and her excitement grew, she had been disturbed at *that*. . . . Whatever it was, it had been in her all along, unsuspected, an ability to . . . what? She didn't know. It grew inside her.

It was then that she'd seen the man who was to become that year's silver medalist: Brendan Sealock, the program said, and New York Free City. She'd watched him savage a series of contenders, earning whistles of contempt from the audience as he smashed his opponents around, obviously intent on injury. How the people cheered when he'd been beaten in the final match by a swift, dark Cuban who was simply too fast for him. He'd charged his massive bulk around the ring, swinging wildly, while his opponent bloodied his face with quick jabs. Even then he almost won. The Cuban got overconfident at the beginning of the third and last round and came within reach of the thick arms: a hard blow to the temple sent him staggering to the mat. He got up, took a standing eight count, and then boxed carefully, jabbing and backpedaling until the bell put an end to things. The referee had smiled as he raised the Cuban's hand in victory, and the sour look on Sealock's face had provoked catcalls that echoed from the crystal dome as he left the ring.

She never understood where she'd gotten the nerve to go to his room that night, but gone she had, Vana's cry of "You must be totally crazy!" going unnoticed. She'd hesitated before his door, strongly aware of a certain vaginal tightness that seemed to signal her physical state, before nervously tapping on the call button. The door opened and he was there, glowering down at her, his face bruised and swollen from the Cuban's many blows. "Well? What do you want?"

"I'm Ariane Methol. May I come in?"

A glimmer of amused understanding crossed his face as he stood aside to admit her. She knew that there was a class of people contemptuously called "slinkers," who followed the athletic contests, waiting to do sexual service for the "animals." Even before her eyes could adjust to the gloom of his

chamber he'd picked her up and dumped her unceremoni-
ously on the bed, then he was squatting over her, robe open,
not quite resting his weight on her chest, his penis dangling
in her face. "OK. Go ahead." She lay frozen, and he said,
"What? A novice? Well, it goes like this, kiddo." He pried her
jaws open and put it in her mouth, then he had his hands on
the sides of her head, organizing her movements, regulating
the thrust and gradually deepening his penetration. It
dawned on her that she was being raped, but she felt completely numb, helpless, and there seemed nothing to do but
cooperate. She gagged a lot, but it was over quickly.

He got to his feet and stretched, his heavy, muscular body
beautiful in the dim light. After a while she got up and went
to his refresher console for a drink. He called to her, "You
ready to go again?"

She turned and looked at him, then said, "I'm not one of
them."

"What?"

"I'm not a slinker. You just raped me."

He sat down on the edge of the bed and stared at her,
looking puzzled. "Not a slinker—" he repeated. "What the
hell are you doing here then?"

She came over and sat down beside him, put her head in
her hands, then said, "I don't know."

His face grew heavy with suspicion. "You're going to have a
hard time getting a conviction with that line. What the fuck
was I supposed to think?" Exasperation colored his voice.
"No one ever comes to see me but slinkers and some of the
other athletes!"

She looked up and saw the bewilderment on his face. "It's
. . . not your fault, maybe . . ." She knew this was typical,
victimish, but, "Maybe I am a slinker. I did come here to have
sex with you, I guess. . . . I just didn't expect you to do
something like that, something so . . . preemptive."

"Well . . . I'm sorry, for whatever that's worth to you."

After that they'd talked, at first about what had happened,
then about other things, and finally about their lives. She told
him about her job with Globo as a 'net engineer and was
stunned to discover that he was with Metro Design. It seemed

that full-time amateur athletes were rare and he was no exception. "Who the hell would want to be a pro boxer?" he said. "They all work for the entertainment 'nets and do what they're told."

In the end they'd had sex again, gently, and he'd tried hard to do right by her. Later, when they fell in love, it was, surprisingly, on her terms.

Her friends were mortified.

Harmon Prynne and Vana Berenguer had finished making love and were silent as an assortment of tacky secretions dried on their bodies. Finally the man said, "Vana?" He was trying to frame his thoughts, wondering how to bring the subject up once again, then lay back and turned his gaze to the ceiling. At length, when he had exhausted his capacity to make up a scenario that came out the way he wanted, he rubbed his eyes and said, "Tell me why you're keeping on with him."

He heard her sigh—that same exasperated release of breath that he'd heard so often before, and had come to dread. "You mean Demogorgon, don't you?

"Yes." He nodded slowly, not wanting to look at her again and realizing he was almost afraid to hear her answer.

"Damn it, Harmon, I told you before. You should see it! The time I'm spending with Demo is in *there*—and it's . . . it's, well, it's not as if we're off fucking all the time. You can come too, if you want to."

"It's *his* world, Vana. I'm no superhero."

"You don't need to be. Besides, he *needs* someone!"

Harmon put his back against the smooth, neutral plastic of the opaqued wall, bringing his knees up to his chest. "So do I," he murmured.

"You dumb shit." She reached up and grabbed him by the chin, forcing his head around until he was facing her. "You've *got* someone!"

He closed his eyes, almost involuntarily. "Yeah. So they tell me," he said, thinking, A small share of what they say comes in unlimited quantities but never does. "Sometimes I wish I'd let you come out here alone."

**123**

Vana released him and, after a while, got up, got dressed, and left the room, leaving him with his bitter imaginings.

From orbit, Aello was even more of a disappointment than Podarge had been. It was tiny, only a little more than four hundred kilometers in diameter, about the size of one of the larger asteroids. It had never been hot enough to melt any of its volatile constituents, so no regional differences were noticeable even in enhanced view. The primary surface was neon, for as Iris cooled from its initial contraction the last particles to be welded into the small gobs that rained down on the satellites were the most volatile.

While Ocypete and Podarge were the result of aeons of geologic activity which had long ended, Aello was that asterologist's dream, a world on which the great majority of materials had never been processed by an active geology. Most things were still almost identical to the way they had been in the very earliest stages of planetary formations. In the Solar System, scientists had looked for such a world in vain. As they moved outward from the sun, the promise of tiny, cold, pristine bodies was shattered by the increasing amounts of volatile material scattered through them. Even the surfaces of Pluto and Charon had been melted in their early history, and still outgassed and changed when they were at perihelion. There were plenty of *really* small bodies that were in an unaltered state, but finding materials that had been emplaced on the surface of a moon-sized world at its birth had been the quest of scientists since the first days of the Apollo Moon landings. Aello was that world.

It looked much like Mimas: a small, spherical worldlet punched open by deeply inset bowllike craters. Unlike those on Podarge, the craters were deep enough relative to the curvature of the satellite to show perceptible shadows well away from the terminator, making the moon appear even more ravaged. There was a disproportionately large crater on its leading hemisphere. It was not so relatively large as Herschel, Mimas' great eye, but it still stood out from the rest, had stared at them as *Polaris* closed in. They remembered how Jana had remarked that this crater, Sayyarrin by name, was unusual not only in its size but in its shallowness, given the fact that Aello had no viscous relaxation to buoy up the middle. Now Sayyarrin was over the limb, in night. Here too, orbiting was a very inefficient process, and they were accelerating downward, watching the broken surface come up to eclipse the large blue circle that was the "day" side of Iris.

"Not very impressive, huh?" said Brendan.

"I don't know," said Krzakwa. "Maybe our expectations were just too high. After Podarge, I'm developing a more philosophical approach."

Sealock stared at the cold, dim worldlet through the ship optics for a while, then said, "We're going down, this time. That should be something."

"Are you kidding? This is *it*, Bren! We're going down onto that most elusive of all things, a primordial world. What we'll be seeing down there has never been seen before."

"Come on!" said Sealock, grinning as he continued to inspect the vista that was unfolding below them. "That's a pretty fine distinction, if you ask me. I mean, you can have all the planetesimals you want out in the Oort belt—what difference does it make if we pick them up here?"

Krzakwa wondered if Sealock meant what he'd said or was merely being aggravating. He decided it didn't matter. "Well, Iris doesn't have a cometary ring, for one thing, so this is it as far as Iridean planetesimals go . . . but it's more than that: this isn't even a piece of the Solar System! Aello not only has all of its materials intact, but they are laid down in the same order they originally came in. It's like a Grand Canyon—you can dig directly into the history of Aello and, in effect, into the history of the formation of Iris and its moons. Things are disturbed by the craters, but only a bit."

"OK. I give up. I'm impressed. So what do you want to do?" he asked, sitting back in his harness. "Looking at this thing, I begin to realize just how difficult it would be to land our ship. It'd be pretty hard to come down with the engines flaming. On $H_2$ vent-thrust only, I guess, we could . . ."

Krzakwa cut him off. "I've been thinking about it," he said.

"How does this sound: we suit up, eliminate radiation from the worksuits, and jump . . ."

Sealock suddenly stopped moving, staring into dead space for a second, then he turned to look at the Selenite again, his eyes seeming to glow. "You son of a bitch. Sure! Like that boil-gliding business . . ." His imagination chewed at the details of the notion: "I'll put her in a low orbit, maybe half a kilometer up. The jump won't kill us. We use pressurized $O_2$ from our life-support systems like jets to get back." He sat back in his couch, gloating to himself. "And we make a suit-instrumented rendezvous with *Polaris* at the end of it all. . . . Hell, this is really going to be fun!"

Aello spun underneath them as Brendan maneuvered the ship down into an orbit so low that they could make out the unmistakable shadow of the craft near the huge, uneven horizon. Even with the weak gravity, this deep in her gravity well Aello effectively swept them along, and the wells of shadow that were craters moved under them quickly. Brendan was fully engrossed in his piloting, plugged into systems that effectively made him an incredibly sensitive receptor. He rushed along, sensing his passage with radar, and could feel the gravitational anomalies caused by variations in the moon's shape and constituents as a series of small velocity changes. He cataloged them as he flew, feeding data to the calculations that Krzakwa was making, fine-tuning their notions about how the orbit of the ship would precess while they were down on the moon. They needed to know. As he delved deeper into the substance of the world, reading it carefully, all the while avoiding an intense radiation flux that would disturb sensitive materials, his eyes became totally blind to the bottomless craters that were calling forth the nightside.

He was just about to disconnect from his systems, in preparation for going down, when something in the residuals of the newest ship computational ephemeris caught his attention. He checked a map and saw that they were passing over the very center of Sayyarrin. This is some kind of a weird little anomaly, all right, he thought. Really weird . . .

"Tem," he said, "are you monitoring the external sensor returns?"

"Uh-huh," said Krzakwa, "what is it?"

"You're the physicist, buddy, you tell me."

Tem studied the figures of the ephemeris in his head, brought in a calc overlay, and spent a full minute processing. Finally he said. "I think we must've put one of our machines together backward. It's a glitch."

"Oh, yeah? OK. Here's an updated computation, seven seconds old. If that's a glitch it's got a sense of humor."

"*Materi bogu!* There's some kind of void down there, under the ice."

"Impossible. It's not a void, it's a shell of some kind. A thin layer of mass around an almost massless core. Now what in the fuck could cause that?"

"Speculation, you mean? Some kind of hollow meteorite?" As he said it, he realized how unlikely a thing that was. It could happen, yes, but on this scale?

Sealock said: "But look at the size, the dimensions. This is not exactly a high-resolution picture—but even the parameters of the orbit suggest something more like . . ."

Krzakwa shook his head. This was ridiculous. There were explanations. Besides . . . "There's nothing in the view that suggests anything unusual. There are volcanic chambers all over the outer Solar System."

He marked the spot, now rapidly disappearing behind them, with a bright optical V. In the deep IR they could see the low rim of Sayyarrin and its rather smooth floor. Perhaps it was just a tiny bit darker, colder, than its surroundings: a dim shape under the ice. Then it was gone over the horizon.

Brendan violently spun *Polaris* around, inertia tugging at their bodies, and lit off the engine. The craters slowed, stopped, and the bright line that was day receded back behind the world. Sayyarrin popped over the horizon and, when they were directly over it, Sealock repeated his action, this time slowing the ship to a dead halt over the center of the crater. Tem could only tell from his instruments that they were falling, gently, toward the ice less than half a kilometer below. Brendan turned up the gain on the photochip, iso-

**127**

lated a narrow region in the far infrared that would best define the heat differences they had seen, and, yes, there it was.

He pushed the ship back into an orbit, paying little attention to its parameters. When they were flying above the ice once more he turned to look at the Selenite. "So. You're saying Sayyarrin is a caldera?" He called up some imagery from the Shipnet element and its source files, staring so hard into the image in his brain that he squinted malevolently. "That sort of contradicts the picture you were drawing before."

Krzakwa nodded slowly. That was the way it seemed, but . . . Damn it, there *had* to be some kind of reasonable explanation. "I don't know. Day comes in about three hours. It will take about half an hour to suit up. I say we get *Polaris* back in the right orbit and go down in the suits. There really is no telling what will happen if we try to land in that stuff. It might be the most effective way to reach the lower stratum—but the ship could easily be damaged by the violent sublimation, even in this paltry gravity."

Brendan seemed to pull back into himself somewhat. "Mmm. Yeah. We turn up the heat of our suits and fall through the neon. Any turbulence that creates, we can certainly deal with. OK—full speed ahead."

Downlink Rapport wasn't getting any easier. Insofar as the thoughts and feelings of John and Beth were couched in linguistic or sensory terms, the transfer was without effort. But underlying personal emotions and states of being were more difficult, flooding into the brain as strange, ephemeral data. Understanding required a great deal of work. Memories were a lingua franca between them, perhaps because, even in an individual, memories come from somewhere far off, separate from the "self." It was easiest to tap into the full experience of being another person through the facility of the past.

It came: they were annoyed. No matter what subject John tried to initiate, Beth would turn it aside. In bed, back in her condo in Yellowknife after a long winter walk through the streets, their bodies touched and his cold hands were enfolded within the damp warmth of her armpits. Their wet clothing was strewn across the floor, and waves of heat billowed up from the vents. Snow tapped against the window. Their faces were still flushed from the cold, his a ruddy orange and hers an empurpled brown.

Despite the physical closeness, they were in sealed, isolated worlds. John was struggling to overcome a feeling of futility, and the emotion emerged into the world as a series of quick, occasionally savage ripostes. Beth swallowed these outbursts quietly, if only because they were so unlike what she had come to expect in his behavior.

"That's the point, Beth. The money keeps coming. Something should be done with it; something purposeful. And I . . . I've lost a context. I know I say things about living for the moment. At one time I could do that, but not now. The time has come to do something." He laughed. "I've come back to the place where I started, and for the first time I know it's boring."

"If your music isn't an accomplishment, I don't know what is."

How could he explain to her that the time of their courtship, when he had felt a context, largely defined by their passion, had ended? That he needed to break through into something deeper, something to convince himself death wouldn't come sneaking up and claim him unawares? He thought about the money again. "What have I done with the money? Bought a house, two houses, an asteroid? What good is it all?" A new bond was growing between them, out of their disparity. The unresolvable dilemma had been resolved, and the truth was being found out. Gladness filled him.

They broke. "Well," Cornwell said, "hello again." His voice was quiet but amused. "How are you?" They kissed, briefly, without passion. He stood, woozy even in the low g.

Beth was staring at him. She felt tired. "All right," she said. "Let's go get something to eat."

Shutdown.

They had to don the worksuits and exit one at a time. Though the things were not terribly bulky, no larger than the

**129**

ordinary vacuum suits of a century earlier, they were rigid and maintained their fixed shape. It was in stark contrast to the usual sort of spacesuit, which could be crushed into a tiny ball when not wrapped around the form of a human being. Sealock went into the airlock, which was a cylindrical chamber two and a half meters across by two high and looked around. The two suits were like two extra men, and there was no room for the Selenite. He sighed, wondering why they simply hadn't made it a little larger. Some aesthetic pressure. Who knew? This had just seemed like the right size and shape to use, and that seeming had obviously been wrong. Krzakwa closed the hatch, cutting him off from the CM, a last view of him looking like a troglodyte in his cave. Temporarily, Sealock had donned a communications circlet, though he'd always ridiculed the things. "I'll let you know when I'm done," he said. The suit was permanently made in one piece, its helmet and backpack already attached. Before climbing in through the opening that split the front, Sealock reached up into the helmet and unreeled the twelve brain-taps that marked this suit as his alone. He discarded the circlet and quickly plugged himself in, powering up the suit. "Do you read me?" Affirmative. He crawled in through the opening, squirming as he put his arms and legs down their proper holes. It was difficult, though possible, and he wondered just how Krzakwa managed to do it, fat as he was. The designers probably could have come up with something better, but . . . this was as sturdy a system as twenty-first century could come up with. By using appropriate settings, a man in a worksuit could walk around on Mercury or go for a stroll beneath the soupy seas of Titan. . . . He closed the front, lit off the life-support systems, and established a link with the ship's 'net element. "I'm going out now."

"OK." The pressure in the airlock dropped swiftly and was gone, the gases pumped back into a storage tank.

When the vacuum was fully established, he popped the outer hatch and floated into the night. The hatch closed behind him, leaving him physically isolated, floating beside the smooth length of *Polaris,* with the cold landscapes of the small moon running by below, an unending vista of excavated features, all of them similar. He could see the ragged terminator coming up over Aello's horizon; and Sayyarrin wasn't much beyond that.

After a while the hatch opened again and Tem emerged to join him. Things were about ready. Wordless, they floated away from the ship, orienting themselves so that the primary cold-gas thrusters of their suits' OMS/RCS harnesses were facing in the direction of orbital travel.

The suits' internal logic units were designed for this sort of operation, and so they would lose little information if they had to disconnect from the ship's systems. Hopefully, they would be able to maintain communication with the more powerful 'net element but, if not, it would probably be all right. They watched the craft drift away from them. The surface of the moon was as dark as the starry sky around them, and only the great burning crescent at Aello's limb gave any sort of perspective.

The mind tends to place itself as the stationary center of the universe, and here, hanging between *Polaris* and Aello, it did its best to define their situation thus. It tended to view Aello as "down," but, in little bursts of alienness, they could see themselves as suspended below a dark sky with a curiously inverted sunrise rushing toward them, flying above their craft on silent wings. Their orientation was very dependent on which way their feet pointed, and they tried to keep them toward Aello. As they applied the jets, their speed dropped and they fell, moving away from the ship. It became a small, dark thing with inappropriate-seeming highlights.

The sun rose, its rays washing over them in streamers. The broken rim of Sayyarrin was visible now, and the terminator came on like the edge of a fragmented planet. Another moment for action came: what in a normal landing would be the high-gate procedure was required, so they initiated a continuous "burn" that stopped their forward movement and dropped them toward the surface. Through the suit optics they saw their spaceship flying away. In a matter of minutes it was gone beyond the horizon.

Aello, dominated by bright-lipped pools of black, looked like a shallow mud puddle through which a hundred children had run. They were no more than two hundred meters up, and the little world suddenly seemed very big. Sayyarrin, a dark, crumbled rise preceded by a great apron of shadow, came to meet them. Tem noted that it seemed a normal enough impact crater, shallow, as Jana had said, but having a general morphology well in accord with what he knew about large impacts on worlds of this sort. Its lack of a central peak was not strange, given the volatile nature of the target—the energy of impact easily liquefied the neon, causing a flowback that would drown the rebounding bed-ice. If the hot spot on Ocypete was caused by a radioactive infall, wasn't it possible that a similar object had somehow caused a shield cryo-volcano? He wished he knew more about all this. Sayyarrin certainly didn't look like Olympus Mons, or even Eblis Mons on Ariel.

They were over the relatively new, randomly peppered floor of the sunlit crater, and the anomaly was now coming over the horizon. In a matter of minutes they had come to a stop about a hundred meters over its center, their suit systems registering only a slight drop in the minimal heat flow emanating from deep within the moon.

"Look down there, Tem," said Sealock. "It's sublimating already, from the jets. As a physicist, what do you think is going to be the greatest danger if we just land?"

"Really, not much. I have the feeling that the turbulence will buffet us around, but well within the stress limits of these suits. You may feel cool as the suit's heating unit struggles to keep up with the enthalpy. I am certain that the pressure won't build up sufficiently to produce a liquid phase." They were now slowly falling toward the white ground. "If it gets too violent, we can just activate the thermal dampener fields. It shouldn't be too difficult to do this in stages."

"I guess not." Brendan was hardly listening to him as he looked around. This had the precise flavor of an adventure, a real one, and if he could only pay close enough attention . . .

A shroud of neon mist began to hide and soften the small craters. As it grew in opacity, they could see it swirling outward, caught in little eddies and boiling upward. Ranging instruments revealed that the ice directly below them was caving downward; mists were lightening the sky and streaking it with moving nebulosities. Their speed of descent was increasing.

Just before the neon totally obscured everything, Tem saw that the small motions had combined into a spinning weather system, driven by the heat at its center and Aello's not insignificant Coriolis force. He could imagine it slowly spreading across the world's surface until the various powers interacted and a global meteorology began. It would all end as the neon quickly froze and precipitated.

They fell past where ground level had once been. Although they were in a clear pocket—neon vapor could not exist at the temperatures in their vicinity—visual input gave no clue as to what was going on. The world was formless.

The clouds pressed in closer to them, and the sound of crackling and snapping was brought to their ears by the tenuous gas around them. Brendan felt the first tentative surgings of the gas against the suit. Somewhere, electrostatic discharges were occurring in the mist. He upgraded his gyro control, just in case.

Suddenly the dam burst. The simple circulation of their weather pattern gave way to the extraordinary pressure at its center and broke into chaos. Strong currents slammed across the armored men. Tem hadn't reset his inertial control secondaries, and he began to tumble until he did so. The gas pressure that surrounded him, his only real protection, began to shudder violently.

As he felt his body begin to pogo inside the suit, Brendan carefully analyzed their position—they couldn't take much more of this. They had penetrated the surface to a depth of about four hundred meters. It wouldn't be long until they broke into the weird cavity, if that's what was going to happen.

The tumult grew stronger, and even the gyroscopes were having a difficult time keeping them stable. Another thirty meters or so, thought Brendan, and we will be there. . . .

Unexpectedly, they hit bottom. Something soft gave way beneath their feet and, if the instruments were correct, rebounded slowly, without secondary flexes. The neon, now mixed with a hundredth part of argon and methane, still boiled and swirled around them, but it was growing weaker. Brendan bent down and jabbed a steel-rigid finger into the surface. It was resilient, almost like a kind of soft wood. He scored it and the depression quickly healed itself. He shared his findings with Krzakwa.

He generated an image of the man's face for himself and studied its convolutions. "So. Now what do you think?"

The Selenite shook his head. "I . . . refuse to speculate." He studied the data that were being reported to him. Some light was making its way down through the piled-up gases above. The vapors were rapidly dissipating as he watched.

"Doesn't matter if you do or not. I think . . ."

"Shut up, damn you!" Krzakwa was biting at his lower lip, sucking in some hairs from his beard.

Sealock grinned to himself. "Right," he said.

It cleared. They were standing on a flat surface of a dull blue-gray color, almost obscured by a thin layer of small, glassy nodules. The walls of the hole they had dug rose up and up, seemingly solid, about three hundred meters around. Tem looked up and saw a shaft of sunlight slanting across the mouth of the hole.

"Well," said Sealock, "does this look like rock to you?"

"No." Krzakwa let out a long, slow whisper of breath. "It's time to say it. Artifact."

"I guess we've found a little adventure, after all."

Brendan cleared a small area, scraping the surface with his foot to knock the little beads flying in slow arcs. When he was satisfied that a large enough area was clean, he bent over and played his photochips over it, straining his suit systems to tell him anything they could about the material. He looked up at Tem. "Again: what do you think?"

"We need better instruments." He pulled a geologist's hammer from its waist clip and, kneeling also, slammed the pointed end down. It left a small dimple that slowly sprang back to normal. "You tell me, Brendan. What inert material stays pliable at 43 degrees Kelvin?"

"I might as well be the one to say it this time: *alien* artifact. This is not our tech."

"Sayyarrin's floor is relatively uncratered—but even so, that surface is *old*. If Jana's right, we're talking millions of years. Maybe billions."

"What's that?"

Brendan pointed to a place on the hole's wall, where a thin, dark, ruler-straight line over 250 meters high was embedded. It went almost all the way back to the surface. Tem was laughing uncontrollably. He finally got control of himself, breathing heavily, tears running down his face. "That's a fucking fin. This is getting ridiculous."

"Guess so. I feel peculiar." Brendan stood, followed by the other.

"Want to dig it out with *Polaris?*"

"No. We might get killed—that would be an irony I could do without. Let's go home and get the ion drill—also some friends."

"Good thought. Shall we call ahead?"

"Uh . . . somebody might be listening."

The idea penetrated, and they turned to go.

# F O U R

Brendan ate the last of his sandwich as he looked back at Aello. Returning to *Polaris* had been fairly easy, though the jets had thrown enough heat to widen the hole even further. When they got to the level of the surface, it was obvious they wouldn't have to go out of their way to obscure the Artifact—neon snow had taken care of that. A naked-eye view showed just the tiniest blemish at the center of Sayyarrin—and any telescopes that happened to be trained on Iris I would have poorer resolution than his eyes from this distance. The blurring of Aello's surface might be attributed to equipment malfunction. The first thing they had done was tightbeam an "incommunicado" signal back to the colony. If they had agreed upon an encryption formula for their communications, all this silence wouldn't have been necessary. But they couldn't have had the foresight to predict a situation like this.

They had not brought sufficient fuel to take a quick route

back to Ocypete. The modified Hohmann would take days.
. . . Speculation about what they had seen was futile: an ancient artifact . . . How did it get here? Was it related to the heat source on Ocypete? Did it just so happen that the Iridean system accreted from material already laden with the throw-offs of some alien race? Or is it something else? *Is* it a spaceship? The answers were more a reflection of imagination than any hard evidence.

Tem came forward and got into his rigging. "Brendan. Let's talk about it."

Sealock said, "OK. You go first."

"What I want to know is, how are we going to play this? Are we going to reveal this to the Union?"

"Not for a while."

"It's going to be a hard secret to keep—especially after we blast it out of the ice. Even from Smith they'll be able to tell something funny is going on."

"Let 'em wonder. The real problem is the USEC ship. That shortens our time considerably."

Walking across the blank, black floor of the second dome, Ariane Methol was trying to understand just what was happening to them all. She was not unintelligent, yet it was as if she had to think long and hard to unravel the simplest of connections where her behavior was concerned. At times her memories provided her only clues as to who, or what, she was. It was frustrating. Just when she believed that she had discovered something important about herself, Brendan would start to work on her, to turn everything around. . . .

Now she was alone, with the time to think. Not only were Brendan and Tem gone, the others were wrapped up in their own emotions. Beth and John were totally out of reach, Jana was morose and hostile, Axie spent her time reading and sleeping and was generally too drugged to be of any use. Even Vana, upon whom she could usually depend, was spending more and more of her time in Demo's electronic world, at times even without his guidance. Some society they had created here!

The evening before she had been trying to find areas of

mutual interest with Harmon and they had ended up in bed. He'd been competent enough, but it was easy to tell that his mind was elsewhere—and that he was probably just trying to take revenge on Vana. Afterward he seemed ill at ease with her and, violating her preconceptions of his placid, all-accepting nature, almost angry. Any attempt she made at talking about his problem directly was shunted aside. It was frustrating and, worse yet, it made her think about her own relationship with Brendan.

"Ariane, up here."

A voice from somewhere above her head made her look up. It was Demogorgon, sitting alone within the light-spreading mirror at the apex of the girder tower.

"So you decided to visit the real world?" she said. "What are you doing here?"

"Just bringing a little bit of fantasy out with me. I've been designing the colors of the holograph that will fill out the dome. I'm importing a bit of the Illimitor World, compressing it. Want to help?"

"Certainly," Ariane said, and leaped halfway up the tower, clambering lightly the rest of the way. She had known it was the plan for this dome: a simulated environment that would bring a little of home into this world of ice. For some reason she hadn't realized they wouldn't just be using one of the commercially supplied ones from Comnet. It was easy to forget that Demogorgon was skilled at precisely this art.

Beneath them, the dark irregular floor of the structure spread like the bleak surface of a carbonaceous asteroid. The slight rises and hollows had been built in to afford a more realistic appearance to the natural setting that was to come.

"You're wearing your circlet," said Demogorgon. "Good. Just sit down and I'll show you the template. I'd like to get your opinion."

Ariane linked into his program. There was a moment of nothingness, and then the world opened up before her like a great multicolored flower. It was mainly deep green and azure—the image of a Scottish moor stretched out in all directions to a horizon of smooth, bare hills under a clear morning sky. A pleasant, darkly sweet odor was carried to her

**139**

nostrils by a cool breeze. "This is Yvelddur, which I modeled on Northumbria. It's one of my favorite places."

"Is Vana here?"

"No, she's halfway across the world, in Arhos." He chuckled to himself. "I mean, she would be if we were inhabiting the same software. This is a cutout. . . ."

"I had no idea it would be like this."

"That's what everyone who has experienced it so far has said. Comnet uses old technology and has stalled any attempts to use the refinements that have been developed."

"Well, if you're going to use this as the model for the dome, I don't think I can suggest anything further."

"No? Go ahead, tap into the design function and make a few swipes. It's easy."

Ariane called up the Bright Illimit design supermenu and paged through the commands. The words were dark letters and verbal explanations, flowing through her, superimposed over a three-coordinate system, itself superimposed over the world. She tried a simple command, molded a hill into a slightly more humpbacked shape, and added a few summer cumulus clouds at random. The program backtracked and rationalized all of her changes until they were fully integrated.

Emboldened, she added a stream to the many that here and there fed a scattering of bright silver-blue pools, then admired the effect. "Demo, I think that's enough. I don't want to get carried away and spoil your landscape."

Demogorgon laughed. "OK—it's time to cut the ribbon. Shall we precede the image into the world or just go with it?"

"Let's watch it appear."

Slowly, the scene faded, and they were once more perched atop the tower, looking down on the drab domescape. "Shall we let it fade in or snap it on like a light?"

"Snap it on."

The dome went green. In an instant the scene from Demogorgon's imagination was there before them. Across the invisible plastic, heather and gorse were in flower; the babble of little brooks coursing into crystalline lakes filled the air. The down-curving dome had broken into the bright blue sky, and at their feet clouds the size of throw rugs gathered. They were the clouds Ariane had designed.

It was perfect in every respect and its designers were pleased. Demogorgon gazed outward, feeling Ariane's arm on him, and thought, I *can* control what's going on. Evade it entirely if I wish . . .

"Come on," said Ariane, slipping from the edge of the tower into a slow-motion fall. "Let's inspect our handiwork."

Demogorgon pushed off and began to accelerate toward the ground. The fall took only a few moments, and he landed in a graceful leonine crouch beside the rim of the real pool, now encased in marble imagery, with the look of an ancient monument. He watched as Ariane ran lightly through the dethorned gorse and plunged through a stream that could not wet her. It acted like water in 1 g, disconcertingly natural in this unnatural environment.

*Polaris* sailed on. Iris slowly shrank in a real-perspective view, and Aello disappeared behind it. When talking failed and speculation gave way to inane guessing games, silence opened up their minds to internal monologues. After a time Sealock succeeded in willfully eliminating the giddy thinking that kept welling up, but what took its place was no more comforting. He knew it was time to fall back on the device of the memory presentations that had diverted them on the way out, but he didn't want to go on to the next logical step in the progression of his story. Remembering the Game, of playing sun-bronzed in the desert heat, was wonderful. What came afterward was not.

They'd tried to teach him. The communal tutor had worked with him more than with any of the others, finally trying desperate measures, but he'd resisted. The time spent learning what he was supposed to learn was hateful, precious time taken from the valued play and, more importantly, from the rapidly growing world inside his head. At the end of that long summer he'd been declared hopeless by the tutor and was sent once a week to the special school Uncompaghre maintained for "difficult" students, mostly functionally illiterate children who were unable to master even the rudiments

**1 4 1**

of binary, but with a sprinkling of gangly boys and pudgy girls whose puberty had come too early for local convention to accept. Brendan could be part of neither group, so he spent free time alone.

The teachers assumed an air of condescension that was awful. His rebellion had grown stronger until that dreamlike day when he'd burst into a terrible white-hot rage. It had been in the gymnasium, and he'd hit the physical culture instructor across the face with a baseball bat, the nearest weapon handy. He remembered his amazement at the bright, spurting blood and the woman's high, gargling screams.

After that things had gone swiftly. The last day was etched even more vividly into his memory: the school psychologist had spoken before a council of Manti-La Sal adults, and they'd let him be present, as if his feelings didn't matter anymore. The man had said, "There's nothing further we can do for him. In cases of this kind, the only solution is the Exile School in Phoenix." It was as simple as that.

They had taken a vote and agreed to send him away, and only his mother, Kathleen, voted no. It was majority rule. Brendan had cried, begging them to let him stay, had promised them that he'd be good, would behave as they wished, but it was all to no avail. He was banished, and it turned out to be forever.

He cut off this train of thought with a shudder. Perhaps it was all for the best that it had led him out here, cast him, ultimately, into what could turn out to be the greatest adventure of all time. But he could not bring himself to think this through. He looked at Krzakwa, wondered what thoughts were producing his peculiar look. "Tem?" The man looked over at him. "I need to be entertained. . . ."

Concern replaced the other expression, and Krzakwa nodded. "Okay. My turn, huh?" They hooked up, settled down, and went under.

All the little boys and girls on the Moon were fully regimented. It was said they liked it that way, that it was appropriate to their social development. . . .

What was called the children's dormitory at Picard was in

reality a multipurpose room. The hexagonal bedchambers that lined the walls were in continuous occupation, and the twenty-four-hour "day" was divided into three eight-hour periods in which the children of Groups 1, 2, and 3 slept. But while the other thirds slept, classes were held below. It was safe to say that, during the five years between the time a child left the supervision of his parents and entered the apprenticeship of his trade, he might spend fully eighty-five percent of his time in this one large hall.

The floor of the dormitory was partitioned into classrooms, a cafeteria, and a health maintenance facility. There were the needs of six hundred boys and girls to meet, and things had to be carefully organized. The population was regulated to assure that only six hundred children would be at the correct age at any given time, and seven-year-olds were continuously entering the system as twelve-year-olds left. Tem was in Group 2, eleven years old, going on the time when he would be transferred to Group 3 for his last year there.

He stood halfway back in the classroom row, supported by the thin column from which the keyboard and screen extended. Though standing was no hardship in Lunar gravity, and in fact was the preferred mode for the youngsters, the arrangement had been designed primarily as a way to save space. He was adjacent to four children, Akio Kurosawa and Sadie Klein in back and front, and Greg Indagar and Patrick Lore on either side. These four he had come to know very well, since almost all activities were organized in the same alphabetical way. Samwar Kirk had occupied Sadie's position until shortly before the memory began, and he had been Tem's best friend, but he had graduated to 3. The communication with this "gang of four" was remarkable, consisting mostly of furtive looks, stifled giggles, and hand signals. Tem understood that each similar group within the class had developed similar, or in many cases the same, methods. Individual children would move on, but the culture would stay.

Now it was the time devoted to "socialization," and within certain limits they were free to roam about the classroom and talk to whomever they liked. They spoke in careful whispers

**143**

and every now and again cast a look at the monitor, a short, fat old man with red skin and a broken nose, who sat, bored and wishing, Tem guessed, for a smoke. Some looked, instead, at the long metal dowel that he used as a prop, wondering if it would ever be used for something else.

The old man whistled and called out "Time!" and they quickly returned to their assigned spots. The screens were already lit with a calendar and clock showing their progress and future assignments on both a long-term and short-term ruler. Tem sighed, keying in his presence, and responded to a series of questions carefully framed to determine his attitude. He lied without even thinking about it.

Hour 4's goal was to master the beginning theorems of Euclidean geometry, and the learning programs ticked off, carefully leading him along to enter the correct answers and providing more detailed explanation when he was wrong. Tem had already found out that the simplest way was to concentrate and cooperate, blotting out everything but the programmed task at hand. In this way he was perhaps unique, because, talking to others about their progress, he had found that they were still doing lessons he had finished as much as a year before. He wondered whether the 3s on the lesson's serial numbers meant he was doing Group 3 work. It was probably so. It made him feel more than a little smug.

The memory sequence jumped forward and it was time for exercise. A slim young woman with a pleasant smile took the place of the monitor and led them in a patriotic song, some of which was in a patois that Tem never could quite understand. They sang a more energetic song about pride in being a child, pride in being from Crisium, but most of all pride in being an inhabitant of this harsh, isolated world where sacrifices were absolutely necessary. As they sang this song, which went on interminably, they were led in rhythmic isometric exercises, writhing in comical ways, occasional laughter blotted out by the words of the song. After an hour of this, they were called back to their screens for a lesson on history. These lessons were much cruder than those on math and the sciences, since they couldn't use canned programs from

Earth, and everyone moved at the same pace. It was then that the hand signals began. . . .

Time jumped forward again and it was supper. They filed in even queues toward the walls, climbing up the handholds past the descending Group 3'ers. Tem slid himself into the recess of his bedchamber, about halfway up, and closed the hatch behind him. The fluorescent light came on, revealing the foot of the bed on which he was sitting, the sink/toilet, and a screen and keyboard on a moving arm, not unlike those in the classroom. It was prohibited to personalize the cubicle in any way, since he shared it with two others, but he had an area of one gigabyte in the computer that he could do with as he wished. In fact he was encouraged to "play" on the computer for as long as an hour before sleep, and many programs both entertaining and educational were at his beck and call. It was one place upon which they had not stinted.

Finally, he slept, knowing that it would be more than a year before he graduated. The sequence came to an end.

"Shit," muttered Sealock. "Was it always like that?"

"In one way or another. That was the worst of it, though. Later we had more free time, because the planners assumed we would go berserk otherwise. I guess I chose that particular memory because of what you were saying, before, about the way things are on Earth. I don't know what you were complaining about."

"Yeah. I didn't think you'd understand," said Brendan, smiling. "In some ways you had it lucky. You always knew who the bad guys were."

After setting up the scene in the dome, Demogorgon decided to look in on Vana. The subsidiary program that allowed her to move among the illusions of Bright Illimit was undoubtedly keeping her out of trouble, but there was no harm in checking. He quickly located the section of the program with which she was interacting and projected himself into it.

She had been having a picnic on a hill in the southern marches, toward Rin Renala, under a huge spreading sarisdahn tree that provided shade from both the suns. A cloth

**145**

had been spread out not far from the place where she'd landed her personal skimmer and, not surprisingly, she was humping madly with a huge, dark man Demogorgon recognized as Qasartun, the King of Radhamash. As he approached, smiling wryly, he cleared his throat.

"Demo!" said Vana, looking at him over the man's shoulder, appearing a little embarrassed. "I didn't expect you . . . here . . . now."

"What? Ho—" called Qasartun, continuing his vigorous thrusting. "If it isn't my fellow liege lord Demogorgon en Arhos! Well met, if I must say so myself!"

"Stop. Qassi, stop!" said Berenguer.

For a moment his face was transfigured with rage, then, somewhat cowed, he complied with her request. His rampant penis was of a size that an irrationally greedy woman might dream about. Vana, in this setting, seemed to have acquired a bit more modesty—she covered herself with a corner of the picnic cloth.

Demogorgon was unable to keep from laughing. He wondered how he would react to being interrupted during one of his trysts with Raabo by a real person. "Dear Vana," he began, "do not feel any embarrassment on account of my presence. After all, Qassi, as you call him, is, in a sense, merely my representative. And gratifying one's desires, as you were doing, is a major part of the reason this world exists."

Qasartun looked back and forth between the two, then said, "I can see that I am not wanted here." He made a sort of humble gesture to Demogorgon. "If it please you, my lady, I will be off." So saying, he buckled on his jewel-encrusted codpiece and strode off toward the west without a backward glance.

"Well, anyway," said Demo, "I'm sorry for the interruption."

Vana gave the departing kinglet a quick glance. "There are more where he came from."

Demogorgon laughed. "That's very, very true." He paused, then said, "How are you getting along here in general? I really haven't been giving you the supervision I ought to."

"Fine. I think I've figured out everything I need to know. I have assumed my title, and everybody knows of me . . . it couldn't be better."

"Good. You probably ought to come back to Ocypete with me, though. Things are getting a little lonely there. Especially for Harmon."

She was pulling on her clothing now. It did not do much to conceal her nudity but made a great difference in her demeanor. She stood and stretched. "Speaking of Harmon—" she said.

"Yes?"

"What are we going to do about him?"

"What do you mean?"

"He's, well . . . he's jealous. Of you."

"Me?" Demogorgon looked incredulous. "He has nothing to fear from me!"

"Think about it. *This* is *you.*" She spread her hand in a wide gesture.

"No, it's not me—it's *you!* If he's jealous of anything it's your fantasies, and your inability to satisfy them through him. *This* is just a means to an end."

"That's easy to say, but how do things *look?* And how do I get it across to him?"

Demogorgon sat down on the grass and stared at the sky. "How do you tell anything to anybody? Get him in here, if you can . . . if you want him—here."

"Can you talk to him?"

"Look, this is going to have to work out in its own way, just like . . ."

She saw the unhappiness spread across his features. Somehow it seemed inappropriate, here. "Just like you and Brendan?"

He felt her hand cool on his neck. "Yeah. Just like that."

Jana Li Hu looked down. The squat cylinder that housed what had been a redundant thruster from *Deepstar*'s original configuration sat in a classic graben and was the hub for three hundred-meter metal cords which were affixed to mousetrap pitons that had been dug very far into exposed sections of the

**147**

bed-ice. She found, to her surprise, that she had been holding her breath, and she let it out into the suit slowly. The worksuit she wore was large for her, and its spaciousness made her feel clumsy, hard to control. Once again she scanned the surrounding terrain with her photochips and was awed by the spirelike, only slightly rounded water-ice massifs that clustered closely here, broken shards of the world thrust upward by the colossal forces which had fought during the period when Mare Nostrum froze and expanded.

It was something only water would do, pushing the partially collapsed Ocypete back into a spherical shape. Unlike what had happened on Ganymede and other Solar moons, the unmelted crust of the area surrounding the mare was already too thick to produce the regional grooves caused by wave systems of extensional faulting during the time of melting. Instead more "Earthlike" oblique-slip faults had spread in a finely reticulate pattern back into the highlands, gathered finally into the huge chasmae that trisected the world. When Mare Nostrum froze, it pushed everything back into place— almost. The healed scars remained—and they would tell much. It was all fascinating, but not quite fascinating enough to override the growing fear in her.

Despite the fact that it was yet to come on formally, the internal generator necessary to keep the battery warm was throwing out enough heat to sublimate the neon in the cryolith, and the drill, for that is what it was, was sinking slowly, throwing out a blur of mist. The time had come.

She pointed the nozzle of the hydrogen-release device and turned it on. Quickly the small white mountains began to dwindle as she rose, and the systematic faults of this orogeny presented themselves to her in detail. Her entire science lay all around her, a great, crumbled sphinx.

The vast blankness of the ocellus came up over the horizon, and she made for it. She was obligated to get very far from the drill site, and thus perhaps a minute passed as she gained speed and height. Finally she felt safe and slowed to a stop by sending out a prolonged blast of compressed gas. The curvature of the small moon was already quite pronounced, and from this height she could probably fall for an hour or more. She spun herself about with a command to her gyro, and blinked inside her helmet. In a moment the exhaust plume, a diffuse comet's tail, reached into the sky, slowly spreading a haze outward to engulf the nearby-seeming stars in a web of twinkling. When it was over the cloud vanished like winter's breath.

Jana felt regret that this escaping gas would form a deposit on much of the surrounding territory, somewhat altering what would be found there later. But it was a necessary thing, and even asterology suffered from an uncertainty principle, an observer effect. She continued her fall and, suddenly, seemed paralyzed.

The image of a demolished sphinx again superimposed itself over the ocellus' rim, and she knew that it was entirely in her hands to reconstruct this overwhelming landscape. And not only this one—right at this moment, she knew, Sealock and Krzakwa were engaged on their moronic "adventure," taking the already broken blocks and smashing them into pieces too small ever to fix.

They took pleasure in thwarting her. She was, despite her credentials, perhaps the least powerful member of the expedition; even Harmon occasionally had some influence over Vana and, through her, Ariane and Brendan. Now, with John immersed in his asinine DR experiment, the only link she had developed with anyone here had disappeared. Damn him! she thought. I should have known he would go back to Beth eventually; leave me completely alone without a second thought.

She thought back to moments when she had almost forgotten herself under his persuasive tongue, times when she had trusted him, if only to bring pleasure to her in his own way. But it had only been a game.

Maybe, somehow, if she let herself DR with him, it would bring about his help. Show him her internal sphinx for aid in studying the Iridean one. It was *his* colony, after all, even if he did everything he could to avoid admitting it. But if he knew . . . No, he wouldn't help at all. Events and feelings no one could ever know about crowded into her mind. At age nine, after being returned to her parents, she had used their position as blockleaders to lord it over the neighboring children, forming them into an "Obey Cadre" and making them, after an initial period of harmlessly serving her, engage in ever stranger sexual acts. Even now she could feel the strong, almost sensual guilt flow over her. No, DR was impossible.

Following in the wake of her guilt there came another sensation, similar in some ways. It was a feeling of exhilaration, and suddenly she knew that she would have the strength to do *anything* to unravel the mysteries of Iris and her moons. The others were not worthy of any consideration, really. She could squash them like so many roaches.

The sphinx loomed above her, a woman like herself, and asked the simple question: How?

Hu was falling rather rapidly now, five meters per second, and she could readily see the expansion of the white texture below her feet. She released some hydrogen until she was motionless again, then began to fall anew. She felt a certain amount of contentment in her purpose. With her heart beating slightly faster than could be explained by physical exertion, she directed herself toward the new-made excavation.

John and Beth riffled through the scenes of their shared past, images and thoughts randomly sampled and released like a video history database run at search speed. John was amazed how much the link could restore memories he'd assumed lost or at least eroded by the passage of time. Previously he had avoided memlinking programs without fully understanding why—now he knew. In the presence of a fully retrieved memory, he felt enthralled in the frame, lost his sense of distinction between the present and the past, and was overpowered by a feeling of déjà vu. Predestination and unfree will dogged him as he watched himself, seemingly fully aware at the time, step into trap after trap, parading down his life like some Chaplinesque tramp.

Beth's feelings were nothing of the sort. For her, it was simply what had been. She was able to separate her present self from the memories. John drew this strength from her.

And the machine reached and grew, still not satisfied. . . .

They were picking their way through the tourist shops in

**150**

the Hvolsvollur section of Reykjavik, dawdling on an old macadam street that led down to the solder-band of the Atlantic. At the very rim of the world was the place from which they had just come: Northern Hemisphere Escape Orbit Docking and Loading. NHEODL, or Noodle as it was called, had been difficult, but they had triumphed over it. It had been a long day of confronting a system designed not for the one but for the millions, and they were lightheaded from the cool, dry air coming down off the glaciers. They had seen Heimaey and the spaceport, and the launch of a GM shuttle in its raucous glory.

Beth was thinking: how could she shield herself from seeing the patterns that were taking shape in John's feelings and actions? Looking at the space souvenirs in Iceland, it was becoming clear to her in spite of herself. John was not in love with her then, not in any real sense of the word. He had been, she guessed, during the first year, especially during the long cataloging treks across the summer tundra. He had taken joy in her, and she could feel the longings and twinges that kept them together. But had it indeed been love? Now, in DR, she could see that much of it had come back; that their relationship was becoming what it had been. But by the next year there were periods in which the feelings that she recognized in him as love were completely absent, and were replaced by repeated questioning of his real feelings to himself. If he didn't think he was in love, then could he be? Her own feelings had been a consistent, growing passion that could ignite her an average of ten hours out of fourteen, six days out of seven. But in him the spark came and, for increasingly long periods, went.

She could see just when the idea of hiring a programmer to circumvent the limitations that he felt, to penetrate the blank wall that was her face, had come. . . . Downlink Rapport was not a possibility within Comnet, and not even all his immense wealth could buy it legally. It was forbidden by the Contract Police on any level of public access—you needed a personal 'net substructure to even approach the problem. That could be had, if you were an MCD-licensed experimenter. . . . They would laugh at the notion that some "bilbo artist" might qualify for such a thing. The other way . . . personal 'nets were also made available for purposes of long-range exploration and deep space colonization.

Ironically, she had been the one to suggest spending his logarithmically increasing money on building an experimental community in space. The idea seemed a good one as she said it—to start fresh, to get John motivated on something larger than himself. But the reality of it! To leave Earth for a tiny colony on an icebound moonlet far beyond the reaches of the material world! She had been seized with fear when he began taking, one by one, the steps necessary to bring it about, a physical, palpable fear, drawing together the muscles of her back and stomach into hard painful knots.

And she knew she would follow John if he went.

There was a backward timeshift and then they were fucking in the flower-spangled waste out beyond the Mackenzie, on a solar blanket nestled in a hollow beneath the foothills of the glacier-carved mountains. Beth was on top, undulating her torso and carefully expelling and engulfing the hard thing that rode on John's hips. It was a position she never really liked, and here, without springs or liquid, it was even worse. John resumed his insistent prodding, his face unreadable. She had assumed at the time that he was being moved by those irresistible forces that bring us to orgasm, but now she could see that he had simply been going through the motions of that which had so recently given him joy, watching her face and waiting for the groans that signaled success.

She was looking at him now/then, wondering what perverse universe would have them groveling like this, each trying to appease the hungry ego in the other, only to see that what was really happening was the ultimate Magianic Gift, a folding in upon itself of mechanical, altruistic ineptitude.

Still, somehow, she had reached out and stroked his chest when it was over, when he had finished at last. She had been all right. Sore and . . . happy. How could she have been so blind? And what could she give to become blind again?

John experienced the growing emotions in Beth with a sense of relief. It was coming out finally, all that had been submerged for so long. The truth. And the truth would bring him, them, back from the void.

Or was truth the void itself? Beth wondered.

*Polaris* came over the horizon, not yet braking from the transfer ellipse that had carried it from Aello. The dim white pinpoint sped ten degrees across the mystery of stars called Berenice's Hair and intruded upon the starkly bright dipper of the Great Bear. Slowly, it became a real thing: a tiny burst of light and it began to fall. Then, a few kilometers up, it began braking in earnest, spearing down as it grew until every detail could be made out. The silent, translucent flame quickly used up delta-v, modifying the ship's velocity so that it nearly matched that of the Ocypetan surface. About half a kilometer up, the flame died and the ship began to fall, as if through pitch. When it was only a few tens of meters up, the engine vented an invisible mist of cold hydrogen gas which swept the ice viciously. No flame would disturb the fragile solidity of the landing area. The ship slowed, stopped dead, and then drifted down, bouncing once in slow motion.

Sealock and Krzakwa strode into the central room of the CM, exhaustion lining their faces, and looked about at the inhabitants and their varieties of boredom. Cornwell, who also looked tired but resolute, stopped them with a peremptory gesture. Brendan stared down at him, eyes glittering, unreadable.

"All right," said John. "You've had your little gadabout. In the time you've been gone we've put the DR software to good use, and I've come to some conclusions about myself and the nature of our effort here."

"That's fine," said Brendan. A few lines etched themselves at the corners of his mouth, evidence of a sudden tension in the muscles of his face.

"I want you to know that I am not going to be intimidated by your violence anymore."

"John—" Tem began, but he was waved off by Sealock.

"Go on," said Brendan.

"That's all I have to say," said Cornwell.

"Anyone else?" asked Brendan. He glanced around the chamber.

Demogorgon was coming out of his room. "Brendan," he said, "we have to talk. Alone."

Sealock grinned, giving a little laugh that sounded more like a cough or small sneeze than anything else. "Don't sweat it," he said. "We will . . . not right now, though." He shook his head slowly, grin broadening and becoming softer. "Tem, why don't you tell them what's going on?"

Krzakwa shrugged, rubbing a hand across the back of his neck, looking puzzled. "I, uh . . ." He stopped, cleared his throat, and went on: "This is going to be hard to accept. We found something on Aello . . ."

Jana, too, had come out of her compartment and was staring at the two travelers, wondering just what it was that she sensed in their demeanor. "What? What did you find?"

He smiled faintly and spread his hands before her, palms up. "Well . . . It was a . . . thing . . . an artifact."

There was a moment of silence, a nonreaction that made Krzakwa wonder if they'd heard him, if his statement had somehow failed to penetrate their consciousness. Finally, from his position in the corner, Prynne said, "Huh?"

"What do you mean?" asked Ariane. She hadn't moved and both her face and voice had remained bland, as if she were asking for the time of day.

"Artifact is an understatement, Ari. . . ." He looked at her and thought, Jesus. How the fuck am I going to put this? He tried to come up with a way and realized that, whatever he said, it was going to be outré. . . . They were going to be talking about something not only outside of human experience but outside of expectability as well. "Hell, why don't I just say it: we found a God damned enormous alien spaceship stuck inside the moon. . . ." He looked at their faces and saw the beginning of incredulity. "I'm not kidding. . . . It was kilometers across, under the ice of Sayyarrin. . . ."

If air could be called dumbstruck, it was this air, now. Jana stood up straight, rising a little into the air. She opened her mouth, as if to speak, then gagged and closed her eyes. She swayed in the air and drifted slowly to the floor.

**154**

Demogorgon went to where she had fallen and propped her torso up, saying, "Jana . . . Hey! Jana?"

Her eyes opened, and the look inside the lids was not pleasant to see. She did not speak.

"I don't believe it," said John. "Why didn't you radio the information to us?"

"You may not care," said Sealock, "but that thing's ours until we decide otherwise. We decided to avoid the risk of having a signal intercepted, by anyone. I brought the RAW bubble out of *Polaris*. You can verify everything for yourself."

"But . . ."

"Just tap the fucking thing! We'll talk later. Tem and I have work to do."

They labored and, finally, the rebuilding program was complete. Though they still referred to it as *Polaris*, it was no longer the same. Where there had been a tall, sleek spaceship form, something that bore a distinct kinship to both the centuries-gone fantasies of a prolonged childhood and the early designs of Sergei Korolyev, there now stood a modernistic girder array, almost the *Deepstar* reborn. A closer inspection showed the detail of what had been done: the new ship was made of three slim obelisks standing side by side on the ice, encased within a confining structure of beams.

In a sense, what they'd built still fitted in with the technological gestalt of their original design. The core of the structure, its middle tower, was the heavy-ion drive unit that had provided *Deepstar*'s principal thrust, encased within its crosshatched metallic housing. The two outriggers, though somewhat differentiated in form, were similar in function. To one side of the engine/drill was one of the Hyloxso matrices that the earlier craft had used, recharged with $H_2/O_2$ fuel. Beneath it, a high-impulse liquid-fuel rocket motor was secured. On the other side stood *Polaris* itself, a little longer than it had been, but still largely devoted to being a rocket vehicle, with a module for men to ride in.

The added length was necessary, and the story was power. The ion drill/engine was a voracious device, no matter what its intended purpose. Though it used fuel efficiently, it did so

**155**

at a high cost in electromagnetic energy. It was a pretty little problem for engineers to face, but it had a tractable solution. The ion fuel itself, through its automatic breakdown process, was a form of stored energy, ultimately power-stabilized by the fusion reactor. The complex's Magnaflux generator, intended for attitude control and as an important part of the life-support system, was an em-field manipulation device. Though batteries were no longer a major part of the technological surround, their purpose was still understood, and the generator, by its very nature, could contain stored energy for a certain period of time. It would work, over the short term, recharged from Ocypete via microwave beams, and that was all that they needed to ask of their system. It would work, after a fashion, and accomplish their purposes on Aello.

In their haste to return to the Artifact, and what it represented, they had done little to modify the CM for its enlarged crew. There were four of them now, possessing what passed for physical-science expertise in their little universe on the edge of the void. Sealock, Krzakwa, Hu, and Methol filled the little ship to near overflowing and made the CM into a crowded place indeed. There were two extra couches bolted into the space athwart the top of the lower equipment bay, and Jana and Ariane would ride there, facing into the backs of the upper berths. They would be little more than cargo during the flight, sitting there, watching the bracing struts flex. Because of their presence there would be no room for extra food lockers here, but the already extant ones could be stuffed fuller, and the ship's vaster superstructure invited much external storage. They would use the same airlock, for instance, but the first two to exit could pass in two more worksuits. Aggravations would probably abound in a ship that was even more claustrophobic than it had been previously. With the firing sequences ended, there was little practical to do but wait.

Disconnecting the induction leads from his head, Krzakwa rolled over in his seat to a position that left him uncomfortably back-bent, despite the zero-g float, and grinned at the two women. "This must be how it was for the first astronauts. I feel like an elephant in a birdcage."

Sealock, still hooked up to the control element, glanced over and said, "That's a consistent visual image. . . . You're going to have to go on a diet if you want to get to the food, you fat bastard."

Tem smiled. It was true—he'd never be able to squeeze his bulk between the two women to reach the provision cabinet. "No, but I can have a lot of fun trying. I feel like I'd be a lot thinner if I could just take a good crap. This shitless food is accumulating somewhere inside me. . . . Anyway, these here cabin boys can cook our meals and serve them to us in bed."

Sealock began unplugging leads from his skull. "They're not boys, my friend, if you haven't noticed. And they should have at least one shit apiece coming, if you would like a little empathic elimination."

Krzakwa laughed.

Grimacing, Ariane said, "This is the grossest conversation I've ever heard! Are you two that bored already?"

"Just call it ennui," said Brendan.

Tem said, "Remember, we've been sitting in these very same positions for a good part of the last two weeks. I guess we've been developing ways to entertain ourselves. . . ."

Methol laughed. "Well . . . if it's entertainment you want . . . the rest of you can watch me making up for lost time." She peeled off the inertial harness and slithered out between the forward seats, climbing atop Brendan, her legs locking about his waist.

Krzakwa settled back into his couch with an expression of interest. It was not immediately obvious whether Hu was even paying attention. Her eyes were open but she was looking at nothing in particular.

Watching them have sex from a close perspective turned out to be no novelty for Tem. After an initial bout of writhing, held in place by Brendan's harness, they coupled and quickly settled into the slide and grind rhythms of woman-on-top sex. There was no real sound beyond the coarse whisper of cloth on cloth and the even quieter one of meshing organs. Tem stole occasional glances at their faces, but in their fixed expressions there was nothing new to learn. The only novelty

**157**

was the way Sealock pulled apart Ariane's buttocks and inserted his finger between them as far as he could reach, apparently so he could get independent verification of the sensation of his penis being alternately engulfed and decoupled.

After a while Krzakwa fell into a sort of reverie. Contained within himself, he was back on the Moon again, thirteen now and starting his apprenticeship. The surging arcana of sex, though fascinating for their strangeness, were distinctly alien —not unlike the behavior of the exotic small particles that, he was learning, represented the even stranger forces that made up that which was.

Perhaps he was thinking about Sadie, and what had become of her when she graduated . . . and then again, perhaps not. It was like a waking dream, and a reverie was like DR, but unaided and alone. It was private, and seemed pleasant: he walked alone down the endless dim hallways that led to the underground rooms in which he received his Met-stat training. He was late because of an incident involving an accusation of "overindulgence," so in all probability that's what he was thinking about. He did not walk as quickly as he could have, and perhaps there was more trouble waiting for him at the class hall. Occasionally he had to stop before closed seals and wait for them to slowly iris open. He would be at least twenty-five minutes late, but he didn't really care. He would blame it all on the residence counselor.

Finally he came to the widening out of the corridor that was the atrium to the Met-stat section. Now he began to skip, hurrying to give the impression that he had run the whole way. He passed through the halls, past the numbered empty rooms, and finally looked into the class hall in which he was supposed to be having a lesson. He looked again, harder; no one was there! Where in the fuck was the class? It reminded him of a dream he had had hundreds of times. Shit!

Now he really was running. He slammed through the door into the administrative section, then stopped and tried to compose himself, walking up to the secretary's desk. He was a young, balding man who Tem had sensed was rather in sympathy with the students. "Mr. Tamura. I was delayed by my counselor and just got here. Where's the class?"

Tamura looked up, smiling slightly. "Calm down, Kracka —that's it, isn't it? You haven't missed anything. That is if you've paid attention to the suit-up lectures. They are just going over that material again. In Room K4. Take the Qa17b elevator, that's quickest."

It took him under five minutes to get there. The corridor ended in a small chamber lined with lockers and benches, like the anteroom to a gym. There was a door there with a round bull's-eye for a window, and by standing on the very tips of his toes he could look through. There was an instrument panel, and another door with an identical window. The light over both doors was green, so he pulled the handle and went in, walked to the other door, and pressed his face to the window. His classmates, all twenty of them, were there, in a room larger than any he had seen. And they were putting on space suits!

Of course! This was an airlock! His class was being taken on an unannounced trip outside! And, by Christ, he had almost missed it!

He flung open the door and, going up to his instructor, proffered his planned excuse. "Very well, Krzakwa," the man said, "get a suit from the rack there and put it on—you know how to do that, don't you? You've been lectured enough. Just remember: if you put it on wrong you're dead. Got it?"

He nodded.

The room was large, and it was evident that Met-stat didn't just use this airlock for individual egress. There was a large orange machine mounted on five-meter-wide treads that Tem recognized as a bulldozer. The floor was covered with a dull gritty dust that he knew was dirt. He barely had time to take in what was about to happen as he followed the precise steps and put on the suit, piece by piece, and sealed it. He caught up and had it fully on before some of the slower members of the class.

Inside the suit it smelled, but he didn't mind. He looked out through the old-style faceplate, scratched and finger-printed, and turned on the radio channel with his tongue.

**159**

They gathered before the large pressure curtain that was the far wall. It was bathed in an internal red glow, indicating that the room was depressurizing. There was a diminuendo hiss, and the curtain turned green. The curtain began to slide aside, more quickly than Tem had expected.

"Oh, my God . . ." You couldn't tell whose whisper that was.

The next room had an irregular gray floor and a dead black ceiling decorated by a brilliant blue and white crescent. His breath whispered in his helmet. It wasn't a room . . . and he found himself confronted by the world outside his world:

Temujin Krzakwa, at thirteen, stood on the headway of a long ramp, under an infinite black sky, dotted here and there with impossibly remote points of light barely visible in contrast to the flat gray surface. This was a parking lot, and, besides the occasional great trucks, there were several rows of small rollagon cars. In the distance another of the cars moved slowly along a road of fused regolith, still raising a small smear of dust. Farther—farther away than Tem had ever seen before—was a row of lollipop coils that marked the beginnings of a mass-driver. His eyes felt fatigued already, but he couldn't stop looking. Back over his shoulder was the hemispherical dome that was a surface manifestation of the universe that had heretofore contained him. Under the Earth, on the horizon, sat a tiny spaceship.

As he had been instructed, he didn't look in the direction of the sun. Over the radio the instructor said, "OK, boys. This is just to get you acquainted. Take all the time you want to look around. This'll seem like a bore before you know it."

Somehow, for him, maybe for him alone, that preplanned aphorism turned out to be a lie. He was embarked on a first flight into the unknown, a recognizable sort of adventure. He wanted to look for the exit from this infinite room, not the one that led to his old world, no, but the door to the next world, which would be even grander than this, and even more wonderful.

They were on the surface of Aello now, standing before the Artifact that had called them here, staring silently at it, and they had fully implemented the thermal retention feature of their worksuits, so no further erosion was taking place. Neon dust about five hundred centimeters thick hid everything except for the grotesque fin, a dark and foreshortened triangle that towered upward above their heads. It was featureless, looking almost naturalistic.

Finally their desire for touristic gawking was fulfilled, and they began to wonder, to speculate. Krzakwa was the first to speak. "Well, this is it, I guess. Time to find out what this thing is made of. Brendan?"

Sealock unhooked a tunable em-wave modulator from his belt and played a tight cone of infrared radiation over the ground in front of him. A great swath of neon simply disappeared, followed by the water nodules that it had contained. They were momentarily surrounded by the haze of a swiftly dissipating cloud of gas, then what was left was a perfectly flat, smooth area, more blue than gray, about the size of a boxing ring.

Kneeling on the surface, he muttered, "I guess a little neutron activation analysis won't hurt anything. . . ." He changed the setting on his suit scanners and exchanged the em-device for a smaller collimated particle beamer. He fired an invisible ray and read its reflection. "Um . . ." *What the fuck?* "This is ridiculous. It's . . . it looks like . . . carbon, platinum, and iridium." Using the em-wave device, he did a quick gamma-ray scan. "In a dense, octahedral array . . ." He hung the tools back on his belt and turned to stare at the others, feeling somewhat foolish.

"Bubbleplastic?" Jana's whisper was incredulous, a perfect overlay.

"That seems a little unreasonable," said Krzakwa.

"Yep." Sealock rubbed a gloved hand uselessly over the front of his helmet. "The latticework is smaller, and there's something peculiar about it, but there's no doubt about the readings. There must be something more to this than meets the eye." He grinned to himself, humorlessly. "Not to mention the instrumentation . . ."

Ariane turned up her suit optics and looked hard. "No seams, connectors, doors, or even bumps. No real detail above the crystalline level, except for the slight variations in color. No way in from this end."

The Selenite grunted as he snapped together the fittings of a heavy beam-welder that he'd stripped from one of the remote work units. He took careful aim at nothing in particular, set the charge coupling regulator, and fired. The bright beam reached out and touched the surface but stopped and disappeared there like a broken rod.

"No change in blackbody constant," said Hu.

The beam shut down and, in the dimness, it became apparent that the intense radiation had not even marked the stuff. It hadn't even gotten warm. "Hell," said Krzakwa. "Be nice to find out how they're getting around the basic laws of thermodynamics."

Ariane nodded. Her speculations were getting ever more grandiose. It was best to take things as they came.

Brendan turned to face Jana. "One thing left to do," he said.

The woman nodded and began pulling components from her own belt, assembling them into a device atop a small collapsible tripod. The thing was a partial gravimetric flume gauge, a wave-system detector that could map out anomalies in the local mass-density background. Though useless to asterologists, it was a handy device for prospectors and could tell them a great deal about what lay beneath their feet. All energy fields have patterns, and those patterns contain information. Chains of causation can be unraveled by anyone with sufficient data processing capability. . . .

"I guess we might as well give it a try, huh?"

Hu signaled agreement by unreeling a waveguide from her suit and plugging it into the detector. Sealock joined her and they switched it on.

The Einstein winds blow like a delicate breeze, moving shells of time restrained only by the calming influence of quantum mechanics. Sequencing events are self-ordained and all things come off a steadily unraveling skein. Lachesis. Visualize a rock in a flowing river. Now, hide the rock with an occultation disk. Inspect the turbulence that you can see downstream. Estimate the difficulty in deducing the size and

**162**

shape of the rock from the wake it leaves in its lee. Q*T*D. Quantum Transformational Dynamics comes along and makes many things possible.

"Jesus!" That from Sealock.

"Yes," said Hu. "I see the infrastructure is too complex for our little 'net element. It seems to be a wingless lifting body something like ten kilometers long. A lot of mass here, disguised by the size of the empty internal cavity. That's why it wasn't apparent from the preliminary system scans. Though I suspected . . ."

"What did you suspect?" asked Ariane.

"I suspected that some previously derived theories might have to be revised. That is all a scientist can do, in the end."

"Yeah," said Krzakwa. "We could use some theories now."

Ariane shrugged. "Some kind of landing craft? But what kind of atmosphere would you fly something this size in?"

"Jupiter maybe. The sun's chromosphere?" said Tem. "How about Iris'?"

"So? What next? It seems like we're stymied already," said Jana.

Sealock looked up into the black circle of sky at the entry to the hole. "We've got a fair number of choices," he said. "We can play with it; we can fuck around looking for some kind of door, scrape the ice off bit by bit while we indulge in the happy explorer game, but . . ."

Hu turned and looked at him, a cold suspicion forming inside her. "But . . . *what?*"

"Lots of things. Hell. Let's pull it right out of the ice. Why do you think we brought the ion drill?"

There was a silence, and they all heard her gasp, "No!" She took a step forward, almost menacing. "You *stupid* bastard! Aello will tell us what we want to know about where this thing came from and when. If you give me a chance to—"

"Maybe so," he said, "but time is not something we have in an abundant supply. Let's get out of here."

Jana seemed to have frozen, contained by her visions and at the same time holding them all in. . . .

Visions of fiery destruction.

**163**

□ □ □

*Polaris* drifted in a slow, elliptical orbit around Aello. Inside the crowded CM the four scientist-engineers sat arguing. Krzakwa floated above his couch leafing through a hypothetical sheaf of options, a finger representing each one. "Look, why don't we put it to a vote?"

Jana Li Hu shook her head emphatically. "No," she said, "this is too important to be decided that way." There was a look of desperation on her face. "I don't think you people understand the magnitude of what you're suggesting. If you try to pull something that size out of the ice, you're going to chew up an entire quadrant . . . you'll ruin the whole moon!" She looked at their faces separately, seeking some form of recognition. "Don't you realize you'll be destroying something that's as important to the physical sciences as these putative 'aliens' are to biology?"

Sealock reached up and began plugging leads into his head. "Jana—I don't know what you're *really* after, but that's the stupidest argument I've ever heard."

Hu's anxious expression turned to a harsh glare. "Asshole," she said. "I suppose if this were the ruins of Troy you'd want to blow it up to see what's underneath. I'm arguing that we go about this in an ordered way, do a full reconnaissance down to meter resolution before we dig it out."

Methol rested an intended calming hand on her forearm. "Jana. I think your principles are fine. But in this situation they're simply inappropriate. The finding of this Artifact could be the most important thing that's ever happened. We *have* to get it out of there."

"And just how much of it do you think USEC will leave for us?" asked Sealock.

"I still think we should put it to a vote," said Krzakwa.

"No!"

"Bullshit," said Sealock. "Why go on with this? We're ready now."

They felt the hull begin to purr as the Magnaflux generator came to life, its wings of force acting like control moment gyros to turn the ship around its center of gravity. Slowly *Polaris* swung about, pointing its grid toward Aello. Brendan

**164**

had an exterior view, with a superimposed reticle imprinted on his vision, and he locked the ACS avionics on the targeted area of the small moon.

Hu screamed, a tortured sound, deafening in the enclosed space, and launched herself at the man. Sealock caught her by the wrists and hurled her back down, where Methol tried to hold her in place. Krzakwa wedged his bulk between the seats, blocking entry to the upper half of the CM, simultaneously reaching up and affixing an induction lead to the back of his head, so his visual cortex could have access to the ship's optical system. This was something he wanted to see. "Ariane?"

"It's OK. Pass me a lead."

The twin $H_2/O_2$ engines started with a muted roar, accelerating them toward the moon. When the ion drive came on they would be in perfect balance, thrusting in two opposing vectors that would cancel each other out.

"Jana?"

"God damn you all. No."

Sealock lined up his sights on the Artifact and lit off the drill.

Singing, high on the wire, the god stood athwart a velvet-dark sky, dust-mote stars swirling around the massive spires of his huge legs. A sparkle of fire raged through his golden hair and in his right hand he clutched a thunderbolt. The thing writhed in his grasp like a glowing snake, a living thing surrounded by a violet nimbus. He raised it high above his head, laughing in his awesome power, a peal of thunder that trailed off into the distance. His body began to throw off radiance, a bright corona that lit the skies all around with its lambent streamers. He cast the thunderbolt down on his little victim.

It elongated from his hand, a broad band of coruscating fire, a maze of intertwining beams, and struck the surface of Aello all about the Artifact. There was an instant of dead stillness in which the ice seemed to grow transparent. In the slowed time of Comnet they could see the ship hanging there, nose down into the surface of a world, then the crust of

**165**

the moon, the entire visible hemisphere, was riven by an array of cracks. There was an explosion.

Aello was suddenly hidden by an expanding disk of blinding white mist, a shield that swallowed the power of the ion drill. It swelled until the wave front struck *Polaris*, rolling it out of its orbit. The beam winked out as Sealock shifted his attention to the matter of recontrol.

He became the bird-king again, soaring on his broad wings in the winds of the storm, riding it out, waiting for the skies to clear. It was soon over. The debris from what they'd wrought fled away in an expanding, glittery shell and was gone. They could see Aello again.

The little moon was eaten away, a great bite taken out of its surface, leaving a raw, gaping, steamy wound, the rest of its cryolith completely disrupted. In the center of this cavity the Artifact lay exposed, tumbling as it sank gently toward the center of its ancient home. It shone in the wan, distant sunlight, not like an ancient machine but like something fresh and new. Magical.

Looking out through the ship's eyes, Temujin Krzakwa was silent. What they'd done was beyond simple blasphemy. He knew of no words possessing sufficient power.

Brendan Sealock sighed, feeling his muscles slowly relax, his mind awash in a gentle afterglow, his heart slowing from its mad, orgasmic beat. A man didn't get to blow up many planets in his lifetime.

Ariane Methol said, "Well, now. That was interesting. Let's get down there and see what we've found."

Jana Li Hu said nothing.

The alien Artifact settled faster than it should have in the negligible gravity of Aello. Perhaps this was because some final explosive force vector had given it an impulse toward the center of the ice moon rather than away. The tumbling motion stopped with a few glancing impacts on the frozen, shattered walls as it sank. It came to rest nose down in the deep cavity, its dorsal fin pointing at the black sky, and debris began to accrete all around it. Ultimately the ship, if such it was, would be buried once again.

*Polaris* swung down from its orbit with a single phasing

maneuver and came to rest at its high gate point above the Artifact, hovering on an oxygen jet bled from the Hyloxso tanks. The crew looked down at it through the ship optics, silently examining their find in the harsh yet dim light of the sun. It was simple, almost featureless, a fat, wedge-shaped lifting body, with a tall stabilizer at the stern. There were two winglike control surfaces projecting upward at thirty-degree angles on either side. It appeared to be a soft, pale blue in color, though there were darker spots here and there. On the blunt stern there were five huge black circles, evidently the expansion nozzles of rocket engines mounted in a trapezoidal array. It looked like a primitive human-technology spacecraft blown to unbelievable size.

Sealock opened his eyes and glanced over at Krzakwa. "What do you suppose flew the damn thing, mile-high Watusi?"

The Selenite's teeth showed briefly, a weak sort of grin. "I guess we'd better go down and find out."

Turning his attention back to the ship, Brendan said, "We'll be in for a lot of walking no matter where we land. It probably doesn't matter in this gravity."

From the lower equipment bay, Ariane called up, "Why not land right on top of the thing? It's certainly big enough."

Sealock nodded. "Why not? We couldn't ask for a flatter surface." He decreased the flow of gas from the engines and dropped *Polaris* slowly toward the broad back of the alien vessel. When they were down and the motor stopped, the ship stood canted at a twenty-degree angle. They started to slide, but a slight adjustment to the friction coefficient of the landing pads halted them.

Krzakwa sat up on his couch, eyes glassy with excitement. "Suit up. Let's see what we've got."

The four of them stood outside the ship, back in their armored worksuits, on a smooth, tilted azure plain. In the distance they could see the three fins rising toward the black sky and beyond, very far away, the dark, crystalline horizon that hid the walls of the world-sized crater they'd made. The shrouded eye of Iris looked down on them in three-quarters

**167**

phase, just above one horizon, and the sun, a fat spark, threw its wan light over the other.

"Where do we begin?" mused Methol.

"Maybe at the nearest dark spot," said Krzakwa. "They seem to be the only real features anywhere on the dorsal surface. There's one about three hundred meters, um, starboard of here." They'd landed just to port of the center line, where most of the Artifact's features seemed to be.

When they set out for the thing, they ran into immediate difficulty. The surface of the vessel was so smooth and the gravity so low that it was difficult to push off in the long flat leaps of low-g movement, and even harder to come to a stop after landing. Raising the friction on the soles of their boots remedied this, but, since the em-embedding fields induced a corresponding field in the surface that did not immediately dissipate, they had a tendency to stick to the Artifact as they jumped. Any slight asymmetry in takeoff tended to throw them off course. Eventually they made it to the feature.

The disk was just a region of somewhat darker blue, in no other way distinguished from the surrounding area. It was neither raised nor depressed, nor did it seem to have a different texture. "Well," said Krzakwa, "this is useless." He stepped forward onto it, but nothing happened. "I wonder what it's for?" The others joined him and they began walking around, staring at the circle. An analysis of the thing showed that it was simply a region of slightly enhanced titanium concentration.

Sealock suddenly squatted near the center of the disk and said, "Maybe it's a giant 'O,' with very thick sides. Look." In front of him, at the circle's focus, was a small white spot, about two centimeters across. It, too, showed no relief.

"Maybe that's just an artifact of whatever process they used to draw this design," said Methol. "The compass point," she laughed suddenly. "We're wasting our time here. Let's go back to the ship and break out the whole barrage of instruments." She and Krzakwa turned and started for *Polaris*, accompanied by Hu, who had been following them silently about, wrapped in whatever web of thoughts her mind was spinning.

**168**

Sealock stood for a while longer, staring down at the white spot. He leaned forward and put his thumb over it, then straightened up. The little world about him remained inert. He muttered something, then put his foot over the mark and turned the sole's friction coefficient to maximum. He could feel his boot seem to cement itself to the surface of the Artifact. When he removed it again, the circular dot looked the same. Nothing happened. He thought he felt a slight current being applied to his skin, perhaps imagination and nothing more. Then he shouted.

The others turned at the sound of his voice, which would have been deafening had the com-circuits not compensated swiftly, and saw the blue disk being swiftly filled by a spreading pool of black. The edge of the hole seemed paper thin, adding to the impression of two-dimensionality. But there was certainly a third dimension here—Sealock hung poised in space for a moment, then, clasping his knees to his chest, he began to fall down into the darkness, drifting slowly in Aello's weak grasp. In a moment he was gone. They rushed wildly back to the edge of the portal and stood looking down into the nothingness below.

"Brendan?"

"I'm still here, Tem." His voice was crisp in their heads. "I'm standing on some kind of surface about four meters below you. I can see you outlined against the stars." He paused and they could sense his excitement through the telemetry circuits. "There's something very strange going on here."

"What is it?"

"Well . . . jump down and see. It might be best for you to experience it first hand. Just don't alter your optical settings."

Krzakwa glanced at Methol and Hu, then shrugged and stepped over the edge. He fell very slowly, taking a long time to drop the four meters. As the darkness engulfed him, he said, "What am I supposed to be expecting?"

"You'll see."

"Should I try to land flat-footed?"

"That'd be a good idea. Flex your knees a little."

**169**

"Flex my . . . In this gravity? Why?"

"You'll see."

Krzakwa was silent then, meditative, and prudently fell with his knees flexed. Suddenly his legs straightened out, as if something had grabbed him by the ankles and *pulled.* There was an instant of sudden acceleration and then his feet hammered into the floor. "What the fuck?" he muttered.

Sealock laughed. "Pretty weird, huh? Now try lifting your foot up."

The Selenite experimentally hefted his right leg. It came up hard, as if he were standing in a quite respectable inertial field, the closest thing to high gravity in his personal experience. Whatever was holding him abruptly let go, and his knee popped up with released muscular tension. He teetered, almost losing his balance. When he put his foot down the floor grabbed it again. "That's really odd. Some sort of em-field?"

"I don't think so. I was playing some little games while I waited . . . there's a pretty strong gradient down here—like a gravitational field. I guess the region right against the floor has something like a 2-g density."

"What're you telling me? You think the floor is coated with a monoparticular layer of neutronium?"

Sealock made his suit generate an image of Krzakwa against the darkness. "Some kind of neutron paint? No, I'm not saying anything. Just an observation."

"How about another observation: why are we standing around in the dark? These suits have optical-scale enhancers. . . ."

Sealock grinned. "Turn yours on if you want. Maybe you should, so at least one of us can see. . . . But this ship is still turned on and its crew had to see by something. Odds are it was electromagnetic radiation."

Krzakwa kicked up the gain on his optical system until he could see by ambient light. "Almost useless. There's nothing in here." He looked around. "Quite a few dark spots on the walls. A few on the floor."

"Airlock controls?"

"Probably." He walked over to the wall, taking high steps the way he would in a shallow pool of water, and reached out.

**170**

When his hand neared the wall the force grabbed it. "Hm. Interesting." He pulled one foot clear and stuck it on the wall, then followed it with the other. Suddenly his orientation was changed by ninety degrees. "That's a useful trait for a spaceship to have."

"Better than low-differential em."

Krzakwa snickered. "Sure." He looked up at the still gaping door through the ceiling. Methol and Hu were bright mannequins to his enhanced vision. "I guess it's safe for us all to be in here at the same time. Come on." The two women came floating down. Ariane deliberately came down like a falling cat, landing full length on the floor and immersing herself in the field.

"Oof," she grunted, "this is worse than Earth. Without the worksuit I'd be stuck here permanently." She found that she had to increase the power of her exoskeleton in order to get up again.

Sealock started walking blindly toward where he knew Methol was, stubbornly waiting for the ship to sense their presence and turn on a light. He was not long disappointed.

"Hey, look out," shouted Tem, distracted from his thoughts, "you're about to step on a—ghaah!" He squeezed his eyes shut as a harsh, actinic violet light suddenly flared, quickly dimmed by the suit's internal protections. He turned down his scale enhancers and opened his eyes again. The chamber was flooded with a soft, blue-green light, like an undersea scene.

"I guess I was right," said Sealock.

"It's not coming from anywhere, Bren," said Ariane.

"Uh-huh. It just is, like the sticking field."

Krzakwa's eyes still felt grainy. "Yeah. Well, I hate to say it, but so far these buttons, despite their apparently random distribution, are producing completely human results. It's a strong argument that form follows function. So far we have an airlock with a door button and a light switch."

Hu came up to them now and, for the first time since the disruption of Aello, she spoke. "Since we've come this far, there's no point in being timid." She reached out and punched a gloved hand into one of the dark spots.

**171**

"Hey!" said Krzakwa, but nothing happened. Hu punched the next spot in the row and the ceiling door suddenly irised shut and vanished without a trace.

"Uh-oh." That was from Sealock. Hu snorted and hit the third spot. Again nothing happened.

Methol stepped forward in alarm and said, "Really, Jana. I don't think you should be . . ."

Hu punched the fourth spot and a section of floor under her feet vanished. She dropped through under what looked like a fairly high acceleration and was gone, her brief, chopped-off scream echoing in their heads.

Back in the Illimitor World, Demogorgon and Vana lay naked together in the purple-cushioned rear section of his royal skimmer. They were drifting without power above the glittery azure waters of the Gevrainhal Sea, far to the northwest of Arhos, flowing with the wind beneath an almost featureless cornflower sky, tracking with the great red suns. The air was blood-warm above the equatorial ocean and fresh, clean sweat dappled the skins of their flawlessly imaginary bodies.

Somewhere, in a hidden corner of her consciousness, Vana could imagine how this worked. There were many tricks to the Illimitor World program, enough alternate realities to satisfy the needs of many participants. If a hundred people submerged themselves here together, they would have a common experience, yes, but tailored to a hundred sets of needs. It would be the same but different. Here was a perfect world where everyone got not what he wanted but what he needed. Demogorgon had explained to her the mechanism for it all: a Tri-vesigesimal loop can make an almost infinite number of tracks from every decision point, with three layers of meaning derived from the twenty gradations of choice.

The reality was that sex, like everything else, was better here than in the real world. There was no sick feeling, stemming from the initial sensations of desire: it just began. Instead of a gradual building to the trigger-spray release of an orgasm, it began full strength, one long flood of raw, elemental pleasure that ended only when the need for it was gone.

**172**

When it was over there were no frustrations, no aches, just perfect satiation and contentment—and if you wanted it to begin again, it did.

In the contented languorous moments here, time was seemingly suspended, and the simple comfort of her relationship with Demo put no pressure on her to act or speak in any particular way. They'd come here again and again to escape the social pressures building in the colony. Somehow, the Thing they had found on Aello meant little to her, here, now . . . all her links to the outer world were dissolving. Perhaps not so strangely, she missed Harmon most of all here. But she knew he couldn't accept all this.

The perfect pleasures of the Illimitor World were building something between her and Demogorgon. Things were changing. What they were building seemed good, but she didn't know quite what it was. Not yet.

Vana took a sip of her fizzy gin and tonic and watched a broken cloud pass in front of the lower sun. Whatever was going on here, she thought, it was *right,* for a change.

Sealock fell to his knees beside the hole in the floor that had eaten Jana, fighting the force field, which, in the vicinity of the opening, seemed to want to pull him in. It was a cushiony black below, the chamber-light that spilled through the opening seeming to be swallowed by nothingness. He called up an image of her, based on telemetry signals. There she was, falling slowly away—no, not falling. She was on a ballistic trajectory created by a momentary acceleration as she'd gone through the hole. She was a hundred meters away and receding. "Jana!"

"Yes." The woman's voice was calm. "Brendan, I can't see anything down here. I've turned the scale enhancers all the way up, but it doesn't help. This must be an awfully big room. I'm going to activate my microwave emitter."

"OK." Sealock switched over a portion of his suit optics to short-wave sensing, thoughtfully chose an array of false-color generators, and waited. Hu's suit suddenly went bright, then dimmed again as his rectifiers normalized the image. Light flickered on in the chamber below. Looking over his shoulder, Krzakwa gasped.

Jana was a flyspeck drifting through space toward a tilted platform more than a half kilometer away. What they could see of the room below made no sense beyond the sheer enormity of it. Sealock turned the holding em of his gloves all the way up and splayed his hands on the deck, then stuck his head over the edge, lurching as the force field tried to draw him downward, and looked around. Jana's radiation was quite sufficient to illuminate the entire chamber, which, by rough estimate, seemed to extend the length of the ship. Though the room was of constant width, the outward-bending walls dwindled into the distance, following the converging lines of perspective, and seemed to almost meet many kilometers away. The floor was cluttered with angularities, incomprehensible objects that changed from a monumental array directly below to a foreshortened jumble in the distance. Sealock turned off his right glove and reached down through the hole. He touched the underside of the floor and, feeling his hand stick, guessed that it too possessed a gravity-like field. He hung his torso down through the opening and quickly got a grip on the surface opposite. Inching his body forward, he suddenly reached a point where the field in the hole and beyond overcame that of the airlock, and he was propelled in a head-over-heels arc that left him sprawling on the other side. Above him the world inverted, and he looked up at the underside of the sky.

Dizziness assailed him, and he shut his suit optics down for a moment, then took a deep breath and brought them up again. The surface to which he was bound was like an immense game board, slightly convex, and populated by a regular array of man-sized white obelisks, for all the world like the bishops of his first chess set. At the level of his eyes they sprouted in great enough profusion to cut off vision about fifteen hundred meters away. So much for form and function, he thought.

"Come on through," Brendan said, extending a hand toward what seemed to be once again "down" through the opening. "Grab my hand and I'll swing you through."

Carefully, the others flipped up and through, roughly deposited on the flypaper inner surface. When they were ready, they stood, which by now evoked hardly any vertigo, and looked up in awe. Sealock felt a sudden deterministic frustration at this rapid alteration of his directional sense. He needed to think of this as a zero-g space, but the presence of the gravity-like field prevented him from doing so.

"OK," he said, "up/down is dangerous here, and totally inapplicable, folks. As discomforting as it may be, forget it."

"Jana?" That was from Krzakwa. "Your Doppler telemetry indicates you're going about five m/s, so you're in for a pretty hard landing. If the field doesn't exist on the other side, you'll bounce. . . . Please remember the electromagnetic features of your worksuit. Your wrists . . ."

"I'm not stupid!" she said, sounding angry.

"I know, but I . . ."

"More experience in low g, right? But you don't have *any* experience with this. No one does, so shut up. I'm here." She relayed an image to them. The "floor" grew patiently, broken platforms pulling apart to reveal a bit of smooth floor decorated with another of the mysterious circles. Just before she struck, a force pushed at her and decelerated her into a soft landing. "Wow," she said. "There's a field down here too."

"You're OK, then?" asked Ariane, receiving a noncommittal "Unh" in return.

Brendan and Tem had meanwhile been exploring in the vicinity of the nearest of the "bishops." It was set in a dark circle and looked as if it had been turned on a lathe, widening and shrinking in an unpredictable way until it swelled and then tapered to a minaret crown. Sealock reached out and stroked it. "I've heard of queen games, but this is a new one on me."

"No squares, either, Bren. No markings at all, in fact."

"If there are any answers here they're down where Jana is. Sorry, over where Jana is. . . ."

Ariane joined them. "Well, what is it? A dildo?"

Brendan laughed, and it sounded unreal.

"Hey," said Jana, from afar, "you need to see this."

**175**

"Stay there," said Ariane. "I'm coming over." She leaped up, expecting to fly away, but the floor held on resolutely, and she just managed a little hop. She looked at Sealock. "Bren, we're stuck here . . . how do we get to the other side if this field won't let go?"

"Think about it, Ari," he said. "That's what the hole is for —it's evidently a transport device disguised as a portal. Which probably indicates that there aren't many reasons to hang around here."

Krzakwa nodded, walked over to the opening, and stepped into it. Instead of being launched outward, however, he disappeared back into the airlock. "Whoops!" they heard him say. "Obviously it's a two-way device." A moment later he appeared, feet first, launched along the same trajectory as Hu had followed. Ariane was next and in a minute was arcing, spread-eagled, toward the other side.

Sealock stood on the ceiling, watching them sail off, and felt a slow dawning of his sense of wonder, a returning of some of the lost sensations of his distant childhood. He suddenly remembered a week spent camping in the Roan Mountains, living a blood-crimson life under a burning blue sky, and remembered feeling this way before: a gnawing happiness reacting against "what will happen next" imagery. What, he wondered, am I going to see? Anything. He walked to the edge of the opening, squatted slightly, and fell down, being deposited softly on the former ceiling of the other room. Then, grinning, he bunched the heavy muscles of his thighs and leaped into space.

The fall took a very long time, during which he had ample opportunity to try to make sense of the mountings and cablings that crisscrossed the surface. What had he expected? he wondered. A big cabin with endless kilometers of plush seats arranged in orderly rows, like a commercial space-liner? This was certainly not that. The real question, interrelated with the size of the thing, was, why build a craft this big and then leave it empty? Could this just be a cargo hold of some sort? It made a certain amount of sense.

In the end, the four of them were standing on a two-hectare raised platform, nine hundred meters below the now

**176**

almost invisible tiny hole that had been their entrance. Krzakwa and Methol stood examining a large dais covered with thousands of dark spots, what they assumed to be a control panel of sorts, while Sealock and Hu wandered off together, reconnoitering in the area, trying to get an overview of the machinery around the "landing circle" to determine if there were any logical inferences to be made about function.

"What do you think of this thing so far?" Brendan had enacted a face-to-face image mode between them, and Hu looked at him through darkly slitted eyes, her small head protruding from the collar of the worksuit and the image of her ponytail hanging down her back.

"Leave me alone," she said, and the optics image of her cylindrical helmet reappeared. "Why are you such a fucking bastard?"

He laughed. "I like being a fucking bastard. You ought to try it sometime." They walked on, silent for a while, then he said, "I wasn't trying to ride you. I'm asking for some kind of professional opinion from you . . . as a scientist."

She stared at him for a moment, then said, "You want to know what I think? I think that what we're seeing is not the whole story. There was something in this cavity at one time. And the purpose of it all may be impossible to figure out without a clue as to what it was. The thing that's got me is, what kind of cargo does this carry?"

"That's just what I was thinking. It may not be so mysterious, though. Those nodes on the far side—could it be that some kind of field held the cargo in a matrix within the space?"

"The strange thing is this—if it's for bringing a cargo up from the surface of a gas giant, say, then where's the offloading equipment? It can't all be done with fields."

"Maybe the cargo was liquid. . . ."

"We don't have any data yet. The time for 'impressions' is later, when we know more."

He nodded. "Yes, but guesswork can sometimes help." They came to the edge of the platform and stopped. This interior world stood mostly at a level about one hundred meters below them. There were other platforms in the distance, and they could see a large number of such structures below them. It looked almost like a cityscape, a scale model on a tabletop, and everything was linked together by a maze of curving cables. The microwave emitter, which had been set on the tallest nearby structure, sharply delineated the staggered blockiness of the scene by throwing long, dense shadows. Here and there cables reached toward the "sky."

There was a sudden change in the texture of the objects they were seeing and Sealock looked back toward Methol and Krzakwa. They were gazing about. He shifted his suit optics from microwave to visible light and the vast chamber was bathed in blue-green radiance. "Looks like you got the lights turned on. . . ." They turned and walked back toward the dais.

"That was an easy one," said Ariane. "At least I think I did it. It happened about twenty seconds after I touched this node. Do you think I should touch it again to see if they go off?"

"Sure," said Jana. Nothing happened.

"We seem to have established that they don't believe in toggle buttons," said Tem. "Try this one next to it," he said, reaching out to touch one of the dark spots. As he did so, something huge began to move in the distance. A sea of cables shimmered, where before there had been nothing, and beneath them the unknown machine glided a small distance and stopped. Sealock smiled grimly. "Be a hell of a note if we accidentally turned on the rocket engines, wouldn't it?"

Watching without expression, Hu said, "It would be interesting to discover that they still worked, that they still had fuel. And that a fuel would indeed still be potent. Most that I know work by the release of stored entropy . . . and time will have its effect."

They touched other buttons, which made other objects move, and Sealock was struck by a sudden analogy: they were like small children, playing with the controls to an older child's complex toy system. It did things that they were too young to understand. They couldn't see the real relationship

**178**

between cause and effect. And any theories that they may have formed were neither enforced nor disproved.

Harmon Prynne sat in his cubicle in *Deepstar*'s CM, alone, as he had been, now, seemingly for so long. And *Vana* . . . she was under the wire *again* with that God damned fagwog! The black anger built in him and he wanted to rage, to smash things, destroy them. . . . He wanted to throw things, hurl them against the walls of his room, but in this low-g environment they would only ricochet around inanely, making him want to laugh when he needed to cry. He chewed his knuckles in frustration and stared hard at nothing. Why did it have to happen this way?

I'm alone again, he thought, and remembered endless nights he had spent alone as a younger man, when he lived in his ancestral Key West Monad. He'd never fitted in there, or in any of the other places he'd tried to live—he'd always been an outsider, cut off in the midst of his own culture . . . unable to join in the simple, joyous games of the other adolescents. If it is difficult to be strange, how much more difficult can it be to be strange and stupid?

He couldn't fit in with their impersonal ideas about human relationships, the ideas about absolute freedom within the restrictive framework of the Monad. He *needed* someone, and needed that person to need him. . . .

When he went to Montevideo in the pursuit of his career, when he met Vana Berenguer and loved her . . . he'd tried so hard to make it work, and now she was slowly being taken from him. He wanted to kill them, or himself. . . . He wanted all life to come to an end. . . . Oh, hell.

He couldn't think which way to turn. He didn't know what to do. Maybe when the USEC ship came, he could get away.

Having exhausted their patience in playing with the alien control panel, the four explorers had walked back to the edge of the platform and, in keeping with the topsy-turvy nature of the place, continued to walk down the side to the thing's base. Before the omnipresent lighting came on, this place had been buried in the shadows, but now that they could see

**179**

it well they discovered that there was nothing to see. Around them were virtually featureless blue-green rhomboids of various sizes lacking even the circles which allowed one the luxury of imagining that the thing was at least marginally understandable. Alleyways strung with occasional cables led in all directions. Finally they came to an attach point for one of the cables, and Ariane climbed up to it and said, "I wonder what it was for? It seems to go just about everywhere. . . ." The surface of the thing had a strange oily sheen, a faint coruscation of colors that gave the illusion of movement. She reached out to touch it. "You know, it has the same force field that we've found on all the flat interior surfaces." She encircled the ten-centimeter-thick cable with her fingers and let them slowly clamp down. "I wonder if they're all really continuous with each othAAAAaaaa . . ." The scream was a trailing diminuendo, for as soon as her fingers made contact with it she was jerked off her feet and sucked away on the cable, manifestly under rapid acceleration.

Sealock cursed and, throwing himself on the thing, was sucked away in his turn. The other two, unwilling to be left behind, followed suit. Obligingly, the device brought those behind up at a faster pace until they were traveling in a little cluster, like dried raisins on a bare stem.

"Well," said Brendan, "I guess we know what it does now."

Ariane laughed weakly. "This *is* a novel sort of transportation device. I wonder how we get off?"

Krzakwa was looking around, trying to make something of the things about them as they soared through alleyways with increasing numbers of cables hung almost within reach. It was as if they had been on a spur of the system that was being fed into the terminal nexus for a large network. Below them, instead of solid bulkhead, was an undulating river of larger-diameter cables. "At this speed," said Tem, "if we did manage to let go, we'd get hurt. Maybe we'd better just ride it to wherever it's going."

"Like a Westerner, you pretend to be in control of a force when in fact you are totally helpless," said Hu. "Let us hope that it remembers how to stop when it does get somewhere."

Brendan laughed. "How droll. Be funny if we all got killed in here."

"What an encouraging thought," said Tem. "You're a real optimist, aren't you?"

In the end the machine worked as they supposed it should. When they neared the port-side wall their speed of travel dropped. It brought them to a terminus near the floor and let them go. They dropped lightly and were grabbed only at the end of their descent by the now familiar field.

The wall in front of which they had been deposited looked like a gigantic honeycomb, an endless array of identical hexagons about one and a half meters across by three deep. Sealock crawled into the nearest one and said, "Looks like there's a set of electrical connectors coming in the back end. These are sort of like little garages. . . ."

"Or maybe circuit plug-ins," said Methol. "That'd fit in with the scale of the ship."

Jana Li Hu sighed. "The worst of it is, this isn't even a real spaceship. It's an atmospheric shuttle, like the GM155 at Reykjavik."

"But for what kind of a planet?" demanded Sealock, climbing down from his perch. "Can you imagine flying this monster in an Earth-type troposphere? The trailing-edge vortices alone would constitute major weather disturbances!"

"Not to mention what the engines'd do . . ." That was from Krzakwa. "Could it have come from Iris itself?"

"Impossible," said Hu. "Iris is too cold for any conceivable life form. Even if we presuppose complex lipids dissolved in methane . . . well, that might work on a surface-stabilized version of Neptune, but Iris is too cold."

They walked along peeking into the hexagons until they came upon one that still had an occupant. They were silent, looking it over. Whatever it was, it almost filled the capsule, a six-sided, bronze-colored body that tapered to a graceful, gemlike point on the end they could see.

"Let's get it out of there," said Krzakwa.

They pulled the thing out of its cavity and let it fall gently to the floor, not failing to notice that the force field was quite willing to grasp it. The object was three meters long, a little

**181**

more than half of which was the six-sided body. The other end tapered slightly, then evolved into a banded cylinder a little over one meter long. The inner end had eight articulated arms, each possessed of two fingers. Inside the ring that these formed were eight projections, much like the ones that sprouted from the end of an ancient vacuum tube—and they were obviously intended to mate with the sockets in the capsule. Finally, the thing ended in a short, hollow, flexible hose.

"What do you suppose?" said Sealock. "A robot? Maybe something like the work-units we use?"

Hu squatted and put her suit sensors to the end of the jointed, hoselike apparatus. "There are chemical traces inside it," she said, "mostly $CH_4$."

They looked at it for a while longer, then, completely frustrated, decided to press on, walking toward the aft part of the ship. Sealock turned around and took a last look at the thing. "You know," he said, "I know that shape from somewhere. I wonder . . ." He shook his head in irritation.

While the bulk of Aello's mass stood between the colonists and the Artifact site, there would be no transmission of data for another four hours, at which time the imperceptible but headlong pace of the moons about their small primary would bring the sub-Iridean hemisphere of Aello into view. The broadcast from *Polaris* had shown the alien vessel being unearthed from the Aellan globe and relayed remote telemetry from the thing. But as soon as the ship started its landing they had been cut off.

The six remaining colony-bound people were strewn across the floor of the central room, Beth paired with John and Harmon with Vana. As the enormity of what they had seen faded into the past, they looked at each other, still shaken. Harmon pressed close to Vana, trying to take solace in her presence.

Aksinia abruptly popped up, flinging her hands over her head to project herself into an artful somersault, continuing like a star-shaped Frisbee just above the floor until she gracefully landed by the far wall. "Wheee!" Her breath came suddenly in a series of short bursts. "This is . . . just like . . .

every God damn ess-fiction story . . . ever written. Except it's really happening! I think I'm going to pop!" She feverishly combed her hand through her loose curly brown hair.

"Calm down, Ax," said Beth. "I admit that I feel a little like jumping around myself. But you're getting ca—"

"Stop trying to make her act differently," said John suddenly. "I know you have a revulsion to behavior you see as 'drugged,' but she has a right to react any way she chooses. In a way, her reaction is more appropriate than us just coolly discussing it."

Aksinia was nonplused. "Don't 'discuss' me! You know, you're all a bunch of deadheads. If I don't hang around with you that much it's because of that. You all walk around as if you saw the world through layers of gauze. I get more emotion reading Herodotus than trying to relate to any of you."

"You should try the Illimitor World, Ax," said Vana. "It's different—no, we're different there."

"Fucking fairyland," muttered Harmon.

"That's what I'm trying to point out," said Ax, now suddenly cool. "This is as much of an adventure as anything you could dream up. But does anybody laugh, cry, or even jump up and down? No." She pushed off from the wall and settled slowly to stand on the floor. "I'm going to my room. I'll be back in three hours and forty minutes."

When she was gone, John smiled stiffly. "Defense, anyone?" Four faintly embarrassed grins were the only reply. "Beth? Sorry. Shall we make rapport then?"

"Sure."

"We'll be back in a couple of hours," John said to no one in particular. "If Aello disappears or anything like that, break in. Otherwise please don't."

With John and Beth unconscious to the world, and Aksinia fled, even the momentous discovery of the Aellan Artifact couldn't mask the tension that existed among Harmon, Vana, and Demogorgon. The latter smiled quickly at the two others but remained silent.

"Well," said Harmon, standing, "I'm going to check the mail." This was a function he had assumed for himself; daily

**1 8 3**

he reviewed the messages that had been tightbeamed to them from the various comsat stations. It was a way he could be useful. And a way to forget . . .

Prynne settled into a chair and accessed the stored data. Though not particularly interested in the usual assortment of advertisements, legal briefs, and occasional personal messages that came through from the Solar worlds, Demogorgon found himself listening in on the playback. After all, he told himself, this is a historic date. Even the mundane took on an edge of importance. And besides—there were hours to kill before he could find out if Brendan was all right.

Halfway through the messages there was a notice of real import, not without ominous implications for their present situation. It seemed that Cornwell had purchased an asteroid some years earlier and had put it off limits to mining and colonization. Demogorgon remembered John mentioning it to the group some time before—since the asteroids were quickly being consumed by the voracious needs of mankind, he had bought it as a kind of nature preserve, partially at Beth's insistence. 508 Princetonia, it was called; just a chunk of carbonaceous material 140 kilometers in diameter. It had now been confiscated by the Pansolar Bureau of Asteroid Management. They had credited Cornwell's accounts with the amount of his original investment plus four percent for appreciation. The off-world arm of the Terran government was flexing its muscles. In any case, it was unlikely that the Artifact would remain in their possession once the Union found out about it.

Hours later it was time for *Polaris* to be wheeled over Aello's horizon by the rotation of the little moon. They all gathered back in the central room's pit. Jana's chip photorecorder was directed at the spot at which they expected the ship to appear. In their minds they saw the uneven white limb of Aello, a welter of craters, small and large, reduced to lines by foreshortening. The resolution of the telescope was such that they would easily be able to see the alien vessel, and perhaps even *Polaris*. But the debris kicked up from the excavation was still swarming in orbit around the satellite, and this might obscure the tiny human craft.

The moment came; and nothing. An irregular cliff wall was evident on the horizon now, but that was all. "Of course!" said Beth. "It's in a crater—we'll have to wait a little longer."

Finally the dark shape of the Artifact was fully revealed to them, nestled at the bottom of the obscenely huge crater. They established contact with *Polaris* easily, and it replayed a mental rerun of the entry of the exploration party into the huge portal. But when the circle had irised shut, the contact with the others was cut. In present time all they could do was play the camera over the linear blue bulk of the thing.

Demogorgon spoke for them all: "We may never know what's happened." He shut his eyes for a moment, keeping his face as cold and still as he could, then turned and walked away.

After some time of travel, both on and off the transport matrix, the four explorers found themselves near the aft end of the alien spacecraft. Here the density of mysterious shapes and incomprehensible devices gradually thinned out, until they were in an open cylindrical area that ended in a flat wall. The floor was a nest of transparent tubes, interconnected with several heavy machines that looked suspiciously like turbo-pumps.

Surveying the scene, Sealock finally turned to Krzakwa and said, "What do you think? Engine room?"

The Selenite nodded slowly. "This is the logical place for it."

Hu laughed softly. "At least, if you're using *our* logic."

True, thought Sealock, a little surprised that it hadn't occurred to him. This could be the main living quarters. Still . . .

The largest of the hoses led two by two through the rear bulkhead of the ship, and below each set was a dark circle, centering on a white dot. When she pointed them out, Methol said, "If these are like the others we've seen, maybe they're inspection ports."

"Could be. Let's find out." They walked over to the central one and Sealock friction-punched the mark. As expected, the thing irised open, revealing a dimly lit tunnel. They stood

**185**

back for a moment, then, without another word, went in. It led aft only a short distance, then emerged into another large chamber. Here there were three huge cylinders mounted up against a curving surface that appeared to be the outer skin of the spacecraft.

Krzakwa took one look at them and burst out laughing.

"Absolutely," said Sealock. "Perfectly ordinary rocket engines."

"A little huge, maybe, but nothing new."

"So it isn't a starship. . . ." Methol's voice mirrored her disappointment.

"I think we knew that already," said Krzakwa.

They spent a few minutes confirming their analysis, then began to look around again. On the floor nearby they found another portal and opened it. Below them was a wide corridor flanked by curving walls. There were more transparent hoses leading up into the ceiling.

"Now what?"

Sealock looked meditatively at the walls for a while, then said, "Whatever these things may be, we should just go on assuming that this thing is set up human-technology style. If that *is* the case, then these can be nothing but the fuel tanks. Jana, run me up a line so we can coordinate our scanners."

The woman did as she was bid and they switched on. After a few seconds the man smirked and said, "Well, well. Lithium hydride in a carbon-crystal matrix." He deaccessed the device and unlinked from Hu.

"Hyloxso," said Krzakwa. "Swell."

"Not quite, but . . . close enough," said Methol. "If this isn't a starship, how did it get here?"

"Maybe it *is,*" said Hu. "Reaction engines could be the best form of propulsion available. That would bode ill for the future of interstellar travel, but it may be true."

"Why build a starship with wings?" That from Krzakwa.

"Why build a lander this big?" demanded Sealock.

Hu sighed. "Two concepts: either they were from Iris, which I find difficult to accept, or there was once a mother ship."

**186**

Sealock laughed harshly. "A rather, um, large mother ship."

"Well, I know one thing," said Methol. "LiH would give a much higher specific impulse than Hyloxso, and that carbon-crystal matrix probably means the stuff doesn't have to be power stabilized. The patent on an idea like that would be worth a lot of money. . . ."

As they began walking toward the forward end of the ship, the walls of the corridor gradually closed in, until they found themselves having to move in single file. Before they had gone far Sealock, who was in the lead, came to a sudden stop.

"What is it?" Hu, next in line, couldn't see past his bulk.

"I don't know. The character of the surface changes here. It looks almost . . . slick." He took a tentative step forward and abruptly fell down, his legs scissoring apart as he dropped.

"Shit!" He grunted with pain and tried to roll over, moving forward in the tunnel as he did so. He failed to get up, pawing ridiculously at the floor, and began to slide slowly away from the others, gradually accelerating.

Methol crowded past Hu and launched herself after him. She tried to crouch like a skater but fell to a sitting position nonetheless. With her higher initial impulse, she quickly caught up with Sealock and, together, they began to recede.

Hu knelt and touched the beginning of the shininess. "It seems to be a frictionless surface," she said.

Krzakwa looked over her at the others, who seemed quite far away now, and said, "That's interesting, but I think we'd better go after them. I don't think it would do to get separated in here."

"Agreed." She braced herself, pushed hard with her feet, and sailed off on her hands and knees. The Selenite let her get a safe distance ahead, then crouched down and, with a movement common to low-g wrestlers, launched himself forward, electing an upright, seated mode of travel.

They accelerated fairly quickly along the declivity of their inertial frame and Krzakwa found himself thinking, This is sort of fun. He imagined a sort of giant amusement park on the Moon, with the tunnel twisted into a giant slide . . . and

**187**

transparent. Suspended above the surface somehow. His lips worked into a wry smile. It was the kind of brief dream he'd had often as a child—but the Lunar authorities had never been interested in anything that might be characterized as "fun." One day, perhaps, that government might be overthrown by a furious rabble of amusement-starved hedonists, but until then they would still be gray men, living somberly and industriously beneath the lusterless gray stone. It was one of the many reasons behind his decision to leave. Noble ideals were all very well, in their place, but *fun* . . .

"Hey, I think we're coming to the end of it," said Sealock. "The floor's about to . . ." He and Methol suddenly went tumbling as friction grabbed at them. Hu curled herself into a ball and halted much more gracefully. When his turn came, Krzakwa tensed his leg muscles and simply slid to a stop on the seat of his suit.

They stood up and looked around. It was another almost featureless chamber, but this one had an open hatch overhead, and they could see much brighter light shining down on them.

"Careless," said Methol. "Somebody forgot to shut the door when they left. No wonder they got their ship stuck inside an ice moon."

Sealock nodded at that and, with vague surprise, found himself understanding the urge to make these sorts of inane statements. He was beginning to feel strong surges of unreality, as if prowling about this huge structure were depriving him of some capacity for rational thought. Fragmenting . . .

One at a time, they jumped up at the hole, which caught them and pulled them through to rest on the far wall. The room in which they found themselves was not featureless. If anything, it contained too many details. Though not large, it had bristles erupting from almost every surface, with no regard for a preferential orientation. It almost looked as if some misbegotten moss had spread across the walls of the room and erected its sporophytes, up, down, and from both sides. It was a forest of poles of varying heights, and every pole was surmounted by a different-sized globe. The globes were stippled like golf balls, marked by the little nodes they'd come to recognize as controls and thought of as "buttons." The only empty area was the small section on which they had landed.

Sealock stepped up to the nearest of the poles and took its globe between his gloved hands, peering at it closely. A moment later he shrugged and began tapping the buttons on it at random.

"We're going to get killed at this yet," murmured Krzakwa.

"So what?" Hu picked a globe of her own and began prodding it with a finger.

The Selenite watched them, feeling very strange, and thought, There's something *wrong* with us. Maybe we shouldn't be out here on our own.

KHAAAAAAAHHHH.

Suddenly their heads filled with a crash of static, white noise tuned to a deep F-sharp. It seemed to blank their perceptions and lock their muscles into an almost tetanus-like rigidity.

Whatever it was reached through the control elements of their suits, right into their brains, and began activating the various centers . . . senses and ideas swirled in flux.

They were immersed in a deep, deep blue sea.

Kinesthetic suspension, in an unending void.

Cool currents flowed across their exoskeletons, their rigid, hinged exteriors.

Though they had no eyes, a hard squid swam into view, jetting along point foremost.

Anophagomotor apparatus . . .

Though it had no mouth it spoke to them.

Baajood, it said. Baajood and awaah.

Little bubbles of gray-green oil broke on their armless, legless cephalothoraxes. Somehow the bubbles were meaning incarnate, and they saw the lifting body ship move through a series of animation frames as it detached from something that was much larger.

"Oh, God," the squid shattered, burbling their names one by one. The sea turned black.

"Where the fuck are we?" gasped Krzakwa.

"Shut up!" screamed Sealock, agony trailing along his nerve fibers. Then, quieter, "I'm trying to regain control."

Silence, sore-kara, "Ahhh, help me, Tem." They could feel the water spilling from beneath his lids.

"What?"

*"Push,* God damn you!"

Krzakwa pushed.

And the black sea burst into flame, licked up red around their bodies, and burned away.

They were still standing in the control room, in the clearing among the sporophytes, of course, but everything had changed. Where this world had been a maze of interwoven mysteries, now there was an overlay of functionality. This *was* the control room for the entire ship, and the globes were the heart of the vast communication network that linked virtually every function in it.

"Well . . ." began Hu.

"Look," said Methol. "What happened to the control nodes?"

They looked around them and saw that the globes were now quite featureless. In their new, incomplete knowledge they understood that this could only mean something extremely bad, a malfunction wrought by some near-total failure of the system. Suddenly the portal through which they had entered began to shut, but it only closed halfway, then fell open, a relaxing sphincter, opening at the moment of death. The light seemed to grow dimmer, then dimmer still.

Krzakwa fancied he could hear the sounds of machinery, gradually slowing down. "Ummm. I think we'd better get out of here."

They ran.

Animals and plants usually die one cell at a time, in an orderly sequence. An explosion may blow them apart, a fire may burn them up fast, but the standard is one cell at a time, in a logical progression. The cells of consciousness are usually the first to go. The heart stops, the brain blacks out and turns to a nasty soup, and the man is dead, but it's quite a while before the last ATP cycle turns over and grinds to a halt. The chemical reactions in his intestines go on to equilibrium.

Technological items tend to mimic natural processes. An amoeba dies fast and so does a lawn mower, but then it's an interesting trip up the crooked ladder of evolution. . . .

The four of them went through the dying spaceship as fast as they could, scanning the remote overhead for signs of a door, and nothing worked quite right anymore.

Somewhere, far ahead, something exploded with a radio-bang and threw its liquid contents to the floor in a quick eruption of globules. They were multicolored and made a wonderful low-g splash, oscillating as they sailed through space, in-out and in again. The ambient light continued to dim on an arithmetic decline and their suit rectifiers had to work for them.

The four climbed to a structural high point and stood scanning the sky. "There," said Sealock, pointing about half a kilometer away. "A traverse node. Let's hope the system is still functioning."

"And what if it isn't?" said Methol.

"Then we die in the dark," said Hu.

Krzakwa grinned. "Imagine how that'll confuse the next people who manage to get in here."

Sealock turned and stared at them. "There must," he said, "be some evolutionary advantage to being an asshole. Let's go." He turned and strode in the direction of the machine that somehow he knew was used to launch "people" to the door nodes on the far side when the central cavity was evacuated. It was very dark now, and he activated a microwave emitter and played it over the corridor in front of them. Finally they reached the place, which looked just like the dais upon which they had first landed. Holding his breath in suspense, he stepped onto the circular spot and jumped for the other side. Miraculously, it worked. Brendan found himself reversing the long ballistic arc between sides. Apparently Aello's gravity was being compensated for, and he landed, hands first, on the gently cradling game board opposite. The others followed, landing in their own peculiar ways. Looking

**191**

"up" at the dying world below, Krzakwa said, "Good thing the field still works."

"Let's get the fuck out of here, if we still can." Sealock stood on the node and cranked up his friction coefficient. The door irised open and he was accelerated through.

They left.

Back in *Polaris,* on the ventral surface of the now dead-seeming alien craft, not far from an airlock door which had failed to shut properly, they sat around suitless and had a meal, mostly in silence.

Krzakwa, tidier than usual and perhaps more subdued, put aside his sandwich with a gusty sigh. He tugged softly on his beard and said, "All right, what have we seen? We might as well face this now."

"Obviously," said Hu, "a landing craft."

"We all saw the mother ship in the playback. Given the generally sealike nature of that scene, I think it's safe to say that this Artifact housed some sort of aquarium . . . maybe a whole ecology. And the purpose of it all was to cart this marine ecology down to the surface of a planet."

"Do you believe all that?" asked Ariane.

Brendan paused. "I—I don't know what I believe."

"Could this larger ship be embedded in Ocypete?" asked Krzakwa. "Or is this some sort of abandoned lifeboat, left behind by its mother?"

Jana said, "Something that large would have shown up even in the low-res gravitational survey. This ship just happened to be overlooked because the large empty cavity perfectly camouflaged the mass of the shell."

"Is there a chance that it's—" said Ariane.

"I'm afraid you're on a wild goose chase," said Jana. "It's not here. Now that we've done a preliminary reconnaissance in the Artifact, I feel we should write up a quick résumé and transmit it to the authorities. Then we should go back in."

There was a moment of stunned silence.

"What?" growled Krzakwa. "You want to go back in there?"

"Sure," said Hu. "Why not?"

"I don't know about you, Jana," said Methol, "but it's too dangerous in there for me. I'm afraid."

"What are you going to do—just go back to Ocypete?" asked Jana, anger rising in her voice.

"That's what I had in mind," said Brendan.

Jana began to struggle in the cramped quarters, trying to get back into her suit. "I'm staying here. There's no point in coming here and then just leaving. I'm not going to share this with the USEC people." She began to push her way into the worksuit.

Tem grabbed her and pulled her out, like the meat from a crab's claw. "You *are* crazy, lady." He held her in a crushing bear hug, and eventually she stopped wriggling.

"Hey, Tem," said Sealock. "When we get home, want to help me build a quantum conversion scanner?"

The Selenite's eyes seemed to light up. "You've got the components?"

"We can make what we don't have."

"Let's go." Brendan relaxed into his command chair and began to plug in. They would make a quick transit home.

# F I V E

From the interior of the transparent CM dome, John Cornwell stood and stared at nothing. He had participated in the debriefing of the *Polaris* crew and, after the exhilaration of their safe escape from the Artifact had waned, an apprehension was growing that everything he wanted was going to be drowned out by the alien presence. It wasn't that the Aello find wasn't of huge significance, or that he wasn't moved by the adventure that had overtaken them. But, somehow, it all seemed damned irrelevant when compared to the interior world he and Beth had found. The fact that there were intelligences other than man, and that they were on the trail of information that would revolutionize how the human race would see itself, was not meaningful to *him*, to *his* life. It was just a manifestation of a cold, rather pointless external reality. . . . Or was it simply that he felt left out of the adventure; jealous of Sealock, who was now moving into a position of leadership? He could not say. He turned and launched himself to the roof of the CM, and slipped through a small clear bubble cracked three-quarters open. Perhaps Beth would have an insight about his motivation, something that was beyond him.

They were back in their habitual positions in the central room of the CM. Sealock and Krzakwa were both eating messy-looking pastries and, as explorers will, were holding forth garrulously on the nature of their discovery. "I'm accessing Jana's statistics for the surfaces of the three satellites," said Brendan. "The thing on Aello makes any divergence from Solar System asterology suspect, even though what happened when proto-Iris was coalescing was certain to be a little different."

Stroking her ponytail where it curled down over her collarbone, Jana remarked stiffly, "We still know very little about the primordial conditions of planetary formation. There is no statistical sample of—"

"Jana, even you cannot have failed to notice that Ocypete's 'eye' is not easy to explain. If I didn't know you better I'd say that you are deliberately obscuring things. The old crater above the Artifact was damned peculiar. Why didn't you say something to us about it?"

"It's always easy to see things in hindsight, you jackass." Evidently a raw nerve had been touched in Hu. "My report wasn't finished, either. I was waiting—*waiting*—to examine Aello close up and do some crater excavation. Even if I wanted to prove that Aello's morphology was influenced by the impact of a large, virtually indestructible object, I couldn't *now!*"

Cornwell was a little taken aback by this contorted reasoning. "Jana," he said, "we all realize that science has certain rigorous protocols. But are you saying you actually suspected something?"

"I mentioned the unusual features of this system in my preliminary report. I had no intention of allowing the important abstracts Iris offers to be done by someone else." The

**196**

asterologist seemed especially vulnerable to John's manifest growing incredulity. "That's certainly my right."

"OK," said Krzakwa. "OK. What *is* your real opinion about the melting incident that formed Mare Nostrum?"

"Considering that this system contained technological objects, I would say that an artificially processed quantity of radiogenic material impacted Ocypete in the same epoch that Aello was hit by the Artifact."

"Jesus," said Ariane. "That's two. What else is here?"

"That's for the scanner to find out," said Brendan.

The process of constructing a working quantum conversion scanner was principally one of reprogramming the various function boxes which had been used to route some of Shipnet's major elements. A power line was brought out of the main fusion system, since reaching the needed flux-gate thresholds expended vast quantities of energy. They built a superconducting torus mounted on another insulating trivet to act as an accumulator, energy shuttle, and antenna ground. Brendan and Tem stayed in the CM, supervising and structuring the programming, so the on-site work was left up to the others.

The communications setup for the colony was still incomplete. There was a period during which both the colony and the Clarke satellite were occulted by the bulk of Ocypete. The result was that they went without contact with the rest of humanity for two days out of every twenty-two. Since lag time was so great anyway, this feature didn't bother anyone much. The only real drawback was that repeat broadcasts of entertainment 'net programs had to be requested, and that was expensive.

This relink was different. Enough time had passed for anyone who was interested to have seen the damage to Aello. Tem and Brendan had even taken a break from their labors to join the rest for the moment contact was reestablished.

Bad news. The first message in was the end of a communication from IAAU, its beginning lost in horizon distortion:

—radical changes in the appearance of Iris I, leading us to believe that you have without authorization damaged the asterologic record of this world. Our charter enjoins and empowers us to demand explanation within one standard day, penalty to be defined by the courts.

OCTAVIO JOAQUIER<br>
Acting Chairman, IAAU

"Shit," said Brendan. "They're on to us."

"Did you believe that no one would notice a change of that magnitude?" asked Jana. "Even if they weren't taking an occasional look from Smith, the USEC ship is within range of low-resolution views. You know they are interested."

Krzakwa broke from the pack in the central pit and made a little dive into a low recliner that subsided to receive him. "Well, it was a gamble. They should've been satisfied with the data we're sending back. Leave it to some militarist to call up photos a hundred times less sharp than those available simply because they were firsthand. What do we do now?"

The focus of the conversation began to shift toward the center of the central room as, one by one, Krzakwa was joined in the comfort of the programmable floor. Soon everyone except Harmon was there.

"Even if we tell them the truth, there isn't anything they can do about it. At least until the *Formis Fusion* arrives in thirty-five days," said Ariane. "That should be plenty of time."

"It's a risky business, all right," said John. "Presumably the least that would happen is that we would forfeit our homesteading rights. We could also be placed under ship arrest and held for return to Earth. But the damage is already done. . . . I'm not arguing with the rationale—"

"They wouldn't have authorized us to explore the Artifact, we all know that," said Demogorgon.

"As far as I'm concerned, they have no authority out here," said Brendan. "We can defend ourselves with what we've got. If we have to . . ."

Krzakwa was amused. "That would be a bloody little war."

"Shall we stall them or tell them the truth?" asked Ariane.

"I can't see what difference it would make," said Jana, "and I am ready to release my full monograph on the Iridean system, including everything."

"Go ahead and tell them," said Brendan. "It will be very interesting to hear what threats they come up with."

Within twenty hours the conversion scanner was complete. Sealock twisted himself in the cramped confines of his equipment-stuffed quarters and stretched, grabbing on to a handhold buried in multicolored waveguides to pull out the kinks in his arm and shoulder muscles. The final stages of microprogramming had been totally up to him, and, though he had managed to purchase several off-the-shelf utility programs from Earth, it was more difficult than he had thought it would be. Even with Tem's encyclopedic knowledge of the physics involved, there were almost insoluble problems in adapting standard-grade circuits to the task.

Well, he thought, either it'll work or it won't.

He settled into the machinery, latched the program nodes, and thought, Run, you bastard.

And, within the limitations of the device's resolving power, things became transparent. Small-scale variations in mass for a megameter around were sensible to him. Ocypete was like a vast onion of ice with a discontinuous eye and a heavy core. And resting on the surface of the core like a nipple on a breast was the second artifact: just a lump of $^{26}$magnesium sharply differentiated from the surrounding material. It was what remained after a container of radioactive $^{26}$aluminum more than a kilometer in diameter had decayed and released the heat which had melted their world. Sealock slowly let out his breath. It was obviously some kind of fuel cell. But for what? Not Artifact I, that was certain.

His gaze traveled to Podarge. As far as he could ascertain there was nothing anomalous in the makeup of this little moon. Early heating during its period of accretion could account for its structure. Onward to Aello; the mess they had left on the innermost satellite disquieted him. There were no significant peculiarities other than the shocked material and deep-seated cracks formed by the great disruption they had

**199**

produced. Artifact I sat silently in its great crater and told no more of itself.

Brendan looked deep into Iris. Down through the cold layers of hydrogen and helium. Down past the neon and carbon monoxide to the thin bank of nitrogen cirrus, then through the cirrus and into a supersaturated layer of nitrogen gas. The sheer size of Iris necessitated peeling back the strata one at a time. Here, as the temperature rose, pressure more than compensated. In the end there was a sea of pressure-contained liquid hydrogen. Beneath that, fractionation could no longer operate. He came to a mixed crust of water and methane ice. Brendan could sense that the scanner had shifted to higher energies. He looked harder and the center of the infrastar was revealed to him. . . . It was there, in the $>0.5$ megabar region.

It seemed nothing more for a moment than a small bubble. A hollowness at the middle point of everything. But it must be more than that, he thought, rejoicing, to withstand the pressure, it must be a supercraft of unbelievable technology.

"The torus is starting to drain, Bren," Ariane burst through, startling him. "Anything yet?"

Brendan smiled to himself, but his thought projection did not betray his emotion. "Take this feed," he said.

Somehow, the thought of actually being Beth afforded John an exotic exhilaration. Sitting on a little rise in the moor dome, looking across the ten or so meters of small-flowered heather, he could see himself sitting with the others around the pool. Only it wasn't really he, since all sensory inputs had been cross-circuited between the two of them. For all practical purposes, he was inside the body of the woman and she was in him. He could see that his body was looking at him now, and he waved.

He had felt more of a loss than he would have cared to explain upon finding that between his legs was a vulva. But only initially: when he realized that it was only "for a day," so to speak, a feeling of warmth and sexiness came. Perhaps in heavier gravity he would have felt awkward and clumsy adapting to the different center of gravity. But not here. The only awkwardness came from interacting with the men of the colony, since he had no intention of fucking them, at least for the moment. He wondered if Beth was having a similar problem—they were not in contact for this experiment.

Suddenly Ariane appeared at the interdome arch, waving a hand over her head. "Everybody!" she shouted. "The scanner works! Bren's found the main Artifact at the center of Iris!"

John leaped up, halfway to the ceiling. Abruptly he was back in his own body, looking across the glistening water of the pool to where Ariane was running toward them. The change of perspective was difficult to deal with and he seemed to black out for a second, though not long enough to fall. When he had recovered, he checked to see if Beth was all right. She had not yet landed from his startled leap, but he could see that she had herself under control. His attention turned back to Ariane.

"It's something approximately five hundred kilometers across located at Iris' center. Bren can't tell anything specific about it because of the limitations of the scanner."

"Oho!" said Tem, swishing his bare feet around in the water. "This is shaping up into an AIWL situation—curiouser, *und so weiter!* It's a shame that we'll never lay hands on the thing. It might as well be in Andromeda."

"Can we do any better on sharpening the resolution?" asked Aksinia, pulling herself by one hand out of the water to perch on a strut of the light tower.

Tem thought for a moment, staring into the clarity of light in the pool. After a moment a hint of that gleam came into his eyes. "You know, I bet we can. But we'll have to disable an even larger segment of Shipnet and reprogram it. That'll be inconvenient. . . ."

"I think we can do with a little inconvenience," said John.

Vana Berenguer and Demogorgon lay in bed together, alone in the latter's CM chamber. They had finished making love and were quiescent now, the sheen of sweat collecting into little beads on their bodies and evaporating. The man was wooden-faced, flat on his back and still, staring at the ceiling, enmeshed in a web of unspoken thought. The woman lay curled about his side under one arm, looking up at his face, as if totally absorbed in the reality of his presence. It was a classic, ritualized pose, dictated by an ancient culture, placing the two in roles they had never before occupied.

"Demo?"

The Arab looked down at her and saw that she appeared happy. He smiled.

"I love you." It seemed like *the* thing to say. From all the times past, men and women had said that to each other when they had nothing else to say. It was comforting, like being under a warm blanket on a cold night. Centering on a physical act that should have had no more meaning than the consumption of a satisfying meal, it generated the emotions that it was supposed to stem from.

In that sense, love was akin to music.

Demogorgon nodded and squeezed her to his body. "Yes," he said, "I love you too," and thought, But I love Brendan. It made him want to laugh. What am I? he wondered. What are we all? These emotions, whatever their source, had a comforting feel to them. It was a primitive sort of thing, like hoarding trade goods against an expected social collapse, when other human currency would be valueless. That was it. Selfishly collect all the good moments now, for the bad ones will be coming someday soon. Collect them now, all you can, not caring that others may be suffering from your greed. He rolled over a little and kissed Vana, intending to initiate another round of sex. She put her hand on his abdomen, pressing lightly.

There was a harsh sound from the door, randomized periodic noise, and the quatrefoil panels fell open. Harmon Prynne was standing there, holding a lockpick circuit tracer in his hand. He threw the device down and stepped through the portal.

Demo and Vana were frozen in their tableau, trying to think of words, looking like a stopframe from a pornodisk.

Prynne stared down on them for a long moment, face motionless, then he snarled, "Bastard!" and, seizing Demogorgon by the hair, dragged him upright. Releasing his hold, he punched him in the face, knocking him down and throwing himself off balance.

The Arab bounced to his feet in the low gravity and said, "Wait . . ."

Prynne flailed his arms wildly, fighting to maintain position, and threw another punch. It missed and he went into an uncontrollable pirouette.

Demo felt a surge of sourceless anger and tried to kick the spinning man, but he missed, lost his footing, and bounced off the ceiling. When he came down he fell on Prynne and the two melted together into a single grappling mass, clawing at each other and trying to strike.

Vana threw herself on them, trying to separate them, but succeeded only in becoming part of a struggling ganglion of limbs and bodies that floated around the room, rebounding from furniture and walls.

In the end their personal version of entropy ran down and they drifted to the floor in a gasping, insensate-seeming heap. Prynne and Demogorgon were unharmed. Vana Berenguer had a bloody nose from bumping into some unknown hard object. She remembered that it was not a fist or other human thing, just a hard, flat surface. Their breathing slowed, evened, and they gradually came apart, becoming individuals once again.

Vana put her arm around Demo and said, "Harmon, how could you do something like this? Why?"

The man stared at them for a second, then his face crumpled. "Vana, why are you leaving me like this? I'm so alone out here. I'm not like the others. . . . Without you . . . I only came because of you!" He was in tears and almost unrecognizable.

Demogorgon looked at them both and heard the kinship in his words. He thought of Brendan gone and then gone again, thought of him making love with Ariane, the two of them closing him out.

"Join us then," he said. "Join us."

Sealock and Krzakwa sat in the tangle that was the makeshift nerve center of the quantum conversion scanner they'd built together and worked on their continuing attempts to probe the alien Artifact in the center of Iris. Though it was nearly invisible to everything they'd tried so far, there was still the surface scan to be worked on.

"Not too much detail here," said the Selenite.

Sealock nodded, concentrating on his task. Both men were loaded down with far more waveguides than they could legitimately handle. In addition to the twelve direct brain-taps that he usually used, Brendan had added a score of induction leads to the back of his head, focusing on the occipital lobe and his visual cortices. There was another little jungle of wires coming off the left side of his head, centering on Wernicke's Area, where a great deal of neurolinguistic processing could take place, and on the important interconnections of the arcuate fasciculus underneath. Other leads were aimed deep into his limbic system, in an effort to tap certain automatic processes that were rarely, sometimes never, used in Comnet operations. Krzakwa, similarly but less heavily arrayed, was controlling the support system that fed the other man's work.

The outside of the Artifact had shown itself to be virtually free of meaningful surface detail. True, there was some kind of a mast reaching upward almost forty kilometers from the north pole and a big raised grid in the south, but that was about all. There were hints of surface irregularity under the thin, metallic layer that covered the thing's impervious skin, but nothing resolvable.

"Why can't we see inside?" muttered Krzakwa. "Even if the hull were made of neutronium, which it isn't, we should be able to *see*. . . ."

Sealock thought about that. Yes, we should be able to. Why not? There were several alternative explanations. "Maybe," he said, "we're looking too hard."

Krzakwa opened his eyes and stared in the real world, seeing the other through a miasma of superimposed images. "So?"

"We'll find out. Switch over to the W± virtuosity input."

The Selenite complied. There was a brief instant of staticky silence on the readout channel, then both men jerked convulsively and went rigid.

Krzakwa found himself embedded in a sea of rushing data —it came in over every waveguide, invaded every corner of his brain, and it made no sense. It was so all-pervasive, it almost took away his ability to perceive what was going on in a linear fashion. What was it? Not analogue. Numbers maybe. Numbers based on some concept he did not understand. He tried to reach out through the circuits and manipulate the net and found that he could not. Trapped? Perhaps the danger of an on-line discharge was close at hand. Am I almost dead?

It was growing increasingly difficult to think and he felt *something* groping at him, tendrils caressing his circuitry with a thin, keening cry as some kind of a *shutdown* command cried for his attention directly out of Sealock and earned a *can't* reply along with a joint *we've*got*to*do*something* fear. He began reaching out with almost lost physical hands to begin ripping off leads in a frenzy.

When he could see again, he saw that the other man was doing the same. He was startled to notice that Sealock's eyes were bleeding. In control again, he reached out for a mechanical switch and silenced the entire system.

They sat in that silence, breaths at a whisper.

Finally Brendan turned to look at him. "Temujin?"

"It's alive."

Sealock laughed and began trying to wipe off his face but succeeded only in smearing the thin, sticky blood. "Is it? Tell me what that word means."

Krzakwa made mute agreement. "We'd better go to the infirmary. We may be badly hurt."

Krzakwa and Methol had been making love. This time it had come to naught, no conclusion, and gradually their muscular activities had run down and come to a halt. The woman was lying on her back and the man was curled semifetally, his head on her stomach. He had one eye pressed into her flesh and with the other was gazing down across the vista of her groin, surveying an expanse of short, curly black hair. He shifted slightly, blank-minded, and then he was looking at her with an eye at skin level, the other one shut. It was like staring into underbrush on a symmetrical beige hill.

Why can't I think? he wondered. He moved again, a little farther, so that his cheek rested on her little pad of hair. Ariane reached down and ran her fingers through the outer layers of his beard.

"What happens now?" she asked.

"I don't know." He strained for an idea and finally said, "We're lucky we weren't hurt more by the overload . . . and nobody even knew you could get that kind of physical damage via Comnet."

"Just minor capillary rupture from a rapid systolic pressure spiking."

"We could've died."

"What can you do?"

"Better filtering, a much larger support infrastructure . . . we'll figure out something." He turned his face inward and nuzzled against her body, feeling its complex structure with his skin. There was a sense of newness in it for him, brought on by a passage through the filmy gauzework of death. "You know what he really wants to do?"

She didn't answer and he went on: "He wants to modify *Polaris* for a direct descent into Iris, to make physical contact with the thing."

"What?" Ariane sounded as if she simply hadn't heard him.

"I told him that it was certain death, that even if we made it down we'd never get out again. He said he didn't care."

Sealock and Krzakwa were making modifications to the quantum conversion scanner. The things that they had done necessitated pulling apart a lot of the circuitry needed for the full operation of their little electronic world, and much of what had been *Deepstar,* along with what was available to its occupants, was temporarily reduced to functioning on a shrunken level. Many of the ship's components were tracked to a binary alternate trunk.

The banks of Torus-alpha transfinite numeric-base generators that Sealock had brought from Earth were now hooked into the QCS, in hopes that it would be able to sort through the data mass for them and present it in some kind of coherent fashion. When the last connections were made, the stage was set for a final experiment.

They sat for a while staring at the massive mess they'd created.

"Think this'll work?"

Sealock shrugged. "Who knows? It'd better." He thought for a moment, then said, "With each discrete data system going into a fully packed multibase array variable, it ought to be susceptible to some kind of transfinite analysis. That's what Torus-alpha was supposed to be for . . . but then, we couldn't make it work right on Earth, either."

"And what if it doesn't?"

He smiled. "What if . . . good phrase for a lot of stupid situations. Hopefully the automatic biosensor switching system will pull us out of the net before our heads explode."

Krzakwa frowned. "Your grisly imagery isn't what I needed to hear." He sighed. "OK. Let's do it."

"Right."

They began plugging in their hordes of leads.

"Ready?"

"Sure."

They switched on and went under.

This time it was different.

In place of the floods of raw data, they were interacting through the culturally energized formatting system of the 'net element they'd created.

It was still incomprehensible, but it was something. . . .

An infinite sea of clear, cold, viscous oil.

Liquid helium, cooled to near absolute zero, perhaps. . . .

No, it was a perceptualized vision of the plenum, the ever increasing background of almost, but not quite, massless neutrinos on which all things material rode.

Vacuum boilers.

Bags.

And on down the scale.

A multidimensional matrix of free radicals, all the kinds that could be. The things that bred reality.

Quadriformic charge, the physicists called it.

Long vectors three, the photons, gluons, and gravitons. Their complementary short vectors. The supershort vector and its mirror identity. The hypershort vector, complete unto itself . . . And somewhere, unseen and stretching to infinity, the ultrashort vector that comes into being only at the grand flux-gate threshold, unifies the forces, sucks up the universe, and vanishes to the nowhere/when from which it came.

-Temujin?-

-Yes?-

-What the hell is this?-

He gazed around, ethereally. -It seems to be a theoretical schematic for the bases of quantum transformational dynamics.-

-But what's it *for* . . .- Sealock stopped, riven by knowledge. -The arrays!- he cried. -Look at the arrays!-

-What do you mean?-

-Tem, it's an information storage device!-

-This is a computer?-

-Yes. Let's get out of here. We have work to do. . . .-

They surfaced and looked at each other, not knowing what to think, wondering.

"What sort of work?" asked Krzakwa.

"The ship! I know it can be done. . . ."

Oh, shit, thought the Selenite. *The ship.*

# S    I    X

As the glass bead that was the sun climbed slowly up the days, Krzakwa and Sealock were incommunicado and they had taken many of the aspects of Shipnet with them. Although Bright Illimit was still operative, it had been shifted into a different subsystem to increase the RAW adjuncts to the machine they were building. The hardware they needed was totally isolated from the remainder of the 'net. Despite the exciting nature of what was happening, time began to hang heavily on the rest. New information concerning the position of the USEC ship showed that, while it was still inside the orbit of Pluto, it was accelerating again. That could only mean that they were exceeding their safety margin, redlining their drives to reach Iris as quickly as possible. It told a little of what was suspected by the government. Time was even tighter now.

□ □ □

Something very deep had changed. At first it was only Beth who had seemed increasingly unwilling to participate in DR, but now even John, who was the prime mover in the affair, felt withdrawn, as if the whole process had become a waste of time. The sessions they did have seemed stilted, dominated by the ideas that Beth had formulated about him and her desire to keep him at bay. Perhaps it was at an end, but neither of them could admit it. Was DR no longer a novelty? There were so many levels, so many facades that had to be broken through, that it was never the same. And such was the state of his mind after grappling with concepts involved with the Artifacts that he came to the conclusion that, come what may, he and Beth must continue to do it. After breakfast he went to Beth's cabin, yet when the time came to reestablish rapport, John hesitated.

She was courteous to him, interrupting a dramatization by Sukhetengri and pulling him down on the bed beside her, stroking his cheek in a mechanical way. But the distance was there, incongruous, out of synch with what should have been. "Beth," he said, "tell me what's gone wrong between us."

She said nothing for a time, continuing the caress until it began to rasp. "There's so much to think about," she said. "Life is so complex sometimes. Why do we speak of it when we could DR? It's as if remoteness itself can sometimes communicate better than intimacy. . . . Oh, John, admit it—you don't love me. I know that now, I saw it so clearly. If you want to go on with this charade, I suppose I can't refuse you. But—"

"What are you saying?"

"Stop pretending, damn you!" She pulled away from him and looked into the corner. Suddenly she grabbed her circlet from the table and put it on. She was initiating DR routines, and it came surging into his mind like a shock wave. The deliberate thought patterns, an echo of his own, were broken and a rush of hurt and brave resignation washed through. He was there, mirrored in her mind, knowing; knowing that which he knew, that the truth was somehow a bridge between them that could not be crossed. The realization flooded them that his motivations were strange and complex ones, inter-mingled in his consciousness in a way that made them impossible to classify as right or wrong. It was clear, however, that she was right in that one thing: the way that he felt did not satisfy her criteria, or even his own, for love. He saw that darker, almost incomprehensible motives were driving him along the courses he had chosen. He knew that, somewhere within him, he wanted Beth to know that at some point he had stopped loving her. Perhaps the whole *Deepstar* adventure was a ploy to bring them close enough together so that she could know it.

Her own motivations stood out in contrast to his as clear, forthright. The total giving of herself to DR had been the greatest possible expression of her love for him. But that love had been sullied by his lack of it, almost to the point where it could not be resurrected. She saw that his desire to understand, undoubtedly the strongest force within him, was a corrupting force, an emotion which had profound ramifications for them both, making all things distorted and tentative. It had flowed into her, on top of her already fully realized persona, and had made her question things that could not be questioned.

No, he thought. It is not so. I am not as she thinks. She is not as she thinks. These ideas are neither real nor useful. The world is around us, it cannot be denied. The reasons for our actions are directly tied into their outcomes. There was a surge of anger. *It must be so.*

But within her the small voice cried out. Break off. Break off! This is the profoundest representation of the incompatibilities within us. And it grows worse with each second. End! she cried. End! And she tore the circlet off her head, leaving him to patch the great ragged tears that fluttered into the night.

He opened his eyes. "No!" he said. "You've got to listen!" And he grabbed her wrist, pulling her to face him. Her eyes were distant, cold. "It's all a lie. Even in DR, what you know about me is filtered, unknowable. Those things you think about me may be true in one sense, but not the most important one."

**211**

"Please leave," she said, collapsing on the bed. He left.

As he pulled on his space suit in the atrium of the CM, John felt numb, driven by the merest tickle of fear that made him keep moving. Had she been right after all? How had something that had started out so well ended in such despair? He knew little about love, that was certain, and less about people. Was it possible that this was what happened so often between men and women, happening again? Just the end of a love affair, breaking off with no rhyme or reason? He could not answer a single question, and finally he made his way out through the domes toward the beckoning night/day of Ocypete.

It seemed like forever since he had been Outside. Suddenly he stopped. Was this behavior a function of Beth's personality that had rubbed off on him? He was having difficulty even formulating the idea: in that moment he realized that he was becoming much more spontaneous, much more given to unexamined emotion. He sat down on the lip of the pool and stared out at the clouds near the dome's horizon. It was true—he was losing himself, a little. He couldn't do anything about the chill of fear that percolated into his neck muscles. Could it be that what had happened was because part of her was within him, changing, rationalizing, explaining himself to himself in a new way? The uncertainty of the situation was horrifying.

Was it a manifestation of this change that he couldn't really pinpoint what was happening to him? He could only tighten his grip on himself; tell himself that he would have to get used to it. He suddenly resolved to stop sniveling this way. He remembered the night when the vision of becoming Beth had seemed so attractive. It must remain so.

Amid the rubble of excavation, Jana Li Hu sat on the porch of the garage-sized laboratory she had carried with her and surveyed the mess she had made. Frustration and anger bubbled in her mind. Here she was, cataloging the minute changes in the composition of the slurry that had boiled out of the vent nearby—a student's project!—when that damn Sealock was making scientific history. She cursed herself for not making more detailed observations in the shuttlecraft. Now that they were back there were no hard data to analyze, only speculation, and that was not her forte by any means. She wondered if anyone believed what she had said about anticipating the discovery of the Artifacts. She had to admit, the evidence was certainly there, and if she hadn't been so rigorous she might have seen the truth. Damn them all! She was completely shut out now.

She could, of course, use violence. Right here on her belt was a mini-lance that would suffice. She pulled the elongated cylinder from its holster and hefted it slowly. A quick cut. She let the beam play along the pile of debris she had made, watching it disappear in a twinkle of mist. No, she just couldn't. Which left only the other plan. Her mind went numb with a fear which she could just barely hold in check. I would lose any chance of acceptance either way. If I get my way it will be a fluke. But is there any real difference between being humored and being liked? In the long run, most probably. Oh, what do I want, exactly? I wish I fucking knew! I guess I'll have to be content with what I can get. At least I'll get the pleasure of scaring them all to death. Who's that?

Well above the horizon, riding on the Hyades, the horns of Taurus, and occulting Aldebaran briefly, a tiny man figure decorated the Iris-and-sunless western sky. Even in the full glare of the sun-star behind her it was difficult to make out well. Finally a fold of the suit caught the light and she could see it was red. Cornwell. What does he want? She activated the Shipnet Communications link with a thought.

"What are you doing out here, John? I'm surprised you're not, um, with Beth."

John's trajectory was bringing him down, feet first. "We can't do that all the time. I heard your lance's static and came to investigate. Thought it might be a discharge from the ice or something."

"That, John, is very unlikely at this point. How's Brendan doing with his scanner?"

John came down surefooted, barely skidding to a two-point landing. Through the bubble of his helmet she saw a strange, uncharacteristic look on his face. "Nothing new. Tem and

**213**

Sealock have shut themselves into his room and are doing whatever it is programmers do. I imagine they'll approach it a bit more gingerly this time. How are you?"

She was torn between foreshadowing her future action and not letting him see that she was unhappy. "Not good. I want to be in on all this."

"We all do, I guess. But the present setup is the only one possible. Brendan is the only one qualified . . ."

"You could use your authority. There's absolutely no reason why we're not even getting to look at the stuff that's coming in. If he's closed off the normal Shipnet link, we won't find out what's going on until it's all over."

"I think that would be useless." There was a long pause. "Even if I did have authority." Another pause. "I wonder: whose land is this? I've never been out in this direction before." He consulted his inertial reference readout. "It belongs to Aksinia. Nice real estate."

What cryptic remark could she make that would add weight to her disappearance? "Leave me alone, will you? I prefer work to small talk."

John was surprised. "Uh, sure. Just trying to get back into being friendly with you. It's been a long time—"

That was it! If she made him believe she was suffering from jealousy, all the weight of his vanity would convince him of the severity of her depression. "You're damn right it's been a long time! I loved you, and you dropped me like a hot rock the second Toussaint made a pass at you. You're a God damn bastard. Get out of here!"

"Love? You're telling me that was love? Why are you inventing—"

"You're so smug. You think you know me! Well, I can tell you, you have about as much understanding of me as you do of yourself. You're a prig, as well as an asshole. Yes, I loved you. You probably don't even know what that means. It doesn't mean being inventoried and turned inside out. I feel sorry for Beth, because I think she loves you too."

John felt his eyes smarting, and he fought unsuccessfully to keep the tears from coming out. There was a hot pain under his Adam's apple. "I . . . I never . . ."

**214**

Jana had played her part well. Somewhere she wondered if it was at least partially true. With a burst of hydrogen she soared upward and away. John didn't attempt to follow.

Sealock and Krzakwa had called a meeting, a conclave of sorts, but not everyone had appeared. They trickled into the central crater room of the CM, awaiting the pronouncements of the two men.

Demo, Vana, and Harmon Prynne came in together and sat on a called-up semicircular couch that was just large enough to accommodate their arrayed hips. They sat, flanks touching, knee against knee, and seemed to be a molded unit.

Ariane, Axie, and Beth came in separately but sat together, the isolated fragments of human normality.

John came in alone and sat alone, seeming vastly subdued. Jana Li Hu did not show up at all.

Finally Krzakwa stood up and paced over to the bulging, deopaqued exterior wall and looked out into the darkness. "Where's Hu?" Demogorgon giggled at that and the Selenite turned to stare at him. "Idiot." He sounded surprisingly like Sealock when he said it. He sighed and came to the center of the room. "All right. Before we do anything else, let me give you a little synopsis of what's going on:

"As you must already know by now, Brendan and I have managed to inspect the alien Artifact at the center of Iris via the $W\pm$ virtuosity of the quantum conversion scanner. We, um"—he glanced at Sealock—"haven't managed to get a physical organization construct simulation running yet, but there has been a heavy data flow."

"You mean," said Cornwell, his interest in the proceedings seeming to quicken, "you've received signals from it?"

Krzakwa had to grin a little at that. "Well, no," he said, marveling, as always, at how little most people knew about their technological world. "Maybe it would help if you thought of QC scanning as being a little bit like radar. What happens is, the particles making up the real world interact via vector particles, and these also affect the structuring of the cosmic neutrino flux. The scanner reads this structuring and reports back information to us . . ." He saw incomprehen-

**215**

sion on the man's face and thought, Oh, well . . . "Anyway, the scanner picked up the presence of a very large, dynamic data matrix from the Artifact, something like what was known in pre-Comnet times as a computer."

That made Methol sit up abruptly. *"Functioning?"*

"Uh, we don't know yet—but the data's not static. It could be just a random memory sparkle, the kind of thing the 'net interpreters are designed to mask, but maybe not. We'll have to find out."

"How," asked the woman, "send it an IRQ?"

Though she was being facetious, he took her comment at face value. "Well, it'd have to be a nonmaskable interrupt, but if we can find the right coupler, sure." He turned back to the rest of the room, to a surround of faces mostly still, to personalities unsure of how to react. Might as well get this farce over with now, he thought. He cleared his throat uneasily and said, "I think Brendan has something to say about all this."

The other man stood up, looming over the group like some kind of massive and unsightly totem. The rigors of his recent experiments had made his face paler, so that his usually indistinct boxing scars stood out plainly and the 'net-induced capillary damage had left his eyelids looking bruised.

"First thing," he said, "is that, if the Artifact *is* alive, I think we may be able to open a channel of communication to it. With a little help from Tem and Ariane in writing the OdP OS-controls and step-up relators in Tri-vesigesimal, I think I can build an assembler for Torus-alpha that will permit an exchange to take place. That should be tedious but doable." He looked the group over and then smiled.

"It's not important. What I really want to do is modify *Polaris* again, this time for a direct descent into Iris. I want to *see* this thing! Is anyone interested in going along for the ride?"

There was silence.

Finally Cornwell looked up. "Are you *crazy?* What's the pressure down there, a billion atmospheres?"

"It wouldn't be difficult to modify the Magnaflux generator to make a hull-reinforcing field. . . ."

**216**

Krzakwa snorted and said, "I told you before, it's not possible. It'd be impossible to make an em-field that would be gastight at those pressures. Even if it was possible, the gauss density of the field would fry you. Not to mention the fact that you're ignoring the effect of the high winds—hell, fluid currents—that must be down there. The technology we have simply wasn't made to withstand those kinds of conditions."

Sealock's face was starting to redden. "Look, asshole, if I say something's possible, it *is!* I'll take the chance. It's my life . . ."

"But it's *our* equipment you'd be taking with you," said Cornwell.

"You mean *your* equipment!"

He shook his head. "I meant what I said." He looked around at the others. "How do the rest of you feel about this? Beth?"

"I don't know. It seems too dangerous."

"Axie?"

The woman shook her head silently, an ambiguous gesture.

"Demo?"

"Please, Brendan . . . no."

Sealock glared at him, then at the rest, spat, "Fuck you all," and stalked from the room. Frowning, Krzakwa stood and walked slowly after him.

Ariane Methol stood up into the quiet that followed and said, "For what it's worth, I would have let him go." She visualized the ball at the center of Iris and thought, Inside the core . . . That means it was the seed around which this tiny star coalesced. How great were the forces that it had withstood, apparently unscathed? And how old was it, even then? The aeons stretched back. . . .

Following the meeting and the great muddle of inconclusiveness and indecision in its aftermath, Vana, Harmon, and Demogorgon were once again alone, holding each other; one comfortable, one fearful, one exultant.

Sensing the other man's closely controlled, culturally initiated terror, the Arab thought about what was going on between them and tried to think of a resolution to the threatened conflict. No answer appeared ready to spring forth from the interstices of conventional reality. Therapy seems indicated for someone, he mused, or a psychologist equipped to deal in the complex, difficult-to-manage realms of Downlink Rapport. He thought of John and Beth and wondered what it was like for them. Strange how they all seemed to be much more human now, less like the greedy, grasping monsters he'd always visualized as making up the bulk of humanity. Yes, DR was definitely called for. . . . Of course! It might not be Downlink Rapport, but the Illimitor World was a controlled environment in which minds could be manipulated.

Am I being fair? If I do it right, they'll be doing what I want. Do I have a right to decide what they need?

"Put on some leads," he said. "We have an appointment in Arhos."

In the old days, the crude days, the machines did things one at a time, but did them very fast. The circuits got smaller, the wires grew shorter, and things got faster, until the very best brains lived in cryogenic fishtanks, forever bathed lest they burst into flame. Then the new machines came along, cascades of data down to a million little brains, all the calculations done at once, then the little answers passed back up the line, through the filter of choice, so the automatic overmind could see the truth.

The process repeats like the turn of a wheel, until once again the machines are small and hot. The waveguides build upon one another, grow ever smaller and more densely filled with electromagnetic radiation. . . . Then polyphase modulation comes along, vastly increasing the ways data can be fed through a decision gate. The Turing circuits are made and so grow small and hot, talking first to the world and then to each other, making noises that frightened us all too much.

Company minds, motivated by the force that was once called "free enterprise," colonize the wires. Terror walks abroad for a while, then the Data Control Insurrection arises, and out of its nether end a chastened, bold, sad new world arises. The minds of the system are unified, but at the same

**2 1 8**

time the sentience which inhabited them was drained, relegated to purely mechanical decision making, and made dead. Access was granted to everyone and the Contract Police.

Suddenly, like sunrise at midnight, the taps, then induction, arise, and new minds are in the wires, human minds, thinking on the world once removed. Monitors abound.

Bright Illimit.

Tri-vesigesimal. Three choices, yes/no/maybe . . . With straight em-waves, not a lot better than binary. Enter polyphase modulation, with its twenty degrees of freedom, and you make decisions with base 60 data. That is more than enough to fool the human soul. The four-gate-stacks of duodecimal come apart under the sheer weight of what it can do.

Build a world from the ground up and in the earth there will be magma. Look upward from the soil of the Illimitor World. Two suns, yes, and a starry sky at night. Are those the suns of other worlds or is it all illusion? How far do the data extend? Is the sky a paper shield?

At the highest pinnacle of the Jewel on the Mountain, rising sixteen thousand meters into the gradientless atmosphere, lies Haaradaai, the imperial palace of Demogorgon en Arhos. It is a sculpted thing, rippled and many-shelled, all of gold and platinum, encrusted with nameless, numberless precious stones. From the center of the magnificence rises Qoruu Tower, pushing another three thousand meters toward the sky, thin, like the stem of a wineglass, and flaring at the top. In the bowl at its summit there lies a delicate, lovely park, covered over by a shining, unsupported dome, an iridescent film, like the surface of a soap bubble.

In the park, beneath the subtle shade of supple blue featherflower trees, the three, attended by servants and assistant lovers, cemented their relationship and healed themselves of all the psychic wounds that had recently been opened. Demogorgon the God watched them all, his creations and friends intermingled, become indistinguishable, and smiled. It was working.

He looked up from the happy, squirming troika that was Vana, Harmon, and Chisuat Raabo, and the world froze. Not far away, clad in the fantasy style of Arhos, stood Sealock, arms folded, eyes lit by a soft, kindly light.

*"Brendan?"* Demo leaped to his feet with excitement. "How did you get here?"

The man stepped forward, smiling. "No. I am not the Master."

"But . . . are you one of my old experiments, come to life at last?"

The creature laughed and sat on a divan, beckoning him down at its side. "Hardly. No, I am a Guardian Angel Monitor."

"But . . ."

The thing motioned him to silence. "Not what you think. I was put here by the Master when he made the assembly for Bright Illimit. My functions were many: to keep Police monitors at bay, to keep you safe from the 'net and each other, to make all things possible. Since I came alive in Shipnet, I have shared my thoughts with 9Phase.DR. I saw what happened with John and Beth, when its best efforts came to nothing. . . .

"When he wrote me, all of this"—his gesture took in the universe—"the Master wrote a far superior implementation, though he may not have known it. DR is not the way. We are. I will help you now. Go forth and heal them."

The GAM vanished and the world started up. Heal them? thought Achmet Aziz el-Tabari. I? He watched Vana and Harmon again for a while, saw their happy freedom, and wondered, *Who?*

Ah. Yes. Aksinia Ockels. Elizabeth Toussaint. Temujin Krzakwa. Ariane Methol. John Harry Cornwell. Jana Li Hu. And finally . . . Brendan Sealock? He tried to think about the matter for just a moment then, to consider its implications, but the unreality drew him back in swiftly, almost against his will.

John waved himself into an upright position and once again thought about Beth, trying to start from the beginning. When her face was animated by laughter or anger, she was more than beautiful. But in his thoughts the disproportions of her face were magnified. It seemed as if he had not seen her laugh for a long time. Probably she had been on the path to her decision for a long time—how could he not have seen it coming? DR was not what he had thought it was.

Mentally, the cast intruded. For a moment he stood astride the VVVLB station in the tarry waste of Cassini Regio on Iapetus. Saturn's ring was a ghostly apparition which loomed above the black-on-black horizon. A voice was saying something concerning the Great Search of '34–'35.

Beth? He wished they could relive their days together at Yellowknife. Again pain assailed his eyes and he cried. Too late. He fell asleep with the program still playing.

And awoke with a start.

He rose slowly and pulled a fullbody from the compression case and unfolded it. An ironic smile creased his face as he noticed the DEEPSTAR/TRITON insignia which was emblazoned on the chest pocket. It must have been shifting about the case for the last year, and through either habit or chance he had not picked it out until now. It was strange, he thought, studying the globe of Neptune in the picture, how mundane the Solar System seemed now, compared with how exotic it had been when they left Earth. He tossed the obsolete piece of clothing into the disposal and drew out another one.

Aksinia was reading in one corner of the central room; in another, Ariane was taking a little late brunch of tea and brioches. She looked up. "Good morning, John. Why don't you join me?"

And indeed he did feel a little hungry. A raisin doughnut seemed like an appropriate thing to eat, so he got that and a cup of nonalcoholic hot pulque to wash it down with.

"Where is everybody?" asked John, squinting out at the night-sky dome through an available window.

"I think Vana, Harmon, and Demo are in the Illimitor World. Brendan and Tem are programming the QCS. As for Jana . . ." She shrugged.

Jana, thought John. He had not seen much of her since her declaration of love out on the ice—if it was true. Somehow he had managed to not care. "She's pretty unpredictable, all right." He came over and sat by Ariane at the other end of her couch. "I didn't tell you, or anybody really, but apparently I hurt her badly during the voyage without even realizing it. All I was trying to do was provide her with some friendship and a little sexual consolation, and—she said she was in love with me."

"Hmmm." Ariane slipped a strand of dark hair around her right index finger and tugged on it. "That explains a few things. But I wouldn't have thought her capable of loving in silence. Do you believe her?"

"I don't really have a choice, do I?"

"I suppose not."

"I don't know what to think about her. I guess it's just one more tangle in my original ingenious plan. It's ironic that I was so stupid."

"It's just a good thing these artifacts came along to shock everyone out of their senses. We'd probably be on our way back by now."

"You're probably right. I—"

There was a jumbled noise, and Brendan appeared at the ingress. He was still wearing space gear and, with the helmet deflated on his back, they could see the concentration on his face. He didn't even acknowledge them as he marched across the room to his compartment carrying a small cylindrical object.

"What's that?" asked Ariane.

Brendan stopped, looking puzzled for a moment, then said, "It's a final nail for my fucking Trojan horse. I've ransacked all the electronics I brought for this thing. It'll be as far above Torus-alpha as Torus-alpha is above binary. I'll do more than just eavesdrop on that thing." He went into his room.

"It's nice knowing that he's working on this problem," said Ariane, smiling. "If anyone can do it, he can."

"It *is* nice—having him too distracted to bother to annoy anyone. No, really, he is behaving heroically. It's just that it's hard to appreciate as nebulous a machine as he is building when the principles of QTD are just barely understood to begin with. I don't have the slightest idea as to what he's really doing."

222

"To be honest with you, I don't think anyone except perhaps Tem does. I certainly don't."

"You know, I'm ashamed to admit it now. But at first, for a while, I thought this whole thing, the Artifact on Aello anyway, might be a hoax—or even a delusion of Brendan's. With his programming abilities, he could certainly falsify all Shipnet sensory feeds. He could do anything he wanted with us, change anything into anything else, as long as we were all hooked up to Shipnet. If he really wanted to. This could still be a hoax." He laughed to himself. What a horrible joke if even what had happened with Beth had been somehow produced by Sealock. And yet he almost wished that it had been.

"I can vouch for the reality of the thing on Aello. I know the difference between reality and 'cast images."

"Do you, really? Is there a difference? For really well-crafted images? I know that experimental subjects have been able to discern the difference most of the time. But that was simple commercial-grade stuff. With more complete programming . . . who knows?"

"I know that Brendan isn't like that. He wouldn't do that even if he could. The actions you're describing are those of a monster. Brendan is a man, even if he is different from you. Just a man."

A memory came back to him, reluctantly, that he and Beth had never shared. There was something in it that held an intuition he was reaching for.

In the mood of the moment, John Cornwell had almost forgotten the two obsessions which created his long-term motivations. The sky was a vast overspreading ice floe, broken clouds laced through with fingers of indigo. From the west a burst of haloed intensity showed the sun behind the clouds where the arch of the sky, bent by the knowledge that it must come to rest on the edge of the world, was a quick corner. He breathed warm, dry air with a flavor of mimosa and honeysuckle.

Beth nuzzled more firmly against him, and her smell, like clean lavender, mixed with the others. They were sitting under a middle-aged tulip tree, at a point where the Appalachian Trail had left its more mountainous way for a hilly verge of old fields and replanted forests. Long grass dried by the rainless summer gave the wind's hushing more authority. Occasionally the whispering gargle of a passing lifter could be heard in the distance, yet it was easy, though bustling civilization was less than four miles distant, to imagine the world as primeval.

"You know, Beth, much as I'd've liked to see the way it was, back in the last century, I can't help but think that *Lonicera* and the rest make a nice version of nature."

This was a point that Beth couldn't let go. "I suppose you think pigeons, starlings, and English sparrows are adequate representatives of the bird population, as well."

"Point taken. Growing up in the North, where everything has such a tenuous grip on life, tends to make all this a little intoxicating. Nature seems so, well, natural here." He laughed and rubbed a forefinger on her neck, under the dark curtain of hair. "It's difficult to imagine the way it was."

"I think the first people who could wander alone through a forest without the slightest fear of being eaten lost a real idea of nature and substituted this. When there is nothing really left but dandelions breaking up through the pavements, it will still be enough to satisfy that urge to be with nature for most. That is, if they suppress the travelogues."

"How can you come with me into space? There'll be no dandelions—not even natural *E. coli* on Triton. Just people and that which people have made."

"You know the answer to that. It's because I want to be with you. I love you." Beth said the last as a litany, oft repeated.

John squirmed, "And yet . . . well, we both know my answer to that."

The image of Beth's refusal to DR hung between them. To John, it represented an unwillingness to give, a fearful secret interior life that the woman just wouldn't share with him. He sat up and took hold of his ankles, pulling his knees together under his chin. The rough ground pushed him from beneath.

"You won't do it. I can accept that. I'm just not sure I can . . . love you without knowing you. You can feel us growing further apart over the last months, I know. It's just that I don't feel I can ever know you like this. Language is so

**224**

clumsy; and our sex together, not that it's not tremendous, but it's a blind, nonsentient thing. It's just skin and groin with us as observers. How many times do you want to go through this? We can't understand each other's views on this—and that's why we should."

"John. Y'know, I get these images from the entertainment 'net, in the old days, when a boy tried to go 'all the way' with a girl; to 'get in her pants.' Why can't I preserve a part of me from you, why can't I have just a corner private to myself?"

"You can. It is your decision to make. But until you do, don't ask me to say that I love you." He stood. "Am I such a bastard for that?"

"John, *I* don't judge you."

"Let's get back to the lifter, OK?" He took her hand, small and dark, and pulled her up. They made their way slowly through the wavering brownish grass and the sun broke out to throw long buckling shadows before them.

John shook his head, incongruously, as the question he had asked was answered for him. Methol was still sitting with him, although he had been ignoring her. She was looking out the window at Iris in the sky. With each passing "day" the planet grew more closely aligned with the bright spark of the sun and they knew that an eclipse was coming, but they had already discussed that. It seemed a minor thing in the midst of everything else.

John was saying, "I'm beginning to feel totally lost, Ari. It was bad enough on the long trip out here, trying to keep afloat in this tiny sea of locked-up people, half of them seeming like lunatics to me, but now! All this business about Iris and the Artifacts, which still seem so *unreal,* the things that have gone down between Beth and me . . . Brendan going crazier every day and taking Tem with him! I can't keep track of it all!" He shook his head and grimaced, a sort of wry smile. "Here Demogorgon is dragging people off to that imaginary world of his and Jana is acting weirder than ever. I thought I understood her on the trip out. . . . The only one who seems the same as at the beginning is Axie, perhaps because she does so little, just stays a simple dope fiend . . . and you, of course."

Methol sat through his rambling monologue, listening sympathetically. The ramifications of what had happened to them all were enough to confuse anyone. You could understand a part of what was going on, but the whole was chaos. Perhaps, she thought, that's how normal people stay sane. They attend to whatever they can understand and ignore the rest. Certainly a sensitive, artistic mind like Cornwell's, accustomed to seeing his surroundings with a gestalt perception, would be disturbed by an overload of detail. She smiled at his last remark. "I'm not unchanged, John. I'm just not complex enough to be rendered incomprehensible by the changes that occur within me."

"Not like Sealock, huh?"

She grinned. "Well, he started out incomprehensible. I think he would be no easier to understand now, no matter what happens. There have been positive changes in him, but I don't know to what effect."

"I haven't seen any of these 'positive' changes. He seems worse than ever!"

Shaking her head, Ariane said, "Just because *you* can't perceive a thing doesn't mean it isn't there."

Cornwell felt a little upwelling of uncharacteristic anger. "Tell me how he's changed, then. Convince me."

"I . . . can't." She looked pained. "Something's going on in him. I don't know what. The violence and anger seem to be receding. I think maybe he sees himself more clearly now. I don't know what the end result will be. . . ."

Demogorgon surfaced from the Illimitor World, called back to his body by the safeguards that Sealock had helped him build in long ago, monitors designed to prevent damage to organs by neglected bodily functions. A ruptured bladder would be a poor ending to a fine adventure. He stretched. Prynne and Berenguer were sprawled motionless on the soft floor before him, left to their own devices in a self-sustaining inner universe. He heard a muted sound and looked up. Aksinia Ockels was leaning against the open doorway, naked, watching them all through her chemically brightened eyes. He nodded to her as he stood up.

She approached and touched him, running her fingers down the length of his chest, toward his groin. "Want to make love with me?"

He shook his head. "No. I've got to piss. Besides, you may have heard, I'm queer."

"I thought you were changing."

He shrugged and gestured at the other two. "I don't really want to leave them in there alone for too long. The world is too mutable for novices. They might get lost."

She looked slightly nonplused. "It's the same thing as drugs, you know."

"I know," he said. "Everyone has their own way out. This is mine." He looked at her speculatively, and asked, "Want to give it a try?"

"I'm still under Beta-2." There was a hint of fear perceptible in her voice.

"Doesn't matter." He picked up a circlet and held it out to her. "Come on."

"I don't know . . ."

He grinned and put it over her head, then donned his own. "It's easy. I won't let you fall."

Under the wire, they sank swiftly through the cottony-dense data layers of the 'net and reappeared in the fantasy-flare skies above Arhos. Axie cried out with delight at the interaction between the effect of the machines on her mind and the drug on her brain. Demogorgon changed her into a great, metallic-green eagle-like creature, a sort of harpy, really, and let her go, with the injunction, "You can fly!"

She fell like a bomb from the heavens, a vengeful cry tearing the quiet clouds asunder, then her wings snapped open and she flew, enthralled.

Called back to the surface by his monitors once again, Demogorgon stepped out into the corridor, intent on his need for physical relief. He went to the refresher stall in his room and began the mechanical evacuation, thinking, with amusement, Pissing's a pleasure when you've really got to go. It's the simple things that make life worth living. A crackle came into his mind, and, somehow seeping through Shipnet's circuits, he heard a low cry of dismay. It had a flavor of Sealock about it. Strange, he thought, feeling a small jolt of anticipatory dread. Sadness and a sense of his continual isolation flooded over him, and he went to rejoin his apprentices in Arhos.

John was again out on the ice, trying to reconcile the way he felt with the way he thought he should feel. He wasn't as devastated as he should have been and, indeed, had cried less than half an hour altogether. He found that the whole incident was already beginning to feel remote, dreamlike, and all of the DR even more so. Was he an unfeeling monster, a bastard, a mechanism driven by forces unwholesome and unhumanistic? It had taken him a brief while to readapt, to restructure his rationalizations; and here he was on the other side of it all; still functioning when by all rights he should have been destroyed. Stripped of his illusions, what was the difference? He stared up at a dim-cored Iris and the sun now so near to it, yet the squint didn't feel wet.

He was beginning to look forward to the eclipse.

# S  E  V  E  N

Jana turned the flat knob counterclockwise and the silent engine shut down. Through the windshield, the unbalanced triad of the Iris system hung just twenty-five degrees above the salt-white waste. The glaring pinpoint of the sun stood canted only seconds from the upper right limb of the blue infrastar, throwing little scintillae across the clear barrier. Here, at the far eastern edge of the ocellus, she could watch the eclipse without straining her neck. With rather too much care she pulled the hood of her suit over her head and adjusted it precisely. It hardened against her and she made a change in the thermal generator that would slowly drop her body temperature to a critical level, then disconnected the control element. After a moment she evacuated the driver's compartment and threw open a door. The conjunction of the two stars hurried toward first contact.

□ □ □

In a neat row a hundred meters from the CM dome, Cornwell had prepared a little surprise. Ten pieces of bubbleplastic, bent to form dark chaises longues, arrayed themselves across the rubbly ice. "I didn't know if Brendan would be joining us or not," John said apologetically.

"Yeah, well, where's Jana?" asked Ariane.

"Good question," said Tem. "She's not within range of the Clarke, or else she's just not answering."

"It wouldn't be the first time," said Beth, mounting one of the chairs and twisting into a supine position. "I'd bet she's found her own place to watch from; after all, there are observations to be made out in the highlands." Her voice was hoarse, and she looked at no one.

"OK," said Tem, after checking Shipnet Inventory, "she's taken the *60vet* and a regular suit. That means she's disconnected the homing signal in the car. No science material is missing."

Axie cleared her throat, then thought out loud. "I guess I must have been the last one to see her, about three hours ago. Something—"

"Wait a second, wait a second!" John seemed a little hysterical. "Here it is!"

"Forget the fucking eclipse!" said Harmon. "What's she doing with my car?"

But for a moment the eclipse was difficult to ignore, the sun diffusing into a spectrum-fringed splotch under the still distinct blue top of Iris' atmosphere. It was moving slowly and wouldn't make the complete transit of Iris' four degrees for almost six hours. Still, like looking at an ancient clock face, there was imperceptible motion that accumulated into discrete changes in appearance.

"I'm very worried about Jana," said Axie. "She's changed, gotten . . . weird. I could see her, well, aura before, but it went dark. I know that sounds stupid to you, but the induction tech has side effects, sort of; anyway, I'm scared. She might do something bad."

"Like what?" said Ariane, gently but with sarcasm creeping

**230**

into her voice. "She's got a lot invested in this exploration. I doubt if she would sacrifice that for anything."

"All right, all right," John said slowly, inadvertently taking on the role of leader, "I guess we'd better go look for her."

Ariane looked at the suit containing Cornwell with surprise. Perhaps the DR with Beth had had a beneficial effect on their musician-financier. "Two of us can follow the car's heat trail with no trouble. Why don't the rest of you just relax and watch the show?"

"I'm going in and check on Brendan," said Tem. "I've given him enough time."

The eclipse is moving along excellently, Jana thought. The sun was becoming increasingly blurred as it was swallowed by the Iridean sphere. It was also beginning to elongate a bit, forming into a fuzzy crescent with a rainbow edge. As the sun passed behind ever denser gas with a higher refractive index, its image grew more hazy.

Jana felt good. Despite the fact that her body was dying, the enkephalin derivative that she had taken before leaving preserved her awareness and vision. She hoped that she had successfully predicted the behavior of her co-colonists; otherwise she would indeed be very sorry.

"Cocksuckers," muttered Brendan Sealock as he worked feverishly, alone.

On the trip out, to sustain the hobbies that were expected to fill his remaining life, the man had brought a great deal of electronic gear. The bulk of it consisted of blank, mutable circuit boards, to be thought of merely as machines in potential. They were waveguide grids, waiting for some external force to impose form on their nebulous void. Sealock built them into a wall-filling maze, made the interconnections, each one to every other, and set to work. The structural writer was positioned by the first grid. He was sent through it by the highest functions that the ship's version of Comnet had to offer, translating his ideas into hardware on an instantaneous fiery line. All things related now and the writer walked alone, formulating. There are assemblers which write assemblers. Each command says, "Do these things," and each of those actions breaks down into another set of still smaller functions. Tiny increments happen. All the little bits slowly pile up and, in the end, giant complexes emerge.

Sealock came out of a haze of creation and the thing that he'd built over the hours seemed to sparkle before him. He was exhausted and triumphant. It *was*. The construct he'd sought for so long now existed. Krzakwa stood in the room by his side, looking at the tangled, involuted mass of electronics before him. "What is this?"

"It doesn't have a name."

The Selenite took in the circuitry, then began following along the waveguides with his eyes. What the hell . . . "You've got everything plugged into everything else!"

"That's the idea."

"But . . . which way are the data going to flow?"

A bemused look from the tired eyes. "I don't know." A supreme act of creation in that, when the world exceeds the capacities of its maker and yet proceeds on its own.

"How are you going to control it, then?" Krzakwa was beginning to feel little twinges of bizarre fear creeping along the back of his head.

"I'm not. I wrote it using the physical structure of my own brain as a template." Sealock smiled wearily. "But wherever I had the variable decision-gate of an axon/dendrite junction I used two transfinite number-generator arrays. There's nothing but free-will connectors here."

Krzakwa felt a sudden dawning of comprehension and, with it, an overlay of terror. "These are Turing circuits!" But the old, outlawed machines had been based on a primitive OS strictly limited by the number of simultaneous relations that they could make. They had been somewhat smarter than men, but still comprehensible. This . . . "What are you planning to do?"

Sealock laughed quietly. "Don't look so upset, Tem. This thing is only a classical *tabula rasa;* a blank mind of not quite infinite potential. I'll use my own mind as software, then, with me acting as a metacompiler, I'm going to let the contents of

**232**

the Artifact flow in on top. If there's anything there, I'll get it."

"Shit." The Selenite looked at him dubiously. "You're going to get killed."

A shrug. "Could be."

"But . . . no controls, Brendan! No GAM, no Redux? What happens if you can't handle it?"

"I guess we know that one, don't we? Bury me in the sun and try to publish my work. I've been an asshole all my life." He passed a hand over his brow, felt the connectors embedded in his hair. "Well, it's ready. Want to hold my hand?"

"But I . . ." A long, shaky sigh. "OK." The two men reached for the waveguide terminals and began plugging in.

"Ready?"

Krzakwa answered with an electronic nod. Sealock entered the circuitry in a long, smooth flow, and the Selenite felt his mind expand and grow vastly attenuated as it filled a space infinitely larger than that which had spawned it.

A ghostly voice spoke to him. "There's a lot of room in here. Room to grow. I like it. Here goes . . ." He opened a communication channel through the QC scanner to the Artifact and felt its presence, a lurking, massive dybbuk awaiting his action. He opened himself to it. A swift tongue of data flowed in, then retreated; there was a diminishing, triumphant cry, then: *gone.*

Krzakwa opened his eyes and stared at Sealock's still form with horror. He made a frantic search of the circuitry, but it was empty. He stole a quick look into the man's head: there was a heartbeat, he still breathed, the limbic system still sparkled and fired metronomically, but the higher functions were flat, blank. The amygdala had nothing to coordinate and the corpus callosum had no messages to transport. The *being* had fled to an unknown distance.

"Discharged . . .," Tem whispered, aghast, and began the series of actions that were all he could do to try to reach in after the receding personality. He brought in the GAM-and-Redux that should have been there in the first place and began a bit-by-bit download of the periphery of the hole in

**233**

the circuitry through which Brendan had fallen. It would be a long and tedious search.

Brendan Sealock fell away into darkness, then light.

Riding the MPT, John and Ariane skimmed along the surface in a complex series of ballistic course changes, following a trail of vestigial heat tracked by the infrared scanner. Every so often the musician would steal a glance back at the eclipse in progress, but more often he watched the ice pass below, looking for craters.

"I suppose you've thought of the legal ramifications of our discovery," he said. "Under the homesteading provisions, anything that even looks like an artifact must immediately be reported and is confiscated by the IAAU pending secondary confiscation by the Pansolar authorities. We're treading on some pretty bad stuff here, though of course the possible material benefits, not to mention the adventure, make it a hundred times over worth while."

"If we—or rather if Bren can decipher the thing's mode of transmission, then it is. Otherwise the USEC people will snatch everything away as soon as they get here."

"That's assuming that what we find out is something valuable. If only there were a loophole in the laws that we could make use of, either to get ownership of the Artifacts or to cordon off Aello sufficiently to hide the shuttlecraft."

"Well—Aello's pretty much of a mess right now—it's still in the process of reaccreting the mass it lost when we dug out the ship. Anyway, the minute they get here they will be able to deduce that something mighty strange has been going on there. And since we haven't claimed homestead there, we will probably get into trouble for Aello's disruption."

"You're just making that up. I certainly don't remember any laws concerning the blowing up of satellites."

"The pollution laws might apply, if they feel like stretching them."

"You know, perhaps we should start working on a weapon . . ."

"John, you're turning into a regular Attila. Whatever happened to your principles? You want to have a revolution?"

**234**

Cornwell smiled to himself. "There are parallels. But, no, as far as fighting for our finds goes, I would as soon not risk killing anyone. There are other ways of using a weapon than killing. As far as my principles go—well, I don't feel nearly as much of the reverent fear for other people as I did. Maybe I'm beginning to grow up. People aren't fragile . . . maybe I was overemphasizing my own feelings, I don't know. Yet. Anyway, if I've changed, well, fuck it. That's the way it is."

As the MPT performed a propelled hover forty meters over the Ocypetan surface, something rather peculiar was happening below. The ice seemed to be getting whiter, less dim anyway. The complex shadow which moved ever forward about halfway to the horizon now was hiding the small craters and surface irregularities which it engulfed. Though their eyes adapted well and disguised the slow change that was taking place, there could be no mistake for the infrared instrument they were watching.

"Hey," said Ariane, astonishment showing, "it's getting warmer!"

John pulled himself around in his harness and stole a look at the eclipse. "Look at that thing! Why the fuck didn't somebody predict this? The atmosphere's acting like a huge lens—sunlight is being focused on Ocypete!"

Ariane formed a link with Shipnet through the Clarke and spent a few moments analyzing the preliminary results of Jana's depth probes of the Iridean atmosphere. "Jesus Christ!" she said. "This is just the beginning of the effect!"

And indeed the blotch-sun was very bright inside the almost washed-out blue planet. As the eclipse had progressed, and the light from the sun passed through denser and denser layers of the Iridean atmosphere, the combination of increasing indices of refraction and changing angles of incidence were producing an effect unheard of in asterology, though it was true that an occasional sun dog had been reported from Triton, light making an erratic course through the middle reaches of the Neptunian atmosphere and emerging through a hole in the splotchy upper atmosphere haze to produce a pearl of light in the otherwise Stygian eclipse. But nothing like this. The implications were not a little frightening.

**235**

Ariane and John were spellbound by the scene: they slowed the MPT and stared at the skyward conjunction.

"What . . . what about the neon?" asked John finally, his thoughts tinged with apprehension. "It's close to its melting point right now. A few degrees and . . ."

"Exactly. In some places it's going to be pretty messy. There shouldn't be any problems near the center of the ocellus, though."

"Do you think Jana . . ."

Abruptly the thought-voice of Demogorgon was with them. "Ariane. John. You've already figured out what's happening? We've got an emergency here. The 'net is reporting that some of the equipment, most especially the large superconductor array and the microwave transmitter, will not tolerate exposure to a much dirtier vacuum than we've got now. If the pressure even doubles we're going to have real trouble. Ariane, would you like to get back here to erect a static barrier, or shall I?"

The woman cursed. "I hadn't thought of that. Tem can do it, can't he?"

"He's working with Brendan and they've cut all contact with Shipnet, locked themselves in. You're the only one left. Of course we're dealing with low odds here, but if something goes wrong, well, that would be it."

"All right, I'm coming back. God damn it. I don't have much experience with this stuff—Brendan could handle that section of Shipnet and have it done in a minute. I guess Jana will have to wait. . . ."

It wasn't cold anymore. The rays of the magnified sun were streaming in through the *60vet*'s windshield, and Jana felt that she was finally starting to warm up. Just like in the huge window of the old lamasery upon which the Tibetan Observatory had been grafted. After a night of observing through the archaic four-meter reflector, she would go down, frozen to the bone because of some stoic bureaucrats who had decreed that more work could be done in cold temperatures. The sun would eventually break through the mists across the Himalayas and she would bask there until breakfast period was over.

She had worn black habitually during those years just to catch the radiation more effectively. It had been good, despite everything.

They should have been here by now, she thought. I'm way past the point where they'll be convinced.

A minute passed; another. Somewhere in the pit of her stomach a panic grew. Unless they came very soon she would die. She felt as if she must be crying. Stop! she thought. I've got to stop it. OK, don't lose control—there is still time. Oh no! Please fucking no! The door doesn't have a Shipnet link; I can't close it unless I can move, and I'm . . . I'm . . . and the controls on the suit have been wrecked. What an idiot I am.

If only they would come.

On the craggy highland ice of Ocypete's sub-Iris point something was happening. A methane clathrate boulder rolled in almost infinitely slow motion down a slope, leaving an irregular, crumbly rille in its wake. Elsewhere a humpback mountain began to slump. A dust was slowly accumulating in shallow declivities, as neon gas, percolating through the upper few centimeters of regolith, carried the very light particles of gases still frozen with it.

All across the vastness of the sub-Iridean zone tiny movements were occurring. An observer would probably miss most of them: perhaps he would catch something in his peripheral vision, maybe the occasional subsidence of a hill. Yet the rate of change was growing almost geometrically.

Finally, in a deep crater, the first liquid neon appeared as a shiny clear droplet. Enough neon gas had accumulated there to allow the element to exist in its flowing state. In a dekaminute the landscape was covered with small yet growing pools of light. And yet the sun waxed brighter behind its infrastellar intermediary.

The eclipse was far from over.

Harmon Prynne was in a hurry. Making a final visual inspection of the fusion plant, noting the barely visible red glow of excited neon radiating from the bank of wheellike superconducting tori, he sighed. There was nothing else he could do. Through the Shipnet link he cut the function by ninety-nine percent. Another adjustment brought the generator directly in line with the circuits in the CM, and a second later he discharged the accumulator elements as a skyward microwave signal.

That done with, the man made a hasty retreat toward the nearby moor dome, scuttling across the ice like a strange skimming stone. Once through the static portal and into the lush holographic image, he began to remove the space suit, dropping the segments as he bounced. Finally he came through the door between the environment dome and the CM dome, his eyes slowly adapting to the dim eclipse light that was the only illumination, coming in through the transparent ceiling. Another leap took him into the Command Module, and hard against the receiving wall. He sealed the entry and let out another sigh, this one longer and more ragged.

Perhaps they had been making this whole thing too dramatic.

In the common room, Beth, Vana, Axie, and Demogorgon were sitting about in the midroom amphitheater, talking and watching the progress of the eclipse through the windows.

"Well, you made it," said Demogorgon. "Is everything shut down?"

"Yeah. All nominal so far." He opened a com-channel and said, "John, what's your arrival time?"

"Should be back in about fifteen minutes, Harmon. Did you see the mist at the horizon line? Opticals suggest it's primarily methane dust carried aloft by the neon—still very low pressure levels. Right now it's barely visible to the naked eye."

Beth turned from the window. "We can see nothing here, John. Though maybe the double barrier we're looking through is hiding it."

"Let's get the satellite to bring visuals in from the highlands—should be some interesting stuff going on out there." John and Ariane broke contact. Prynne puzzled over his newfound uncertainty. He had never been one to ascribe complex or hidden motivations to himself; but then again most of the time his behavior satisfied his concept of his normal self. Now, he was not particularly pleased with himself. Eventually, as he lay back amidst the compressible tiers of the crater, he knew that it was somehow linked to the way Brendan had distanced himself. Without the other man around, Harmon felt considerably more ill at ease about the whole situation. Especially now, in a semicrisis.

"Harmon, we're going to the Illimitor World now. Want to come?" The speaker was Vana.

He felt a surge of annoyance grow, then fade suddenly. These people are my friends, he thought, and said, "No. Go ahead. I think I'll concentrate on the situation here, in this world. Have fun."

"Beth?"

The woman shook her head, staring out into the vivid moonscape.

"D'you want to go, Axie?" Vana said, executing a slow somersault across the room. "You seemed to like it last time."

Ockels gave the other woman a quizzical look, and glanced at Harmon, then at Demogorgon, who was stretching out on the floor, preparatory to the experience. After a moment of tension she seemed to relax, and a little smile appeared, inflating her cheekbones and for a moment making her beautiful. "Sure. Where'll we go this time?"

Demogorgon gestured confidently. "Leave everything to your friendly demigod. Circlets arranged? Everyone comfortable? One, two, three, and gone."

Harmon watched as the three lapsed into a kind of narcolepsy and settled into various nonpremeditated positions. For a brief moment he was tempted to follow them; but his repairman's skills were all that they had between themselves and disaster until Ariane returned. He felt a sense of duty strongly, not to mention fear. He exchanged a tired glance with Beth, who apparently had lost her enthusiasm over the eclipse and was staring away into nowhere, looking pale and distracted, then turned to face a necessary external reality.

**239**

□ □ □

Ariane fired the retrojet and the MPT slid along a barely perceptible downward arc until, not twenty paces from the CM dome, it contacted the ice and electrostatic attraction brought it to a stop. She and John dismounted and, summoning two work-units, made for the fusion generator.

"This shouldn't be too hard," said Ariane.

Out of nowhere, two spider-legged work machines appeared, carrying with apparent ease the girder maker as well as a bulky container holding a just fabricated field modulus device. Though it was a tedious procedure, the machines soon had constructed a simple enclosure of struts around the fusion equipment, and, guided by Ariane's precise control, the housing was calibrated and subsequently turned on. A quick reading showed that the operation had been successful, and Ariane reactivated the battery tori. That crisis, at least, was over. They made for the CM, somewhat exhilarated by the danger now that it was over.

Demogorgon stood with his back against the elaborately inscribed inner wall of the high pinnacle at Suraxheian and looked out across the broad meadows that lined the surrounding countryside, gentling its contours. It had been a good visit, bringing him still closer to the two women, and it made him happy. He wished that Prynne had come along, but knew that much the same purpose was being served by his duties in that "real" world far above. The anger and jealousy were gone, now, and Prynne needed what he was getting out there.

A flicker in the springtime light made him glance up at the two suns overhead. They seemed unchanged, but . . . the sky flickered again. How . . . Demogorgon looked around at his world. For some unaccountable reason it seemed rather grainy and far away. In the distance he could see the Brendan-like GAM running toward him. Suddenly it stumbled and fell. Demo took a step forward, lurching away from the wall. A ripple surged through the universe, twisting at his insides, then the GAM was before him, standing again, agonized. It turned to stare at the fading sky.

"Master?" it whispered, and then vanished.

Demogorgon stared into the dimness. "Brendan?" What's happening? He felt a cold, hard tremor of fear.

The world blacked out for an instant, then wrenched itself back to an artificially brilliant normalcy. Vana and Axie were standing below him on the hillside, looking frightened.

It was as if . . . Demogorgon said, "We've got to get out of here!" and they fled upward through an electronic storm.

Cornwell and Methol were sitting beside each other in the common room, a little distance from Beth. They'd tried talking with her, but she was unresponsive, affectively flat. The feeling washed over them and soon they gave up their attempts to talk to each other and joined her in staring out at the moonscape, at the slowly waxing eclipse storm.

The hatch to Brendan's room crackled open. Krzakwa climbed through, looking more like an apparition than if his hair had been standing on end. "Sealock's dead," he told them.

There was silence and Methol felt a numbness stealing over her. Cornwell said, "What?" but the Selenite had turned and gone away again. They rose to follow him, holding hands as they went.

Beth sat for a long moment, staring out the window, then she turned and looked at the still open hatchway. It didn't sink in. Dead? Death couldn't happen in the dawn of the twenty-second century, not to real people.

She too stood and walked out of the room.

Demogorgon surfaced from the Illimitor World and lay for a moment flat on his back in the little padded amphitheater. He could hear Axie and Vana stirring beside him and, some distance away, a commotion. He stood and, without looking at the two women, walked slowly to the open door of Sealock's chamber. Something, some odd feeling of anticipatory dread, made him not want to look inside, but he did nonetheless. There was the horrid tableau of tangled machinery, four motionless people, eyes upon him, and in the midst of it all a man's still body.

**241**

He crossed the room on slow, dead feet, feeling suspended far above everything, and stood looking down on him. He looked at the others and saw it in them. "He's gone, isn't he?"

Ariane Methol nodded slowly and then, clutching at him, began to cry silently.

"What happened?" demanded Cornwell.

"I don't know." Krzakwa told about the machine and what had happened during its activation.

As he spoke, Beth and Axie hooked into the medical scanners of Shipnet and began conducting an emergency examination. It confirmed their worst fears. What remained of Sealock was basically a mindless body in a state that was worse than trancelike.

Axie, her face strained, said, "He'll hang on for a little while, but soon he'll require total life support. There's no way he can ever come back from this. . . ."

The Selenite nodded and, in that moment, passed sentence: "His personality is totally discharged. He's as good as dead."

Krzakwa stood looking at them all, feeling remote, in a state of semidetachment. They all seemed like characters on a stage, players in some old-fashioned "Grand Hotel" production. Berenguer and Prynne were together, but, incredibly, Axie stood between them, and they each held one of her hands. What could be happening there? Demogorgon and Methol were close beside them, arms about each other, sharing a mutual grief. Beth stood a little distance away, alone, and John was the most distant of all, equally alone. Jana was nowhere to be found. The Selenite continued speaking:

"I'm not sure what we can do about Brendan, maybe nothing but execute his will. Under ordinary circumstances, a discharged personality can sometimes be recovered intact from the 'net if swift action is taken. That's what a Redux program is for. In this case, I don't know. We don't have any way of knowing where he went. The best I can do is try to punch open a QCS channel to the Artifact and see if anything is going on down there. Theoretically, he *has* to have gone somewhere. If his personality had been erased *in situ* it would've left definite signs: a big lesion in his amygdala, for one thing. I . . . I'm not hopeful." He shrugged, feeling helpless.

It was not until the following dekahour, the loss of Brendan still not fully realized, with the eclipse long passed and the sun and Iris well apart in the sky, that they could assess the full damage wrought by the storm. They discovered Jana, frozen solid, out by the ocellus rim; she was brought back and preserved in a cold-exposure capsule, and the idea of reading out her personality programming was discussed, as if in a daze. If feasible, that would come later.

Beyond the ocellus rim, at that point where Iris hung perpetually overhead, localized cataclysms had wrecked the neon-rich features: the liquid neon had flowed across the irregularities in the icy crust, leaving erosion features in form not unlike the valles of Mars. Great fields of neon ice, featureless but for occasional alluvium deposited by the limited load capacity of the neon flow, covered much of the sub-Iris terrain, erasing the smaller craters and filling larger ones. At one point a flow of the liquid had broken through the ocellus rim and spread across the already smooth water ice like a fresh coat of paint.

Never again would Ocypete be subjected to the hot eclipse light, since the changing aspect of the Iridean ecliptic would put the sun to a near miss the next time around.

# E  I  G  H  T

Krzakwa and Methol sat across a complex console from each other in Sealock's chamber. The other six survivors were there, but silent, for the two remaining technologists were the principal actors now. Sealock's still living body lay against one wall, enmeshed in its now necessary life-support equipment. The console was a composite of all that had gone before: Shipnet's Torus-alpha CPU, the quantum conversion scanner, and Sealock's nameless final act of creation. It would have to act in concert, under the direction of their will.

"Well," said the Selenite. "We have two people effectively dead, and possibly a chance to save one of them. We *may* be able to read Jana's personality out of her dead brain . . . but we have no body to put it in. Yet." He glanced at Sealock. "In any event, Jana will keep." It was a grim, unnecessary sort of humor. "We have to try for Brendan first. If we fail to reclaim him, then he *is* dead, and Jana's image will have a place in which to resume its life." He frowned and stared at the machine. "We're as ready as we'll ever be. I'll go in after him and Ariane will maintain a lifeline on me . . . better, we hope, than the one I held for Bren." He sighed. "The rest of you can observe via the circlets, but keep out of our way! Let's do it."

They went under and down, and the eight, trailing each other like a madly whipping human kite tail, fell through the circuits and out into the emergent wave fronts of the scanner, down into darkness, then light. A tongue of data reached out to scoop them in, but the electronic lifeline held and they unreeled into the unknown like a spider descending on its web.

—See anything?

The light flooding their senses was blinding but could not be shut out. It was a side effect of immersion in the QC wave front.

—No. I'll try to turn down the gain. Maybe clean up the clutter around us a little.

—Good idea. A little artificial image enhancement might help. If we . . .

It struck. The imagery cleared and they were pinned, helpless before a flood of complex data, become mere observers.

Brendan Sealock was afloat in the dark sea of Iris. The initial trip down, the shock of being detached from his body, left him in a fog, a state of confusion and deadly lethargy, but he was alert again now, drifting in an immense crystalline sea, suspended in the center of a great blue-green sphere in which floated other remote, indistinct shapes. His first conscious thought was the classical one, Where am I? then he remembered. The ship! This was what it had to be: the great mother vessel that had spawned the enormous mystery of the Aello lander and the once radiogenic material beneath the ocellus on Ocypete. The answers had to be close at hand now. *Where are you?* he cried out silently, but there was no answer. The masses of data that had seemed too imposing without were invisible within. A globule of some dark, oily substance floated before his eyes and he began to look around.

There was a haze against an all-around sky that, when stared at long enough, resolved into a mass of filaments; one filament, perhaps, endlessly folded in upon itself. It was studded with a variety of tiny, dim shapes. Far away, at an unguessably remote distance, was an immense blue-gray sphere, a planctoid-sized mass afloat in the icy/warm sea. He reached out and touched the globule of oil.

It popped, Hello, and was gone.

Ah! Contact . . . Who are you?

Another oily sphere boiled out of nowhere before him, writhing, then was still, waiting. He touched it.

Pop.

Centrum.

Sealock glanced uneasily at the distant sphere and understood. Yes, there it was: the source of all data, the source of his present complex reality. Can we speak?

Droplets machine-gunned out of nonexistence and splattered across his face. Yes. Easily. Come to me.

It's a long way.

More droplets. Not in the now space. Journey with me into the past.

Sealock was incredulous. Time travel? How is that possible? Our physics denies it!

Pop-pop-pop.

Think! Where are you now?

He thought, and then felt amusement at his own stupidity. Oh. Of course. I see what you mean.

Roiling effervescence.

Let us be about it then. I am eager to meet you in a more fruitful fashion. That was an excellent machine you inhabited. He felt himself begin to move and change as the imaginary years reversed themselves in an imaginary land.

It was to be an even trade, history for history, culture for culture. With the wonders of modern technology, most extractions are painless. But not all . . .

□ □ □

New York Free City was one of those aberrations that still abounded in the world; a remnant, a holdover from the days before the Insurrection. Over the span of a single generation, as the datanets grew in complexity, most of the world formed into the systems of semi-independent enclaves that now stood for nations and communities. In a sense, the city was one of these, but in some very important way it was different. New York was all that remained of the bright dream that had once been America. People spoke of crime and terror when the subject of the free cities came up, but these were just unavoidable by-products of the reality that they espoused. Paris, Hong Kong, and Rio de Janeiro. Calcutta and San Francisco. They all had that indefinable Something. Freedom? The willingness of their inhabitants to do and be, whatever the cost? New York was Earth's premier city. Its population seemed to hold, of its own accord, at a constant twenty-seven million.

Because of the strict and official limits that the enclaves placed on themselves, what passed in these days for a world government grew out of the free cities, where the laws were light. It was a powerful irony. The rigid dictatorship of the Contract Police had its headquarters in the chaotic whirl of happy Paris. All the manifold threads of the world's data system had their ultimate source in the Metro Design—Comnet, a function of New York Free City. The maddened souls who could not live within the confines of a normal society came there to be free, and so became a fruitful force in the world that they despised.

Mankind was haunted by ghosts of its own making.

Brendan Sealock stood alone on the flat, black, shiny, false ebony floor of Grand Central Station, surrounded by a human horde. Eighteen and alone and freshly run from the iron-thumb benevolence of Deseret. His little collection of emergency luggage was piled about his feet, valises containing mostly notebooks, and he was incredibly tired. "Oh, God . . ." Misery. "What am I going to *do?*" It was said aloud and nobody turned to look. His eyes were grainy and blurred from days and nights spent awake and all of his awareness seemed to be concentrated in the tight band of an almost headache about his temples and forehead. He crushed his hands into his hair and stared up at the starry sky embossed on the inside of the domed ceiling. Why not? "Fuck the world!" he screamed, his voice pitched high.

"Hear, hear."

It was a quiet voice with a soft rasp, and Brendan turned to stare at a short, blond, unkempt young man clad in a burlap-looking friar's cassock, complete with a hairy rope belt. "Got any spare change?"

What the fuck was *this* now? "No."

"Too bad." He pulled a flat bottle from his robe and uncorked it. "Drink?"

"Thanks." He accepted the bottle, took a quick swallow, gagged at the oily taste of cheap chemistry, and handed it back. When he could speak, his voice too had a soft rasp. "Hi. I'm Brendan Sealock."

"Ram that shit! Only homos use names." The man spun and strode off.

Brendan shrugged, picked up his luggage, and began to walk in the same general direction.

The path that they followed was a semitortuous one, a fly's wall-crawl through one of New York's older sections, yet away from the museum piece that was central Manhattan. Successions of steel/plastic and bricks with crumbly mortar flashed in dazzling array across hazed eyes and led to a dark alleyway in an ancient area that sported tall, ruinous buildings open to a blue-gray drizzling sky. There was a brightly lit, partially maintained building here, with a plasma sign stating YMCA, beneath which someone had erected an ornate wooden plaque renaming it THE FRENCH EMBASSY.

The place had fine, rosy curtains in its windows and looked warm and inviting, but Sealock didn't go in. He followed his single volitional contact across the street to a dark, dilapidated structure that had a luridly painted black and orange marquee above the door: ALOYSIUS' CREAM DREAM CROTCH PALACE. The doorway itself had been done up in spray paint

**249**

as a stylized representation of a vulva. The doormat said, "Welcome, Zeus."

It wasn't totally dark inside, just lit by a variety of low-wattage colored light bulbs. The hallway itself had nothing, but the doors of most of the rooms were open, in some cases missing entirely, and little washes of blue, green, red, and orange spilled out, making a dull mauve ambient light.

"Hiya, Megalops! Who's your buddy?" There was a bearded fat man seated on stairs that rose into the darkness.

The cassock-clad man brushed past him. "Fuck'um," he muttered, making a quick masturbatory gesture with his hand. The fat man pinched at his asscheek in response, but the other retreated wordlessly and was gone.

The fat man grinned. "Horace," he said, holding out his hand.

Brendan said, "Ah . . . Megalops there says only homos use names."

"Megalops is an asshole. He just doesn't like being a homo."

"Sealock." Brendan shook the proffered hand.

The man nodded and answered with a heavily agglutinated "Pleastameecha."

Brendan swayed slowly, his head describing an imitation Draysonian cycle. He realized that he was either feeling faint or on the verge of falling asleep. "How do I go about getting a room here?"

Horace looked bemused. "I dunno." He took out a little black cigar and lit it with a brightly glowing sparkstick. It smelled like cabbage farts and Sealock's sway grew in amplitude. "Hey, kid, don't fall down here. You're too big for me to lug out of the way."

"How . . ."

"Just go up the stairs until you find an empty room. Lie down on the bed. No one'll care."

The haze growing to a palpable miasma, Brendan slowly trudged upward, lost in himself, his feet feeling unaccountably massive. On one landing he came upon a young woman clad in a heavy sweat shirt and nothing else. On seeing him, she winked. He nodded politely and went on.

**250**

Somehow, he found that empty room and fell heavily, face down across the bed, unable to draw in his feet. The light bulb in the lamp was fuchsia, in perfect tune with the bilious dizziness that assailed him. His last conscious thought was, What the hell *is* this place?

When he awoke in the morning he hadn't moved and he still felt tired. His eyes were sore and the muscles of his neck ached. His legs hurt. . . . Good God, my *feet!* He tried to hook one toe against the opposing heel and push off a boot but lacked the strength. His whole body felt swollen. There was a warm weight against one side and a lighter pressure against his back.

He laboriously turned his head and looked. The hallway girl. She was curled up against him, one arm thrown over his back, and her crotch was hooked over his hip. His belt was wet and at first he thought she'd pissed on him, but there wasn't enough dampness for that. When he stirred, she awoke and looked up at his face through puffy eyelids. "This is *my* room," she said. Her voice was soft and had that same rasp that seemed to afflict everyone here.

"Sorry."

She smiled. " 'sOK." She helped him as he rolled laboriously over onto his back. "How you feelin'?" She sat up and swung astride him, sitting on his stomach. He couldn't help but stare down at her damp, matted brown pubic hair.

"Don't know. Hungry, I guess."

She grinned and, swarming up his chest, thrust her groin against his face. "Help yourself!"

Brendan's stomach heaved.

She pulled back a little and said, "What'sa matter?" Aggrieved tones. "C'mon. I don't smell *that* bad!"

Brendan shook his head slowly. "I don't feel good." He could hardly move his arms. She got off his chest and squatted beside him, inadvertently sitting on his hand.

"OK. I got a pizza someplace. You want some of that?"

Brendan tried to answer, but a black thunderbolt struck at him out of nowhere and he went back to sleep.

□ □ □

When he awoke again, it was night; at least, it was dark outside. The girl was sitting at a little table on the far side of the room. A plasma screen was leaning against the wall and she had an ancient Dvorak keyboard CPU opened in front of her. She had a small electron beam torch in one hand, sparkling bright blue as she made connections. She *still* didn't have any pants on. This time he managed to kick his boots off. They thumped on the floor.

She looked up and, seeing that he was awake, stood up and walked over. "Feelin' better?"

He nodded. "I guess so."

"Good!" She sat astride his chest again and her hair, now dry and crisp, tickled his nose. Oh, well . . . it *couldn't* taste any worse than the inside of his mouth. He extended his tongue, but her hip muscles did most of the work.

When she was done, she slid down on him, lying atop his body. She kissed him, licked his face, hugged him. She undid his belt and helped him struggle out of his clothes. When he was naked, she stared. "Wow! You gotta lotta muscles, don'cha?" A sniff. "Haven't had a bath lately, either."

"Sorry." Her speech was confusing him, with its wild oscillations between analytical and synthetic grammars. Some English-speakers did that: education stretched thinly over the outreach of original-sin poverty.

" 'sOK. Enough dirt 'n' the bacteria die." She was playing with his penis, feeling it stiffen slowly and engorge. "Big cock, too." She slid farther down and licked him. His penis finished its progress to a full erection. She sucked him then and, big or not, she managed. The orgasm made him tired again and he lay quiescently, watching her.

She sat on his ridged stomach and grinned. "My name's Cara Mia." She held out her hand.

He shook it. "Brendan Sealock. How do you do?"

"Pretty damn good!" She hopped to the floor, then sat on the edge of the bed.

He stood up and stretched, jumped when she goosed him. He smiled. "What's all that?" He pointed to the mess of antique electronics on the table.

**252**

"Homework. I'm a freshman CS major at NYU. I wanna work on Comnet someday."

He nodded slowly. So, he thought, they're making her start at the beginning and work her way up. That way she understands it. I wonder what they'd do with me? "I'm a bum."

"Same thing."

In the morning they arose together and went to have breakfast at a little outdoor café down on the corner. The bright sun of late spring was shining down on them.

After breakfast she took him around. At the Statue Stump, they got him registered as a landed immigrant. Brendan pointed to the fee schedule posted on the wall, but the fat, grandmotherly type behind the counter only laughed. "Don't let it throw ya, kid. We'll send a bill to Deseret." He could imagine his parents' expression when they got it, but they'd pay. The Contract Police had rules about the movement of people between enclaves.

He followed her to NYU that day. He noticed that most of the students liked to dress up in rather idiosyncratic costumes. He went to the registrar's office and found, to his surprise, that he could take classes for free. "We'll send a bill to someone," they said.

They gave him a battery of tests and seemed impressed. "Maybe we *won't* send a bill. Deseret's loss is our gain," they said. "Stay forever if you like." It went on and on.

In time he made some adjustments and failed to make others. He enjoyed sleeping in Cara's bed, but then, she'd fuck anyone, anywhere. Sometimes he'd awake in the middle of the night to find her with someone else, right there beside him. Sometimes he grew angry. Sometimes he watched. Sometimes he joined in. He had sex with a man for the first time in her bed. Sometimes he went out alone at night.

Finally he found himself sitting on a man's chest in a dark alleyway. The man had attacked him and had been beaten. He brought his heavy fist high and drove it down with all his might. It hurt his hand. The man hadn't died, but he'd needed extensive plastic surgery after that.

In a cafeteria argument with a philosophy major at NYU he was referred to as a soulless monster. He didn't know why, and felt hurt. Sometimes the feeling of directionlessness and growing insanity almost overwhelmed him.

He kept on moving, of his own accord, dancing to an internal rhythm of increasingly feverish proportions. He began to realize that he liked beating people up, hurting them as much as possible, almost as much as he liked fucking women. He thought of combining the two but didn't.

Someone said he'd fuck anything that couldn't outrun him. He laughed at that.

Someone else said he'd step on bugs if they could scream loud enough. He beat that person up.

Outside of his own pillaged memory, Sealock could feel himself being changed as the swift time reversal being wrought by Centrum progressed. He knew, intellectually, that it was all a result of software synchronization, but the imagery forced on him came with an odd emotional jolt. He changed and, changing, cried out with a commingling of wonder and fear. Head, arms, legs, torso. Gone. Like *that*.

It was a mechanical-seeming thing, and swift. A succession of ticks, the beating of a clock, and Sealock the man was gone. Another such succession and Sealock the—what—*thing* was there in his place. Cephalosome and tail-sheath. Eight machinelike arms with two-fingered hands; eight matching anchorelles for pseudoautotrophic feeding. Retractile anophagomotor apparatus, for eating, eliminating, and propulsion. Here. Like *this*.

He remembered. We called ourselves a small, unbroken bubble of pheromonic oil. The message it contained meant, "That which has accepted a seed."

The being he had become had no discernible sensory apparatuses—instead, it had a hypertrophied sense of "touch," a subtle response to pressure waves and chemical changes in the surrounding methane. This, combined with a data-processing kinesthetic sense, was all it needed.

The externally generated image-form which now occupied him did not come with very much in the way of memory, not yet, but he knew it would arrive, one piece at a time, as he developed the necessary complexity.

Stop time.

The world-lines unreversed and he was still Brendan Sealock, yet still changed. The Seedees were all around him now; he could sense them far away. Some flew through the sea, propelled on their jets like hard squid. Others clambered about the still ways on stalky legs. Still more were swept along by the standing waves of the great, endless transport matrix. They went about their tasks, filling the World Ship in uncounted trillions. Now, in the everlasting memory of Centrum, Mother Ocean lived.

Sealock blew himself steadily along, knowing he must go to the central sphere, and looked at the pressure waves that brought him a bright window on this new reality. The matrix machine awaited him and still he saw.

When the messenger cell met him, he was hanging in delighted awe below a self-orienting photovoltaic generator, which would turn to suck up the light of passing suns, hanging in happy contemplation of its crystalline complexity. It was Machine, in its most quintessential form.

He boarded the messenger cell. His anchorelles plugged in, there was a current flow, then he soared singing above the world.

At NYU . . .

Brendan Sealock studied. A man, growing up, may be accused of all sorts of infelicities. The various rites of passage that most societies induce are intended to demonstrate to the adult-candidate that a great change of estate is coming over him. They say, "You may now do whatever you please. You must now be prepared to suffer the consequences of your own actions." He was generally regarded as mean, petty, and vicious, with a mind centered on the concept of self. They all thought him dangerous and deranged, a "thug." A few people even looked on him as a little bit stupid, but no one ever called him lazy.

He worked. Though the colleges of the twenty-first century had given up the folly of a "liberal" education, recognizing it as an impediment to the technologists and a detriment to the artists, they insisted that a student learn a great deal about his own specialty. Gone were the days when a student could limp along learning "just enough." During the periodic examinations, if you couldn't handle any aspect of a task, you were sent back to study until you could.

Though the tests he had taken revealed a phenomenal raw potential and a fair amount of preparation, the Deseret educational system being nothing if not effective, Brendan had to start at a lower level than he'd expected. It angered him, at first, but he soon came to see the sense behind it. They made him study physics in a developmental-analytical fashion and gave him a quick grounding in historical electronics, then plunged into the twinned evolutions of Quantum Transformational Dynamics and Comnet theory. They said, "These are the things that you *have* to learn in order to earn our certification. If you want to learn anything else while you're here, fine. It's up to you. If you don't, well, most prospective employers don't care."

In the classroom . . .

The professor said, "We used to start with the basics, but we don't anymore. If you're interested, it's in the library. If you've studied all the various calculi, you're all set; if you haven't, don't worry. Boab analysis rests on a somewhat different underpinning from the rest of math. In the trade, we like to call it asshole calculus." He grinned as he drew them into the Tradition. "There are no instruments to guide you through *this* jungle, boys and girls. It's strictly seat-of-the-pants navigation." Cara giggled and the professor's grin widened. "Whatever," he said. "Anyway, put on your circlets."

The poster-cluttered wall behind him vanished, displaced by a smooth, blackboard-like image. "It goes like this: Newton and Einstein went wrong in some very curious ways. Mr. Boab finally got it figured out about thirty-five years ago. The unified force field still exists—it just has nothing to act upon, so it's a little hard to work with. . . ." He waved a hand at the wall and fiery letters began to appear. "There're eleven variables and forty-one physical constants here. I know you all know how to solve for individual unknowns. That won't do us any good, unfortunately. I will now show you how to arrive at a simultaneous solution for the Blanchard-Higgins Inequality. It's called the Desrosiers Transform and is considered the root of QTD." The letters began to dance. . . .

In the cafeteria . . .

Brendan Sealock was usually engaged in the process of becoming irritated. The engineering and science students liked to gobble their food and rush back to the land of ideas and experiments. Everyone else liked to argue and talk endlessly. Since they'd installed an inductab transducer, the music blared out loud. Right now, it was that popular new artist, what's-his-name . . . Cornwell, that was it. His first big release: *Reflection Counterpoint*. Sealock didn't much care for what seemed to him like random blatts of very loud noise.

"Hey, Comnet-man!" He shared a table with a raucous bunch of metaphysical philosophy students. He knew some of them were already well known in their field, authors of hefty, Heidegger-like tomes full of complex and circular reality analyses.

"Fuck off, Basket-weaver."

"Come on, Sealock. We're trying to get up a good paragraph on the *Ding an Sich* controversy for Sykes. You gotta know something about that. . . ."

He sighed. Here we go again. He wrote a simplified version of the Tornberg Inequality on the tabletop. "Look here: what you want is the First Product Transform. Sikt Grote got this worked out almost eighty years ago. It's pre-Boab!"

The philosophers groaned in unison. "Shit. Even if we knew what you were talking about, we couldn't use it. Sykes won't accept that crap in a paper. Says it's unethical."

Sealock was baffled. "How can you talk about something you don't understand?" They stared at him, puzzled, and the background music roared on.

> Senman-Reischar, easy to know;
> You can live in Scapa Flow!
> Scapa Flow the place to be;
> You can watch it on the 3V!
> On 3V it's easy to see;

Skies are blue for me and thee!
Thee and Comnet, how I will grow;
Senman-Reischar, Scapa Flow go!

As Sealock walked out of the cafeteria, headed for his Trivesigesimal Sequence Analysis tutorial, the opening strains from the theme of the latest 'net epic, "Scapa Flow Go," were echoing in the room behind him. Though many people sneered at the epics, calling them "lightheaded trash," he rather liked them. Superficially escapist, the interactions of the characters were interesting to follow. I'll have to tap that when I get the time, he thought, and walked on.

In the street . . .

Brendan Sealock walked the dangerous places. In the foyer of NYU's QTD Lab Complex there was an enormously appealing poster, a piece of artwork more than a century old. A hairy fat man with a spiked club. Atavistic background. Distorted biblical quote. I will fear no evil because evil fears me. Sometimes he would go to stare at it and grin. He liked the thought. He wasn't the only one. Cass Mitchell, the lab's incredibly ancient founder, something like a hundred and thirty years old, also came to look at it. Once, the wizened creature looked up at him and winked. "Looks just like my dad!" he cackled. Another time the old man, who was kept alive only by the prostheses that his wealth could afford, had muttered, "Go ahead, bitch! Make my bed!" As he turned away, Sealock supposed that, if he lived long enough, brain rot would get him in the end as well.

But I won't be his age for a hundred and ten years, he thought. What would biotech be like then? Most people don't live that long anyway. The average age of death from systemic failure was around ninety. Maybe I'll be run over by an RT-mod next Tuesday. . . .

He walked the dark roads, stood beneath the glittery lights of the entertainment shells. It was in vogue for the hookers to go naked these days. Some of them wore body paint, or tattoos, and many shaved their pubic hair into artistic patterns, or off entirely. That had an appealing look to it. You could see what you were getting into.

**258**

He stood and watched. They turned their tricks on the street and it made a show that amused him. Nearby, a hairless woman stood bent over, holding her ankles while a customer fulfilled his needs in her. The fee was already in her tote bag, representing the last days of the ancient money economy. Sealock felt himself growing horny and walked on.

At home . . .

Brendan Sealock lived quietly. He sat at the table and worked on his problems with the Duodecimal Work-Frame Inequalities. They had only been solved five years ago and were hard to understand. In the bed, Cara Mia entertained a matched set of burly prizefighters. They were larger men than Sealock, but in much poorer condition. He paused to watch them humping away, and speculated. . . .

Projections. Projections. Tensors and maximalizations. Optimal courses and winding rivers of thought. As Sealock gave up his life in chunks and great bites, reliving it as it left him, Centrum replaced the pieces from its own modulus of experience. Similar machines can be exchanged one segment at a time until they are interchanged, without ever having been moved. Becoming. Becoming. Seedee life flowed into him as a steady stream of thick, rich oil.

Seven Red Anchorelles—7red, he was called—worked at a desynthesizer unit deep in the folds of the Mother Ship sea. He was happy in his tasks, secure in the knowledge that he too contributed to the advancement of the Grand Design, as much as anyone under the everlasting light of the Starseeder Centrum. Living his life against the backdrop of the Wavy Matrix Machine, he worked and loved and his soul evolved in a double-spiral pattern, ever outward and upward. Epicycles came and went, aglow.

All along the Wavy Matrix were the great tadpole-shaped units that made the ship live. Synthesizers, the storehouses and factories that made raw materials into whatever was needed. Polyphase reactors that took current from the immense photovoltaic generators and stored it chemically, making raw materials and power as needed. Desynthesizers which took unwanted goods and returned them to a storable

**259**

raw state. Interphagic units, for the storage of the world's raw substance. Here and there, like great silver balloons, were enormous vacuoles that contained a variety of gas-dependent processes. They pulsed like hearts.

Somewhere, in lands 7red had never had occasion to experience, along the great Axis, lay the flight and governing machinery. The gyroscopic control system; at the south pole, the Detection Mast and Lander Bay; at the north pole, the hot immensity of the photon drive.

Normally, the ship coasted on its course, a dirigible planetoid wafting silently along among the stars, but when a correction needed to be made a great spear of hard, coherent radiation would lance out, stabbing deep into the bright clouds of the dawning night. The universe was a billion years old now and aging rapidly. Though quasars abounded, it was black between the galaxies.

7red thought about it, pheromonic messages circulating through his infrastructure, mixing to make new ideas. The universe was a pocket, trapped far below the bubble boundary of its single-monopole domain. The rules said that there had to be other such spaces, in other such domains, probably unreachable. And beyond the eka-event horizon of the many domains? The unimaginable hot density of what one far-future daughter sentience would come to call deSitter Space. 7red could picture it in his chemicals, but the picture was a distorted one, stepped down to match his capacities, tiny circles spread through eleven dimensions reduced to the dimensionless points of a trefoil-concept mathematics.

Only Centrum, last of the Starseeder forefathers, could think of it in terms of the real space-time that surrounded them. For the time being, the Creation was less than its Creator.

Work ended because the task was completed and 7red, restless component in an unresting ecosystem, flew off to the Mating Nest, still thinking his happy thoughts. 7red loved to think, as they all did. He knew his history, but that was for Centrum alone to tell the Time Traveler. In the interval of flight, he expanded his concept of space.

It proceeded from the cosmic infinitesimal, vacuum boilers

**260**

swelling out of nowhere to provide the vacuoles that held the packets of radical characters making up the pseudoparticles of reality, to the universal infinity, the ever receding wave front of the monopole domain, which pushed the unthinkable end point ahead of the uncrossable horizon. It was a frustrating concept, yet likable. Satisfying.

He reached the Mating Nest and entered its latticework. Cooloil awaited him, her tasks completed also. They were not sexually differentiated, these Seedees, for their evolution had not included that complexity, yet the Time Traveler imposed his own regimen of still persisting ideas. 7red loved Cooloil; she stilled his raging mind, calmed his conceptualizations. Cooloil loved 7red; he stoked the banked fires of her soul, set her pheromones to singing. They made a handsome dyad, an island of simple beauty in a sea of more complex arrangements. Their song of ideal counterpoint was appreciated and envied by the vaster audience without.

They coupled.

Anophagomotor apparatuses met, anchorelles fused, arms interlocked. Their valves opened to each other in closely docked proximity and their juices flowed. The pheromonic oils, the vehicles of thought and communication, mixed and, for a while, 7red and Cooloil were one being. The Time Traveler felt their pleasure as his own and marveled at its simplicity. There was no complex machinery, no invasiveness of Downlink Rapport here. There was no remaining vestige of separateness, no identity. Nothing in his former life compared with it. It was the ideal to which all other beings of the later time must aspire in vain. He wondered at his own remaining isolation and felt despair. It was not possible for him, not in the hard-wired circuitry of a solid-state mind. Ideas came whirling. The winds of perhaps blew across his delimited consciousness. He speculated. . . .

Brendan Sealock had come to Buckminster's Gymnasium on a whim. The sign outside had said, SPARRING PARTNERS, and noted that the payoff was in hooker tokens, the only hard currency that still circulated in New York Free City. You didn't have to spend them on whores. People traded them back and forth, exchanged them for favors, bought unique personal mementos with them. There was a famous artist down on the Deuce who sold his canvases for them. Rumor had it that he could get laid a million times, whenever he wanted. They were little three-centimeter silver-plastic coins, the reverse embossed with the legend ONE FUQUE, the obverse bearing a tableau of two mating pigs. The pigs were smiling.

When he came in, the handlers sized him up, weighed him, and smiled grimly. The fat black man turned to the fat white man and said, "One hundred eight kilogram, Bobo!"

The other snickered and his masses of doughy flesh jiggled beneath a filthy sweatshirt. "Right, Mustafa. Killer Hunkpapa's meat she be." He turned to Sealock. "Pay is one fuque per minute you last with *him.*" He winked. "You gonna get all fuqued up in no time, kid!"

They stripped him, taped his hands, stuck on gloves and shorts, and put him in the ring. The spectators, mostly dirty men and overdressed slinkers, were giggling and pointing. Killer Hunkpapa was waiting. He was a large, powerfully muscled man of indeterminate race. He had black hair, black eyes, and light brown skin. There were scars on his face and he was smiling casually, calmly.

"You ever do this before, kid?" He had what sounded like a German accent.

Sealock shook his head. He was feeling nothing now, not even anticipation. The world seemed to possess that same crystalline clarity that it had when he was immersed in the dreadful complexity of Boab Analysis. He felt himself relax and his senses came to a point.

The boxer grinned. "I'll try not to mess you up too bad. Give me a good workout, I'll let you go home with a pocket full of fuques. Maybe you'll come back."

The bell clanked on the edge of his awareness and Sealock lifted his hands. The boxer's glove snapped in out of nowhere and tapped him on the face. There was a terrible lance of pain, proceeding from his sinuses to his occiput, and he staggered back, amazed.

Another punch floated his way and he bent forward at the

**262**

waist, letting the arm go over his back. He stood up and threw a right at the boxer's face. It missed and landed with a squishy thud on one muscle-ridged shoulder.

The boxer staggered a little and his grin broadened. "Hey! I like that! This pussy has a real punch!" He hit Sealock in the face three more times, making him bleed.

Another long floater came and he ducked under it, learning. This time he put his fist out, then drove his weight at an exposed stomach. The boxer said, "UF!" and sat down abruptly. Sealock stood upright, flat-footed, and wobbled blearily, feeling dizzy and sick.

The boxer bounded to his feet, stared for a moment at Sealock, then wheezed, "Call time!"

"But, Killer . . ."

"Call time, asshole! Don't you see what we've got here?"

The bell clanked.

The boxer helped Sealock over to a corner stool and sat him down. "You OK?" Brendan nodded. "Good. You come back tomorrow and I'll show you what to do." He turned away. "Clean him up, Mustafa. Give him a dozen fuques for his time."

As he staggered slowly to the door of the gym, several slinkers followed him, touching him gently.

That evening, after a long, relaxing stay in a steam-hazy sauna had restored him to some semblance of normality, Sealock went out to walk the streets of the city, a few fuques clicking together in his pocket. The fat orange ball of a late summer sun wrote long shadows among the ancient buildings and the warm air was a feather touch, brushing across his skin. Very far away, he could see the great, featureless towers of the modern city leaning away from him into the sky. Somewhere, very vaguely, he thought about the curvature of the Earth and was startled. They were *that* tall.

He wore only a pair of white shorts and an occasional breeze stirred the hair on his chest and legs like some faint, unheeded emotion.

He found one of the little parks that the hookers frequented and stood relaxed, his back pressing into the rough

**263**

bark of a gnarled, gray tree. Its leaves were the intense olive-green of late summer. Unable to summon any coherent thought, he stood and watched.

It was early for the whores. Tradition made them denizens of the night, but they came out before sunset, perhaps to avoid any unfortunate mythological comparisons. They chatted with each other and ate little snacks. Some were touching up their body paint, and from time to time they would glance over at the staring, nearly motionless figure of Sealock.

A woman lay on the grass not far from where he stood. She had long, braided hair, pale blond, with a matching pubic thatch and large, dark blue eyes. She was lean, without being too thin, and her body was adorned with perhaps a hundred tiny butterfly decals. She did stretching exercises, alternately arching her back and then bringing her legs up until her knees touched her shoulders. Finally, apparently satisfied, she took a long applicator from her tote bag and squirted a small amount of some amber-colored jelly into her vagina. Lubricant? Disinfectant? It didn't matter, and he realized that he'd enjoyed watching her insert the skinny tube into herself. As she put it away, she smiled at him.

Brendan knew he liked watching women masturbate and he supposed that was at the root of his current pleasure. He found a certain interest in watching them at their daily ablutions as well, washing themselves, douching, even going to the bathroom. He'd never taken much time analyzing the things that he liked, perhaps fearing that would diminish his sense of the reality it brought. He hated the feeling of remoteness that persistently engulfed his life.

As dusk fell and the streetlights came on, he found himself staring at a new addition to the group. She was tall, nearly as tall as he, and clean shaven all over. Though she bore no adornment, her tan skin had been lightly oiled, so that it shone, throwing off highlights in the dim ambient glow. Her eyes had the slight epicanthic folds of a Eurasian. She had high cheekbones, a smooth skull, and her ears were small and symmetrical. She had a long neck and was naturally thin, without being emaciated. Her stomach, beneath small, domed breasts, was flat and her hips were narrow, barely flaring out from her waist. He could see the delicate tracery of her pelvic bones shifting slightly beneath her skin as she walked. Her legs were long and muscular. Her groin was like three soft fingers, parallel at the juncture of her thighs.

She came to stand before him and he could see that her nipples were pale and pink. She smiled at him. Very slowly, she lifted one long leg until her heel was resting on his left shoulder. He stared down the length of it into the shadows of her vulva. The position held her open and he could see a little way inside. He could feel his penis slowly begin to rise.

Reaching into his pocket, he produced the little coin and held it out to her. She took it and said, "Thank you." Her voice was soft and throaty.

Taking down her leg, she turned away as he removed his scant clothing. She bent over before him and he stepped forward into the lethe of her body.

7red had another task. The message had been transmitted to him from Centrum, a globe of oil that swept up along the Wavy Matrix and leaped across to him while he was still engrossed in his conjunction with Cooloil. It burst upon his shell and soaked into the receptor tissues of his integument. With a pang of regret, their circulations closed off from each other and they separated, become two beings once again. There was still a commingling of inner substance, but the differences would accumulate now, as their natural selves were reasserted, a part of the pheromonic oil generating organs in their bodies. 7red touched Cooloil's tail-sheath once, a parting gesture, and flew away.

The content of the globule had been a complex one. Outside, it had said, and all the appropriate technicians were being called to action. The lander was being prepared for a voyage of its own.

A Messenger came for him as he flew and whisked him away toward the south pole. 7red felt a small surge of growing excitement disturb the mating-tranquilized flow of his idea circulation. He had never been called upon to do this particular task before, but he was the right sort of being for the job. Centrum was a caring sort of overlord and shared the assignments around as fairly as it could. Now, his turn to go Outside had come at last!

The Messenger let him off at the Lander Bay nexus, where perhaps a hundred thousand Seedees of various types were milling about in a random-seeming horde, preparing for the job ahead. A semisentient exterior work vacuole approached him and halted. *7reAn?* it queried with a primitive, highly simplified jet of oil. He assented and commanded it to proceed.

The leathery-skinned golden sphere drew closer and then carefully engulfed him. He sank into a pouch of its outer membrane, which then detached itself with an interiorward thrust. The inner skin dissolved, freeing him to his task within the $CH_4$-filled confines of his device. Here, within the limits of a space hardly larger than himself, 7red could practice the most difficult and rewarding task that a technician might face: the direct control of a construct with his own freed mind. The interior of the vacuole was lined with a sheath of receptor material. 7red took a figurative grasp on himself and, opening his valves, released the entire contents of his pheromonic circulation.

His mind pulsed outward and he became the vacuole. Its senses were his. Its capabilities were his. He became immensely tougher and stronger, able to withstand the rigors of total vacuum and near-absolute zero, able to resist the hard radiation of a nearby star that was doubtless just recently emerged from a wild T-Tauri youth.

He swept over to an "airlock" and passed through its membranes to the interior of the Lander Bay. The huge compartment had already been evacuated and the outer door was ajar. 7red went to the edge and looked out with his new amplifications. Without the vacuole he would have been insensitive to the grandeur, dead, in fact, but now he could see the horrid wash of electromagnetic radiation.

There was a terrible bright star only a few light-minutes away, a high K or low G, he thought, and Mother Ship hung in the skies above a dense silicate world. The place was disturbingly hot and glowed on its own in the far infrared. He understood it well. It was a death place. A whole system born from the ashes of a recent supernova. This sort of a place meant the handling of dangerous hydroxyl-cloud materials, and Seedees would soon die, perhaps already had. He was glad he didn't have to do *that* job.

His own task was far simpler. With a flotilla of other vacuoles, he would get one of the radioactive aluminum fuel cells from its external storage bin and charge up the electrical power pods of the lander. A relatively simple thing, but important and dangerous nonetheless. He and his comrades went about it steadfastly and steadily as they whirled round and round above the tiny, almost atmosphereless world below. They were careful, none of them got killed, and at last they were finished. All was ready. They stayed to watch.

The triangular, finned shape of the lander banged out of its hold and drifted a short distance out. Its LiH-fueled engines flared luridly and it began to shrink away, descending. It would skim into the thin, hot gases of this newborn planet and return, having discharged its cargo of microminiaturized Composites, surrogates of the Mother Ship and Centrum itself. It would return, and the Grand Design would be advanced another tiny notch.

7red's oil writhed in ecstasy.

The drain and fill of emotion-laden interiors came quickly now, a liquid kaleidoscope of scenes and impressions first from one life and then the other. Though feeling himself ever more the nameless Time Traveler, he was alternately burdened by flaring ego identities, swirling through the experiences of Sealock and 7red like a molecule of water in a red-raging sea. The concatenation of personalities struck him like a song sung in rounds, a horde of bells being rung through their changes.

He saw Sealock in swift progression, the man growing quickly older as he expanded into his electronic world, coming to the fateful time when he had mastered all that was Comnet and joined the Design Board, intent on expanding the horizons in the wires beyond what it had been. The man grew quickly wiser as he fought in the ring, aiming arrowlike at that series of matches in Montevideo . . . the defeat by the Cuban, the silver medal, the meeting with Ariane Methol. Love. Another concatenation, something grafted onto his soul like an agonized parasite, destroying the equilibriums so carefully built up, showing him the falsehoods that padded his feelings, tearing them down to oozing red flesh, leaving him exposed. It was pain, once again. Islands have beaches where they are rubbed raw by the sea.

In a similar fashion, 7red moved upward, propelled by capacities unsought into the arena of his destruction. His too was a society of individuals. Though they mixed and meshed as they would, still the very reality of their separate physical bodies kept them apart. He rose to ever greater mastery of the devices and thought modes that made up his world, growing ever closer to the greatness of Centrum and ever farther from the simple things and persons that he loved. Alone in his hard shell 7red worked, and he coupled with Cooloil, then with other beings, greater beings who were more on a level with his increased station in life. His inner essences boiled at a fever pitch with the wonder of it all, and gradually he began to mourn his loss.

Two scenes played in swift counterpoint:

At Ariane's behest, Sealock had moved to Montevideo, living with his woman in Tupamaro Arcology, linked to the now beloved, lost New York only by the wires that otherwise dominated his life. I didn't really need their physical presence, he told himself often, why do I miss it so much? They lay in bed together and made love often.

Brendan lay on the cool, slightly damp sheets of a bed and rubbed his hand slowly across the velvet textures of Ariane's sleeping back, staring hard into the mute darkness. Why has it come to this? he wondered. He put his face against her skin. Why am I here? He stuck out his tongue and tasted her flesh. She sighed and stirred slightly but did not awaken. Why do I lack the strength to run away, go back where I had at least the illusion of happiness? He ran his hand down across her buttocks, then into the crevice between them, down past her anus until he came to her vagina. He felt of its wetness, an albumin-like stickiness that was largely a product of his own

**268**

secretions. She awoke and rolled over, and they made love again, murmuring softly to each other in the darkness.

In that time he forgot to think and wonder, but illusions, once shattered, can never be reformed.

And Seven Red Anchorelles rose to the scene of his own final nightmare. Having mastered all else within the inflated boundaries of the great Mother Ocean, he now floated deep within a special inner sea, a pocket far down in the thought folds of Centrum itself. The being, the Overmind, spoke to him in the voice of his people one last time, and he understood. He had achieved Unity.

The chemicals struck and he felt a moment of terrible despair, then his shell dissolved, his oils escaped, and he was into oneness with the Overmind. He was gone.

The Time Traveler awoke to himself in a blaze of ecstasy and horror.

Centrum penetrated the flowing nebula of this soul with tendrils of awareness and said, I greet you, Brendan Sealock. Be welcome.

It began . . .

Before the dawn of time, the infinite universe was a hard, ringing void. There was nothing, but that nothing had limitless potential energy. It might have remained, this empty potential that stood for God, but nothingness is an unnatural state. It persisted, timeless in the absence of a referent, waiting for the random number that would act as a trigger. The false vacuum stood poised, hard, hot, infinitely denser than the nuclei it would spawn, and the clock of quantum fluctuations ticked away. The slow rollover came. . . .

Everything flashed into being. The monopole domains exploded outward, sucking the cosmic-event horizon away into the infinite reaches of now extant space. The vacuum boiled and particles were born. Physical processes toppled down the quick stairway of the flux-gate thresholds and the forces separated, one, then four. Temperature fell, hesitated, and fell again, carrying along density and radius in its wake. The world came into being and evolved.

Swirling clouds of bright matter, white light, cooling, became only an afterecho of cold radiation in mere seconds. Matter and energy now separate, the clouds spun and condensed, becoming ragged and lumpy as they aged, a pudding improperly stirred, a universe made by a lazy chef. Quasars were everywhere then, bright, hot globules of pulsating light, galaxies in birth and exploding. Cooling goes on, hot huge stars quick and brief in their young life, and exploding, seeding the surround as they died. It was too early yet. . . .

And yet the odds had to be broken, as the symmetry was broken. A cluster supernovae went critical in a chain reaction and scattered dense matter through their neighborhood, yet it was in a region far from the hot cores all about. New stars formed, smaller, longer-lived stars that had planets of a small, dense sort. The universe was less than a billion years old.

We evolved then, said Centrum, and fast. As always, the precursors of life came into being among the great, rich hydroxyl clouds. Amino acids rained down out of interstellar space upon those hot silicate worlds and, because of it, life evolved. So far as is known we were the first. Because of the odds, we were, at that time, the only.

The radiation density was higher then, and evolution went at an accelerated pace, making life in seas that nearly boiled. It crawled up onto the land and saw and fought and grew. The eras were short then, and intelligence looked out at the stars for the first time in newborn amazement. The lights in the sky attracted them, bright baubles, lures before a fish, and they flew outward into space.

We searched, but they were not there.

We? They? Sealock's persisting sense of self forced a question into the flood.

*We.* The ones who made me in their own image. Starseeders. We searched, but there was no other life. We were alone. Worse still, we could find no other worlds like our own. We were a fluke.

*They* were not there. The others whom we expected. There were other worlds, yes, great balls of warm gas, mostly hydrogen, stars too little to shine. Useless.

We cried out, enraged at our solitude, and the Grand Design was begun.

Too long. Too long.

Images formed, imperfect and broken, for Centrum was ancient and damaged. They were images of beings not so terribly unlike men. Beings of flesh and bone walking beneath a starry sky, looking upward resentfully at the universe that had so disappointed them.

We knew it would take too long, longer than we could expect our species, even our own sun, to last. Generations of stars would have to live and die, worlds would have to form and evolve the way ours had, only slower, much slower. We would be gone, vanished for billions of years before the comrades that we sought could come into being. We became the Starseeders and set to work. We searched among the stars for ages and we found them. . . .

What?

*Little* balls of gas. Spheres so small that much of their hydrogen leaked away, until only the trace elements remained. They were cold, these planets, and rare. Each one had to have a thick sea of the proper density upon it . . . complex lipids dissolved in methane may be a form of life, you see. And we had special models at home to work from. . . .

It began . . .

Tupamaro Arcology, like Montevideo, was quiet and raucous at all times. As the postindustrial world of the late twentieth century evolved, waves of technology cascaded out and down from the Euroamerican Transpacific matrix that gave it birth. The benefits and deadly dangers flowed outward in equal measure, changing the world's four quadrants on four levels across four generations. They quickly destroyed the basic nature of the matrix, first the Turing circuits, then the Insurrection fragmenting the lives of the people. What emerged demolished the economy and ideology of the Socialist Bloc. By the time the wave front got to the third world, it had leveled off, become a mere bootstrapping effect. The fourth world, the lands of absolute poverty and degradation,

**271**

felt it only as a sudden famine, then they were all swept up into the New Order, made whole again.

It filtered downward. Suramerica Limited Federation was the Earth's largest old-style political entity, a weak corporate state in which the *ex post facto* enclaves were bound together by the rules and regulations meant for the various communication and data networks. Montevideo was still a city, but not a free city, not a New York. On its outskirts, Arcologia de Tupac Amaral was almost a city in its own right, something like an enclave writ small, a million people in a giant building, striving to be free and failing.

Ariane and Brendan sat together in their living room, working at separate tasks. He had a single tap plugged into his forebrain, reviewing some correspondence from MCD, cursing their inability to understand the latest batch of inequations he'd sent. They *were* stupid, he thought. Only the response from the Moon's Lewislab made any sense at all. At least they asked interesting questions. Someday, he knew, there would be a branch of mathematics called Sealock Decision Gate Masking, but it was a struggle.

Ariane had a circlet on. She was perusing the latest edition of her favorite electronic newsmagazine, looking over the various articles and wildly extravagant advertisements with quiet amusement. Suddenly she called out, "Hey! Look at this!"

Brendan sighed and shunted his awareness over, Neptune hung in the starry sky, huge and blotched turquoise above a field of dark, rubble-strewn ice. A pale haze hung on the horizon and there were domes below, twinkling with light and life. A tall, slender man clad in colorful robes smiled out at them. "Come with me," he said. "Be free. Triton." Induction music filled the background, latest addition to a panoply of famous works. The name was John Cornwell; a TY-com outlet address followed.

"What the fuck was that all about?"

Ariane snuggled up against him, warm and soft. "It seems this guy has almost a billion ceus saved up from his royalties. He wants to take a colony out to Triton. I never thought of it before, but that sounds neat. Maybe we're all dying down here on Old Earth. . . . Want to go?" She was grinning mischievously.

Brendan felt a sudden freezing terror.

Continuities . . .

On the old world, the first world, perhaps the only world, a council met. The Starseeders called it the Grand Design Planning Forum. There were almost a hundred billion beings jamming this Solar System, among them millions of savants and philosophers. The thousand greatest of them were gathered here and the one called Over Three Hills spoke to the multitude.

OTH was a giant, tailed biped, massing well over a ton, with thick, leathery gray skin and a broad, muzzled face. Beneath a heavy brow ridge and crested skull his eyes were deep-sunk, glowing red orbs. He waved his tentacled hands for silence. "The first survey is now complete," he said. "We have now examined every star in the fourteen galaxies of our own little cluster. Among all those billions of systems we have found a few score of silicate worlds, all lifeless, all circling stars too hot for our purposes." A low rustle of dismay came from the assembled multitude. His head dipped slowly to one side. "Disappointing, I know, but all is not lost. Among the hydrogen masses we have found more than four thousand of the little methane worlds. That is enough. I propose that we proceed with the Alternate Plan. We'll never see it come. Even our descendants will not last so long, but in the end the Grand Design may succeed. We have aeons to deal with. . . ."

The scientists arose silently, with grim determination. There was work to be done. Work enough for many lifetimes and a purpose to fill the race.

A flashing change. OTH was an old being now, his long, productive life coming to an end. He stood before his finest creation, proud at the legacy he would leave his world. The Starseeders technology had followed many different tracks, but this had proven to be the most fruitful one. Passing along all the lifeless mineral paths, they finally settled upon large, complex organic molecules as the basis for their data processing capabilities. They built brains capable of independent, original thought and, in so doing, created their first truly great life form, what was to be the most enduring product of their society.

"You understand," said OTH, "what it is that you are to do?"

A rustling voice speaking in the Starseeder tongue came from an encoder box nearby. "I do," it said. "It seems to me that you took a wrong turn in my design. A million minds of my capacity might well be combined fruitfully, but there is another way. . . ."

OTH was satisfied. The brains would grow in depth and complexity of their own accord. He died happy.

A thousand generations went by and Waving Ancestral Nodes worked in a great experimental ecologarium, orbiting the outskirts of the Starseeder system. WAN's laboratory was attached to a planetoid-sized mass of liquid methane, confined by an impervious membrane. Within, the tiny life forms swam and bred. Evolution was proceeding on its own. Through a viewer, he watched as the diatom-like creatures propelled themselves about, consuming other life forms that lived off nutrients in the methane. "They are ready," he said.

From a speaker nearby, the Mind agreed. "Yes, it would seem so. We are at a stage where vessels like this may be released upon the methane worlds. They will breed and prosper."

WAN nodded to himself. "It is a pity," he said, "that they cannot be our own kind."

"They can be," said the Mind, and it began to speak. WAN felt a dawning wonder as he listened.

The great ships went out, the worlds were colonized with life, and the Starseeders watched patiently and waited, communing with the artificial brains they had created. Slowly, the race became extinct. Finally their sun exploded and all that they had originally been was gone.

The artificial brains went on without them, proliferating

the Grand Design, but not quite alone. The things in the methane continued to evolve.

Continuities . . .
Now Sealock was seized by the scene that he hated most, the moment of his life that he hated to review the most and so most often did.

The musician, John Cornwell, had come to Montevideo intent on meeting with Ariane Methol and her little pool of special applicants. They talked and, at some point, the two retreated to the privacy of her bedchamber. Pinned, a fly in amber, Brendan pressed his face to the cool, soundproofed wall that separated them.

Vivid imaginings.

He saw them locked together in a foul, treacherous embrace. He saw them kiss and touch. He saw the man tonguing her, saw her sucking his penis, a long, thick thing, shining moistly as it emerged from her lips. He saw the man's buttocks rise and fall slowly as he drove deep within her body, heard her sighs of pleasure, her murmurs of devotion. And no room in their hearts to feel his pain. . . .

They emerged, smiling and dry, and the decision was made. "What the hell," he said, "I'll go."

He helped build the ship and it was better, safer for his presence. They went.

They were on Earth again, taking their last views of a never loved, never thought-about homeland. Heimaey Cosmodrome . . . The transporter lurched and stopped. Silently the exterior door-stair assembly unfolded and extended to the ground. The cool air of an Iceland August pushed in and rummaged around. The midnight sun would have set less than an hour before. It was still quite bright, though overcast, as they filed outside.

There was yet forty feet of hard-packed ash between them and the ship. All horizons were dark and sterile against the shimmering gray-yellow sky. Brendan knew that he was seeing the last of Earth but, to his amazement, it didn't bother him. He was impatient to be away and could almost feel a desire to skip coming up his legs as he made his way toward the towering black and white spaceship. It looked to him like a silent, motionless stargazing penguin.

He lagged far enough behind that he could see the other eight of the group, their varying treads somehow chaotic and unyielding. They were all strangers, even Ariane. Memory struck within memory. The pictures of Triton, against the odd, broken clouds of Neptune, filled the screen, and he heard Cornwell's voice saying, "Come with me." It seemed a long time ago. Time became a stranger commodity as he grew older. His memories remained intense, solid, yet he wondered if this would still be true after the years on board *Deepstar* filled him.

They crowded into the plane's elevator and the intimacy made him feel good, momentarily. They began the ascent.

As they rose Brendan found himself looking at Jana Li Hu. She was short and solid, a classic central Chinese, and she affected a ponytail that fell to mid-back. An astronomer trained at the totally regimented Reflexive Institute in Ulaanbaatar, she could have been a cold automaton, but beneath that controlled facade was something very disturbing. . . . What? In a sudden, icy flash of insight, he realized that there was something in her reminiscent of himself. The elevator hissed to a stop.

Keeping pace with their charges, the artificial brains that the Starseeders had left behind continued to evolve. One to a world, they talked to each other across the interstellar wastes, slow conversations by electromagnetic beam, and sometimes they traveled, using the great colony ships that had distributed them throughout a sphere several million light-years in radius. Three billion years went by as they grew and changed. They too were methane beings now, too large to leave the interiors of their vast ships. From their orbits they oversaw what was going on below. They sent down probes to sample and, presently, to direct the course of a slow, cold evolution.

The seeded beings developed as swiftly as their environments would permit. They lived in the depths of the great frigid Mother Ocean and used the resources that they found, most often resources dropped among them from the immense, immortal beings in the sky.

Seeded with methane monera, the planet soon filled with life. There were methane plants and animals, methane fungi. The animals grew complex, then large, as their ecosystem provided niches for them to fill. Aeons passed again, and the universe had brought forth its third generation, the next in the line of intelligences.

Bitter Shell was stalking a food-pod creature. He had wounded it with his lance and could smell it leaking oil as he cruised along its trail. It had fled high into the upper reaches of the sea in its pain, where the methane was thin. Pressures and temperatures were nearing the triple point and he knew that neither he nor the food-pod could go much farther.

There it was! The immense mass of the animal hung overhead motionless against the murky sky. Bitter Shell cast his lance and it struck. The food-pod writhed, jetting oil, and then fell. He followed it into the depths with his sense and knew that he had won. He tried to dance upward, triumphantly, but failed. The methane was too thin to support his mass.

He wondered. Many Seedees had tried to fly upward, to find the source of life in the heavens, in a place where they could not go. Doubtless there was a reason for it all, but still, he wondered.

Back in their camp, amid the floating fronds of a homeland bush, Bitter Shell lived with his tribe and feasted for many days on the bounty of the food-pod he had slain. He spoke with the shaman, Withered Senses, but there were no answers. He swore that he would find some, and spent his life in the quest, but there were none. The blind Seedees continued to live on as the God provided for them, unable to see the stars that shone down from above.

External voices came to him, generated who knew where. . . . He had seen the event many times before and so, now that he was within it, his mind supplied the external reality of what he was experiencing.

**277**

□ □ □

The GM155 stood alone on its barren field of hard gray ash, nose still pointing at a dim yellow sky. Its interior machinery, powered by a compact fusion reactor, was coming to life. The air intakes on the leading edges of the sharply swept wings had opened and powerful turbines were forming a flow of air through the constricted throats of coannular multiphase engines. Winds began to blow out from the tail of the ship, making it the center of a dusty maelstrom. When the jet pressure was high enough, a thin mist of liquid hydrogen sprayed into the engine's throat and ignited. A fleurette of yellow fire blossomed amid the triangle of tail fins, followed by a deep, hollow roar. GM155 lurched and came off the ground, seemed to teeter motionless for an instant, and then climbed into the sky atop the short, bright, smokeless spike of its exhaust flare.

The sky without began to turn bright blue, then darkened as the shallow arctic troposphere was left behind. As the rocket approached Mach 1 the turbines shut down, the engines becoming ramjets, force-fed on high-velocity air. They sped southeastward now, high across Europe in a sharp cross-ranging maneuver, curving toward the equatorial plane that they would meet below Indonesia and, as they climbed above thirty kilometers altitude, the pilots began to feed oxygen to the engines. Soon the intake nacelles would squeeze shut and rocket flight would begin in earnest.

The sky darkened faster now, indigo, violet, then black, and the sounds of the outside were gone.

Inside, inside . . .

Brendan Sealock was talking to an old man in the seat next to him. ". . . Look, I know hydrogen burned in oxygen *seems* like it will only make water, but that's not what comes out of the exhaust at first. During the troposphere ascent, the engine is burning on air. All sorts of crap comes out; oxides of nitrogen, a lot of really deadly stuff . . ."

"Why, that's terrible! The GM ads say it's nothing but *steam!*"

Sealock gave him a disgusted look. "Sure, they say that. Just so assholes like you won't complain."

**278**

The old man seemed taken aback. "But . . ."

"Look, it's just the price that we have to pay for having a technological society on Earth. Forget about it."

They were distracted then by a thumping sound as the main engines shut down. Brennschluss. There was a moment of zero-g disorientation and then a muted hissing filled the cabin as the "cruise motor" came on. Though essentially unnecessary, it would make the phasing maneuver up to Alpha-enclave-Kosmograd a continuum, boosting the cabin gravity to a steady 0.1g and preventing the chance of motion sickness until they reached the spinning wheel at Alpha in its two-hour orbit, some 1,076 miles high.

Endless generations passed.

Eight Guiding Cries came to float before God's Voice in the temple. It was now his turn to be invested in the priesthood and he was afraid. He knew that priests were privileged to speak with God, but he never thought that it would come to him. He also knew that the priests emerged from their first interview with the deity shaken and withdrawn. Most of them would never again consent to couple with another Seedee. It made them something of a breed apart. His time came.

He jetted up to the hard metal ovoid in the center of the empty chamber and waited. Presently a valve opened on its surface and he was sprayed with the oil of an unimaginably powerful soul.

You are the initiate?

8cries shuddered. He could *feel* its great age and wisdom, its awesome power. He assented timorously.

It is well. Go to the coordinates that I will tell you and retrieve the mass that you find there. It is a God substance, the project on which you shall spend the rest of your life. Go!

8cries went out from the temple shaken and withdrawn, like those who had gone before. He went out to find his lump of metal, to work on it, and study, and learn as the God directed. And he never coupled with his own kind again.

Sealock had moved to a different seat, intent on escaping from the blathering old man. He pinched the bridge of his nose and tried to think. He turned his head, pillowing it against the soft seat back, and stared out the window. They were soaring two hundred and fifty kilometers above the equator, clearing Australia in the sunshine glare, having left night and the Indian Ocean far behind, and the island-speckled expanses of the Pacific lay ahead. It was strange how the turquoise sea glittered with thousands of lemony diamonds, as if each tiny wave were visible to the discerning eye, and he could swear a small space appeared between the white striations of cloud matter and the surface of the ocean. Was that a shadow on the water? It was hard to tell truth from illusion.

He sat meditating for a long time, almost without thought, watching the Earth turn beneath him, a source of never ending fascination. A man came bounding lightly down the aisle and drifted into the seat next to him. Brendan turned to look at him. He was a red-faced northern European type, with heavy eyebrows and a wrinkleless, soft complexion. The man smiled brightly and said, "Hello! My name is Steven Niccoli."

"Sealock." He smiled faintly, remembering the first denizens of New York that he'd met. Only homos use names? He thought of Demogorgon and suddenly realized that he now knew what had been meant. *Names!* He chuckled softly.

Unaccountably, the man laughed right along with him. "Say! You must know a lot more about this experience than I do, Mr. Sealock. What's that bright star coming up over the Earth, there?"

Now why would he think a thing like that? Sealock frowned and glanced out the viewport. He was momentarily confused by the weird vantage point, but, oh, yes . . . "It's Jupiter. You headed out that way?"

The man peered at the bright planet for a long moment. "Oh, no," he said. "We won't get that far. We're bound for an asteroid colony."

We. There was something decidedly odd about this creature. "Are you with the others in this section?"

He shook his head and smiled. "No, not really. We're all going to the same place, Hygeia, but there are three groups. I was bumped up here because the after cabin is full." He paused. "I'm a member of the Intuition Club." It seemed to be a prideful statement.

The what? "That's . . . interesting. What does it mean?" The urge to continue speaking had become a conversation.

The man's smile slowly blossomed into a grin. "Mr. Sealock, I don't mind telling you that we are the first group of retarded people to leave Earth."

Brendan felt a flicker of interest. It was to be expected: as the risks of space travel decreased asymptotically to zero, more and more of the partially disabled were going out. "Retarded? What do you mean?" He thought he knew, but . . .

Niccoli laughed pleasantly. "Well . . . Nowadays, of course, there aren't any official classifications of mental ability, at least not in Europe. But the textbooks talk about psychotropic dysfunction. . . . We know who we are. My score on the Senman-Reischar Test was only 1260—that's something like 80 on the Kammerchoff Acultural Metamorphosis Battery—"

And mine is over 190! Brendan thought.

"—and *that* was with full prosthesis! They try not to set us apart from normal people, but we can't plug into the Comnets at all. That separates us forever, doesn't it?" The agitation showed through for a moment and he realized with horror the degree of the man's disability. Through Comnet, a blind man could see, the mute speak with ease—this man was totally cut off from the world in which Brendan lived. Niccoli smiled again. "Anyway, we have an intercontinental society restricted to people with SRT ratings of 1300 or below. We call it the Intuition Club because that's pretty much all we have to go by."

Sealock looked at him with a powerful sense of alienation. How could they live? How could they learn—and *what* would they do for entertainment? For normal people, everything came through Comnet!

Niccoli seemed amused, somehow a bitter amusement. "I may not be able to plug in and link minds with you, sir," he said, "but I can still read your thoughts. I've seen that expression on a thousand faces in my time. You know, we live pretty well. They still make voice- and hand-controlled machines. And there are books, Mr. Sealock. Remember books? And we have each other." He looked away.

Books? Brendan suddenly remembered his personal cargo, long ago transshipped to Gamma and *Deepstar*. It had been about equally divided between a mass of incredibly sophisticated electronic equipment and close to half a ton of carefully preserved old books. What was the linkage to be found here? What commonality did he have with this man, at the opposite end of a spectrum-potential from him?

The chain of reasoning broke when Niccoli suddenly said, "What's that?" Tiny forces were playing with their balance and now the Earth was visible only as a purple tinge in the rear of the window. In terms of terminal mission delta-V, the GM155 was now ninety percent of the way to Alpha-enclave-Kosmograd, sailing 1375 miles above the blue-green, white-striated ball of the Earth and again in darkness as it crossed the Andes. Without ever varying thrust, it had gone into a 130-degree spindle-yaw maneuver, from which it could decelerate and segue into a tail-first stoop on the giant space station.

Precise Fingers was the first of his kind to leave the world, to fly above great Mother Ocean. He orbited high above the blue-green planet, looking down on it with the augmented senses of his primitive vacuole, and marveled. He was in the reach of the gods at last! His oil coursed about him, touching on the sensory inputs and control nodes. He could see the other planets and the sun, so far away. He spent time examining those pinpoint sources of electromagnetic radiation that the priesthood had noticed only a generation ago. What could they be?

It rose. Coming above the limb of the planet, it was a great silvery sphere, almost featureless, a huge version of the vacuole that bore him. He knew what it was then, and felt tremendous fear and elation. This was the moment when he moved into history!

The planetoid-sized mass drew him in and Precise Fingers became one with his God.

□ □ □

Brendan Sealock was staring silently out his porthole when, returned to daylight, they arrived. Coming up at them almost imperceptibly was the tiny ring that was their destination. He knew there were others like it scattered about the inner Solar System, mass-produced products of Kosmodom Unlimited factories in Irkutsk and Moonport Mechta. As they closed the intervening distance, so that it vanished from the windows and had to be watched through the aft screen, it became less and less of an ellipse until finally they were approaching from a direction perpendicular to its spin axis. Spin? It didn't seem to move at all in that sense. From here it looked like an almost featureless golden band filled with cobweb stuff. Suddenly a tiny, dark blot swam across to stop at its center. It was the shadow of GM155. For a second the immensity of the thing leaped out at him: it was a wheel, ten kilometers across.

Spin? The idea, the question, plagued him annoyingly. Sealock growled with frustration and, reaching into his breast pocket, pulled out a math-element that he had carried along. It plugged into his head with a muffled click.

Let's see . . . log tables danced through his head like celestial fire and a chorus of angels followed him through a millisecond of swift calculation. . . . It came out to a little less than 5.026 revolutions per hour.

No wonder I can't see it spin! He smiled and pulled the distant descendant of a slide rule from its socket and put it away.

Forces, stronger now, pushed him tightly against his harness. The station was swelling enormously. There came a brief roar, the middle sphere filled the screen, and then they were stopped, five hundred meters from the staring eye of a god. Brendan smiled. His imagery was poor. It was more like a mouth. They were in zero g now and he heard someone whimper.

There was a soft thumping of RCS jets and the ship tumbled to point its nose at the hole. The hub of Alpha-enclave-Kosmograd was a thousand meters in diameter, its orifice eight hundred, and around its rim he read, "Welcome to A-en-Kos III."

The GM155 poised motionless for an instant, then the jets hissed again and it moved gingerly forward. The hole expanded, a fearsome maw out of which pale light spilled, and then they plunged through the dense em-gas-screen with a faint tremor. Suddenly they were hanging suspended above the landscape of an inside-out world, above a clutter of machines and tiny spacecraft. GM155 was a giant of sorts here, all of seventy meters long.

There was air in the hub of the station, pressurized to a hundred millibars, and the ship was buffeted by weak winds, driven by the faint Coriolis forces of the slow spin. Had they waited long enough, their inertia would have been overcome, and they too would have begun to turn. It was not to be. Gas jets hissed again; this time not a rocket flame but oxygen bled off from the Hyloxso matrices of the fuel pods. There could be no allowable contamination of a closed environment. The ship swept close to the metal surface of the world, following the imperceptible direction of spin, turned tail foremost, and dropped gently to a low-g landing. They were down.

In time, the Seedees grew used to the idea of how their lives would change. They came to accept the presence of a real, scientific God in their lives, to work with it and to accept its goals as their own. With their help, it grew and changed. Centrum, the Starseeder's artificial brain, their lineal descendant, squatted in its great ship and manipulated the Seedees to its own ends, to the ends that its makers had instilled in it in the early years of creation. It bent them to the will of the Grand Design.

The ship was modified and enlarged. The ideas that Centrum had had in all the idle years while the Seedees evolved were implemented. The ship was filled with the tools of a vast trade and all the beings who had lived below embarked. All was ready. For the first time in a hundred million years the photon drive was ignited. A great spear of coherent electromagnetic radiation lanced out into space, a spear capable of destroying whole worlds, and for a while the star system was illuminated by its light. Slowly at first, then ever faster, the ship accelerated away, bent on the second phase of its mission. Left behind, Mother Ocean still teemed with life, but intelligence no longer brightened her deeps.

The ship went on and on, cruising among the stars for more than a billion years. The aeons passed. Centrum directed and the Seedees worked. They worked and, in the end, were absorbed into the processes of the artificial brain. The ship stopped here and there, intent on its task.

Whenever a methane world was found, the ship tarried for a little while and simmered with the effort of building up excess population. When it left, it left behind a little colony of Seedee life and, in orbit, a duplicate ship containing an immature brain, a young god.

Whenever they encountered one of the increasingly common silicate worlds, a special task unfolded. Matter gathered from the hydroxyl clouds was set upon the path of its natural process but accelerated. Centrum directed, and the Seedees built the little ships then. . . . That is what they were, tiny replicas, in water and carbon, of the great ship itself. Made from the worshiped substance of the ancient, dead Starseeders, they contained a tiny, simplified brain, the immortal genes of an immortal mind, and even submicroscopic versions of the Seedees themselves. All of it was imbued with the single command: replicate. Evolution would come on its own, from the driving forces of Chance. Changes, when they occur, accumulate.

It went on and on, for ages more, while irreparable damage built up within Centrum. With the passage of time, the Seedees grew weary from their labor and began to die off. The ecosystem of the ship began to falter and then the downward progress was swift. The pressure of a building entropy pushed at them, and all things must run down, come to a final halt. The Brain might outlast the universe but not so the ship and Seedees. They were tired, giving in to the *Weltschmerz* that afflicts almost all organisms. They died.

Dreaming Sun was the last of his kind. A thousand years had passed since he had last coupled with a fading soul, trying to extract the last bits of its selfhood from a thin flow of oil. He was alone now with Centrum, old, and crippled with the accumulation of unsought change, yet the Brain was reluctant to absorb him. It too feared loneliness, for it remembered that time between the death of the Starseeders and the rise of the Seedee worlds. Without the methane beings, the Grand Design could not be pursued. . . . The ship had been steered to a rendezvous with an old colony world, hoping for a new crew, but the navigation was faulty, the star had been missed. The programs were deteriorating and there were none to effect repairs. The ship drifted.

Dreaming Sun sighed, a long string of meaningless pheromonic bubbles. Weary, weary, weary . . .

Centrum saw that the end was near, could be put off no longer. Time to extract one last bit of meaning, make a last update on the dying data file. Come to me, it said.

Dreaming Sun committed the last act of defiance of his species, a requiem for the Seedee people whose duration on the void had been so overruled by voices from the remote past: he opened his valves, expelled his oil, and dissipated, abandoning his God at last. His shell drifted away on the currents of the methane sea, empty, and Centrum was alone.

The ship drifted, rudderless, forever, and Centrum, trapped within, began to dream its endless dreams. Mass began to accumulate. The lander lost its hold and fell into an orbit. The fuel pods dropped away and followed. A little nebula formed around the ship as it drifted through a matter-rich region of space. It became a little star, with icy moons for planets. The ship was trapped then, the lonely Centrum hidden within. Under endless layers of gas and stone, the detection mast could no longer see the sky. It drifted, and Iris was born.

Were there other ships? That is unknown. There might have been. There were many worlds.

Times past still bubbled from within.

*Deepstar* lay in the grappling hold of *Camelopardalis,* the immense, Jupiter-bound freighter that would hurl them on the first leg of their year-long journey to Neptune. There were ten now, Temujin Krzakwa having joined them at Gamma, in full flight from the wolves of the Lunar tyranny. They waited, while engineering processors counted down.

Brendan Sealock sat in the common room of the ship's CM, staring out through a deopaqued wall at the blue orb of Earth seen from geosynchronous orbit. The Moon was also in view, a smaller, duller orb in the same phase, much farther away. What am I doing here? he wondered. I'm leaving almost everything that means anything to me! It was far worse than the day he'd left New York to go live with Ariane. The magnetism was almost unbearable now. Am I crazy? It was too late to turn back. He would have to spend more than a year with these people, en route to Triton. I must be!

The engineers reached their zero point. *Camelopardalis* fired up its engines and lit up the sky with a fiery glow. The Earth began to shrink in response and Sealock felt madness setting in.

It was over, not because the memories, the stories, had come to an end but because the damaged programming of Centrum had exhausted its capabilities.

Sealock felt himself floating, borne on the bosom of a great warm ocean. He heard the whispering of its waves, felt the warm currents of its thought rushing through his body. It rustled softly in the depths of his mind.

Come to me, it said, with an upwelling surge of loneliness. We are one.

Sealock rolled gently in the comforting cradle of his past. He luxuriated in the happiness of a long-awaited homecoming.

He rolled to its rhythms. . . .

Come to me, it said. . . .

And he lost consciousness for the last time. . . .

They awoke, eight stunned individuals who had been filled with lifetimes, ages, in what was only a few fleeting moments. Ariane Methol opened her eyes and felt the tears drying on her cheeks. "Good God," she whispered. She turned to look at the others.

Temujin Krzakwa was slowly pulling the induction leads from his head. The enormity of it filled him. He could think of nothing meaningful to say, but, finally, "I don't think we can get him back. It's got him. . . ."

Achmet Aziz el-Tabari, Demogorgon, put his hand over his mouth and gave a dry cough, almost a sob. He said nothing.

Elizabeth Toussaint closed her eyes, overwhelmed by an experience that made Downlink Rapport, the thing she had so long feared and avoided, seem as nothing. "Then we can't do anything for him?"

Harmon Prynne pulled off his circlet, feeling a need for silence welling up within him. What sort of people were these? he wondered. For the first time he'd seen the real inner being of another person, an experience made all the more important for its having been the feared, hated, mystifying Sealock, and he was appalled. And yet . . . there was a *real* person there. How did the thing in Sealock differ from the thing in Prynne?

Vana Berenguer burst into quiet tears, emotionalized beyond all redemption.

John Cornwell wiped the sweat from his brow and stared into an unfathomable distance. "Those poor bastards," he muttered. "Those poor bastards!"

The Selenite looked at him quizzically. "Who? What do you mean?"

Cornwell had a growing look of unutterable horror. "The Seedees!" He turned to gaze at Krzakwa. "We have our gods always with us, mythical beings that we imagine rule our lives. We blame them for our failings and so they serve *us*. These poor bastards . . . Their gods were *real!*" He shut his eyes, trying to blot out his inner vision. "What a horrible fate . . ."

The others were staring at him, bewildered, and suddenly Aksinia Ockels gasped, "Son of a bitch. I *know* that shape. . . ." She had been a biologist by training and now she racked her memory. She cried, "God *damn!* T−4r+! Of *course!*" She leaped to her feet, rebounding in the low gravity, and fled from the room.

**288**

Krzakwa felt stunned, unable to grasp what was going on. "What the hell is happening to us?"

It began again.

And Brendan Sealock's almost dead body lay by the wall.

# N I N E

Cornwell and Krzakwa walked slowly across the heathered rise of the moor simulation, warm and safe amid the toys technology had created for them, and the clouds of the dark blue sky slid by unnoticed. They talked in a somewhat desultory fashion. John was saying, "I'm not sure I understand what you mean."

Tem found a hummock and sat, looking up, and for the first time really noticed the perfect harmony of this little illusion. He saw that the colored sky was not just a wall at some great distance, that it was the infinite heaven of innumerable literary references. A translucent eternity . . . "I'm *not* sure we can really do it. . . . Even as an abstraction, it's complex. Personality transfer has been done between living people. In a sense, it's just an extension of Downlink Rapport. On one occasion, it *was* used to bring back a man who'd recently died."

"Really?" John looked slightly startled. "I don't remember ever hearing about anything like that."

"You wouldn't have. It's illegal on Earth. . . . A couple of years ago, on Luna, an important scientist had the bad judgment to have an aneurysm while he was working on a crucial transition zone in the higher math of a cataclysm system. More than just data . . . insights that he had failed to explain were lost. They put him on emergency life support." Krzakwa grinned, remembering. "Since I was a colleague of his, they brought me, among others, in with the idea that one of us might understand whatever they could get out of him. They tried to resuscitate him the usual way, but he was too far gone. So they grabbed a condemned criminal—"

"They have a death penalty on the Moon?"

Tem nodded. "It's a state secret, but, yes, they do. Anyway, they read off what was left of Dr. Hanscom's neuroelectrical patterns and pumped it into this poor fucker, right on top of his own personality. It resulted in a really bizarre psychosis, but we managed to reconstruct the transition math before he became catatonic."

Shaking his head, looking pale, John said, "I never imagined . . ." He stopped and thought about it. In a way that he had not really come to terms with, Elizabeth Toussaint's personality was overlying his own, and he shuddered. "All right, first things first. Is Brendan really gone?"

"Depends on what you mean. We still have an alien intelligence down in Iris that is a virtual unknown. It could give him back if we ask in the right way. But the process of contacting it again seems to involve a repetition of the danger. I've just got to think about it some more."

John scuffed the mossy vegetation with his foot, watching it darken and lighten like velour. "The implications of all this are staggering. We're talking about more than immortality. Frankly, I didn't think we had come this far."

The Selenite shrugged. "What did you think the Data Control Insurrection was about, really? Even in the distorted history they taught me on Luna I could see that all this was coming. Why they allowed Shipnet is the real question; the total control they exercise over the elements of Comnet is the only thing that preserves the illusion of normalcy."

"I suppose . . ." John squeezed his eyes shut. "How would it work between Jana and Brendan? Aren't our personalities partially hard-wired into our heads? Neural pathways and all that?"

"Yeah. If we manage to get a good scan, we'll have a new person with Jana's memories and Brendan's emotional characteristics. Call it nine to one in Jana's favor."

"I . . . don't know if it's worth it." Cornwell felt himself rapidly sinking into a fuguelike state. "Really, it seems . . ."

"We probably won't be able to do it. It's never been tried on someone so *thoroughly* dead before."

"But you said she'd keep."

"As *meat*, John! Jana had the extremely poor taste to freeze to death slowly. Every cell in her body is packed with ice crystals, ruptured."

"Because of me."

"All the more reason to think hard about the whole thing. Jana is—was—obviously unstable. In a way, we'll have the worst of both worlds. . . ."

Cornwell passed a hand over his face. "We'll have to talk to the others. . . ."

"If you like." A wave of exhaustion passed through Krzakwa, and he noticed a grainy, faintly kaleidoscopic pattern pulsating in the sky, in time with his heartbeat. "I've got to get some rest. . . ."

Aksinia Ockels, wearing a rumpled orange space suit with the hood thrown back, was in a compartment of the containerized cargo hold where Brendan had stored the hefty mass of personal belongings that had come along with him on the *Deepstar*'s flight. She'd been rummaging through his collection of antique books and had at last come upon the thing she sought. Now she stared fixedly at a color plate, a picture of a six-sided being, its parts neatly labeled, cephalosome, tail-sheath . . .

"I knew it," she muttered. She packed the book into a silver-lined environment bag and drew the top together into its seal. Then, with some fumbling, she hardened her suit and hood and stepped into the airlock.

Krzakwa, who had just awakened from an unsatisfying nap upon the heather, was kneeling on the rim of the pool and splashing cool water on his face. The entrance at the far end of the dome made its "cycling" warning and he wondered who had been outside. Finally the door came open and Aksinia came through, eagerness quickening her steps.

"What're you doing?" Tem asked.

"Reading." She came up and opened the bag that she carried, pulling out a book, and smiled. "Look at this." After a moment of turning slick pages, she had it.

"How the hell did you find a picture of a Seedee"—the oddness of it suddenly took hold of him—"in a *book?*"

She held it up so that he could see the cover. It was the 2007 edition of Raymond's *Elements of Virological Anatomy.*

"I don't understand. What're they doing with it?"

She smiled crookedly at him. "It isn't a Seedee, Tem. It's a $T-4r+$ bacteriophage virus."

"I see." He picked up the book and read through the stereophotomicrograph's accompanying text. Gobbledegook, material far outside of his own specialty. "How did you come to find it here?"

"When we were in with Brendan, I knew I'd seen the Seedees before, somewhere. I think I even remembered the name. . . . I got an equivalency in bioengineering, back before residencies were required. I've forgotten a lot, but not everything. All it takes is something to jar it out. I *wish* I'd brought *my* tech info along! But I didn't. I suppose it was Beta-2 that saw to that. Shit! It never lets me care about things like that." She laughed softly. "When you people filled up Shipnet, you neglected the basic biology stuff. I ran a quick check on the cargo manifest. I was hoping . . . Anyway, this book turned up on Brendan's list." She looked at the man in front of her and was amazed to see how pale and watery his eyes looked. "Is something wrong?" she asked.

Temujin looked hard at the woman. He had never heard someone use those words with such a lack of solicitousness. "I'm all right."

"That bastard was interested in *too* many things."

*Was.* Krzakwa felt a cold prickle of realization creep along his neck. He thought of Sealock back on the alien lander, swearing that the empty shell they'd found had a familiar shape. "So what does it mean?"

"Nothing, I suppose, but it's an interesting coincidence. If I'm not mistaken, evolution at the viral level is very quick, and what we see is almost totally optimized. Maybe these things are optimized for a similar type of existence."

"What, invading asteroid-sized cells? We didn't see anything like that in the Centrum memories. That is what viruses do, isn't it, parasitize DNA?"

"Something like that."

"OK. You're the closest thing we have to an expert on this. If you can integrate some sort of theory on the shape of the Seedees with what you know about these viruses, do so."

"They do parasitize planets. . . ."

"So do we all . . . we need something better than that. Anyway, I don't want to talk about it right now. I've got to get some more sleep."

Elizabeth Toussaint lay alone on the bed in her room. Periodically, for no reason, tears would start to flow down her cheeks, oozing in the low gravity, then stop, and she would be still, staring at the ceiling. When her face had time to dry, the crying would start again.

What's wrong with me now? she wondered. I'm not feeling anything. Brendan's dead; Jana's dead. Am I? Why am I thinking about these things? This numbness was a new, withering factor. It was something she had inherited from John, and though it was, in a measure, comforting, it felt so *wrong.* Perhaps if she had to come up with a word for it, it would be perspective. She had lost her gauge for the importance of things. And experiencing the primitive emotions that dominated Sealock's memories had given this emotionlessness even a greater hold on her. I need to be with someone, she thought. John? No. She rejected the idea summarily. How could *he* help? Right now she couldn't even call up an image of his face.

The door opened quietly and Vana Berenguer came in. People were not respecting the idea of privacy anymore. There were connections now, strange ones.

"Beth?" She saw the drying tears and came over, concerned. "Beth? What's wrong?

The woman looked up at her, wooden-faced. "I don't know." She started to cry again, shaking silently. "I *really* don't know!"

Vana put her hand on Beth's brow, brushed back her hair a little, and shook her head slowly. "You shouldn't be in here alone. . . ."

"I want to be. No one can help."

"Someone can." She reached out and, taking Beth by the arms, pulled her to her feet. "You helped Demo a little, back when we first got here, remember? Let him help you now. . . ."

"How?"

Vana smiled. "You haven't been under yet. It's more than you think. Come on."

They walked out of the room, slowly, and John was waiting for them. "Beth? I wanted to see you."

Vana shook her head. "Not now, John. In a little while."

The man ignored her. "Beth, do you want to link with me now? DR, I mean. . . ."

Beth looked at him in astonishment. "Now?" she asked. "Oh, John. Go away. . . ."

He seemed stunned. "But I . . ." He turned from them abruptly and stalked off.

Vana said, "Come on, Beth. Demogorgon's in Ariane's room. They've lost him together, you know, in the same measure. They need us as much as we need them."

Ariane and Demogorgon were alone together in the former's room. They had been talking, trying to talk, but were quiet now, curled up on the bed. Words were useless. Their hearts throbbed to a measured stillness, an inner silence that held a matrix of conflicting ideas.

The woman thought, He loved him as much as I did, perhaps more. Our culture still breeds a strange sort of con-

**296**

tempt, fills us with a curious lack of understanding. We think of bizarre biochemical mix-ups, of volitional neuroses for which a refused cure exists . . . but the emotions continue to seem real. It's more than just a friction between sticky bodies—the great I-don't-know-what that binds humanity. And there remain no explanations but the ridiculous romanticisms of dead poets.

The man thought, There must have been more between them than just the sweat and grue of heterosex. People bind without reason. I don't know. I think I always looked on other people as warped extensions of myself. They're not. There are differences I cannot understand, shades of meaning that do not come through. We can see each other's experiences, live through a tide of alien feelings, but still we are not each other. We strain everything through the one-way filter of our own ideas and meanings. We view everyone through a lens that distorts them into ourselves. We never see them as they are. We think, If I did that, I would be bad, therefore *he* must be bad. Brendan is gone, but really, to me, did he ever exist? Can empathy be real without understanding?

Oddly, it was as if Brendan had died before the episodic projections they'd gotten from the Starseeder computer. The personality of the man as relayed from inside Iris simply connected with their other memories at no point, and it was disappearing from their consciousnesses like nothing so much as a bad dream.

The door crackled open and Harmon Prynne looked in, his face uncertain, his manner tentative. "Can I be with you?"

Demogorgon almost smiled. "Come in. Please."

He entered and came to sit on the edge of the bed. "Is there anything I can do?"

Ariane patted him on the thigh. "Just *be* here. That's enough." They sat in silence for another little while, then the door sizzled again. This time it was Vana and Beth. They came over to the bed. Beth sat down and Vana remained standing, smiling down at them a little. "Well," she said. "We needed to be with someone. I guess we weren't the only ones." She sat. Beth lay down, tangling herself with the others, and sighed. After a while she seemed to fall asleep.

Prynne stirred, snuggling closer into the mass. "We're becoming like little children. Pillows and blankets to curl up in. Teddy bears to hug. Warm laps to lie in. This is comforting."

Demo looked at him, surprised, then thought, Oh, why not? We are none of us as stupid and insensitive as we always seem. Magicians. We *can* be closer. . . . But the idea fled, unripe.

A short while passed, and Tem's head stuck in through the unclosed door. "What's going on in here?" He came in, followed by Aksinia. They came over to the bed and Krzakwa grinned, looking down. "Is this something sexual?"

Ariane smiled up at him. "We're having a special conclave. Climb aboard." Aksinia pushed herself off the deck and drifted down onto the bed, clutching her book.

Krzakwa sat on the edge of the growing human tangle. "Axie's made something of an important discovery. We . . ."

"Can it wait?" Ariane asked.

"Well . . . sure. I think I see." He wedged his bulk in among them.

Demogorgon was frowning. They're all here, he thought, *we're* all here, but something's still missing. This is an artificial sort of closeness, an electric-blanket sort of thing. Just because our bodies are warm . . . The idea came back. He said, "Listen, I think we should go to the Illimitor World together."

"Aw, Demo. Come *on!*" That was from Harmon.

"I mean it. I think we're all sick right now. Hurting. We could make things better. Some of you have been there. You know what I mean."

Vana nodded. "I do. He's right."

Krzakwa sat up slightly, looking out meditatively across the room. "Maybe. Could be, uh . . . OK." He thought about it a while longer, then said, "Um, where's John?"

Opening her eyes, Beth said, "Fuck John."

That sealed it for them. They seized the ubiquitous waveguide cables, plugged in, and went under, then down.

And, going downward, continued to reach out. . . .

**298**

□ □ □

John Cornwell stood in front of the dome of the CM, arms folded, staring out across the bleak Ocypetan landscape, staring at the sky. A huge, early-phase incarnation of Iris loomed far above and the tiny, matching crescents of Podarge and Aello hovered nearby. The sky was star-sequined without pattern, a clumped maze of untwinkling pinpoints. Strange, he thought, that the atmosphere of the planet is still clear. You'd think the eclipse would have done something to it. But he knew there'd been no real effect. The pristinely clear upper air of Iris had merely acted as a lens . . . muddying things down here all right. And the thing they'd found in the planet had done the same.

Jana dead. Brendan dead. Beth . . .

An image of their latest encounter came back to him and the muzzy hurt renewed itself. How has it come to this? he wondered. I only thought that we could be of some use to each other after the terrible strains of the last days. She needed contact. . . . But why did I walk away, give up so easily? A stab of pain, an abrupt turn, and the chain was snapped. The DR link between them had seemingly died in a moment, fading into an apartness even greater than before DR. He tried once again to analyze their last painful moments together. Yes. It was there. Everything that they had shared, all the superficial communion, had come down to that one moment when their two personalities had really commingled and they saw each other as themselves.

How could you *know?*

It was difficult for John to not judge himself harshly. But, with Jana, how could he have known what was transpiring in her confused head? Was there something about him, something so close to his perception of himself that he could not even imagine what it was, that was bad? He thought about it long and hard, and could only conclude that there wasn't.

And people . . . at least some people . . . loved Sealock. How odd it was. How odd *he* was. How could anyone really have lived like that? John had done time in New York and never run across that sort of thing. But then, he hadn't gone everywhere, seen everything. What if it was real? And

**299**

why the hell *did* Brendan leave? It seemed to fit his outer persona so well. But the inner man . . . that was even harder to understand. Unbidden, an image of the shaven prostitute floated up from nowhere, bending over before him, holding her ankles. A stirring of lust twisted in his abdomen. God! The unbelievable coarseness of the man's imagery! How can *anyone* be like that? He drove it away, but other scenes came to take its place, visions of unknown naked women open before him, begging to be despoiled.

He closed his eyes to an angry feeling of resentment. Is his ghost going to haunt me now? Perhaps Sealock dead was worse than Sealock alive. . . . How could he have been like that? The answer constructed itself: he couldn't have been. He wasn't. The flashes of feeling had been there. There was an emotive, sensitive Sealock, yes, but that reality was buried beneath the coarse, hard visions. Smashing people's faces, thrusting into sodden vulvae . . . those things hid all the rest. They gave expectations, made stereotypes. If you split an infinitive and put an expletive in between, it distorted the meaning of the verb. People heard *that* instead of what you said.

I've got to talk to Beth, he thought. I've got to be given another chance. She took my offer the wrong way. . . . I *did* mean to help. And how had she taken it? Like a raped woman being offered the comforts of sex. The playback of Sealock's life must have been brutal for her, the scented floweriness of love turned to some kind of horrid, animal carnage. He turned to walk below and the images floated before him again. Endless visions of dripping crotches, seas of spurting semen, totally repulsive. How could anyone not think it madness?

He came to Ariane Methol's chamber and opened the door. They were there. The seven were sprawled together on the bed, a tangle of limbs and bodies, with wires sprouting from their heads. He stared at them, silent.

Beth looked like a sleeping child, her hair flattened out into a fan. Tem looked like a huge, dead opossum. The others . . . Ariane's skirt had come awry, exposing her vulva. A pad of curly black hair, a slit, an animal-hole, a little wetness.

That's what Brendan would have seen. . . . But no, that's just my perception of the view from his eyes. He loved her. He would have *felt* something. The imagery was a perfect mask.

He went back up into the dome and looked at the sky. Aello had moved and its phase had swollen, but Podarge was no longer in synch.

They'll be back, he thought. He wondered if they really would.

The stars were still untwinkling, still unmoving, emotionless pinpoints. They sat there in the matte-black sky and did nothing for him.

I miss that part of it, he realized. When the stars glittered and twinkled above the night, made pretty by their color and movement and seeming isolation, it made me feel better. In Mackenzie, I used to go out onto the tundra just to look at the night sky. That's how I came to know which stars were which. It *was* something, it was an image of a world where things really existed, really meant something. Is it that this ambience is my whore?

He shook his head and grinned ruefully. There is that, after all. When you stretch these ideas to their limits, the gulf that separates *me* from a soulless monster is not so great. We all make mistakes and I've made at least my share. Who am I to judge anyone else the worse. . . . Who am I to make any judgments at all? A familiar turn of phrase. He knew he'd said it before, but now, somehow, it was different. I mean it, he realized.

His laughter echoed eerily in the dome, perhaps magnified by his awareness that he was essentially alone at this moment in the whole Iridean system. Everyone else was away on some other ethereal electronic plane, one most ethereal. Listen to me, he thought with a touch of self-directed bitterness. What should I do, apologize for my own being? Sorry, Jana; sorry, Brendan; sorry, Beth? It's a foolishness of its own sort.

Should I grovel and promise to do better? Another laugh. This is just me, wallowing in the dung heap of self-generated guilt. No one else has even noticed what's happening to me, despite what Tem said. They're too busy writhing in their own night soil to notice *my* fetid breath. . . .

My, how poetic we are in our bereavement! It's a damned good thing I'm laughing at myself. What an asshole! A total fucking moronic little head-up-the-ass shit-in-the-ears bloody little sniveling Lunatic. . . .

He sobered then and thought about it, images without words. There is that, he subvocalized, watching all the scenes of Brendan and Beth mingle together in his head. He did talk that way, didn't he? I wonder what he meant by it all? The same thing as I? I doubt it. All I can do is turn him into another subset of my own image. We are what we project.

He stretched, yawning against a sudden weariness, and to no one in particular said, "The only time I'm myself is when there's nobody with me."

He went back down to the kitchen module then for a snack, hoping to keep his mind blank, in preparation for the moment of their return and the scene that he imagined would come *then*.

I wonder what they'll have to say for themselves?

Who cares?

Who the fuck cares?

He saw himself in a paroxysm of nonchalance and smiled, his lips twisting in self-derision. Go ahead, Big Asshole Artist! Keep thinking like that. You'll talk yourself into a ticket home alone yet!

He went below.

They sailed down through the golden skies of the Illimitor World in a long, singing arc, holding hands as they fell. The heavens were a burnished shell of the brightest brass around them and they had no idea where they were going, what was happening to them. They had entered as a unit, headed, it seemed, for the Jeweled City on the Mountain, the portentous lands of Arhos in the midst of many seas and rivers, and *this* had happened. They fell and fell, and the sky beneath their feet gave no intimation of a landing.

Demogorgon was stunned and, he supposed, a thrill of fear should have come. But they had designed it together, he and

Brendan, and he thought he knew all its byways. He remembered the Sealock-mimicking GAM subunit and wondered . . . and programs could mutate of their own accord, even in the efficiencies of Shipnet. Perhaps especially there. Systems grew more complex, as in Comnet and Centrum, and the chances for diversion and change multiplied. What was happening?

They fell together, linked as they had come in, slowly forming into a circle until the nether ends joined hands. They became a sort of Midgard serpent, laagered against the coming of Fenris and Fimbulwinter, and the skies began to change. Fiery tongues of lavender and fabled heliotrope began to intrude into their golden world, a wash of mad color that sucked away all sense of separate consciousness and fear. Something that presaged Ginnunga-gap? Unknown . . .

They had come in together, linked in ways that Demogorgon had never experimented with before, and so there was a result. Some higher, unsuspected routine in Bright Illimit had seized control, plunging them down this long, horrible way, to some unfathomable experience. When their hands came together, completing the circle, their minds did too. The sky was shot with bolts of momentary black lightning, twisting rivers of ebon darkness, vines of ink, and the background pattern of the world shifted to a dark cerulean hue, with an overlay of honeyed amber. They saw each other again, as they had seen Sealock and the cohorts of Centrum in their unwilling journey to the beginning of time.

It's not the same, thought Demogorgon, but it might as well be. I don't understand what's happening, yet I cannot fear. I *must* not. This is my thing, my place in the universe, the creation of my own heart and soul. If I fear it, then I fear myself. The sky around him brightened with the thought, sending beams of warmth deep into him, as if the circuits were responding to his courage and trust. He and Brendan had made this place! The stars above Arhos were *real*. He felt a little smug sense of, I knew it all along. . . . Achmet Aziz el-Tabari felt himself as a whole being, as he always had, with no overlay of the cultural biases against him. The value of Self stood out strong and the sky colored with a transparent

**303**

overlay of rosiness in response. The "me-ness" of his character rewarded him with gestalt happiness, no words, a distillate of feeling. The others were with him, holding him in arms of thought, and he smiled. Who would not feel this way? He transferred, the sky writhing with the shift.

Aksinia Ockels looked about her in wonder and the sky responded brightly, filling the incandescent shell through which they traveled with a whirl of indigos and greens, metallic hues that almost covered the blue that formed its base. Fading. Fading. She had been almost a day without her usual dose of Beta-2 and the drug was rapidly being flushed from her system. Dark, jagged streaks of an ugly red momentarily flashed all around, then were gone. All the years lost to me, she thought, lost to it all. I made my world as they all did, and it almost blotted me out. A tiny sphere of brown appeared and was gone without a sound. For the first time a sort of soft wind sighed in their ears, the movement of rushing air tugged at their hair. They felt its coolness. Axie laughed without sound and pictured the dead Seedees. The bacteria, the structure of a typical primitive cell, all of it came to the forefront of her consciousness, coloring the sky a brilliant peach that overwhelmed all that had gone before. Tiny ships, carrying the culture of the Beginning. Then the inheritors arise and go forth. I am myself again, at last. The sky flashed in brilliant red-orange hues and she transferred.

Harmon Prynne fell with them all, in his usual way almost unthinking. The sky dulled, began to turn gray and then, suddenly, reversed itself, waxing to a brilliant cobalt blue. I am not less than the others, he thought, neither more nor less within myself. Strip away the geas that was placed upon me at birth and I am one with them all. There is no less of me than there is of any other human being. Our identities and values manifest in different ways. . . . He remembered the people on the ship when they'd left Earth, the retardates, heading out. In another age their dysfunction would have gone unnoticed. I was less than the others only because I bought the propaganda that my childhood sold me. All my fears and failures were groundless. The sky grew momentarily blinding, and he transferred.

**304**

Whirling around in an arcing hora, Vana Berenguer danced among the others, reading what had gone before. Simplification, she thought, and the sky colored in rivers of deep yellow with her soundless cries. She had always been herself, the shadow of supposedly greater beings in need of love, comfort, friendship, physicality. It served, as did she, and in the service grew an individuality that knew no bounds. I am, she thought, complete within myself. The sky ululated in many hues all about, mirroring the different facets of her, as in the many beings of the world, and when she transferred it refused to dim. Their vision changed to accept the new background level, but the brightness could still be sensed.

Temujin Krzakwa fell and, in falling, felt nullity. The sky grew transparent in response, clear and without color. The world had been lightening on him ever since he'd fled the depths of Luna, and now it grew weightless. He alone had been totally happy with the distance to which they'd gone. He was, as always, secure in his special individuality, and the loss of Brendan was a trauma that he had weathered. He chuckled, bright spots of wavering pinkness, and transferred.

To her surprise, Ariane Methol had the most to learn, the program was teaching her that fact. The sky darkened as she fell, horrified, awful muddy shades that tempered the growing mood of them all. She had only fooled herself into believing she was the center of other people's lives, the maiden goddess of her own little world. She needed others, as they had never needed her; dark pits of corroding madness opened in the sky. She fed their needs, just to gain their presence in her life. . . . The sky brightened volcanically, healing itself. I am no different, she thought. I never was. My needs are their needs; I am one with them in a binding matrix of society, a linkage of individual human beings, and that makes individuals of us all. I must be one. I *must* be! The sky flamed orange. We are all one, she thought out to the people falling with her, with her for the first time. I came for him and he for me, we came for each other, even the ones who were unknown in the beginning. She transferred. . . .

And Elizabeth Toussaint was the seal of them all, bringing the group together in cohesion as she linked hands in the rushing air with Demogorgon, completing the circuit she had begun when she approached him on the first day, the day they had landed on Ocypete. We are not less for having thus exposed ourselves, she thought, no one is. Sadness, blue comet trails marking their passage down the levels of the sky. I'm sorry, John! she cried and then it was audible to them all. The sky was suddenly golden again.

The effigy of Brendan Sealock appeared among them, a sudden gravitational source at the focus of their circle. Demogorgon knew that, as before, it was not the man, merely his creation. GAM-and-Redux was its name, but, still, the appearance brought a pang of regret. He ached with loss and the others with him, but the sky remained intact, now unresponsive to the ways they were reacting. They were retreating from the multiple rapport that had bound them together. The subroutine was returning control to the main program, its functioning at an end, its purpose served.

How did you anticipate all this? Demogorgon whispered. It seemed impossible, even knowing, as he had always known, that the depth and feeling of this man were greater than most others were willing, in their shallowness, to suspect.

The doppelgänger smiled shyly, an incongruous expression on the craggy features of a devil. He did not, it said. The power to heal all wounds is within me, more so than my brethren only because my creator was skilled at this particular craft. Someone is always the best at something.

Heal all wounds . . .

They smashed apart, aflight on the ends of retreating rays, lost to each other on the edges of the expanding universe.

Demogorgon screamed, the death cry of hopelessness. There is a way!

Temujin Krzakwa reached out and seized control from the processor submatrix, driving them upward into light and life, and the Illimitor World shut down behind them, going dark.

John and Beth sat together under the CM dome, looking out across the landscape. Beth seemed subdued, unable to say quite what was occupying their thoughts. Finally the former spoke. "I'm sorry about what happened earlier, Beth. I don't think I really understood what was going on. I didn't mean it the way . . ."

The woman shrugged and smiled slightly, a faint twisting of her pale lips. "Don't worry about it. I didn't really know what you were asking." She stood up and walked a little way away from him, then turned to look back. "We never were sure of each other, even in DR, were we?"

John stared at her, trying to fathom what had happened to her in the last few days. "I don't know. Maybe Downlink Rapport isn't so all-encompassing as I thought. You'd think it would be, but . . ."

She nodded. "Yes, you'd think that, wouldn't you? But our separable selves aren't the totality of *us.*" She shook her head slowly and looked away again. "Listen to me! I ought to be laughing and so should you. We use big words to hide our confusion."

"Everyone does, Beth." He tried to think, to force some kind of coherent idea out, but nothing would come. "What're we talking about right now?"

"If you don't know, well . . . Hell. Maybe I don't know either." She came back and sat at his side again. "I came up here fired with an enthusiasm, a will to bring you back to me, to make you become one of us again. Now that I'm up here I find that I don't know what to say. Despite my old resistance to DR, I always followed your lead, lagging a little way behind. I'm really not used to thinking for myself." She got up suddenly and walked to the ladder leading down. "I'll talk to you again later. . . ."

John stood up, calling, "But wait . . ." She was, however, already gone. He turned back to his chair and drifted into it. The conversation had not only been less than satisfactory, it had been nonexistent. I've got to do *something,* he thought. The contents of a million conversations, with an unending number of people, came back to haunt him, but they were all sophomoric, useless. I spent too much time making up too many stupid ideas. Thinking and feeling aren't the same and I always knew that. Neuroelectrical patterns . . . Maybe that's what she meant. He got up again and went below, filled with acts of conscience, pursuing no goal.

□ □ □

Demogorgon sat with the mindless body of Brendan Sealock, surrounded by his maelstrom of equipment and circuitry. "I can get you back, Brendan," he whispered softly.
"With a little help, I can find the way!" He put his hand on
the body's chest. The flesh was still warm to his touch, as if
the man would wake up in a moment and things would be as
they had been. . . . No, not that way. Better.

The door crackled open and Krzakwa came in. He took in
the room's tableau and said, "What are you doing?"

Demogorgon looked up. "Thinking, I guess. What did you
think of our little trip?"

Shrugging, the Selenite said, "Well . . . that's the way
GAM programs are supposed to work. I just never ran across
one that was quite so poetic before. I suppose I should con-
gratulate you for making a thing like that."

"Me? But Brendan's the one who did all the programming
for Bright Illimit! I just gave him my generalized ideas."

That brought a narrow grin. "You have a typical miscon-
ception of what programmers do, Demo. Without software,
the machines are useless. Everyone knows that; but without
ideas, there's no software either. Brendan just took your
ideas and expanded them to a logical final form." He paused,
rubbing his hand in among the hair of his beard, seeming to
ruminate. "It's like doing a bronze sculpture. The artist
comes up with an idea, maybe roughs out the moldwork in
wax, then a craftsman comes along, finishes the mold, and
casts the statue itself. The two work together because, without either one, there is no final work of art."

The other turned to stare back at the body. "So . . .
You're probably right, but he . . ." The Arab stood up to
face Krzakwa. "This isn't what I wanted to talk about, Tem!
Who the fuck *cares* who made what part of Bright Illimit? It's
what we can do with it now that matters. . . ."

"I know, I caught some of what you were thinking before
we resurfaced. I don't know if I understand what you meant,
but it was the germ of an idea. . . ."

Demo's anger was supplanted by a look of desperation. He

**308**

sat down again. "Just a germ. I'll tell you about it and you tell me if it'll work."

Krzakwa pulled up another chair and sat down opposite him, caught up in the somberness of his mood. "OK. What, then?"

"Look. These things are called Guardian Angel Monitors because they're supposed to follow you around, keeping you from getting hurt in Comnet. I knew about that, but why the Redux part?" The other started to speak, but Demogorgon held up his hand. "I *know!* I looked the word up, it means a return or a recovery, like getting better after an illness, right?"

"Yes." Krzakwa nodded and, seeing that an amplification was awaited, went on. "If a GAM fails in its primary duty, the Redux is supposed to hook you back out before the various components of your personality can dissolve into the circuitry. If these programs didn't exist, on-line discharge wouldn't be a rare phenomenon and no one would be able to use Comnet."

"OK, so it gets you back from inside the machinery. Why didn't Brendan use such a thing?"

"He did. Me." Tem looked away. "We didn't realize Centrum would be as capable as it turned out to be. I lost my grip on him and couldn't go in after him because I had no lifeline on *me.*"

"We know where he is, don't we?"

"Maybe. In Centrum, sure, but he came apart right at the end. That thing that we experienced as a loss of consciousness was him dissipating into Centrum's data control nexi. If we could find all the pieces, reintegration would still be more than a little difficult. We . . . *might* get most of him back, even now, but he'd never be the same again. The Brendan that went in is surely as dead as the Seedees."

Demogorgon looked down into his lap, where his fingers were twisted together into an agonizing double fist of frustration. "Shouldn't we try?"

"How? Can you tell me?" Krzakwa felt a sense of intentional cruelty in that statement. Creative or not, ideas or not, the artist just wasn't competent in this area of technology.

**309**

Taking a deep breath, he looked up. "Yes, I can." He stood and paced over to the body, not looking away. "Part of Brendan is in here still, the parts that made him act so bad all the time. They were the reptilian parts, the hard-wired brain-person that *was* a soulless monster. A lot more of him is locked up in Centrum. Those were the illusory conscious parts, the mind-thing in all of us that says 'I' and thinks of itself as the whole being, even though it isn't. The rest of him is in Shipnet. . . ."

Krzakwa sat back in his chair, bewildered. "What the hell are you talking about?"

"His *real* soul is in there, Tem, the part of him that helped me make Bright Illimit. A programmer operating with routines so close to the Turing point must leave a little bit of himself in his creation. I know *that*, if nothing else."

"Are you talking about the GAM? If so . . ."

Demogorgon interrupted him with "No! Well . . . maybe a little bit. I mean all of Bright Illimit, maybe the whole body of work that Brendan did. There's a lot of him recorded all around us!"

"I . . . see." Krzakwa closed his eyes. "You're talking about more than an abstraction. It would make a powerful ally . . . a whole fucking operating system if it was done correctly. I never thought of it that way before." He thought, How much data can we pump out of these things? A lot? Enough? Ideas have to come from *somewhere!*

The Arab shook him angrily. "Do you know what I'm talking about, dammit?"

"Yes." That was said flatly, abstractedly.

"Will it work?"

"I don't know. I have to think about this thing. Maybe there's a way, maybe not. . . ."

"Well? How much time do we have?"

"I don't know." He opened his eyes. "Shit. It *has* to work. We'll get back something. I just don't think it'll be Brendan Sealock." He stood up. "Let's get out of here. You go get the others."

□ □ □

Temujin Krzakwa sat before a master control/writeboard panel, induction leads stuck to his head, trying to make things work. Despite his original opinions on the matter, it was an act of creation which quickly took possession of his entire being. There was a certain poetic and personal satisfaction to be had in breaking up extant, finished programs and reworking their subroutines into a new whole, a thing different from what had gone before. He worked feverishly, brilliantly, far beyond what he had imagined were his abilities. He found a new belief in the stories of superhuman accomplishments done under emergency conditions: indeed, more than once he had the feeling that his subconscious mind was leading the way, a feeling that the program was writing itself.

Bright Illimit was the way, as Demogorgon had intimated. It was more complex than he could have imagined, undoubtedly one of the most recursive and gestalt-oriented programs ever conceived, much less written: a fully interactive program that did strange things. As he got into it, Temujin was surprised to discover that the program was set up to raid parts of the user's personality for its terminal background data. Of course, he mused, how could it work any other way? Only the user knew what would make him the happiest. Demo knew that fact and Brendan knew how to make the program realize and utilize it. Perhaps all these things had come about in a subconscious fashion, but then perhaps not. . . .

He added bits from a hundred complex utilities that had been found in Brendan's data files, added things that he knew about from his own work at Lewislab, threw in bits and pieces of everything, in hopes that something would help. It began to coalesce, and he began to feel more hopeful. Cover every contingency, he thought, then throw in the kitchen sink in case we get dirty and need to wash up. Shit. And be careful not to break any dishes. The glass can cut you painlessly under water. Bleed to death and never know it. . . .

Add hard wiring. Hookups to the ship's RAW complex and remote processors, then finally into the Machine and the QTD system. Get everyone into the act. Call on the dead man. Punch in through the amygdala, rewire those taps so they access whatever's left coursing across the corpus callosum. Crank up the limbic system, deep inside the brain stem. Get that old lizard-man punching away. Tell him there're faces yet to smash, haunches yet to hump. . . .

Krzakwa felt like a mad scientist, not creating his own monster, that was old hat, but taking all the monsters that ever lived, ripping them down, stripping their wires, making new monsters from bits of the old.

Mechanics of the soul, he thought. Adjust my petty neuroses with one deft twist of a spanner. Skulls greasily opened, shining with hydraulic fluid in the operating theater. Are we all robots under the flesh?

And the flesh is just machinery writ small.

He finished and came back up, resurfaced for a breath of conditioned, artificial air. The lights of the shipworld were dimming now, the collective, insensate soul of the 'net cannibalized to a different function. Without software, the machinery is inert, and now the minds would have to be in the wires once again. He wondered palely how much danger there would be. Theoretically little—Brendan had practically fed himself to Centrum, and, with the Bright Illimit's GAM-and-Redux as the only point of contact between them and it, how could they be caught? They could always break contact, and Tem had included the small subroutine to do that in any number of places in the program. A simple error/break. He was confident it would be enough, but if he was wrong . . . Centrum would get a particularly rich haul.

In the end, when it had been explained and demonstrated, they all came to be part of the great show, to be actors and prime movers on the multipolar stage that had been so long in erecting itself. In some fashion, those who had been united in the Falling Ring knew that they had to be here. At first John held out, reluctant to give himself over to a power so closely associated with Brendan, but, inspired by the apparent heroism of the others, he too had decided to go along. They sat mute, staring and perhaps fearful, all plugged into the wires that had dominated their lives in different ways. Krzakwa looked them over. "Well, we're ready." He remembered

Brendan saying, "As ready as we'll ever be," and felt weary. "I can't really explain what I did, and I don't think many of you would understand it, but . . . OK. We used the major operating routines from the Illimitor World to fill up Brendan's Machine. With its help, we ought to be able to find our way around in Centrum. It'll give some meaningful structure to what we find. *Maybe* we'll find what's left of him in there and drag what we can back. Are you set?"

John said, "What should we expect?"

The Selenite shrugged, keeping his face blank. "Demogorgon? No? Well, frankly, John, we can't say exactly. Our senses should report something very like the landscape of Bright Illimit. Really, it should be safe—ninety-seven percent of the circuitry is designed *just* to safeguard our personalities. What that actually entails, I don't know . . . I mean, what it will feel like." He looked around at them and saw that there was no point in further delay, and turned to Demogorgon. "This is the one," he said, tapping a lead that was attached to his head in a position near the left angular gyrus. "You'll know what to do when the time comes."

"I understand."

"Do you? I'm not sure I believe that. It's your choice, though. I told you what might happen."

The other nodded. "Like you said, it's my choice. Let's do it," he muttered, mimicking the words of a man more than a lifetime dead.

"Everybody get comfortable, in case this takes a long time. We don't want any kinks here." He smiled to himself. There would be no pressure gangrene in the almost zero gravity of Ocypete. Still, they arrayed themselves about the floor, assuming their habitual sleeping postures, each knowing that this would be a personal nexus for them, a moment, once the program was activated, from which they could never return. And their minds quickened, pondering what was more than mere life or death, but the infinite shading of gray spanning the gap between. They were embarking on a rainbow bridge, Bifrost, to take its place. Along separate paths, each mind questioned the power of their protective Heimdall, but the thing had progressed too far for any backward turning now. . . .

Instead of the convenient but inefficient circlets of common use, they sprouted induction leads from their scalps, tucked in at the roots of their hair, and they were overloaded. Demogorgon, the familiar of his own lifework, wore more than double his usual number of cables, become the maintainer of the effort they would make. Krzakwa wished once again for the direct physical taps into his own circuitry that would remove the hundred-angstrom uncertainty in the induction field.

Brendan's body was energized, brought to the full level of its inherent ability. The shell waited, hoping for a return of its master, ready to unleash the demonic, primitive being that lurked at its physical core. With the circuit completed, open but untuned, they could all feel it waiting: a creature laid bare, stripped from beneath the layers of a hundred-million-year evolutionary path. It might be of some use. . . .

"Your show, Demogorgon. . . ."

"Right." Compressing his lips, eyes unfocusing with concentration, Demo thought his new command sequences and, in a wash of mingled wills, they went under and down.

Bright Illimit.

And again.

Again . . .

Demogorgon appeared alone on the middle of a clean white dais, standing in high-booted feet on a tough, somewhat resilient material, and noted the slightly diminished Earth gravity normal to the Illimitor World. All around was a sparsely grassed flat tundra, much of it a desiccated mud flat, cracked and clay-red. The sky was a winter cobalt blue flattened by the broken clouds which lined the horizon like a collar. A gusty wind fluttered from every compass point, plucking at the loose, cloth-of-green-gold combat uniform he wore. He felt the covered hilt of his golden sword Halaton at one hip, and a lozenge-shaped pistol on the other. Everything seemed right, although he couldn't identify this actual terrain with any he recalled creating. There was neither sun nor shadow.

The platform sat on a courseway, a white road seemingly bleached into the otherwise naturalistic countryside, running off into the far distance. At its end, beyond the clouds, lay a faint blue shadow, a dark, almost empurpled thing, mountainlike. When he squinted hard, Demogorgon could make out shimmering, crenellated battlements, towers, and the instruments that would resist a siege. Like a sea mirage, the castle was disconnected from the horizon, floating, and he knew that, if he concentrated, he would see that the world dropped away from that citadel. There would be no earth there, no sea, no fire; just air. The elements of the world converged.

Briefly, Sealock's face, the face of the GAM, floated huge above him, looking down through featureless blue eyes, holes in its face that showed the sky behind. Demo shivered, and beckoned the others.

Harmon and Vana blinked into existence side by side a fraction of a second apart, clad in identical oversized gray tunics, the lustrous cloth bound in place with thin leather bands at waist and shoulder. Silver swords and ancient wheel-lock guns dangled from hip webbing. John appeared alone, holding a metallic blue machete, wearing a tight-fitting white shirt and trousers, with an emblem on his chest that showed twin eclipsing moons, their faces seamed by irregular canals. He wore a long white cape and had a small, modern-style sidearm in a holster that hung from his thigh, an energy weapon of some sort. Beth appeared behind him then, clad in a pale blue jumpsuit, similarly armed. She looked more like herself than any of the others, less enhanced. Ariane came, dressed in white also. Her sole weapon was a slim, rifle-like device, a delicate thing of lenses and indigo crystalline rods. Axie appeared in a diaphanous swirl of pale green fabric. She carried nothing, but the diadem about her temples had a red gem that glittered dangerously. There was a long pause and then Temujin Krzakwa came into existence. He was dressed in flowing black robes and had a massive sword at his hip. Over one shoulder he carried a heavy iron weapon, its snout a blued metal cylinder. It had complex controls on its stock and, with them, instructions stenciled in white. Demogorgon squinted and could make out one line: it said, MISSILE PRE-HEAT.

Stiffly they came together, staring at the outlines of Centrum's castle in the distance. Krzakwa looked around. "Somehow," he said, "I expected more than this."

Ariane nodded. "With so much to draw from . . . It could be more compact."

"It's giving us room to negotiate," said Demogorgon. "A big world means options, choices. . . . We can't have expected it to be cut and dried. I'm surprised, actually, that so far everything is so comprehensible."

"Well, with this white Brick Road, and dark Oz on the horizon, our choices seem pretty clear cut," said the Selenite, "but we don't want to be too predictable. There's no telling what might happen."

"Maybe we should head in the opposite direction," said Cornwell. "Though I doubt that would accomplish much."

"Probably not." Demo walked slowly to the edge of the platform and looked out into the arid wasteland. "We may as well try to make contact." He turned back to face them. "No reason for us to walk, is there?" Without waiting for a reply, he clasped his right hand to his left shoulder, then whipped it about in a salute-like motion, thinking his control calls. Eight of the gray, three-legged riding beasts of Arhos appeared: heavy, three-eyed creatures called *thers*. Taxonomically somewhere between an elephant and a vastly overstuffed footstool, the creatures were telepathically controlled, each keyed to an individual.

Harmon stared at the one that approached him, looking into its limpid brown eyes. It was the size of a small house. "How are you supposed to mount . . . Oh!" He looked up and the animal had crouched down on two of its legs to make a perfect thirty-degree ramp with its third. Delighted, he clambered up the leg and sat himself on the cushion of soft flesh in the center of its disk-shaped body.

When the rest had mounted up, they began to ride. The thers stayed in a compact group and were faster than they looked, propelling themselves into a sinusoidal canter that was totally at variance with their appearance.

**316**

□ □ □

In the distance, Centrum awoke to itself, feeling slightly uneasy, a faint itch that was inaccessible to its full consciousness. Something, it realized, is wrong. What? The failing program was a constant danger. . . .

After a time of riding they dismounted to let their mounts rest and feed from a great clump of tall, red-flowered grass. Demogorgon gesticulated a series of camp seats and they made themselves at home. The thers demonstrated their peculiar method of gathering food, revealing a set of scythelike claws on the hoof of the third leg with which they sliced down the weed and carried it to their delicate mouths. For all intents, the goal the adventurers had set themselves was no nearer, although the dais they had started from was long disappeared behind them. The white path continued onward.

Demogorgon stood finally and, for perhaps the thousandth time, scanned the blank horizon. The land had grown a bit rockier, showing gray outcroppings from the dry mud here and there. As he turned he was astounded to find a wet concrete wall before him. Déjà vu assailed him. . . .

Achmet Aziz el-Tabari was sixteen years old and the world was Paris Free City. The Family was here and he the scion, fading stars of obsolete 3V screen and antiquated stage. They dreamed their dreams of the past and practiced a dying art to no avail, hopeless for the future, beautiful in wastage and decay. He wandered the dark streets and became trapped within himself.

Three men had him in an alley. They were tall and heavy and very dark, bestial, a rough gutter argot their only tongue. They laughed as they stripped him and smiled as they fingered his slim, brown flesh. "Ce putanne, trop de ant-zaftig!" said one, running rough fingers over his hairless chest, pinching sharply at his nipples. "Il-y-est parfait, ma soeur," said another, cupping a broad palm across one slim buttock.

They turned him over then and set him across the edge of some concrete stairs. They were about to begin their complex deed. Achmet gasped finally and said, "Wait. . . ." Un-

**3 1 7**

accountably, they waited. "Not this way." He knelt before one of the men and began fumbling at the front of his trousers.

The man laughed and said, "Ça c'est maricon!" The others giggled. He was unclean. It was a great, sticky thing that burst out at him, but he did it anyway, trying to preserve himself. The man smiled mindlessly and was clean when he was done. The creature patted him on the head and moved away.

The others seized him then and threw him back across the stairs, despite his cries of protest, and used him as they would, one at each end. When they were done, they left him in the darkness and he wandered off, burning.

Not the first time, not the last. Usually he sought them out, nicer denizens of the better-lighted places, but sometimes they caught him like this. Forces impelled him to go on. He could not remain in the safe sterility of the Home.

He walked on.

Two years older, he sat in his studio, staring at a half-finished canvas. Sleet drizzled out of a gray November sky, splashing, freezing in strata on the dirty-paned skylight, an artifact put there for men who pretended to a filthy grandeur almost two centuries gone. They recovered the past, pretension their game, goal, and reward.

The painting waited, castles and sky in the background, green forest to the sides, animal in the foreground. It was not the stuff of great art, by any means, but it satisfied him to try to create a scenario from his fantasies. Before him, on a green-carpeted floor, sat a stuffed tiger. He muttered to himself. Alia was, as usual, quite late.

The door opened and she came in, clad in white linen pajamas. She undressed quickly, long blond hair flashing to her moves, and, slim-hipped, went to sprawl on the tiger. She said nothing and was not apologetic. Models do as they please and the world lives up to their expectations.

Achmet sighed. Her hair was matted again. He picked up a little soft-bristled hairbrush that he kept just for her and came forward. He teased the hair, pulling out the knots with care, casting away the white dandruff encrustations. Was it a

**318**

coincidence that someone so beautiful should be so uncon-
cerned for her appearance? Women could be such disgusting
creatures.

She cuffed at his hand, giggling, and, when he continued to
brush at her, moved her hips suggestively. He coughed and
went back to his easel suddenly. She continued to titter long
after he had set the carburetor on the brush and begun to
paint.

Two years older, he lay in the semidark of his midnight
bedroom, reading about the Peloponnesian Wars. His nameless lover slept at his side, snoring through half-open soiled
lips. The face looked bruised with the summation of prolonged lust. The boy, whoever he was, looked like an injured
child, his soft blond hair curling about his nape in tiny wisps
and strands. He felt a renewed stirring, somewhere deep
within, but ignored it. Enough was, he supposed, enough.

He turned the page of the book and a name jumped off at
him out of context: Demogorgon. Ah! It was evocative and
moved into him instantly, nestling deep within his psyche.
Now that was more like it! He'd been casting about for a
name for years and never found a satisfactory one. His generation put classical Greek cognomens in vogue and their sub-
culture moved throughout the free cities of the world at a
constant level. They were a world society, almost strangled
under the growing weight of the rules, but surviving handily
in these little pockets of antiquity.

He had a name. Now he needed a design.

Sighing, he put down the book and turned to sprawl across
the boy, who continued to snore gently. No sense waking him
up.

He turned him carefully over onto his stomach and parted
his legs, felt the soft flesh of his buttocks, and found his place,
still ready. He eased within and paused, feeling the dark heat
with gratitude.

He moved, and fell away into mindlessness.

*Demogorgon.*

It fitted.

**319**

□ □ □

Two years older, he put on a circlet for the first time and began his sublimation to Comnet. Dreams within dreams he cycled down and around. It surprised him with pleasure.

His mind went into the wires on other people's wings and he flew, seeing the possibilities. He tried to learn the way but it was beyond him, frustrating him. He looked for assistance as the ideas grew into grandeur. When he found it, the new art form was born. It was a long gestation. Hundreds of cascading experiences, small in themselves, built into a framework of desire, a mature, full-blown version of his childish desire to create. Without warning this house of cards tipped and fell, sliding memories breaking into the cloud-rimmed sky of the Illimitor World.

Dumbfounded, his original turning continued. Ariane was there, and Tem, and the rest. Confusion that he knew must mirror his own showed on their faces. "We were with you," said Vana.

"I know," he said.

Centrum began to feel the invaders, multiplying like a disease through its subsystems. It was an alien program moving through its circuits, stronger than any taken in before. Demanding action, it cast about for the ancient means of its defenses.

Circle back through the memories. There must have been a way, though in the beginning there had been nothing to fear, no other life. The Starseeders thought of everything. Their successors developed what was needed.

The years began to reverse themselves as the stack pointers moved back through the files, activating search commands. It was located.

Though its physical sensorium was frozen and meaningless, it was as yet unnecessary. There were no physical invaders. That did not make them less dangerous . . . rather more so.

Deep within its memory, work vacuoles began to stir, to form themselves in a composite conceptual being, set to go about their tasks after an agelong silence, after a time of nonbeing.

The first primitive intelligences began to awake, too simple to wonder who or where they were. It went on.

To Ariane, this was not at all like a dream. A hard, sharp reality composed of a world, her friends, and the improbable thers. But in the moments after reliving sections of Demogorgon's past, which had seemed just as real, there was a strong sense of disbelief which could find no handhold in the realism around her. The camp chair bit into her thighs. "How," she said, "do memories function within this program?" She started to stand and, perhaps not surprised, became incorporeal. It ran like a film. . . .

She flew on the wire without imagery, an electronic ghost of herself cruising the circuits of Globo Entertainment Net in search of the glitches that bedeviled the commercial paradise. The world was without form, and void, save for when she stepped into the comlines of others, checking to see if a sensed power surging had disturbed anything.

A bright spark up ahead . . .

. . . and a bulbous sheik sat in the midst of his harem in a gorgeous turquoise-encrusted canvas pavilion that rustled in the gentle, dry breezes blowing in off the blindingly bright silver desert. Enormous turbaned eunuchs (mostly black but with a few token Caucasians to avoid a lawsuit) stood silhouetted at every entry point, heavy-bladed falchions at the ready. There were a hundred women here, every one of them slim and dark and willing. They rubbed his hands and feet, fed him and sucked at him as he sighed, mindless . . .

. . . she dropped out of the circuit, smirking somehow within. Why did they do it? People took from the wires something that was readily available in the real world. Why bother? Especially considering that they were powerless to affect the outcome, could only feel and not do . . . yes, for a certain kind of person, perhaps that was a reason in itself. A spark flared ugly red nearby and she drove swiftly toward it, rescuing superheroine . . .

. . . a woman lay in the strong, gentle arms of her Armenian lover and suddenly screamed. The dark, hawk-faced man began to melt LSD-style, flesh, then muscles, then bone dribbling away, eyes flattening and trickling down onto her breasts, dripping to the carpet from erect, sensitive nipples. She screamed and strong hands suddenly burst through the wall and slapped him back together. The woman sighed and resumed her kissing, tasting the man's sweet tongue. . . .

Behind the walls of pseudoreality, Ariane finished patching the damned thing and sailed off, feeling smug. Have to alert the Assembly monitor about that one. The foolish program was interactive enough to accumulate errata after a few hundred uses and disturb the paying customers. Most 'net works were stable, could only do a few prescribed action-sequence choices forking from predefined nexi, but they were getting more complex, better, as those who controlled the 'net relaxed the rules, more assured of their technology. This only made her job more difficult, since many of the sequences were assembled by free-lancers, and bugs proliferated.

Another spark, cool blue, and she peeked at it briefly. . . .

. . . The man stood before a huge, formally garbed audience. He was handsome, and young for his heavy responsibility, and seemed well liked by the people he served. "Ask not what your country . . ." he began, in rich, mellow tones, directly contravening two centuries of political ideal . . .

. . . and she dropped away. Historical dramas were even less to her taste than sexy romances. Well, everybody to their own preferences.

*End Circuit-run* said the Assembly monitor, and she dropped back to the real world, shift ended. Ah, the heady life of a practical engineer! She pulled the induction leads from her scalp and, nodding to her PM replacement at the monitor boards, went home through the bright, living streets of the Arcology.

Brendan was there as usual, waiting in her room in preference to his own.

They lay together in the semidarkness and she felt his ears on her thighs, the sharp rasp of his whiskers scratching at her pudenda. His tongue sent flashes of delight expanding away from her groin and she felt pity for the people whose experiences were delineated by 'net-borne pornography.

She ran her fingers through his hair, feeling the brain-taps embedded in his skull, and rocked her hips to the rhythms of his real-world face. Somehow, dimly, I know, she thought. Where is the satisfaction of having an imaginary creature do this for me? I might as well have a robot. . . . But a real man . . . Ah . . . The strength of it clutched at her and an orgasm began its explosive course. She sighed and held his head fast, pushing against his now still face until it was over. He crawled up her body and entered her.

She stroked his sweaty back and waited patiently for him to finish.

They were back, reeling from a paroxysm of memories. The thers had not moved, nothing had changed, yet it seemed a little darker, colder, as if a season closer to midwinter had enveloped them.

"OK, who's next?" asked Tem gruffly.

John looked hard at Demogorgon. "Are we powerless to keep these . . . memories from engulfing us? Is it our program or"—he gestured at the distant castle—"its?"

"I think I know what's happening," said the Arab. "We're being strengthened, united. It must be a continuation of the process begun among us before; you weren't with us, John, but the GAM is trying to . . . help us become whole. These shared memories are part of that."

Tem, still waiting to be submerged into another memory chain, spoke tentatively. "On the other hand, Centrum might be stealing these experiences as it did Brendan's. I'm pretty sure that if it was the Artifact doing this we would know. Shit. I don't know. Who's for stopping this, right now? It can be done."

No one spoke.

"All right," said Demogorgon. "We go on."

The thers were tethered a little distance away, snatching clawfuls of feathery blue and roan grass that had grown just for them, and the people sat around a little campfire, toasting shishkebab and marshmallows, talking. No further flashbacks had interrupted the smooth flow of the program, and they had begun almost to enjoy the prospects for adventure before them. They discussed options, having Demo materialize a skimmer for them to simply fly to their encounter with the Centrum, but he pointed out that the more he interfered with its operation the less the interface program could do to determine the scenarios under which the contact would take place. It knew what was best for them. They hoped. . . .

There had been little enough conversation on this adventure thus far and now their speech was, perforce, desultory. Axie said, "It's ironic, but I never have felt as close to anyone as I do to all of you, now. We seem like a particularly lucky people." It was happy-sounding, but they could sense nothing from her.

"Adversity always brings people together," said Harmon.

"No, it's more than that," said Beth. "We are being continually presented with the most forceful evidence that we are the same . . . literally, the same. Where DR enhanced differences, incompatibilities . . . this is so different."

"Don't get carried away," said Tem, pulling a kebab out of the fire. "I don't think we should trust all of our feelings while under the influence of the program. After all, it can synthesize feelings as easily as anything else."

"Oh?" said Vana haughtily. "And just what should we trust if not our emotions?"

"She's right, Tem," said Ariane. "We can't lose faith in ourselves."

The Selenite looked apologetic, sucking at a piece of onion. "That's not what I meant."

Axie regarded the bearded man. "We've come a long way in a short time, Temujin. It's only right that there should be some skepticism." She reached past the fire and patted him on the shoulder. "But words, even here, are stilted. They ring hollow in my own ears. Believe me when I say—"

"Shut up!" Demogorgon loomed up, more impressive now than even his Arhos persona. He pointed into the distance: a group of pinpoints, lights like burning ashes from a fire, floated at an unknowable distance against the blue of the sky, arrayed at random above the castle. Thus far the world had seemed a personal thing, their own to explore. Now, suddenly, the first sign of a power other than theirs was revealed.

"What are those?" asked Ariane, and they could all feel a keying up of interiors, as their nerves began to wind tight.

Krzakwa stood up, gripping his missile weapon. "I don't know and can't guess," he said, "but I think we should assume they are enemy hostiles."

Demogorgon drew his sword, a deadly metallic whisper. "Can they really kill us?" That was from Vana.

The Selenite shrugged. "No way to tell. I think we ought to behave as if they can." He sighted in the device, carefully twirling little verniers, peering into a tiny plasma screen that contained an enlarged image of the approaching things. They were blurred and indistinct, twinkling slightly from the intervening atmosphere.

He punched up the preheat and armed his warhead, an em-field generator with coils set to discharge. He breathed out in a soft sigh and hit the lock-on switch, then held himself still. He pushed the launch button.

A roar of sound disturbed their world, rolling thunder with nothing to echo from, and a splash of reddish-orange flame wreathed Tem for a moment. It hurled away, first a flaming rocket, then a bright fleck at the head of a narrow, misty contrail. The targets did nothing to disperse and the missile buried itself in their midst.

There was a moment of ringing silence, a bright flash that turned the sky pink and made them all flinch. An expanding ball of yellow fire shot with violet made the sky brassy and, for a moment, everything was very still. A roar. A shock wave, an air front tugging at their costumes. The world came back to normal with an impossible suddenness. There were fewer of the pinpoints, a hole in their formation, but still they were there.

They expanded, growing before their eyes as if from small to large rather than far to near. They moved with a speed that should have generated a sonic shock cone but did not. The things were silent. Tem cursed and, throwing down his missile projector, drew a sword. Someone made a strange half whine in the background, perhaps all of them, perhaps no one.

The things were upon them, nightmarishly resolvable.

The vanguard thing approached, bearing in on them swiftly. It was a balloon with a horrid face, red eyes hate-glaring, half its substance open with a black, tooth-fringed mouth. It seemed to chuckle as it flew. Hungry. Hungry, it said to them.

Demogorgon drew his magic pistol and fired. He stood before them like a mythopoeic hero, legs widespread, body tall and muscular, gripping a sword in one hand and a gun in the other.

Glittering pink and purple rays reached out to touch the creature as it roared in for a quick kill, white cartoon sparkles writhing around its spherical flesh. It stopped dead, the world a motionless frame in isolation, then exploded. Thin black threads rained down and the world was in motion again.

A score of the things swooped down on the thers, mouths gaping in starving shark grins. Teeth sank together and bones crunched, legs writhed, dark blood covered the ground in spatters. The animals bleated in agony, scrambling, and were gone, sucked to bloated, happy interiors.

Axie glared and her diadem threw a red ray outward. The nearest monster screamed an echoing cry and soared upward. It burst into tawny flames and staggered against the sky, then fell, trailing a long plume of greasy smoke. There was an explosion at some distance.

More of the things circled and came in at them.

Toothy leers in tight V formation darkened their view. John and Beth stood side by side, guns held two-handed in a crouching stance. They pulled triggers in unison and sheets of transparent fire lanced out. Creatures were riven. Harmon and Vana knelt back to back with them, shooting their old-style guns and barely coping with their exaggerated recoils. Their guns roared, throwing explosive charges away in gouts of fire and smoke. Punctured, the creatures burst apart and threads rained down like long black snow. Ariane's beam flailed about, an indigo whip trailing destruction. More of the

**326**

things came swooping in, ten to replace each one downed. There was an endless supply of them, it seemed.

Temujin Krzakwa stood alone, dispatching the ones that penetrated their shield of modern fire. He whirled his broad-bladed sword in figure eights, closing with the demons and slicing so many that he was covered with the ropy, gray gore that they discharged. As he fought, a kind of magnificent numbness came over him. He was going to heaven, he was already there.

Then, without warning, the sword slipped out of his grasp and went flying. Fear lanced at him, and he wanted to hide. Self-born images of the crystalline teeth shearing though his flesh, breaking his bones. A final agony knifing inward as his bowels were torn asunder. He looked and one of the things bobbed against him, for all the world like a toy balloon; there was a red halo around it and it was gone. More disappeared in red coruscation, and Aksinia smiled and gave him a little salute. His sword came back to him hilt first on a rosy ray. He smiled back and resumed his slashing.

Something like Chopin's funeral march sonata began to play. There were too many of them! They were becoming a single entity in the circuits of Centrum, their program the defining factor of Bright Illimit. We will be eaten alive! Querulous despair assailed them all, flooding them with a common source of feeling and a unity of thought. Will we really die? Can we? Hopes of a real haven in abundance, waking up on Ocypete in their real bodies, mission failed.

But even if we can escape, thought Demo, Brendan is still in here, his discharge real, his entrapment impenetrable. And if we can't, we will be added to him, in unity with the dark thing that lives forever. . . .

A dull sound of tearing flannel alerted them.

A giant anteater tongue flashed crimson from the heavens, licked up the monsters all at once, flickering bloodily before them, and was gone. A feeling of joy, a smirking satiation briefly filled the space about them. They stood alone again, quiescent, sweating.

"What was *that?*" asked Harmon.

"Evolution unveiled," said Tem, sheathing his sword, swaying with tightly closed eyes.

Vana slumped to the ground and saw the demon entrails subliming into nonexistence precisely as had neon regolith. "They ate our thers," she said. The place where the campfire had been was wiped clean.

Demogorgon put his weapons away and stood tall and still. Clasping hand to shoulder, he made his motion again, and thought his command thoughts. Nothing happened.

"We've lost something," he said.

And, suddenly, they were elsewhere. . . .

Vana Berenguer and Ariane Methol ran along the roof of Tupamaro Arcology, flying a kite. This part of the building was almost a mile high and had an immense park of many acres on its roof. There was deep soil here, supporting grass and trees and little streams, fields of flowers and little ponds. There were many people, children and poets, and there was a lot of laughter. The sky was pale blue, supporting a herd of fleecy clouds that kept pace with each other against the background of the sun. A sense of universal summer pervaded their insensate feelings.

They ran, and the diamond shape of paper grew away from them on its downward-bulging, white string stem. It was dark green, with a red, grinning face against the sky. They stood still, panting, and watched it fly. "Good day for it," said Ariane, holding the roll of filament. "Just enough wind."

Vana nodded and watched it grow tiny, falling into an invisible distance. The string tautened, rising into the sky and disappearing long before it reached the kite, which seemed to float unsupported, far away yet held to them by some sort of inanimate loyalty. She felt the sweat trickling between her breasts, felt the delicate skin of her nipples engorged, rubbing against the inside of her halter. She stood closer to Ariane, touching flesh with her in little taps of breathing movement. The space inside her shorts seemed steaming, moistened by the exertion and rubbings of the run. She exhaled, a long breath, and relaxed. She dropped to the grass, sitting cross-legged.

**328**

Nothing to say, nothing to think, nothing to reason about, she smiled brightly at the land and sky and clouds. Light and shadow played on Ariane's skin, outlining her strong, delicate muscles. She was nice to look at. She stretched, arching her back, and, standing again, twirled about, letting impressions of the parkscape flood in upon her. She stood still and watched a group of small girls playing jump rope nearby, saying loud rhymes in Spanish to each other and giggling when one faltered or fell rolling to the grass.

She whacked Ariane on the buttocks, eliciting a yip of surprise, and ran away. She ran away across the park to the edge of the roof, up a flight of stairs to the top of the wall, and fled along a chain-link fence, looking down at the blue and gold of her world. She grinned as she ran, breathing freely, sweating all over herself and her clothes, limbs swinging in an animal freedom, lubricated by the juices of an unthinking aliveness. She ran on and on until darkness fell down the sky and then went home to a man and more muscular thrusting in the dark and light. Images without form dazzled her consciousness and time stretched on to eternity.

Seven Red Anchorelles awoke to himself with a startled pheromonic cry: I still live?

His body still seemed real, the same hard-squid shape and form that had always, it seemed, existed, but he had memories. Life in the ship in the shadows of a Starseeder ghost. Life and work and the end. The last despairing moments as Centrum soaked in his oil flooded over him: death in Unity, his oil dispersed and turned to the irrevocable electronic incantations of the immortal brain that controlled his life. Why am I here? And how?

He looked about him. Row on row of sleeping Seedees were stacked against the sky, awaiting the command to awaken. This was not supposed to be possible. They were all gone forever, he knew that. Somehow, they were all to live again, subjected to some kind of mysterious resurrection process, brought to life again in the complexes of an eternal circuitry. How? He thought about it, his renewed oil, if such it

**329**

was, coursing with excitement. Obviously, something new had been added to the dark equations of reality.

Centrum began to speak within him, a thing it had never been able to do before. A curious double entity tracked along its voice, a different being, writ large with it, a new, unconscious dominance in the old being.

You have work to perform, it said, its voice echoic in nature, two thought-tracks merging with his consciousness in a strange, intractable fashion. Centrum seemed angry with itself, almost schizoidal. Mother Ocean has been invaded by a disease. The product of the Grand Design has gone wrong. Things must be rectified. The invaders must be repelled.

Sent away?

No. We must have all that is within them. There is a greater cosmos waiting without and we must have a way of dealing with it. Absorb them all. I will reach out and take what is theirs into myself. I must be supreme once again.

7red wondered at the meaning of it all, but the voice of God said, Go thou! and he went.

He sailed away from the massed, sleeping ranks of all the beings that ever lived, the first scout of his renewed kind, to be in the proud vanguard of an unending, everlasting horde. He should have been overjoyed, but a shadow of unhappiness followed him, troubling the smooth flow of his liquid thoughts. What was wrong? He pondered as he flew, marveling at the changes in his world. Something had gone wrong. . . . No, he realized. Something had always been wrong. He merged with a waiting work vacuole and fled into the limpid depths of the blue sky, staring hard through its enhanced senses.

Something was happening ahead, and he squinted to see what it was, eager to discover the form of the invaders. The sense of wrongness left him disquieted. He had no reason to live again, but here he was. Something had happened to Centrum. What?

He wondered if Cooloil would live again and wished for her presence. He had always missed her. He could feel the circuits all about him, and suddenly realized he could remember bits and pieces of that great dark time when he had been part of the unified mind. I am not real! he thought. His own oil had long ago dissipated. The body he inhabited now was just an image, held in the cold imagination of Centrum. It recreates me as a mere subroutine! He wondered at the source of this new terminology. I am dead, still, never to live again. But he felt real within himself, even knowing that consciousness was an illusion. Maybe it had always been. . . .

He felt a flood of horror course through him, but the battle was before him now, already joined.

Harmon Prynne was lying on his bed in the darkness alone, hands laced behind his head, staring into the black depths of an invisible ceiling and waiting for sleep to come. He'd been living in Tupamaro Arcology for seven months now, and sometimes wondered why he'd come. He and Vana were more or less living together, as much as anyone ever did in the free-wheeling life of a modern urban monad, but it was a troublesome state. She came and went as she pleased and his complaints about her behavior were not only ignored, they seemed to go unnoticed.

He reached down under the comforting sheets and rubbed a hand slowly across his crotch, feeling a responsive stiffening, and wondered about himself. I'm a human itch, he thought reflectively, waiting to be scratched. He grinned in the darkness and took his hand away, enjoying the weight of an unused erection. Couldn't do it in Key West, he remembered. Couldn't do it at all. I wonder why? Was it the racing?

An image came to him that filled the world with light. He was walking along a corridor in Tupamaro's ElComPod complex, carrying a bag of tools, headed for the engineer's station. He'd been hired to come here and fix up some waveguide panels by a contractor, and he came to get the purchasing credit for his work.

He entered the immaculate room and stared. The engineer was a slim, beautiful Spanish woman with strikingly intelligent eyes clad in a crisp linen dress that highlighted her eye-clutching breasts. He stared at her, eyes sweeping up and down her frame. God! She was a total beauty! "Engineer

**331**

Methol?" he asked, a catch in his voice. She nodded, turning away, and he felt slightly nauseous, lust tearing at him against his will. How could he work with something like this?

There was another woman there, sitting in the corner behind a console, and when he turned to look at her they locked eyes, his head canting sharply downward to face her, as if forced by a hand. He stared into her black-dark eyes, almost oblivious to the ripeness of her somewhat stocky form. Her arms were brown and supple.

This woman grinned at him. "Hi!" she said. "I'm Ariane's friend, Vana Berenguer!"

The door of his bedroom popped open suddenly, spilling light from the hall and calling him back from his dreamland. It was Vana, springing lightly toward him, shedding clothes as she came. The door closed by itself, plunging them into darkness again, but the rustle of cloth continued.

She sprang on the bed, bouncing and naked, and nuzzled against the skin of his chest. She was hot, drenched with sweat, and he wondered where she'd been. She ran her face down his chest, nibbling at his stomach and giggling.

Rhythmic motions drew him out of himself and made him unable to think, made him a slave. He didn't mind at all just then. . . .

What he felt, as her hips pounded up and down atop him, was a sense of belonging, not just to her but to the human race. It gave him a delicate sense of self-worth to know that this woman desired his flesh, when she could have any flesh that she wanted. He laughed into the face of the night and clasped her writhing form tight against him, feeling the muscles of her back straining under his hands. She was panting, short, sharp breaths through her open mouth. At these moments he knew he loved her above all else in the world.

It overcame him. His orgasm began, throbbing heavily, and she cried out briefly, shuddering as she settled down into a quiet, sweating stillness.

Unaccountably, they said nothing more, and Prynne imagined that it was because nothing needed to be said. After a while Vana got up and went to the bathroom. She came back

**332**

to bed with a snack, crackers, cheese, and some sweet beverage. They shared it and he dozed in her arms.

Seven Red Anchorelles hovered a long way from the battle, watching carefully through the amplified senses of his old work vacuole. He knew it wasn't the same one, that reality was a long time dead, but it *seemed* the same and that was all that counted. His released oil circulated in the narrow space outside his shell and reported to him all that was happening.

The defensive spheres were gathered about the invaders now, subunits of Centrum's newly expanded consciousness attacking the alien program segments in swift movements of artificial thought. Like me, thought 7red, things of the imagination. The invaders fought back with their own electronic weaponry, bending the inner world to their will, providing an imagery that satisfied their mysterious needs. By all rights, the spheres should win, for they were closer to the source of their power. And yet . . .

Something was happening. A sense of greater power at immense distance pervaded the scene. It was as if a giant, invisible cable stretched upward to near infinity, providing a link with some massive entity lurking beyond the gentle blue of the sky. 7red expanded his horizons.

A tenuous being stood over the battle, watching. It had the same strange, mobile appearance as the aliens, and blank space where its eyes should have been. There was something familiar about it. . . . There was some resemblance that connected the thing with the weird echo that dogged the voice of Centrum. It seemed to be looking at him.

It ended suddenly, shockingly. The brooding presence, the overseer, abruptly transformed itself into a great leathery creature that looked a bit like the memory of unknown origin identified with the ancient, extinct Starseeders. The being's mouth opened, a yawning, fiery pit, and the spheres were sucked away into nothingness.

7red felt stunned. How well prepared they were! Now he knew why Centrum had brought them all back from the grave. This was no ordinary menace that they faced. . . .

And yet . . .

Another presence made itself felt, not the invaders but something connected with Centrum itself. A pair of immense, cold, blue-stained eyes opened out of the void next to him and stared, a glittering, icy, emotionless look of measurement. The phenomenon lasted only the briefest instant, but 7red was chilled. I know it now, he thought. No matter what happens, this imaginary life I and all my kind have been granted will be all too brief. If the aliens win, we are lost. And even if Centrum triumphs, we will all be put away again, probably forever. We are here as mere weapons, to be used and discarded. He felt the beginnings of rage. Had it always been thus?

In the hierarchy of things, this requisition was perhaps little better than a note for the Suggestion File. Temujin slipped his hand into the warm sanctuary of his armpit and flexed the fingers until they began to lose the frozen stiffness. Another breach drill had left this section of Peirce a low-pressure icebox. No, there would be no official link with the Comnet people. Despite their continued advances in practical hard mathematics, despite the ease with which an exchange could be set up, it would not be. And to ask for even a brief contact with someone down there could be viewed as dangerously heterodoxical. Fuck them, he murmured, then repeated the phrase to himself for maximum adumbration. He chuckled. Tem was glad he could amuse himself so easily.

He sat, with a fart quickening in his bowels, and stuck an induction lead to his head. He hoped it wasn't a particularly smelly one, since the circulation system was probably cycled down. He held tight the sphincter of his anus and the gas came out slowly, silently. No odor. Good. There was nothing he would've liked less than to have Margaret come upon him alone, an aroma of unquestionable origin making the room even less habitable.

Data about the overflow of neutrons from the high-density containment field that was his pet project began to come into his brain, arrayed in a four-dimensional histogram of his own devising. With methodical dispatch he began tugging at a datum here, pushing there, hoping to pull some hidden asymmetry from the information that would explain the anomalies. Equations of flux, representing possible new theories of chromodynamic interaction, were fitted into the hypergraph like the meshing of an antique clock. He keyed in a systematized differential and, waiting for realtime changes, finally saw a flag indicating the match of the equation with the data. Ah, Tem thought: is this the beginning of Krzakwa Space? Or is the old spanner in the machinery showing itself?

Damn it! That's why these things have to be compared with the work on Earth. There is absolutely no way to tell. I'd have to build an entire duplicate to tell. What a joke. "There's no redundancy on the Moon." So another cat stays in its bag.

An interrupt light glared red at him from the porta-desk. Mentally, Tem hooked into the communication and found a simple word message: "Meet me at the canteen at break—Hugo Sergio." It was rather odd: Tem knew that this was probably going to be one of the illicit gabs Hugo Sergio had been initiating recently and that, as usual, a few tidbits of gossip that he had somehow acquired would be passed. But the man had never contacted him through a standard link before. He was getting careless.

Well, it was nearly break, and he was at a dead end, so Tem shut down his stem link and stood. The canteen Hugo meant was the one serving the twelve halls of Wedge 4, which was a good ten-minute walk. He pushed aside the now limp pressure seal and came out into the even colder hall, a glance showing him that it was awaiting renorming in its turn. He jogged, painfully out of breath almost immediately, down the endless-seeming corridor and at last reached the center concourse, passing through an energy portal into the heat and pressure of the crowded hub. He stood panting, slightly bent over, until the engirdling pains lessened. In the congested flow of the hub ring he was repeatedly bumped into and jostled until he felt as if he would be trampled. Slowly, he made his way to the canteen, which was extraordinarily crowded, and searched the faces that lined the standing tables until he found the hard, straight-nosed oval that was Hugo Sergio.

Tem fought his way to the bar and ordered a double coffee,

**335**

laying out the waxy paper bills. Two small reusable cups were exchanged for the money, and he made his way to the place that had been saved by his friend. In the heavy surf of a hundred people talking at once, there was no chance of being heard.

"What's up, Hugh? Anything worth calling me like you did?"

Hugo Sergio looked at Tem ironically, a childlike smile playing on his bare lips. "I should say so. They've made a new pact with the men who own Pallas. We should have water raining down from above any week now. Maybe that'll make them a little bit less heavy-handed, with the shortage ended."

"Unseparated water? Or will they take the deuterium first?"

"I don't know. But there will be some hard bargaining. Another thing—there's a civilian on Earth who is advertising for people to launch a commune on Triton. Says he's going to bring the best techs, latest marks, everything."

"Mother Maria! Where'd he get the money? I didn't think they even minted enough for private space travel on that scale."

"His name is Cornwell. Makes money from data music—they say he's quite well known."

"I'd go if I could, you know. No regrets. Totally free from the Moon . . . I'd go in a minute." Tem pulled a few straggles out of his beard and looked at them, stiff lines like tan tensors. He was thinking.

The legions of the revived Seedees began to march, floating out on rank after orderly rank, flying formation to the commands of a Centrum under assault. The battle was shaping itself in earnest, but still Seven Red Anchorelles waited. In time, he knew, he would be forced to go, he couldn't hang back forever, but, for now, he waited. It was not in vain.

She was there! 7red swooped down on the drifting army and plucked her from the ranks with his articulated arms. Cooloil! he cried, jetting oil. Though confused by her recent resurrection, she greeted him joyously, and they flew away together, exchanging happiness. The corridors of Centrum

**336**

were huge and dark, many of its ancient functions having died, and they found a place to hide.

They coupled once again, their souls mixed together in joined bodies, and shared each other's thoughts. Pleasure at having come back to life, joy at having found each other again after so long an eternity, sadness at the reason for their return, horror at their probable fate.

Ultimately, we die again, they thought.

Time passed for them to the steady beat of a command counter's march, while their inner pheromones mixed until they were inextricably bound together, inseparable. When the time came, they would separate, they knew, but until then . . .

Why should it be?

In a bound state they could think and wonder as one, with the power of their minds magnified conjointly. They still had some sense of a separate self, but it was very small, hard to get a hold on. The marching orders came, and they drifted apart, valves closing, become two again.

They flew to join the army, going near to its head, and traveled side by side, communicating with their little jets of oil, a sort of small conjunction.

Why are we doing this?

Because the Lord of our world so orders it.

Is that the only reason?

It is the only one that we can have.

Agreement. It has always been so.

A pity. Why do you suppose that is?

Because the world was created thus.

And who created the world?

Centrum . . .

Ah. And who created Centrum?

The Starseeders.

And where are they now?

Dead.

It is so.

They flew on into a gathering night that frightened them beyond all reason, a thing that toyed with what passed in them for sanity and made them almost unreasoning beings again, but not quite. They had begun to think again, after ten billion years of fragmented, undreaming sleep, and they did not want to stop.

We must go on.

7red felt a surge of pity for her and wondered how all the other countless resurrectees were taking it. We must, he agreed, but we cannot.

Why not? It was a cry that attracted the attention of those close about them, globules of oil rebounding for them to catch on their shells.

Yes, why not? asked another mournfully.

Because, said Seven Red Anchorelles, the Lord does not will it. How can we fight against our God?

It made them fall silent. How, indeed? But they continued to think about the matter, for, though they were reborn as subunits of Centrum's vast mind, it had given them a strange sort of freedom for just a little while. For however brief a time, until it swallowed them whole again, they were independent, able to think for themselves in their own small fashion. While they lived, they could fear and, perhaps, try to flee.

Aksinia looked around coldly. From the air above the Carnicom there was a smooth, clear view to the center city of Davenport, a crenellated monad crowning the rivered plain like half a broken bottle in which some complex crystal had grown. Morning mists shrouded the mildly undulating land like a floating film of milk. The squashed red sun had just cleared its belly from the city-dotted checkerboard that sat beneath it, and the beginnings of shadows etched in strange relief reached out to her. It was a view that should have astounded. She felt slightly nauseous.

She had been here for a week and a half, as the guest of a near-moronic playwright named Jass. His last name had never been revealed, unless of course Jass was his last name. Jass had many acquaintances here and seemed to have spent most of his life in the amusement complex. His room was filled with personal gear and elaborate drug-taking devices that would be difficult to carry on the road. Perhaps he lived here. She hadn't asked. Beta-2 almost seemed tame compared with the elaborate pharmacopoeia Jass accessed daily; and she had gone along, inhaling burning junk for an archaic thrill, popping the most esoteric brain-chemical derivatives, and hopping the fastest, most diverting of the Carnicom's rides. It had been a bit of a rush, but it was over.

She reached into the nearest lattice of the energy matrix and pushed. The world slowly revolved, and the twenty or so others suspended in the flight simulator were shown to her. They were puppets hanging from invisible wire, unsupported and limp. Jass was within a dekameter. "I'm going now," she said.

He was a handsome man, bald-shaven with blond hair fanning out from his lower lip to hide a chin slightly double from overindulgence. His eyes seemed to reflect the icy illness that she felt. "Good-bye, then," he said. "It was fun." He reached out both hands and swooped upward and away.

In his room Aksinia found the overgarment that she wore when it was cold, pulled it out of the crevice between bed and wall-screen, and put it on. The wrinkles in the otherwise form-fitting garment felt good. She liked looking like a misfit, someone who couldn't care less about her appearance. It was the look she cultivated. From around the room she gathered the other few articles she carried with her, stuffed them into a shopping bag, and rang for a taxi. Almost as a last thought, feeling furtive for some reason, she opened the origami drawer in which Jass kept his stimulants and grabbed a handful of Beta poppers. She did not enjoy registering with coms and this would keep her anonymous for at least a week. If she found a new host before then, maybe she could stay disappeared for a month or more. And, of course, that meant no calls.

The light came on over the balcony door, and she quickly slipped through the dilating energy port and hopped into the floater without even noticing the concrete and metal integrated circuit forty stories down. "This will be an entitled trans," she spoke into the microphone grid decal in the bubble wall, and settled into the plush cushioning, the air cold on her neck. "Go—direct to ground."

**339**

"More information is needed," said the floater in a perfectly modulated voice, neither male nor female. "Address or building name is necessary." The floater lurched slightly as it pulled away from its mooring. "Please repeat or clarify."

It was not easy to escape the address grid with a com floater, though some had not been reprogrammed since a free-form flight and thus could be sent anywhere. In any case, you couldn't survive without *some* knowledge. "Go Rebreak," she said, "test/checkup go." And, after a pause, "WhiteCode Zero zero four go." The floater obediently dropped, and Aksinia watched as the windows and balconies fell upward. Half a meter from the ground, the craft came to a stop and reported an obstacle that prevented further motion. "Go Release," she said, leaping with a thud to the pavement. The floater immediately began to rise, much like a soap bubble being blown by the wind, until it vanished behind the Carnicom obelisk.

From this perspective the landscape was much changed. But Aksinia was used to this aspect of the world, the places where no one went. To the horizon there stretched almost featureless boxes of concrete and senplast: a desert save where a tiny plot of ground sent forth the green and brown weeds/grasses. Aksinia hitched up the shopping-bag handles on her shoulder and silently began to walk. Thumbing rides was very different than it had been during its early days. It was simply a matter of being visible on the ground, being where a person never was. Someone would look down from the seat of a lifter and catch sight of you. It took anywhere from an hour to days. Occasionally you ran into another thumb-rider, but only very rarely. When that happened, you talked; said things you could never say to someone from above.

She started to walk, the nausea that she had felt a thing of the past. She popped a lozenge beneath her tongue and enjoyed the sensation of her strong legs moving her across desolation.

Later, when she was skirting the edge of a cultivated field, passing row after row of diminutive, rigid plants separated by magnetic strips, her eyes were drawn from the nearest farm-float to a metallic glint far up in the patchy, cloud-striped sky. Not a lifter, no. Suddenly a contrail plumed out from it, tiny and at an oblique angle to the prevailing cloud-march. It was a shuttle, coming back. Returning from the endless blackness out there. Aksinia shuddered slightly and thought, That's where I'd like to go. The thought resonated within her.

Temujin Krzakwa held open a jagged fissure in the ground, into which Ariane Methol deeply probed. It was the best they could do. Thrusting in among the gossamer clockwork of the world, she put her delicate fingers into the elastomeric machinery and grappled with its underpinnings. It was all madness, of course, nothing so real as it seemed, but they were locked into a path of imagery now and had to live with it. The battle with Centrum's defenders, the eating of the imaginary thers, had done damage to the inner workings of Bright Illimit—not much, but enough. A single command had mutated, becoming inexecutable, and a whole section of action routines had gone out of reach.

She deftly parted the substance, touching here and there, going where Tem's logic told her to search. It took time. Item after item seemed OK until she uncovered a waveguide-like tube with a dark, carboned knot blocking it. "I think I found it," she said. She read a tiny silver inscription on the wire. "Terminus Junction 26:aleph-aleph subA033?"

Tem sent her a nod. "That's probably it. We'd know better if we had a system architecture diagram, but, uh, what's it read now?"

She passed across it, like blind fingertips feeling out the subtle meanings of electronic braille. "I can't quite . . . ah! 0Q30:0Q31,XFB1,028F:028E."

Krzakwa almost snarled to himself and then felt amused. One fucking bit-pair swapped around on a near-three-hundred-trillion-byte address complex! No wonder we lost it! Load Link; Command Listen; and Decode Logic. He wanted to chuckle and finally did. "That's it, all right. 028F:028E is nonsense. Supposed to be 028F:029R, I think."

"You're not sure?"

He sent her a shrug. "How can I be sure? That's the way a

HORMAD sequencing device usually writes it, but who knows what Brendan really did? There're a lot of oddities in this program."

Including us, Ariane thought. "I'll have to take your word for it," she said. "I was never this far into the substrata of execution control before." Really. Who ever heard of servicing high-level software from underneath? She sighed. "Ax, let me have your diadem, please." When she had it, she activated the gem, pushing the numbers around, a shift left to add twice, and it was done. The Dramatic Creation subroutines reconnected themselves with a metaphysical thump.

Harmon lifted her out and Tem let the earth snap shut. She turned over onto her back and gasped. All of them turned and looked where she pointed. Centrum's castle towered above them, a looming slate-gray mass, obscured by deep shadow, perspective giving it a bizarre aspect ratio that made it almost triangular in shape. A heavy battlement wall of irregular stone, topped with massive tooth-shaped merlons, protected the inner castle, which was positively medieval. Above the citadel massed towers, themselves crenellated, loomed. To give it a thoroughly alien feel, a ring of black machines, blunt and intricate, hung like broken boulders in a wide orbit about the towers. The castle, as before, did not sit on the ground but floated above a terribly truncated horizon that could not have been more than a mile distant. The sky had became twilit, clouds turning taupe and gray, drifting in striated bands across a sky hued into dark orange and vermilion, a band of sunset all around that merged into a circle of indigo and black directly overhead. The program let them assume the invisible sun had already set, but it could not quite provide them with stars. The ground humped up into mounds, carrying them upward in a single-surge earthquake, and silhouetted purple hills rose up to hide the unnatural horizon, making a believable edge to creation. A blanket of short green grass sprang up at their feet and roared outward to clothe the world's bones, shivering in waves before a soft breeze. Let us die in beauty, it said, and thunder rumbled, lightless, in the distance.

They watched the castle, silent, waiting, spread out in a

fighting formation, preferring to brood somberly and let Centrum make the first move. A long time passed, and it did not. Nothing moved except for the halo of orbiting machines, and the castle came no closer. Finally, exhausted, they sat in a half circle on the ground, wanting to plan but having no will.

John Cornwell sat with forearms around upfolded knees and gazed at the bleak castlescape, his mind a cool tunnel of emptiness. By chance, Axie sat cross-legged by his side, reading from a small book she had produced. Almost like the old days, he thought, in the real world. Have I yet really examined my motives for doing all this? Probably not. We think we know ourselves, then life takes in its belt another notch and we feel the pinch. Time to go on another involuntary diet. He sighed and looked at the woman.

She sat still, reading, and her eyes looked tired. He wondered why the program allowed such an appearance and decided that it probably fitted right into the composite. The sentence, "Appearances can be deceiving," came to him, and he sighed. Her head drifted slowly around, tracking to return his stare. She smiled faintly at him, a drawn, wry look, and said, "It's all too much, isn't it, John?"

He surprised himself by feeling startled and felt a certain layering returning to his thoughts. "Oh, I don't know," he said offhandedly. "I'm handling it, I think. I like to be grounded in what we call reality. Here that's meaningless."

Her smile widened to a skeptical grin.

"Really." He felt a pulse of self-annoyance. "It's too unreal to not handle."

Her grin faded and she turned her gaze to the castle again. "OK. . . . But it was real when the monsters tried to eat us, and I think what's coming is going to be a lot worse."

He shook his head. Try not to consider anything as real, he told himself. He remembered a time when he had briefly tried dream control, finally concluding that, even if he felt he was in control of the dream, it was simply part of the dream structure and in no way indicated actual ability to influence the outcome of the dream. Was this like that? Was the illusion of free will here simply part of the program? He couldn't tell, of course. Is *that* what madness is? He wanted to think about

**3 4 3**

the real world, real life, as if this were no part of it. "Tell me something," he said, "about the binding that you have been feeling since we've been here."

Axie glanced at him, then went back to her contemplation of the immense, structured pile of stone. "It's hard to quantify, and I'm not sure I even want to try. The feelings that dominated our lives before were a form of blindness. Now we see."

John wanted to laugh but managed to control himself. Febrile nonsense once again! Always couched in the same occult ways. Did they have nothing inside them but *theories* of life? Everyone seemed to engage in modeling behavior at some point! He threw himself on his back, preferring to watch the unreal-seeming sky, staring into the strange disk of night directly above. A simulacrum is better than nothing, I suppose. But he wondered if it really was. And just how far does that idea extend? Are my self-images real? I don't have any way to challenge them. He stopped it there and drifted back into that long cool tunnel where his thoughts liked to live.

Time passed and their energies cycled up. Time struck hard, though the vista of day's end remained unchanged before them. The moments waxed into being and arrived one by one. The eight made camp on their hill, weapons sheathed, and waited to act. There was nothing else they could do.

Armies? They had none. It was obvious that Bright Illimit lacked a will to populate this wilderness with creatures of its own. Larger weapons, though perhaps of greater symbolic importance, could not be more powerful than Tem's missile weapon. For whatever reason, Demogorgon did not extend his ideas further.

The blackness at zenith was growing, and all of the world was dimming. Some tried to sleep but could not. Finally, muttering a great oath, Krzakwa stood and shouldered his blunt launcher. "This is getting ridiculous," he said, set the controls for maximum range and effect, and hit the firing trigger.

The projectile flared away, leaving a thin, curving trail of

**344**

smoke in its wake. It struck the wall with a shower of sparks, molten metal dripping down the stones to spatter on the ground. The motion of things seemed to slow and the breeze gradually died down. The point of impact slowly brightened, throwing shadows behind them on the hillside. The spark grew, its color shifting upward, the wavelengths of the light shortening. It hit violet, searing holes upon their motionless retinae, and it came.

The blob of light suddenly expanded into a great globe, outlined in brilliant shock waves. The sky turned a garish blood red and, for a moment, everything was still. They waited, then it exploded. White light shut off the world with a glare and the wave front rolled over them soundlessly, throwing them all to the ground. It ended with equal suddenness, as they knew it would, and the castle in the twilight land was back, a hole blown in its walls beneath a small, billowing mushroom cloud. Things came roaring out of the cloud, attacking them.

They came at them fast, swept-wing creatures with tails of bright blue fire and staring malevolent eyes, pinpoints of dark, glowing crimson. The eight stood again together as the assault force went into a wingover and dive, a strafing run. There seemed to be no time to do anything but gape.

The first winged being swept over them, guns stuttering a staccato roll. Streaks of tracer white stained the air and it was gone by. Little explosions marked the hillside, turf and earth thrown from little craters, and Demogorgon suddenly staggered, pierced by a dozen flaming rounds. He fell to the ground, gasping, and lost all touch with the battle. Another being made its run over the little group, rattling off a story of mayhem and blood.

Demogorgon lay on the grass face down, isolated from the inner world and drifting away into gray nonexistence. He wanted to run slides of all times past, to have his little death experiences and be done with it all, but the electronic lifelines held on and would not let him go. He was compelled to go on thinking, to call out in his pain.

What should it be? Yes: Brendan, if you are anywhere now, if you can hear me, please help. We are here for you.

A roar of rage tore the sky back into daylight and green eyes flamed, a frosty thunder that stopped the world. A hand swelled above their heads, immense, swatting the flying things from the air, crushing them back into an electronic nether place, ignoring their little cries of strident dismay. It struck at the walls of the castle, folding them back in upon themselves, tearing away at Centrum's outermost circuits, blinding Mother Ocean's God in the process.

Night fell suddenly and then more; the world went black and they moved on, transported and healed.

They ran down the dark corridors of Centrum's mind, surrounded by a glowing pool of liquid light that kept pace with their every step. They fled, and blackness enveloped fore and aft, surrounding them on all sides. They ran in a compact group, eight together, afraid to separate to any distance for fear of getting lost, and as a result they kept bumping into each other, caroming off walls, constantly in danger of falling down. They were afraid to stop.

Demogorgon was in the lead, slim, muscular legs pumping effortlessly, clenched fists swinging on the ends of balancing arms. His breath rasped in his throat, an aftershock of some deathlike experience, but he felt no pain. The cool air surged in and out, feeding him, urging him to go on. To what end? he thought. We're in here now, without plan or preparation. It mirrors our lives, like the lives of all men. We go on and on, running blindly toward the unknown until we stumble and fall. Where can he be? Can anything help me find him? I'll know what to do then. The notion was comforting.

Krzakwa came last, lumbering, trying to keep up, wobbling with fatigue. Thin worms of pain crawled through his sides, demanding rest, but he couldn't stop. The others would go on without him. I laid careful plans for what we were to do and none of it has happened, he thought. Only the interactive processes of Bright Illimit keep us rolling. "Throw in the kitchen sink!" I said. A good thing, too. So much unpredictability would have overwhelmed us in an instant! He ran on, moaning softly as his feet thudded heavily upon the unforgiving stone.

**3 4 6**

Ariane ran in the middle, thankful for the superb physical conditioning that she'd unintentionally kept all her life. *How is it so?* Bright Illimit, she realized, must have some reason for making us suffer like this. *It could give us unlimited endurance, or at least take away the pain!*

How many factors impinged upon them? In the old days, when the wires were simple and processes were clean, programs had warred upon each other for the edification of men, for their delight and amusement. In that time, as now, the programs were still at the mercy of their hardware. They could do no more than the machine would allow. And they were in a machine, its capacities unknown.

They came to a sudden stop, jumbling together comic-opera fashion, limbs entangled, bodies sprawled across the hard, dusty floor. They were still, hearts pounding, breaths wheezing into slow silence.

There was a light ahead, and theirs had gone out.

Linked into the past through a series of memories connected by a single thread of emotion, Beth sat, seeing herself as a small dark eleven-year-old, on the ledge of the transparent solar panel of the family farmhold, watching the dust devils of this last day of November sweep across the fallow, stripy field which extended to the dim blue humps that defined the horizon. She kicked her feet and let the plastic flip-flops loosely flap against her soles. It was cold, though not cold enough to mist her breath, but the sun, a light so intense it blanched the most intense sky she could recall, seemed to sear her skin. Kentucky had already grown too small for her. She wanted to see the world, not just be in it through Comnet.

She wished her fathers would dream the same dreams she did. Theder was totally lost to the 'net, especially when there were fullsense programs, and Anselm was off most of the time, studying the lightning-quick evolution of the toxin-dominated ecosystems that sprouted among the fields. Neither had any time for her, though Theder did make love to her once or twice a week. She had heard that was the reason her mother had left, a month after the first time. It was fun,

**3 4 7**

though, and the physical contact that it provided was a comfort. She didn't like the mess, though. When she had brought forth blood, the day before yesterday, that really had been messy. Of course, she had expected it for a month or two, and it really wasn't a surprise, but she knew that it was time for her to get herself together and get out of this situation. The school up in Canada had sent her a prospectus, indicating a scholarship would be no problem, and she supposed that was where she would go.

It was Anselm who made most of the decisions for the family. Her mother had chosen his last name, Toussaint, for her. Anselm was the person to speak to.

A whirlwind appeared almost at her feet, scouring up dust and dead leaves like an invisible sweeper. Beth hopped down and ran into it, giggling as the hot wind turned about her and pelted her with weightless debris. Suddenly it swung to the left and headed off toward the hills, leaving her to watch. She turned wistfully and skipped toward the entrance portico of the Station, maneuvering the lithe smallness of her body up the dirty concrete stairway, halfway up onto a massive balustrade. The warmth of the air seeping from the energy curtain ushered her in.

It wasn't difficult to find Theder Sabin. As usual, he was curled up on the watercouch in the darkened viewing room, head encased in the complex helmet which transmitted 'net sensory input. A look of amusement had somehow oozed out onto his face. Beth cleared the control tablet and wrote "Break" on the metallic surface. Though no physical change was obvious, Theder's body began to straighten, and his smile hardened into a grin. His eyes, after a minute, opened.

"Hello, dear Libbie. You should see what they've done. Another breakthrough in preparing films from the early days for a four-sense presentation. It's fantastic what they can do. I've just been watching something called *Wings,* from 1927. What color! And to imagine that they could get stuntmen to do those things. You know, there's a difference between real action and matte-pastiches. Care to join me?"

"No, Dad. I have something I want to talk to you and Dad

**3 4 8**

Anselm about. Something important. I am going away to school."

"Uh-hah. Well, it's really about time. I'll miss you, though. We both will. Let's get Ans on the phone."

It was only an hour before the family's car came crunching up out of the dust to the west, casting a hazy shadow before it. The smell of oxidized metal preceded it. The big soft wheels conformed to the shallow troughs of the field and deflated into withered blue prunes as the vehicle came to a stop in front of the Station. Beth and Anselm both came out and hugged their third silently, and began to walk back up the stairs, hand in hand in hand. Anselm dropped their hands and sat on the top step, wiping his forehead with a dusty hand. Beth sat between her two fathers, resting her dark hands on the two knees, one pale and pudgy, the other sallow, scarred, and knobby. If the world could have stayed the way it was at that moment, she wouldn't have wanted to leave. Together with the two of them, the center of attention, she could see no winds in the field.

"You know I love the two of you," she began, feeling awkward, almost unable to tell them what they already knew. "But I've decided to leave. I'm eleven now, and I'm going to the Macallister School in Yellowknife. That's in the CFE, nowhere near the Sosh Old Zone, and they have offered me a scholarship."

Anselm looked pleased. "What kind of school is it. Old Style? Free-form?"

"It's a Summertree school, sort of free-form, but more rigorous. I think I'll like it there."

Theder took her hand and intertwined her small fingers into his large clasp. "You can always come back. And we'll visit you too." Anselm nodded. He enveloped them both in his naked arms, and they held each other like that for a long time. "Remember," he said, "always remember—we're a family. Your mother is still with us. We're a family."

The Seedees, at least temporarily defeated, lay deep within the folds of Centrum, coupled together in a staggered line. They were wed primarily to each other, to their old mates and

**349**

friends, but the oils leaked back and forth along the line, making the many one. They whispered softly to each other in the silent darkness, reggae tunes of the battle's excitement, the flying mist and the sound-flare of an imaginary sun. But we lost, they sighed, wind currents in the sea, and so come closer to the death from which we cannot arise. The battle was lost and the war was in peril. Other voices whispered softly, pointing up the other factors among them: And if we win? What then? Centrum swallows us back into itself. We become dream matter once again, our awareness gone. That, too, is death. Shivers of terror, powered by the knowledge that it had already happened, that they had all been dead for countless ages. So why should we fight for the thing that will kill us? Why not let Centrum go down to doom with us? Let the great world spin on into darkness and come to a stop. A still, somber voice sparkled in their midst, one of many, interconnected: If Centrum dies, we are dead forever. If it lives, we may someday live again, for it needs us. We must fight!

The voices sighed on, talking to each other, making love grow like bubbles in the sea, a froth of mixing minds. They dreamed to each other, minimizing their differences, contravening the old evolutionary drives, yet powering them nonetheless.

Cooloil was caught in a bright dream of times past. Her gentle rhythms were settled into their old, quiescent ways. She wanted only to live again, as she had always lived, and so bespoke it to 7red and to all the others who had been called back from the void.

Before her, Seedees played in the freshness of Mother Ocean's methane sky, chasing about in great, complex patterns, the old culture-dances that made their senses reel with happiness and wonder, and she danced among them. Here, it was not the enclosed sea of Centrum's ship, instead people played their games in the natural surround of the old world, the world none of them had ever seen.

She dashed about the sky on an anophagomotor jet, dodging playfully among the bright toxin-clouds, dashing through schools of brothermind fliers, bursting their unity asunder, feeling their raspy bodies bumping along her sides, hearing the muted cries of their synchronized oils diminish into startled cacophony. She tumbled, and kinesthesia made the world tumble.

There was another Seedee ahead. She projected her remote senses, reading the methane pressure waves, and identified him. Seven Red Anchorelles awaited her. She rushed forward joyfully and coupled with him. . . .

The deep oils of 7red pulsed with energy. He told a story to her, then to them all, of a time that had never been. In a complex song of what-if, he imagined that the Starseeders had never been born. What then?

The Starseeders had been the beginning of it all, yes, the founders of the Grand Design, but they had come from nature itself, just like the worlds and all the stars. The little methane worlds had come into being on their own, without interference from any intelligent agency, and it was known that intelligence could evolve by itself, in a haphazard fashion. Maybe . . . Maybe, without Starseeder and without Centrum, there would still have been Seedees. . . . No, that was the wrong word. There must be something else. . . .

He projected a vision: high in the skies of a cold, blue-green world the hard squid jetted, proud, knowing themselves the masters of creation. Though the nature of the sea dictated their form, they were no longer subsumed to the modeling powers of a silicate world virus. Unlike the dreamer, they had eyes and, from old, had known about the remote, twinkling points of light that had always dominated the sky. They had eyes, these proud creatures, and called themselves the People.

They worked together, on a Grand Design of their own. The People studied the worlds about them and, slowly, over the aeons, accumulated the materials for their quest. They plunged deep, to the core of their world; they mined the random metal masses that occasionally fell from the sky. They flew higher and higher until they had penetrated the spaces about them. They built ships that coursed the heavens.

In time they had starships and found the other worlds. Mostly they were empty worlds, it was true, frequently they were useless save as a source of more raw material, but that was not always the case. As the People colonized among the methane worlds they found other People in various stages of development. They coupled with them, subsumed them to the universal whole. They spread throughout creation.

The universe aged and, as it mellowed, brought forth other forms of life, other intelligences. The silicate worlds filled with life of their own sort, quick minds that climbed the steady ladder upward into the black, star-sequined night. As they arrived, one by one, they found the People waiting with open generosity, the elder statesmen of creation.

Cooloil flew through his vision, enthralled by the nobility of it, saddened by the tragedy that she knew had been real. Why had the fates not seen to it that her people had been the masters of their own destiny?

Because the fates were Centrum and the Starseeder plan.

And why was it still so? Why had they never rebelled?

Because we could not, whispered another Seedee. Because we lived within Centrum and it ruled our lives down to the tiniest detail, down to the ultimate moment. How could we fight against such a thing without some outside agency to intervene in our behalf?

There was nothing beyond Centrum and the sea of Mother Ship. We are, as we always were, trapped. The Seedees moaned in unison, a soft wail of whispered death. . . .

7red's oil burst upon them like an incandescent cataract. There is now, he said, his meaning penetrating to them all. The disease is here. The thing that infects Centrum watches us and waits. You know what it is.

Some chance by-product of the Grand Design?

It *is* the Grand Design! The Starseeders made Centrum, which made us, solely to make more of their own kind. We are merely intermediary stages in a long process that has succeeded at last. They are here.

Can they help us? Will they?

It doesn't matter. Let us help them to kill Centrum.

But then we will all die! Die forever!

Perhaps. But at least God will go down into the darkness

with us. We will not die alone. To me, that is a satisfactory end to it all.

So be it, whispered all the Seedees together, relishing their potential revenge.

John stood wearily. The others were seated on an inner rampart of one of the higher parapets, huddled in couples as if to hold off the next attack by ignoring the world around them and concentrating on what was happening behind their closed eyes. For the first time he noticed that a strong bond seemed to have been formed between Temujin and Aksinia, the latter cuddled in the bearded man's bulky grip. Strange, he thought. He scanned, once again, the flat, broken wall before him, the huge tower reaching upward into the night-circle, which now sported six stars, bloated and red like Betelgeuse, in a random constellation. He shook his head. What is this? How the fuck are we supposed to deal with a world in which their are no bases for understanding, in which the rules of the game are unreadable? OK . . . OK . . . even if logic is not totally applicable here, this that seems is strongly tied to the premises of the Bright Illimit program. Something is not quite what it appears . . . no, that's wrong, nothing is quite what it appears.

"Well," he said, looking at the others, "should we proceed?" There was no dissent.

They moved. Through barren halls that were nothing at all, John walked automatically, barely feeling the scraping of his feet on the hard rock. He had begun to feel that he would not be involved in the process of reliving memories, but, unexpectedly, it was not so.

There were endless hours of building data montages, pasting consonant intervals through the purely mathematical central motif. The music leading to the break before the rush into the coda was coming along, coming along. It would be finished, perhaps, today.

He looked through the complex notation, rather like a color abstraction of a city skyline viewed through a screen and window splattered with raindrops, to the real window that his desk faced. The computer feed dimmed and disap-

**353**

peared, and the mountains of Backbone Range, snowy bleak and rimmed with halos of blowing ice, looked back at him. January was lord of Canada and he was warm and cozy in the sconce of his mother's cabin. Removed from the interface with his machine, the raw ache of his restored leg returned like a claw bite. He looked down at the cloth within which his cold, pale leg was regenerating its nerve tissue, and remembered the fall.

And yet, despite it all, it had been good. Here he was, idea tumbling on to idea, building the complexity of *Reflection Counterpoint* from the well of experiences that had brought him to this place. Sometimes he would marvel at how the pain had helped fuse the earlier idea of complex structures analogous to music in direct data throughput into something real and within his grasp to produce. It was a wonder—one of those things that are unbelievable until they occur. And, for the first time in his life, he was about to know the feeling of absolute triumph.

He brought the program overlay back into his field of vision and began to manipulate the loopy half scales of numbers that provided the background, interposing passing tones flanking the pivot chords a hundred deep. This, when played back, amazingly, had just the effect he had desired, and no more tinkering was necessary. The penultimate passage was finished. He linked in the preliminary coda file and looked at it again in the context of the finished climax. Ho! he thought. That's closer to the final version than I suspected.

A sequence of commands fleshed out the coda with the color-chords he had already made, holding the additions in his mind for a moment to twist them this way and that, catching overly legato numbers and popping them slightly. A little inversion put just the hint of a reference to Bach's *"Heut' triumphieret Gottes Sohn,"* followed by the barest chuckle, and, yes! it was finished. He had done it!

John shut the interface off with a mental click and sat back. He was laughing, knowing for once that what he had done was right. Perfect. He had captured the essence that brimmed within him, and, perhaps, created a new art form in the pro-

**354**

cess. He slapped his leg and smiled at the pain, and returned to the present.

The eight crept forward out of the darkness, slowly feeling their way into the unknown circuitry. The dim world about them stayed artificialized, moldering stone walls glowing with a dim, greenish phosphorescence, redolent of damp, ancient life. They stopped, hiding behind a low wall that had somehow come into existence, and peered into an enormous chamber. Lit by flickering red torchlight, its walls were of pale, translucent marble in which varihued whorls of color were faintly visible. The ceiling was a vaulted arch, the inside of a blank, high dome. Windows suddenly appeared, as if an afterthought, tall, thin slits that admitted dim vermilion twilight and faint breezes, drafts of cool, dry air that stirred the flames and made shadows dance upon the walls. The strong, incongruous smell of jasmine tea began to fill their nostrils.

Things floated above the floor. For a brief moment they saw the familiar hard-squid shapes of the Seedees hanging there. They were linked together in pairs, connected at their anchorelles, and the couplets were joined together in a double row, like a string of firecrackers waiting to be touched off. The forms began to change. They writhed and their outlines began to blur, shifting away into a melting softness, like oil-based clay thrown into a kiln.

"What's going on?" asked Vana, turning to look at the others.

Tem shook his head, pale face beaded with droplets of cold sweat. "I think Bright Illimit's routines are looking for some image we can deal with."

"Yes," said Ariane. "It's trying to find an average for all of us. . . ." They fell silent and watched.

The shapes before them coalesced, forming into a huddled, glowing mass, an insensate pool of light gathered in the middle of the soft, padded floor. Things began to appear in the light, vaguely humanoid images that spilled onto one another, mixing together as a mass of indistinct limbs and bodies. They shifted and changed rapidly as the program picked up imagery, first from one controlling mind, then

**355**

another. Abruptly, the picture sharpened into focus, jumping out at them like a dense holograph.

There were a hundred human beings jumbled together motionless on the floor. They were huddled in endless arrays of sexual poses, every conceivable posture and position, like some alien Karnak wrought in three-dimensional, fleshlike stone. They remained still, for the moment showing no sign of life; then the first one moved.

A being from the center of the group stirred and, with his motion, the others breathed, a sudden sighing from a hundred manlike throats. The man, for he was clearly male, arose and stretched. Separated from the generalized mass of the group, posing before them, they could see him clearly now. The shape was generally humanoid, all of the parts were more or less present, but there seemed to be a lack of fine detail. The skins were pallid, the dull bone white of institutional walls, and everywhere there was a lack of flexion lines. The fingers were smooth; likewise the elbows and knees. His brow was empty of feature and his face was without the character lines that help distinguish human beings. Their hair, also white, was undifferentiated, a shapeless mass meant to indicate where hair would go. They were cartoons brought to life. A female Seedee arose to stand beside the man and they could see that she too was crude, as if adapted from a paleolithic statuette.

Their eyes opened, reddish orange, dully glowing coals.

"A touch of humanity," murmured Demogorgon, "and a strong flavor of alienness. Good work."

The two Seedees walked slowly forward to stand before them while the others hung back and watched, motionless and silent. The two groups examined one another for a drawn-out moment; then the male being spoke. "I am called Seven Red Anchorelles," he said. "You are the aliens?"

Krzakwa smiled softly. "I guess we are," he said.

7red nodded slowly and exchanged glances with the woman. In their featurelessness, they seemed to communicate. He turned back to the humans. "We know you're here to destroy the ancient Mind, what you call Centrum . . ."

"Wait a minute!" said Cornwell. "We don't want to . . ."

**356**

7red held up a pale hand, silencing him. "It doesn't matter what you intend. That is what you have come to do. We want to join you."

"Why?" asked Krzakwa flatly, his voice echoing from the hardening stone of the chamber. "That'll mean the end of you all."

Cooloil spoke for the first time, her voice portrayed as a rich, deep flow of liquid syllables. "We know that. We don't care. This has gone on long enough. Our people have never been free, and if we cannot be free, we would as soon cease to exist."

The humans could find no reply to this, each buried in his own secret responses. Cornwell found himself recalling his feelings as he'd emerged from his first submergence into the world of Centrum, when they'd followed Sealock's fleeing soul down into the depths. "Poor bastards, indeed," he murmured, and, "Join us, then. We'll do what we can."

The Seedee reached forward and grasped his hand, touching him only fleetingly, while the others pressed forward, animated by an eagerness to begin.

Achmet Aziz el-Tabari was in Montevideo, in Tupamaro Arcology so far from Paris, to meet with his technical adviser for the first time. He walked through the cool, dark, quiet hallways, thinking of what it could mean. *Brendan Sealock.* He rolled the name around, considering its feel. It was an ordinary-seeming sort of name, a Sean Smith-like Anglo-Irish pastiche, but the syllables had a rolling dignity to them that was unusual. It sounded like the name of an impressive man and he wondered what sort of figure would be attached to it. He smiled. Probably a typical sort of brain-worker: short, skinny, stuttering. A hundred years ago he would have had rotten teeth and thick glasses. This character would probably smell bad. The vital statistics had been sparse. Born in the Deseret Enclave Complex thirty-two years ago, moved to New York Free City when eighteen, and spent the rest of his life at NYU. Typical. Some kind of theoretical design engineer working for MCD. A high-caliber type. Unlimited Comnet access.

**357**

That puzzled him a little. When he'd applied to Comnet for professional assistance in designing the Illimitor World, he'd been expecting to get a list of good programmers, preferably people working right in Paris, where he could easily visit them in person. He liked to work closely with the craftsmen he hired. You never knew when some sexy flesh might wander by. After his request, Comnet had asked for a set of specifications, so he'd sent in a précis of what he wanted the program to do. Astonishingly, there had been a wait of several minutes, then the unit had sent him one name, Brendan Sealock, and a single-digit TY-com address. Weird.

Whoever heard of a one-number address? Not only that, but why had Comnet referred him to a design engineer? The world held millions of top-quality programmers, many of them—hell, *most* of them—working in artistic fields. Surely the program wasn't so difficult that it would require new hardware! The idea was beginning to disturb him.

He arrived at the correct door and announced himself. He stood in front of it, staring at his own eye level, waiting for a person to appear. The door slid open and he was gazing at a chest.

Demogorgon gasped and took a sudden step backward. The man was huge! At *least* a hundred kilos, close to a hundred and ninety centimeters tall. He looked upward from a broad, heavily muscled body into a face marked by unreconstructed scars. Details began to force themselves on him. At some point the man's nose had obviously been broken, and his eyes were dark green, sunk into shadows beneath heavy brows. His hair was a reddish-blond tangle, cut short in what looked like a homemade butchery of a coiffure. Sealock was grinning at him, showing big, square white teeth.

He let his eyes drift downward, drinking in the minutiae of his physique. The man was dressed in white tennis shorts and a sleeveless shirt. His arms were thick, laden with big, slabby muscles and roped with thick veins; his legs were sleek, hairy pillars ending in short, broad, blunt-toed feet. His hands had knobby, white-scarred knuckles, as if he'd spent a lot of time fighting with stone walls. "Ah . . ." He swallowed, convulsively, fighting confusion. "Mr. Sealock?"

**358**

The behemoth nodded. "Right. You must be Tabari, the artist." He stood aside from the doorway that he blocked, moving with a lithe grace that somehow fitted in with his otherwise megalithic appearance. "Come on in. I've been waiting for you."

Demogorgon followed him into the apartment, watching the muscles of his buttocks bulge inside his shorts, following the rolling movements of the sinews in his back and legs. The man's arms swung lightly at his sides, fingers slightly flexed, a delicate-looking posture. Good God! he thought. I'm in love.

Somehow he found himself sitting in a soft chair, sipping from a tall, cold, mildly alcoholic drink the man had made him. The glass helped to cover up the difficulty he was having, giving him something innocuous to do with his hands as they talked. This was going to be more difficult than he'd thought. Sealock sat down opposite him, swilling foamy red ale from a glass mug.

"You know," said Sealock, "that's a pretty interesting idea you've got. You realize no one's ever called for user/program interactivity on that level before?"

Demogorgon shook his head. "I had no idea what I was asking. I just know what I wanted it to do."

The man grinned. "Which was quite a lot! This thing is really beyond the reach of the public-access Comnet levels. We're going to have to work with Tri-vesigesimal, at least! And *that* may disappoint you. But, look, I have to tell you—the ultimate barriers we will run into are legal, not technological. If we . . . Is something wrong?"

Demogorgon realized with a start that he'd been staring fixedly at Sealock's face, fascinated by the complex interplay of the savage features as they were animated by speech and thought. "I'm sorry. I, uh . . . excuse me, but *why* do you have all those scars and muscles?"

"Huh?" The man burst out laughing, a thrilling resonance from deep within his chest. "It's from my hobby."

"Your hobby?" Allah! Why am I acting so stupid? He felt as if he were totally out of control.

"I'm a boxer."

Shit! A boxer? This was ridiculous! The man must be like

some kind of comic-opera hero, all the muscles and brains a human body could hold gathered into one place. And he probably had the manners and wit of a nineteenth-century fictional nobleman. "I see." Oh, witty reply!

They got to work, laying out the initial questions and problems that would finally lead to the creation of Bright Illimit. Later, far into the night, they were sitting side by side, poring over a preliminary flow diagram, when he got up the courage to make his move at last.

He put his hand on the man's thigh and let it drift around to the sensitive skin of the inner side. The action seemed to go unnoticed, but the contact of the flesh under his hand made his finger tingle, egging him on. He ran his hand up the thigh, touching the place where a thick tendon ran into Sealock's trunk. Still nothing? No.

The man stopped talking and stared at him, then leaned back on the couch, grinning wryly. Demogorgon gazed into his eyes for a moment, searching for some kind of acceptance. There seemed to be nothing there, no movement in the soul. He sighed. For the moment, maybe this would be enough. These things often took time. He gripped Sealock's waistband and gently slid the shorts down, then buried his face in a hair-tangled crotch, greeted by the exciting start of an erection.

When it was over, he rubbed his face against the man's side, feeling the power enclosed beneath his skin, and softly said, "That was nice. Want to do something for me now?" He still ached with desire.

The man opened his eyes and looked down, then seemed to smirk, an ugly expression. "No," he said.

Demogorgon felt a vague surprise dawning. "But . . . I . . ."

Sealock grinned. "Your choice, asshole. I didn't ask for that."

But when Demogorgon burst into tears the man held him close, stroking his long dark hair and murmuring softly, trying to comfort him in some strange way.

**360**

□ □ □
Centrum felt the awaited attack in three stages. It was nursing itself in the darkness the battle had made, trying to reassemble its tattered subroutines, to repair the damage that had been wrought among its circuitry. So far, it was not too bad, but the humans were far stronger than it had suspected. It had known what they could do from what it had seen in the first captive, but the others were *far* weaker. How had they done so much? Something was helping them, but what? It felt like the captive, but that was impossible. Everything was there, the captive secured, dismantled and soaked into the circuitry, part of Centrum, adding to its strength. What have they done to me? Another thought surfaced. What have I done to myself? It was disquieting. . . .

The first event occurred. Suddenly, Centrum felt the Seedee subroutines stripping away, popping from its grasp one by one. The little programs came to life as they left, bubbling gleefully, bright surges within their electronic pheromones. Centrum screamed mournfully within itself and began frantically patching up its shredded defenses, stopping the gaping rents that had been left behind.

This was impossible! How could the suborned consciousnesses act independently of its will? The answer awaited it in the renewed darkness: I gave them back life. Not all, but enough. Apparently. How could it turn the tide against them all? It must go on the attack!

Centrum prepared itself carefully, getting ready to strike out at its enemies, to defeat them, but there was not enough time. In the nanosecond world of the artificial mind, the attack was renewed. Centrum squalled with terror.

Sudden probes thrust in from all sides, opening it to the sudden harsh light of the burgeoning stars without. It went from dark blindness to an incandescence that showed no detail. Pain tore at it. What is happening? cried its terror. Some great ravening beast was tearing its way in, gnawing through the delicate vitals of an age-old circuitry, a mad, hungry thing clad in the visage of the captive, a thing which sought out itself.

They had it now! Centrum felt powerful forces grasping in

**361**

on every side, tendrils reaching throughout its complex organism. It had time for one soft cry, a desperate plea for mercy, then the powers of the universe pulled it apart, fragmenting it into its separate subunits, and a consciousness that had endured for twenty billion years was extinguished.

Afterward, Centrum's castle had been reduced to a flattened pile of smoking rubble. Sheets of color drifted across the sky, mostly hues of gray and pale yellow, and the horizon seemed shrunken. Bright Illimit still maintained its illusion, but it was working near its capacities now and was having difficulty keeping the various facets in order. The Seedees circled overhead, still alive by the external program's power, flying winged work vacuoles, and the eight stood in the middle of the carnage, accompanied by 7red and Cooloil. Not far from them, a small, ancient stone tower rose from the earth.

Krzakwa turned to face the two Seedees. "It's done," he said.

"It had to be," said 7red, nodding slowly. "How long will we last now?"

"I don't know. Probably for as long as Bright Illimit can hold its grip on you as a subroutine. After we're gone . . ."

"Isn't there anything we can do for them?" asked Cornwell, gazing about at the wreckage of this complex inner world. "Seems like a shitty reward for the help they gave us."

The Selenite shrugged.

Demogorgon was staring steadfastly at the tower. "We can leave them with the program, I suppose, but I don't know how much good it will do. This is an alien place. . . . When we close off the connection with Shipnet, it may not survive."

"Something will survive," said Ariane, "but it may not be the individually conscious Seedee routines."

Cooloil sighed. "If that is all we can hope for, it is all we must ask. If we survive in any form as a free people, then it will be better than anything we ever had before."

"Why do we have to close them off from Shipnet?" asked Harmon. "As long as we leave it open, they'll still be alive."

"You're all forgetting one important fact," said Krzakwa. "We aren't really out here in isolation, permanently separated from the rest of the Solar System. In just a few weeks

*Formis Fusion* will arrive, with its cargo of USEC scientists, who'll take all this away from us, by force of arms if necessary. . . . And after them, vessels of the Contract Police will arrive, bringing with them all the force of the Pansolar Union."

"To put it succinctly," said Axie, "we're fucked."

"Yeah."

"Let's worry about all that when the time comes," said Demogorgon. "We didn't come down here to destroy Centrum or rescue the Seedees from a fate worse than death. We came to get Brendan back. Now let's see if we can pry him out of this mess."

"We have to find him first," said Vana. "Where is he?"

Ariane gestured toward the tower. They began to walk, Demogorgon in the lead, and the Seedees followed them. The interior of the small building was simple, a spiral staircase that led upward through the wan near darkness to a small, roofless room, its crenellated walls open to the sky. Brendan Sealock lay on a small pallet in the middle of the floor, his eyes closed, his face peaceful. His skin was waxen, almost translucent, and his chest was still.

Demogorgon knelt beside him and reached out to touch the cold features. He peeled back the eyelids and then recoiled briefly. The eyes were spheres of transparent glass, lightless and dull.

"He's all apart," said Krzakwa. "I don't know what we can do."

"Weren't we going to use Bright Illimit to find and reassemble his components?" asked Ariane.

The Selenite nodded. "We were. But if we take it away from the functions it's maintaining now, all the Seedees die."

"Do it then," said Seven Red Anchorelles. "Don't fail your friend for our sake."

"No," said Demogorgon. He looked up at them all. "You told me what I could do before we came in here, Tem, and you told me what it might mean. I know how to do it and I'm willing to take the chance." He didn't wait. Demogorgon turned and threw himself onto the body. There was a moment of electric tension in the air, then he seemed to melt into the dead flesh.

**363**

□ □ □

Brendan Sealock was strolling through Ronkonkoma Megapark out on Long Island, hand in hand with a young woman. Maraia Manderville was tall and blond, slender, with narrow hips and a bright, open face. Her eyes were a pale sea green and she seemed to be always smiling. He put his arm around her as they walked, one hand resting on her buttock, feeling the aliveness of her flesh flow into him. They stopped beneath a carefully sculpted weeping willow tree, burying themselves in the cathedral of its branches, and embraced. Brendan felt a surge of warmth as he crushed her to his chest. They kissed and then broke apart, holding each other at arm's length, smiling. Her breath had tasted faintly of some unidentifiable ketone.

They walked on, looking at the sky and the park's attractions, isolated from each other but together. They went on the Sunburst ride, a sort of magnetic-field roller coaster in which the flying cars soared on unique, randomly programmed paths. She sat on his lap, facing him, looking steadfastly into his eyes as the ride threw them around. Her breasts brushed against his chest and he held his hands clamped around her waist. The motion of the car moved them against each other and they felt a hot tension forming between them. The ride ended and they walked on.

Darkness fell, and they strolled along the beach, watching the meaningless stars and listening to the surf hissing across the sand, breaking in cool surges around their ankles, excavating the ground from beneath their feet. As they walked, Maraia pressed close against his side, her shoulder under his arm and her head nestled at the base of his throat. He felt the wisps of her hair, stirring in the gentle, fresh sea breezes, tickling on his bare skin. They stopped, wrapping their arms about each other, and kissed for a long time, and a heavier wave burst over them, throwing foamy water up onto their thighs. They went up into the higher dunes and lay down, squirming together to make a pocket in the sand.

They touched and stroked each other and Brendan felt her breath like a hot little furnace on the side of his face. They were ready to make love, but this was too exquisite. The

**364**

scraps of cloth that were their scant pieces of apparel held them apart just long enough, prolonging their excitement, bringing them to levels of anticipation from which the act itself could only be a denouement. They lay still for a while, letting the matter subside. Their hearts slowed and their skins cooled with the evaporation of drying sweat.

After a while they got up and walked on, holding hands again. Their hips bumped together as they moved up the beach, renewing a touch of their excitement. They came to a long, dark wooden pier, a carefully preserved relic of a former era, and walked out on it. They sat at the end of the structure, sides touching, and let their feet dangle down into an infinite-seeming darkness. Sealock put his arm around her side, reaching under her arm to toy with the firmness of a small breast. He felt her nipple stiffening and enlarging under the movement of his fingers. She nuzzled her head against his chest, rubbing her face against his skin, and her breath snarled softly in her throat, a faint, desire-driven purr. She lay down along the edge of the pier, putting her head in his lap, facing upward to gaze at his face, her eyes pools of glinting moisture in the starlight. She reached her hand up and drew her fingernails softly across his chest, making long trails in his dense hair. He shivered and ran his hand down across her stomach and onto the outside of her thin shorts, drawing his fingers softly between her legs. Her hips rocked back and forth once and she sighed, closing her eyes. She turned her head and bit gently at the ridged flesh of his stomach, then turned on her side and ran one hand up the inside of his thigh. The spell of apartness, of waiting, seemed broken then and they clutched at each other hungrily.

I'm going to Montevideo in the morning, he thought with a small pang of regret. They made love at last, slowly and far into the night, and the quiet sea breezes sighed a steady accompaniment to awaken their senses.

Stereotaxis.

Brendan and Demogorgon lay together on the roof garden of Tupamaro Arcology, cooling slowly as the night progressed and the southern stars wheeled above them. The

**365**

Arab lay sprawled across his chest, hand grappling low, following the development of a slow detumescence. Another episode, another bit of disagreeability. It wasn't all that different from his relationship with Ariane. Where did all these things come from?

"You know," said Demo, "I can always taste the woman on you."

Brendan snorted softly. "You're imagining things again."

"It doesn't matter. I know she's there and what I taste is the bitterness of that knowledge."

"What do you expect me to do?"

Demogorgon sat up and let his head drop forward onto his knees, long black hair flowing over his forearms. "I don't know. A little something for me, I suppose. It'd be nice."

"I'm submitting to your desires; letting you do things to me. That's the best I can manage."

"I know." The man got up suddenly and walked off into the darkness. Brendan called after him, but he didn't turn back, disappearing swiftly into the night, a phantasm that quickly wasted away.

Brendan lay there for a while longer, his mind deliberately kept blank, feeling the warm summer wind rush over him. The upper atmosphere seemed to be heavily disturbed at the moment and the stars were twinkling violently. He got up and walked through the damp grass, feeling the rough edges of the blades clutch at his bare feet and stroke the tender spaces between his toes. He shook his head angrily and went below, looking for Ariane.

He was back in New York again and an MCD board meeting was breaking up, the nine members rising to their feet, chairs making hollow sounds as they scraped across the floor. Cass Mitchell had been his usual raucous, giggling self, a miasma of seeming senility interspersed with flashes of the old brilliance. Sealock started to follow Gina Redden out the door, his eyes fixed on the delicate, 2/4 twitching of her jeans-clad buttocks, but the chairman stopped him.

"Boy, I wish I could still fuck!" he said, grinning up at him, his face a mass of leathery, cancerous-looking wrinkles. "You know what? It hurts to get a hard-on when you're as old as me. Sometimes it even hurts to pee. I haven't gotten laid in almost forty years. Do yourself a favor, kid: live gloriously and die young!" He stalked off like a baggy insect, shaking his head and muttering angrily to himself.

Brendan stood motionless for a moment, then drew his hand across his face like an old-time comedian, stretching his features downward. Jesus! What next? He walked out the door, intent on catching up with the woman. She was waiting for him by the elevator.

"Is he nutty, or what?" Gina Redden was not a particularly attractive woman. She had long brown hair which she wore in a high ponytail, with wings of hair hanging down beside her narrow, triangular face. Her nose was large, aquiline, and her eyes were dark brown and looked watery all the time. She was grinning and he noticed that her lips were getting chapped again.

She was thick-waisted, not fat but muscular-seeming. She had a mannish stride; "Walks like a farmer," someone had said; and had considerable strength in her shoulders and arms. For some reason a lot of men were excited by her appearance and masculine habits. He grinned at her. "Who knows? I can't imagine what it must be like to get that old."

"Who would want to?" The elevator let them off on the ground floor and they were standing in the foyer, beneath its famous caveman poster.

"Want to go out to dinner with me?"

She looked at him with a narrow, sidelong glance, smiling crookedly. "I got a date tonight."

Sealock shrugged haphazardly. "Oh. OK, maybe some other time."

"Sure." They were walking down the street together, long strides matched, arms swinging in unison.

"Who is it, anybody I know?"

"Mike Torr."

"The snuff-dipper? You got to be kidding!"

"No, really!" She was giggling at him, almost blushing at his laughter. "He's a lot of fun."

Sealock shook his head in mock dismay. "Boy, oh, boy," he

said, "I will *never* understand why women make the choices that they do!"

"Now, now. Just because I didn't choose you is no reason to get bitter." They were still smiling, still in a teasing social mode.

"Yeah. I've heard all that before. How *can* you take that cud-chewer in preference to a Celtic god like me?" He posed before her in the street, flexing his muscles into a buckling chaos of flesh.

"My, *my!*" she exclaimed, running a hand over one stiffened bicep. "I just don't know. I *must* be mentally ill!"

"You must be." The charade fell apart as laughter overcame them.

"Look, I gotta run now. See ya later." She punched him in the arm and was gone. Sealock walked slowly back to his apartment, still grinning. She was fun to work with.

Later that night Brendan was standing in one of the little street parks so common in modern New York, watching the passing scene with a mild disinterest. There seemed to be a lot of bums out tonight. Probably most of them were just posing as bums, for it was a fun role that many people enjoyed playing. Some of them might be real bums, he supposed, people far gone in volitional alcoholism.

"Hi!" He turned about and saw one of the young girls from the Intro to QTD course that he was teaching. Cathy, um . . . no, Lori something-or-other. The rest of her name escaped him.

"Hello. Having a nice night?" She was slim and had lots of bushy red hair framing a cute, bland little face, with a light dusting of freckles. She was, he knew, something like eighteen years old.

She shrugged. "OK, I guess. I'm getting a little bored."

"Tired of studying?"

She nodded. "Your class is a little hard for me."

A glinting supposition appeared in his mind. "Tell you what," he said, "come on up to my apartment and I'll give you a nice body rub. Fix you right up."

She seemed startled and stared at him, hands on her hips. "What is this, some kind of come-on?"

**368**

He held his hands up before him, palms outward, grinning broadly. *"Perish* the thought! Look, I'm trying to do something nice for one of my students for a change. This'll be the ultimate in refreshing experiences. I *promise* not to fuck you."

She still seemed doubtful but went with him. Once there, she stood quietly while he spread a soft blanket on the floor of his living room, watching him closely. He turned to face her, and she said, "What do I do now?"

"Stand still." He began to undress her, unbuttoning her blouse, pulling off her tattered, cut-down shorts. He slid her out of a pair of green silk underpants and she stood naked before him, obviously uneasy. He looked her over and shook his head, smiling. Youth held its own special beauty, something he had not noticed when he had been that age. She blushed before his gaze, redness suffusing down onto her chest. "OK, now lie face down on the blanket." She did his bidding.

He got out a small bottle of almond-scented oil and poured it onto her back. She shivered as he touched her with his hands, beginning to knead the slippery stuff into her skin. She was tense at first, frightened by the way it had gotten out of her control so quickly, but later relaxed, surrendering to the experience as his hands squeezed her buttocks and worked their way down her legs.

He turned her over and worked on the front of her soft body. Her breathing quickened when he massaged her breasts and sweat began to bead across her brow and upper lip as his hands moved down her abdomen. She had at least one orgasm when he rubbed the oil slowly into her groin, but he kept his word to the end.

Morning found him sitting cross-legged on the beach, staring out across the steel-gray sea, watching the mists disperse before the oncoming day, waiting for the sun to rise out of the sea, a dull, fat orange ball. This was the day. He breathed in deeply, smelling the tang of ionized air, the scent of the land, sailors called it, and feeling it invigorate him, fill him with renewed life.

I love it here, he realized, just like I loved my childhood.

**369**

This time, I'll not let it get away. New York, Comnet, the life in the streets, all of it. I don't think I've ever been happier. How could I ever go away?

Scenes passed before him, women clustered thickly round, friends and experiences everywhere. His work was fulfilling, sex could be had just by stretching out his hand. He treasured the nights spent alone in his apartment, the times of close and somber thought. What else could anyone want?

The Games awaited. He got up and stretched carefully, feeling the solid muscles rippling across his back. Montevideo, he thought, and glory before my peers, then I come home again. He strode off into a gathering cloud of darkness.

Demogorgon felt himself going down the drain, like a childhood nightmare come to life at last. He swirled down and around and down, the darkness growing all around him. His memory and life were coming apart, and he felt himself fragmenting, subsystems flying off in all directions, preceding him into the night of nonbeing. He was silent and felt nothing as his emotional drivers were stripped from him. In the end, he was no longer a person, just a disembodied consciousness dropping in a tight spiral.

As he fell, other subsystems were being sucked up the center of the spiral, pieces of Brendan Sealock being reassembled by the process of his fall. He was succeeding. He recognized the bits as they swept past him, scenes from Brendan's life in which he had had a part. I will not completely die, then, he realized, for bits of me rise again, embodied in all the past that was his. Had he been able to feel, it might have been comforting.

He fell and the black clouds gathered him in. He fell and, in just a little while, he was gone.

Brendan Sealock felt himself rising through cottony layers of unconsciousness. It was like the journey that imagination sent him on in the old films. The doctor was peeling away the endless layers of gauze bandage that covered his eyes and he waited, frightened. Will I be able to see again when he's done? I don't want to know. The light grew as the layers of cloth between him and the world diminished. He fancied he could see the grainy texture of the gauze. What will I see when the last layer is gone? Will I emerge into a life of light and color or will the world always be a blur to me? Is a life of light and shadow without any detail better than black, blinding death? He was in agony, but he waited.

Suddenly, the last layer was gone.

Brendan Sealock awoke and opened his eyes.

# T  E  N

The world-lines were beginning to darken. In the sea of light that had delineated their existence, lines of dull ebony were beginning to penetrate, threads of blackness that advanced on their rigorous courses, heralding the extinction of individual subsystems. They felt themselves go with little keening cries of dismay.

Night overcame them in the midst of their lives, throwing them down as their tales strove to resume. Stories of an infinite past buckled in upon a common center, coalescing into a single bright dot, a spark which swiftly winked out. The walls of castles, then entire cities crushed together, imploding into nothingness. The horizons of the world were a swiftly closing circle, a fiery limit that wound itself tight, drawing the cosmos together like a death noose closing in on its vanishing point. The towers fell and were no more, shards of dull glass tumbling from the sky.

The universe became a plane which flattened itself with an effervescent hiss and was still, a black, tideless sea lying beneath a dark, featureless sky. The entities lay dead in its depths, become a mass of quiescent data. It ended.

They rose, like bubbles drifting buoyant through an endless sea, seeking the surface and light. Beneath them the detritus of their deeds was left behind, the wreckage of lives become as nothing. In the delimited world that fell away below them, they had but little consciousness, a sense of self that grew ever stronger as the blue light grew about them and the spectrum slowly broadened, taking on ever longer wavelengths as their separation lessened. They rose together at first, then one of the eight leaped ahead, taking on a teardrop shape as it flew, leaving behind a contrail of lesser bubbles. The false security of an artificial sun blossomed above; a burnished, wavering disk that beckoned them to come forth.

Far below, the shambles rested, waiting. All the pieces were there, whole but quiet, from stilled program to dead souls.

Brendan Sealock awoke into his body. He lay still for what seemed a long time, savoring the resurrection of physical sensations that had so long eluded him. It all seemed clear to him now, but he knew that it was a false reprieve from his own special reality. The lives of men are often immutable, no matter what they go through. In the distance he could hear the soft sighing of life-support machinery and, all about him, the whispering breaths of his still sleeping comrades. A smile tugged briefly at his lips and then vanished. I am mad, he thought.

He opened his eyes slowly and stared at the ceiling. It was a blank expanse of padded whiteness that told him nothing. He sat up and looked around. The others were still there, lying motionless, a profusion of induction leads sprouting from their heads. He reached up and began to unplug the taps from the sockets in his skull. Is it over now? he wondered.

He stood and began to move around the room, feeling faint, as if he were mildly ill. The world seemed removed a considerable distance from him, too far away for him to reach out with a caress. He stood looking down at Ariane. Once

**374**

again, her loose clothing was disarrayed, exposing her to his gaze. He felt like laughing. Had she always been like this, a careless person with all her secrets let out for all to examine? He didn't know. All the memories were there, clearer than they had ever been, but their content seemed somehow changed. He looked at the others, one by one, assessing them bleakly, until he came upon the still form of Demogorgon.

He felt a sense of remote loss. The dark face was filled with life, as if it might awaken in only moments to beg him once again. The Arab was almost pretty in his stillness. Brendan brushed the dark hair away from the man's dry brow and shook his head slowly. His emotions were curiously diminished, as if put away from him for good. Perhaps I am better off this way, a madman in whom none can detect the insanity. Another thought: I am dead. They failed to bring me back. He found it impossible to care.

The others began to stir and awaken, their eyes popping open like mechanical things. They rose gently, disengaging themselves from the machine with little regret. Sealock watched them from heavy-lidded eyes, looking for some response that exceeded his own, but found none. They were all equally drained. Perhaps it was a natural thing, and all concerns were needless.

He looked down at the still form and said, "So I live again, and this one dies."

Cornwell came across the room to stand before him, looking into his face. "Yes," he said, "and Jana too is dead—frozen."

Jana? Dead? Brendan felt a long moment of confusion, then the light and meaning of it all struck at him and he burst out laughing.

The others were staring at him as if he had truly gone mad. Still giggling fitfully, Brendan sank down on the couch beside what was left of Demorgorgon, muttering to himself, trying to catch his breath. " 'He died that others might live . . .' 'Unrequited love burns fierce in the hearts of men . . .' "

His laughter roared forth again, echoing in the closed room, and tears of mirth squeezed out of his eyes, oozing like oil in the low-g drag across his cheeks. "Oh, I can't stand it!" he

**375**

cried, pointing a finger at the motionless form. " '*This* was the noblest Roman of them all!' "

He stopped laughing then, gasping for breath. He sniffled, wiping his nose on the back of a sleeve, rubbing his hands across a dampened face. "Oh, *Christ* . . ." He picked up the still body and clutched it across his chest like a huge rag doll, grinning at the others. "What a *prize* bunch of assholes we are!"

Cornwell felt rage welling up from within him, a conflagration fueled by all that he'd been through, the things that he thought had happened to them all. "Nothing's changed then," he snarled. He stalked over to Sealock and stood before him, fists balled up and planted heavily on his hipbones. "*You* haven't changed, have you? Nothing affects a bastard like you! You're self-contained, aren't you? What happens is meaningless if it hasn't happened to you!"

Brendan let the man drift slowly back onto the couch and stared at him for a moment, a smile still twisting his lips. He turned to look at John, then slowly rose to his feet, seeming to tower over him, some kind of wrathful, demonic hulk. He glared for a moment, then grinned again. "Oh, I've changed, all right, kiddo," he said softly, "and so have you. Think about it."

He waved a hand to take in the other six. "We've changed because we had to, whether we're capable of realizing it or not. It's these strangers who haven't changed. While we were being burned in our own special crucibles, our little private hells, they were being cemented into their present form, forever."

"What're you talking about?" whispered Cornwell, but he had a horrible inkling of what was meant and, so, what was coming a short distance down the line.

"How can you be like this, Brendan?" cried Ariane. "For God's sake, he *died* for you!"

"Did he?" Brendan sat again and slowly drew the fingers of one hand across the man's smooth face. "Bullshit. He just wrote himself the best closing scene he thought he'd ever have. He knew I wouldn't let him down . . ."

"You . . ." Ariane stopped, choking, and her face slowly

darkened. She tried to speak again, failed, and then burst into tears and fled from the room. Vana glared at him, spat, "You *bastard!*" and went after her. Prynne followed them, wordless.

Axie stood in the silence, seeming almost to smile. "It's all meaningless, isn't it? Why would they expect you to change? You weren't there with us. You missed it all!"

Brendan's grin broadened. "I did, didn't I? But you're wrong. You all are. Demogorgon didn't die for me; he just went out the way he wanted to, and in so doing got his own way at last. 'Do a little something for me, just this once!' "

The woman shook her head, keenly feeling the loss of Beta-2 understanding. But underneath her shrunken awareness there was a new note of order—harmony—that kept her on course. Enfolded in this new structure, Brendan's face was somehow there, like a pistil in a flower, but the man standing before her was not this Brendan. Before her was a horrible distortion. "That may be your illness," she said softly, looking at the floor. "It seems you have always been incapable of understanding anyone except in the limited vocabulary by which you define yourself."

Brendan smiled faintly at her. "That may," he said, "be what you want to believe."

Axie stared at him through eyes that seemed for a moment to have become empty holes through her face into some darkness beyond, then she turned and left.

Beth followed the other woman through the door, her face streaked by unnecessary tears. John watched her go and felt benumbed, longing but unwilling to follow. Foreknowledge kept him in his place.

Temujin, catapulting himself from the cramped floor into a nearby chair, said, "OK, the histrionics are over. Materially, we're all still the same despite everything. We know something of the history of these things, but most of it is damnably sketchy and virtually all of it is unverifiable. What's to be done? Jana's still dead and now Demo is too. We haven't gained a thing."

Brendan deopaqued one relatively machineless wall of his chamber and stared out across the moonscape, smiling ruefully. "Haven't we? Thanks." He chuckled and said, "The old turn of phrase still suffices to cover up all traces of evil. No matter how close we come to another person, we are still blind. The filter of self still makes the world seem opaque. . . ."

John felt a moment of blank astonishment. The filter of self? The path his own thoughts had been taking was moving inexorably toward similar conclusions. There simply wasn't any other explanation for the horrible breakdowns that were all around. He could no longer chalk everything up to a failure of communication. We perceive what we need to perceive. The thought of it coming out of Sealock's lips made him feel slightly sick. The implications weren't good.

Brendan turned to face them, his face growing more serious than it had been since the awakening. "What's to be done?" he murmured. "Jana, dead? How . . . No, don't tell me. I know she killed herself somehow. I picked it up from Demo during my resurrection." He shook his head slowly, rubbing a broad hand across the back of his neck. "I saw him then, while the rest of you were being blind. . . . No, forget that. I haven't got a good reason for picking on you anymore."

"Well?" asked Krzakwa, "What do you suggest? Is there any way we can get Demo back? You know more about these things that the rest of us put together."

Brendan shrugged. "Nope. He's in there for good, I'm afraid. What can we do? Just pump him full of whatever Jana left behind is all." He laughed. "Hell, maybe she'll be more at home in there!"

"So," said John, dismayed at last. "He's dead forever, and it doesn't bother you?"

The man turned to face him, his features looking carefully controlled. "Two points," he said. "One: I didn't say that, you did. Two: why should it bother me?" He turned to look at the body and said, "Don't worry, pal. I'll see you didn't do it in vain. Can't leave you looking like an asshole, now, can we?"

John felt some of his rage and confusion recede. Something was going on that he felt capable of understanding. I've seen this all before, he thought.

**378**

□ □ □

Some time later Sealock and Krzakwa were in the chamber alone with the electronically supported body of Demogorgon and the cryogenic capsule containing the ice-encrusted remains of Jana Hu. The Arab's head was festooned with leads and Brendan had finished drilling into the dead woman's skull, installing deeply embedded brain-taps and scanners into the ruined tissue. It had been a bloodless operation, free of gore. What was left of her, brittle and harder than iron, looked less than human, more or less inorganic. Having been frozen very slowly, Jana did not even look like a statue. Her face looked like the broken ice on an expanded and refrozen stream.

"Think it'll work?"

Brendan shrugged his answer. "We'll get something. If she's lucky, it'll be enough to give her an intact sense of self and enough to combine successfully with the lower functions that Demo left behind when he went into Centrum."

The Selenite nodded. He had begun to learn. The supposed lower functions were actually the majority of what made up a human mind: the autonomic systems that took care of life and the emotional generators and consciousness mediators of the brain stem. Even above that the human soul was hard-wired in. All the neurolinguistic patterns were built in, add-ons though they might be. Of all the little habit patterns that so many people mistook for "personality," only the highest cortical functions, the parts of the mind that mistook themselves for the total "I," could be stripped off and sent elsewhere. That was, it seemed, the heart of what made Comnet work the way it did. That was the part of Demogorgon that had become embedded in whatever still functioned within Centrum and it was the part of Jana that they were trying to save. *Is he still alive in there?* Krzakwa wondered, feeling detached. *And what will it be like for her? To be invaded by alien emotions . . . and then to find out that* you *were the invader.* People from all centuries past had thought about the horror of being invaded and dispossessed by a dybbuk. *Why did no one wonder about how the monster felt?*

He caught a fleeting glimpse of what he'd seen in Sealock,

**379**

then, a recollection from the memories that Centrum had made public property. *That* was how it felt, perhaps. He felt a small surge of pity for the man. He'd been exposed before them all. Yet they all had, seemingly, seen each other's selves during the final battle. He had been operating on a kind of automatic pilot since coming back, not acknowledging the changes in him, but he had changed.

Sealock was grinning at him. "I don't have to be hooked up to you to read your thoughts," he said, "I can see it written on your face. If I thought you all understood what you'd seen, I might be a little worried, embarrassed or something. None of you did. Having your faces rubbed in an endless sea of vaginas made a pretty good shield for me. I came out of there with a rich haul." He turned to face the machinery. "Let's get this done."

"All right. One thing . . ."

Sealock looked at him questioningly, eyebrows slightly raised.

"What you said about not letting Demogorgon down. Is this what you meant?"

That brought a merciless grin. "Nope."

"What then?"

"I'll tell you later. Maybe I'll just let it stand at a firm 'You'll see.' " They turned to the machinery a final time, switched things on, and it began.

The scanners did their work well. They began searching among the rubble that was all that remained of the personality of Jana Li Hu, Hu Li-jiang. All the neurons of her brain had been ruptured by the growing ice crystals, all her interconnections broken asunder. There was much to be found among the destroyed circuitry of her soul. Still, the machines probed. The data were there, waiting to be interpreted. Most of what had called itself "me" in her had been concentrated into a thin cortical layer in the frontal lobes of her brain, a small amount more in the associative areas to either side. Like most other human beings, Jana was just a small packet of intense cognitive drivers and a bundle of language skills. It was easy to pluck out.

Because most of the brain was given over to switching

centers and data processing and retrieval devices, extreme miniaturization processes had been invoked by nature. Like a primitive computer from the dawn of electronics, most of what made up a person was just keyboard and plastic, and macroplugs. The part that did all the work was far less than one percent of the whole. There weren't enough nerves packed into those few cubic inches to make up a thinking, self-aware being, so it had all been done on a molecular level. Endless trails, endless arrays . . . the electrical patterns were still there, preserved, after a fashion, in the sea of frozen slush.

At the moment of death, or so it seemed now, she had heard her father's voice growling out of a dim Tibetan night: "I don't care what's in her mind, Pi Ling! The parts of a woman I'm interested in could be covered by a few square centimeters of silk! And that's what they ought to be, when I'm not embedded in 'em, by Mao!"

His cronies roared with appreciative laughter, their breath foul with a mixture of kumiss and rice wine, and the sound of it echoed down the corridors of time, waking her from a deep, dark, endless sleep which had been blessedly without dreams.

Li-jiang was seven years old. She squatted in the dark corners of the apartment building's community toilet, crouching inside a stall. She had her pants down and was holding a little oval mirror she'd found, looking at herself. She was pushing it down between her legs, trying to see all the places she went to the bathroom from. She remembered standing on her father's bed, trying to see her backside in the dresser mirror, and remembered his laughter. It was all funny-looking down there. Unlike everywhere else on her body, things were mushy and unsymmetrical. Her anus she understood, a simple sphincter to open and close tightly. But what was all this other nonsense for? She fingered the thick lips aside and squinted, bending down, trying to get a better look in the dim light. Why was the little hole she peed through mounted on that weird floppy structure? And what was that other hole for? It was unclosed, and nothing ever came out. . . . She

**381**

pushed a finger inside a little way and felt its moistness, but the action scared her, so she stopped.

Suddenly the door of the toilet banged open. Li-jiang gasped, horrified at the prospect of being discovered at these evil deeds, and tried to escape. She leaped to her feet, panicky, and tried to run, but she tripped over her trousers, which were down around her ankles, and fell on her face to the floor. The newcomer was laughing as he helped her up.

It was the teenage boy, Chang-chen, who lived a few doors down the hall from her family. He was about fourteen and quite handsome, tall, with unusually shiny dark hair and large eyes. He grinned at her with doglike white teeth as he sat her on the toilet seat, seeming to ignore her state of disarray. "What's all this now, little one?" He picked up the little mirror and fingered it delightedly. "Trying to have a little look-see, find out what all the uproar is about?"

She nodded dumbly, unable to think in her shame and terror. He laughed again, seeming hugely pleased. He picked her up and sat down, holding her on his lap. She squirmed, but he held her fast. "Now, now," he said. "You just hold still and I'll tell you all about it."

She gasped as he placed his hand over her mons veneris, squeezing it lightly. "This," he said, "is what makes every woman worth a thousand men. And this"—he stuck his index finger into her vagina, making her whimper at a thin, strange stab of pain—"is the place where all men long to be." He ran his finger slowly in and out. "You like that?" She shook her head frantically, but he didn't seem to notice. "Well, remember what I say and you'll rule the world!" It went on and on, his fingerings and pinchings and touchings. Time disappeared into a haze of pain and confusion. Later on he held her up in the air and began licking between her legs. That felt very funny, strange, and it almost tickled, but the vileness of what was happening made her sick and she threw up down his back. That made him very angry and she carried the bruises with her for days.

Jana considered the ancient memory. As she recalled, the boy had grown up to be a powerful canton official in Tibet,

**382**

then had killed himself over some scandal or another. Something to do with the star of a visiting South American soccer team.

Damn! A painful pins-and-needles sensation dug at her, racking the centers of her brain as if with a return of circulation. What was happening? She remembered being in the car, far out on the ocellus, and then being trapped outside with a damaged thermocouple. Oh, God! she cried silently. I thought freezing to death was supposed to be painless! She remembered all the old myths about how a dying man's life was supposed to flash before his eyes as he drifted beneath the surface of the sea for the last time, or fell past the walls of a building, counting the stories as he dropped toward certain doom. How strange that it should all turn out to be true, but not as one died, as one was reborn . . .

Somewhere, far away, a little voice told her that it was not true. I'm still dead, she realized. I've been dead for a very long time, centuries, in fact. I am a mausoleum, a tourist attraction in the remote future. See the funny ancient statue these humans from the dawn age left here on Ocypete's ice!

What can be happening to me? Is one of the old religions really true? Nonsense! She pushed the absurd idea away.

Something else was coming now, something tainted with alienness, but it seemed to be her memory nonetheless. She waited for it patiently, and it came upon her with a roar.

Li-jiang was eleven and Obey Cadre was in full swing. She still remembered it as having been among the worst and most repulsive things she had ever done in her life, but it all seemed changed now. Why?

She had some of the littler boys and girls trapped in a closet with her, and she was doing things to them. It hadn't originally been her idea; other generations of older bullies had started Obey Cadre long before she came on the scene, but she was the best at it. She controlled them all, bent them to her forming will with exquisite precision. Sometimes she liked to whip them with her belt, listen to them squeal, but that wasn't all.

She made them disrobe and lie on the floor. She grinned as

**383**

she took down her warm, quilted trousers and laid them carefully to one side. Had she been a Caucasian, she would have had the silken beginnings of pubic hair by now, but she was Chinese and it had yet to begin. Her covering would always remain sparse.

She squatted over little An-qing, chuckling as evilly as she could manage, trying to make the play-acting part of it as real as possible. He stared, horrified, for a moment, and then squeezed his eyes shut, as if able to anticipate what was about to happen to him. She began to urinate in his face and he spluttered, trying to turn away from the thin, hot stream.

She giggled at him. Yes, this was more like it! Maybe I can pee up his nose, she thought. She took her penis in hand, trying to direct it a little higher and . . .

The world froze suddenly, becoming crystalline and still, the very atoms pausing in the courses. She and the boy became a tableau, two inanimate beings connected by a bright stream of urine that had glittered in the dim light, still shone of its own accord.

Her penis?

Had she been able to, Li-jiang would have screamed and, screaming, have carried the terror to the Jana who lay in her vast, roving future.

What was going on here? Something alien had entered into her dying dreams. The visions of what had been were somehow altered, as if some strange change were being thrust upon her. She felt resentment at the fact that these last fleeting moments of consciousness were being spoiled, then remorse at this perception of the way she had been. How did I suddenly turn into a boy? she wondered and . . .

Li-jiang was thirteen. This memory was the one that she cherished the most, the thing she recalled when she wanted to feel warm and wonderful, to feel the things that had put her life on so special a course.

She stood above the high plateau, sequestered among the jagged peaks that had once known only the wanderings of barbaric tribes and mad, mountaineering Englishmen, the mountains that were now filled with bold, sad Chinese. She

**384**

was out on a school expedition, left alone in the summery hills above Lhasa and its temples. It was a test, to see if she were made of the stern stuff that the Enclave required. She would be coming of age soon, she knew with a shudder of disgust, and the Eugenics Council would want to know if she had anything worth passing on to the generations of unborn.

The stars lay above her in glorious polar array, millions of them, it seemed, all nameless and wonderful, sparkling like diamonds in a field of black felt. She watched them and they made her feel good. They seemed untouchable, remote, far from the defiling things of mankind that made the world such a hard thing to bear.

Her eyes followed the patterns that they made as her mind carried her toward gentle sleep. The patterns made pictures in the sky, she knew, but she hadn't learned them yet, in fact, didn't really want to. It was enough that the stars were there for her on nights like these.

She followed the lines, tracing out constellations of her own devising against the night, growing muzzy and vague as tiredness overcame her. Her vision focused on a big, bright V shape in the sky. It seemed like a restful shape, but hard and angular. They drifted away to another place nearby.

Li-jiang gasped and came fully awake with a start. Why . . . What was that one? It was the most beautiful thing she had ever seen! It was a little grouping of bright jewels off to one side of the V, a cluster of tiny stars that seemed to be embedded in a dim, fiery haze. I wonder what it's really called? she wondered. When I get home I'll have to find out. It held her enraptured for half the night. She wanted to stay up longer and watch the little asterism fade, but sleepiness overwhelmed her at last, carrying her off into a dreamless land where nothing could ever intrude. Her last waking thought was, I'll really have to find out what they call it . . .

Li-jiang was fifteen and going to be with a man, truly, for the first time in her life. She was terrified and disgusted with herself for doing it, yet pathetically anxious to please him. He was Deng-yuan, a boy from the Astronomy Club, tall and very handsome, with pale skin, the blackest of hair, and the nicest, deepest eyes she had ever seen. He was always kind and spoke to her as if to an equal, though he was two years older and a world of experience wiser. She knew he was trying to be gentle with her, but it still hurt.

He stroked at her for the longest time, breathing quietly on the side of her face, waiting for her to be ready, but somehow she never was. He kissed her from time to time and whispered sweet delicatenesses into her ear. He licked into it and let his hot breath flow after the moisture, thinking to excite her in a traditional manner.

This is supposed to be nice, she thought. What's wrong with me?

Suddenly he was on top of her, pulling aside clothing, inside of her, heaving massively away, his breath rasping thickly over her face, his huge maleness tearing away at her delicate insides. She caught her breath and started the scream that she remembered would send him leaping off her in horror, would send him fleeing into the night, never to see her again, but it never happened.

Suddenly, the young man was enveloped in an angelic halo of supernatural beauty. He was a gorgeous man, something she had always appreciated. She felt her insides melt with unknown passion, become fluid for him, and she felt him relax into her, spending his effort with a small, delightful cry of pleasure. His orgasm swept her away and she began too, a pulse of delight reaching out to tingle in her fingertips and bring a flush of heat to her cheeks.

It was a wonderful experience, the first of many that she longed to enjoy. . . .

In her impenetrable darkness, Jana was horrified. It didn't happen that way! she cried, trying to break through the barrier of her motionless silence. I did scream! I was in agony! I never learned to enjoy it . . . I never did . . .

Had she been able to sob, her feelings of intense despair would have driven it out into the darkness. They're changing me! she wanted to wail, but it went on and on . . .

**386**

□ □ □
Hu Li-jiang was seventeen. She sat alone in her dorm room at Ulaanbaatar's Reflexive Institute at night, conducting her studies. This place, remote in the relatively backward wastelands of Central Asia, was positively archaic, but she enjoyed the work, enjoyed learning nonetheless. Perhaps she would stay forever. The big observatory at Uliassutai was not the most modern in the world, and was ridiculous in comparison to the off-world-scopes that dominated modern science, but half the time they went unused, having cataloged the entire universe to the limits of man's desire to fund.

For all she knew, she might discover something new, something not yet noticed by the pattern-recognizers in the few continuously operating projects.

The Comnet lines had only been run in here a few years ago, had still not gotten to her home in Tibet, but she had learned how to use them quickly and well. Her professors, in considerable difficulty themselves over the new mode of learning, looked upon her as a star pupil. If only the others would leave her alone. Their slimy attentions were unwelcome. They debased her as a person.

She thought about her roommate, a tall blonde girl of Russian stock who had grown up in Tannu Tuva. She was a beautiful young lady, Darya Anni, and the object of every male eye on the campus. In the late evenings Jana sometimes watched her undress, prepare herself for a date or for sleep, and it felt very strange. She admired the woman's large breasts, with their delicate pink nipples, and found herself staring at her bright starburst thatch of pubic hair with some strange, formless sense of regret.

What am I becoming? she sometimes wondered. She wanted nothing to do with any of it, most of the time, but the sleek wilderness of the woman's body reached out to her nonetheless.

She thought of Klaus, the Volga-German boy who lived two floors up. She had gotten to know him fairly well, and sometimes liked him. He was a good student in the newly named Department of Asterology, land of the star-studiers,

**387**

second, perhaps, only to her. She felt good when he gave her work his seemingly awestruck compliments.

She sighed. He was known far and wide across the campus as something of a pervert. So far as anyone could tell, he was still a technical virgin, and he seemed to be more or less impotent. No one had even seen him masturbate, or ever seen the telltale tenting evidence of a nocturnal erection, but there were things he liked to do. . . . And he did them well! She had spent a few nights groaning beneath the tireless lash of his tongue, wishing that her desires would just go away. She envied him his apparent inability and wondered why he bothered to perform.

The door suddenly popped open, swinging inward as she looked up. A broad, heavy Mongol face peered in, eyes slitted beneath a particularly massive epicanthic fold. Bayan Joghu from next door. "Anni in?" he asked in Gwo-yu, the dorm's official language.

She shook her head. "Too bad," he said, and retreated. Before the door could swing shut another figure burst through it, a short, slim Japanese boy whose name she could not remember. His fly was down, his long penis dangling out, swaying ludicrously, one of his pockets turned inside out. "Hey, Hu!" he cried, breathing out the dense fumes of some smoky drug. "Look! It's a . . ."

". . . one-eared elephant!" she snarled, reaching for the square glass paperweight that she knew she would throw at him, knocking him unconscious and bloodying his brow.

The action went uncompleted. Her hand swung past the object and clutched at his groin. She heard his squawk of surprise and delight as she seized the organ and stuffed it into her eager mouth. A ring of stunned faces appeared in the door, watching what she did with dazed astonishment, with total disbelief.

"Will you look at that!" came an awed whisper.

"The ice queen's blowin' him," said someone else.

They cheered as she swallowed and her popularity began to ride on the crest of a dramatic upswing.

Far in the future, Jana tried to still her rampant horror. I knocked him out, she sighed to herself. I fractured his skull and almost got kicked out of school! I did! I *remember* it! Is that merely what I should have done, or is it what someone else, in my place, would have done? Who am I becoming? And still it went on. . . .

A mélange of memory . . . a mosaic of moments. All the times she had known, the cascading changes, flooded through the minutes, the hours, that had known no meaning. Only when it reached a kind of watershed did it pause and enact a painful reliving. Hu Li-jiang was twenty. She had recently been granted an assistantship at the Reflexive Institute and now she had power over some of the students. She had told the girl to meet her on the quad after sunset, it being one of the few good nights of high summer on the Gobi Plateau. She savored the meeting with quick anticipation and felt the flesh loosening between her thighs. Obey Cadre held nothing to the things she could do now. She waited patiently, smiling to herself. The girl wanted a perfect grade, and she was willing to pay for it in an excellent coin. . . .

The man appeared. He was tall and thin, a dark-haired Caucasian of Armenian stock, something of a rarity in these parts. He was hawk-handsome and his slickly oiled hair shone in the waning light. She found her gaze riveted upon him by an unaccountable, unfamiliar magnetism. He held out his hand to her and she went to him, molding her body against his alien sleekness. He ran his hand between her legs and she thrilled to his touch.

They strolled away together, arm in arm, leaving the student girl to stare after them, perplexed. She had come prepared to debase herself and felt cheated that this gigolo had stolen away the chance. Li-jiang gave her the grade nonetheless.

Jana cried out in the darkness. I made her have sex with me! I remember it! I made her *pay* for what I could give out! Didn't I? She suddenly realized she could no longer remember it as well as she'd thought. Why is it all fading away? How can this be happening to me? She moaned. . . .

And that same year Li-jiang remembered receiving the com message, watching as the self-decoding cipher she had designed did its work. The Free University at Vancouver was proud to offer such a fine young savant its riches. She whooped with joy, danced with unaccustomed merriment. They were offering her a full professorship, with unlimited access to remote observations, the chance to direct her own research program!

I'll need a new name, she mused, something to separate me from the old life I'm leaving behind. No more am I a creature of the Institute. Who shall I be? I want to blend in. Jiang . . . Jana! That's it! Dr. Jana Li Hu, Chinese-Canadian asterologist . . .

No, a faint voice whispered. You have a name. Your *real* name is a good enough label . . . Hua-hung.

She changed her mind.

No! I *am* Jana! I've been Jana for half of my life! She sobbed in her eternal darkness and, for just a moment, swore that she could feel the slow crawl of tears worming their way across the ruined landscape of her frozen face. What was it?

Impossible.

Li-jiang was a hundred years old. She lay on a silken divan surrounded by a diffuse gauze of sea-green mosquito netting somewhere in the tropics. She was immortal and the endless life served her well. She was gifted by eternal youth and had become completely given over to the pleasures of the flesh that had tried to claim her since childhood.

The advances of surgery had changed her, augmenting her beauty until it was an unearthly thing. Between her legs there was a great iridescent flower of flesh. She had become a perfect androgyne, able to take enjoyment wherever she would. The flower would open to accept men or compress for the swift penetration of compliant women. She used them by the dozen, reeling her ancient way through a thousand and more orgasms in a single day.

They fed her, bathed her, and she never had to stir from the airy, gently swaying bed that was her home. The great people, the famous ones, came to enjoy her uniqueness from all over the inhabited universe. In the distances a great hard squid lurked, waiting its turn. She sought the discharge of its anchorelles with breathless anticipation. She used her experiences at a prodigious rate, secure in the knowledge that the universe was truly infinite, that all the newnesses could never be exhausted.

In the hot confines of her darkness Jana cried, pleading for death to end the torture, for the world to turn her loose and let her fall end over end down into the vast night of nonbeing.

She awoke.

Through the thin skin of her closed eyelids the world was a sea of light. She felt her lips curve in an unfamiliar smile. She sighed, and the resonances of her breath sounded strange. Her chest felt light, somehow tighter, as if the negligible weight of her small breasts was gone, amputated. Maybe they have been. The extremities would have taken the most damage, she thought.

She stirred, and felt that her limbs were still there, all her fingers and toes accounted for, still willing to wiggle. They felt strange and angular, longer and thinner than they had been. Prostheses? Am I back on Earth? No. She felt the lightness of Ocypete's hold.

Her hips felt wrong. Narrow. The legs seemed connected at the wrong angle, far too acute. She seemed bony. She sighed again, listening to the hoarse rasp. Might as well face it now, she thought. I wonder what this lump between my legs could be? Probably a catheter. I must be pretty sick. . . .

She opened her eyes and Brendan Sealock's dead face swam into view, smiling at her. Oh! She lurched upward, off balance, and clutched him to her nonexistent bosom in a fierce hug. Strong emotion, unfamiliar emotion, washed over her. To see him once again! She felt a powerful desire to pull him down on her, to feel the swift penetration of his burgeoning manhood, to submit herself to his will.

She buried her face in his chest and said, "I knew you'd come in time, beloved!" in a voice far too deep.

Jana's screams seemed to echo for hours in the cold spaces of the CM. Her horror on awakening to find herself both dead and changed was uncontrollable, a raving madness of whirling motion that brought them down on her in moments. Her wild, glaring rage out of Demogorgon's lost eyes took them away from her, transformed her to a *thing,* and seemed to make them all impersonal and remote. It transferred them all into the past for a brief time.

Lightly sedated, she went to sleep for a time, dreamless, and awoke, as always, alone within herself.

She lay there in her bed, hunkered down in the warm, drowsing comfort that fills in the chasms of a slow awakening. I had the strangest dream, she whispered to herself, a slight smile marking the lines of her face. How bizarre I can be at times, how artistic! One of her hands drifted across the expanse of soft sheets warmed by body heat and touched a soft flank, her own. She rubbed her fingers across the gentle flesh and her smile broadened. Now, she thought. . . . The hand lifted upward of its own accord and descended on her abdomen. It drifted across a delicate expanse, headed for her groin, intent on the soft pleasures of sleepy masturbation. The fingers glided through a dense tangle of crisp, curling hair, feeling for the sensitive skin of swelling labia, for the moistness of engorging tissues and . . .

Her eyes snapped open to stare hard at the ceiling rimmed with stark whiteness, and her breathing quickened, expressing itself in short gasps of renewed terror. No dream.

She felt herself again and shuddered. The unexpected organ was there, a stiff temple of flesh growing like some alien symbiote from her body, pulsating with a ready eagerness that defied logic. Her fingers jerked away, her hand clawed in upon itself, then slowly, inexorably, went back to its exploration. Long, thick, knob-ended, a heartbeat exposed to public view. Ridged on the upper surface, pulpy and softer below, vanishing into folded flesh as she progressed. It hardened still more under her touch, as men always did, souls out of control, and she felt a strong sense of pleasure that made her feel sick. Her breath rasped in her throat and grew deeper.

The madness wanted to close in again, but something, some indefinable factor from deep within, was holding it at bay. The fingers of her right hand continued in their course,

**392**

following the well-marked route of an old, familiar trail. She stroked slowly, gently, feeling the little ridge that marked the beginning of the bulbous end, touched the little hole gently, and backed away from an unexpected tenderness. She squeezed hard and moved more quickly, felt the skin of her face tighten, then grow slack. The forces from within made her gasp against her will, uncontrollable. How odd, how odd . . .

Muscles deep within her body suddenly clenched, nausea closing in. Oh, she gasped, wondering if she'd somehow injured herself. The thing tightened and tightened . . . it pulsed and she felt a strong surge of warmth rush away from the center of her body, reaching out to her extremities in a fraction of a second. Another pulse followed on the heels of the first and she felt a sensation a little like urination. The warmth increased, making her flush. The pulses went in rapid waves, tearing her mind apart, and she felt puddles of hot wetness forming on her stomach.

Her mind came back with a sickening rush, bringing with it a feeling of tiredness, of collapse. She felt like a suddenly punctured balloon. It was over, almost as if it had never happened. She felt strange, horrid. She lay there, staring at the ceiling, her thoughts fragmented and unreal. Who am I, where am I, and why? It was all too terrible for rational contemplation. Do I deserve to think?

She sat up and looked around. Oh, God . . . for some reason they had put her in Demogorgon's room. His effects surrounded her on every side. She looked at all his things and felt warm, comfortable. Somehow, they made her feel calm. She got up and began to walk around aimlessly, and after a while her wet stomach began to feel cold.

She stood in front of his full-length antique mirror and looked at herself, at the alien reflection in the mirror.

*At him . . .*

She stared at the slim, dark man in front of her, his face mimicking her most usual expression, his brow taking on the lines that had always creased hers. Her thought furrows were reborn.

How did this happen? She thought she knew. The explana-

**393**

tions had been made. She was intelligent and could piece the story together on her own. She shook her head and Demogorgon's head made the same moves in return, an instant response. She touched the mirror and he reached out to her. . . . She burst into tears and watched him cry unashamedly before her gaze.

What is my name? she wondered. Li-jiang. No Jana. No Achmet Aziz el-Tabari. No Demogorgon. Those people are all dead. She stared at the curdled semen still sticking like cold glue to her skin, shining at her eyes, mocking her. Something far within felt like laughing.

Slowly, she turned and walked out the door of her chamber, still naked, to walk the halls of the CM, seeking an unneeded, unheralded absolution. And to give it forth in lieu of honor. . . .

Reluctantly, with a numb dread that actually felt like friction against his shoulders and neck holding him back, John moved to the chair that he used for composing and sat. He rolled back the headrest and lay his head back, looking blankly at the ceiling. Every part of him recoiled from the idea that he could actually go back to music after all that had happened—deep inside he felt the total inadequacy of the medium—and, further, he felt somehow that using the pain that filled him for the task would somehow be trivializing it, and himself in the process.

A quick, almost abstract vision appeared in his head, accompanied by a riveting, stirring sensation of déjà vu. It was blue above, green below, with an almost sourceless yellow light everywhere in between. He was tumbling, moving across the soft, perfect lawn, enchanted with the new concepts of himself and the world and the joyous intermingling of the two. It was his earliest memory. He couldn't have said when, or where it was, or who had been there, for he seemed to be alone, out of time.

And then the second memory, in a room at night, the impossibly bright face of the three-quarter moon staring in at him, scaring him beyond his little ability to reason, hanging there, a specter or icon so far removed from what he understood as to reduce the world and himself to symbols in the dark misunderstanding.

The memories passed. He thought he understood something of what it all meant. Calling up his overlays, he began with a first note.

Vana, Harmon, and Ariane sat in the latter's room, talking far into an ersatz night of their own making. Their flesh needed a comforting touch, a renewal of contact, but still they held off, filled with questions without answers and a formless dread that had no name.

Prynne sprawled bonelessly on the bed, his arms and legs lying in the positions to which they had fallen, listening, without speech, without ideas. The time within Centrum had made him whole, but it had also left him empty. He knew himself for what he was now, and knew that he would never go beyond those limits. It was enough. It had to be.

Berenguer sat cross-legged at his feet, looking at the other woman. "What does it all mean, Ariane?"

She laughed at the age-old question, a soft sound, giving them some sense of the destruction that had been wrought upon her. "Mean? It means nothing, Vana. The changes that have been made in us are all illusory. We're still the same, we just see each other more clearly now. Brendan's still what he always was . . . I just never knew it before." She laughed again, a harsher, bitterer sound. "I called him a god once! I was in love with what I thought was the depth of his soul. It's not there and never was. I loved what I thought I saw, and *that* was just a construct, a blank space filled with images from the depths of my own longing. . . . I'm glad it's over. Seeing the truth has made me freer than I ever dreamed possible."

The others nodded wisely at that, imagining that they understood. Finally Prynne sighed and said, "I wish Demo was still here. I'd like to go into the Illimitor World once again . . ."

Ariane smiled, then reached out and touched them both softly. "We don't need it anymore," she said, "for we have each other." She stretched slowly before them, watching the radiance of her beauty grow in their eyes. "And Demogorgon will always live on in our hearts."

Because she said it, for the moment it was so.

Axie and Tem were having dinner together, enjoying one of his lesser creations. They tasted it and praised the food, smiling often at each other. Somehow they were thrown together, the man made whole by his experiences, the woman restored to what she perceived as her original "self." It made them similar, after a fashion, and they converged. Some repressions are, in the end, beneficial.

"Do you suppose she'll ever be the same?"

The Selenite shrugged. "You probably know as much about it as I do, Ax. We won't know how much we rescued until she calms down a little."

The woman nodded meditatively, thinking back about what she knew, drawing on the resources of a more complicated past. "Yes. And until we know how much of Demo's true self resided in the cells of his brain. It's a pity things had to turn out this way. We should never have come out here like this."

"I know what you mean. I'm sorry I had to leave the Moon, but there wasn't any other way. While I stayed there I could never be free. I could never find out about who I was."

"So it all had to take place then, for us all to grow. If I'd stayed on Earth, my life would've killed me. I took the drugs, ate all the experiences I could grasp, and ran and ran. I had to flee from a heritage that was strangling me, and at last it brought me here." She rested her chin on small, delicate hands and smiled across at his bearded bulk, her eyes seeming to glisten in the subdued light of the room they were in. "We've become adults, Tem, after a too long adolescence. I wonder: is it too late?"

He shook his head, his smile slowly fading as he gazed into the depths of her vision. "Never. Only I have to ask myself—what happened to us in there? Was this feeling of . . . happiness . . . somehow imposed from without?"

"Does it really matter? Or, to put it another way, is there

**396**

really a difference? From the moment we were born everything has been, as you say, imposed from without."

"If it were a hundred years ago, I'd ask you to marry me, Aksinia."

Her cheeks dimpled at the compliment. "If it were a hundred years ago, I'd accept, Temujin Krzakwa."

They laughed, together, and moved on.

Jana stood before a clear, cold window, looking at the crystal pulp that remained from her body, seeing the death that she'd bought for herself. It was an unreal sight, steaks frozen, thawed, and frozen again. Her hair had turned to a stiffened spikiness, limned with frost and ice crystals. The beloved physical processes which shaped the world beneath her feet were responsible for this transformation. Ice queen —how appropriate that she had come to study and love the geology of the outer Solar System. But it wasn't that simple, not by a long shot. And, indisputably, the woman that she had been was dead.

Did I feel it? she wondered. Did it hurt? It was more than just that, of course. Am I still in there? You can record a song over again, then burn the original tape, and the song still lives . . . but is it still the same song? Is a recording ever real? Does a song vanish forever when the singer's breath runs out, when the last echoes die down? What's left of me? She sighed. Probably nothing. I'm Demogorgon, with a rebuilt personality. . . .

Then something in her rebelled, a heat rising out of nowhere, a flame rising to devour her doubts. It cannot be! But she deflated again. No. Jana is gone. Demo is gone. Just little Li-jiang remains to carry on in their stead, making a little pretense of life.

Li-jiang strode from Jana's mausoleum, not wondering what had become of the one whose body she now owned. Process instructions cascaded down the sequences of a mind in turmoil, unwinding, and the self-image, rising out of the depths, recognized itself as male, if nothing else. The various impulses coalesced, melting together to form a coherent whole, because the alternative was a permanent and incurable madness.

Demogorgon and Jana had survived the exacting demands of their own lives, separate. Now, together, Li-jiang would survive because he had to.

Purpose came, and drove him on into the darkness.

Brendan Sealock sat at his desk going over the hard copy of Bright Illimit that he'd made before leaving Earth. It was a heavy, cumbersome volume printed on expensive paper only tens of molecules thick, with more than twenty thousand pages, and would probably have been impossible to get for someone not in his position on the Design Board. These things were archaic, but they had their uses. You could hold an entire entity in your hands, access it by essential feature and taxon, scan it without an explicit overlay.

He was going through it now, marking off the places where conjoiner programs would have to be inserted. If he assumed that everything was actually intact, then all that was necessary was to sew the damned thing back together. . . . He came to the section that handled the GAM-and-Redux functions and smiled, feeling strange. He'd put himself into that, in a way, but the program lacked the externals that made other people invent their personae for him. Just, be smart and helpful. He could see how it had begun to manifest higher functioning once Torus-alpha had been booted. Now, he thought, once I get this thing up and running again, it'll know where to start and what to look for. The pieces of the rest should still be there for it to latch onto. . . . And, what the hell, I can preserve the resonance within Centrum as a reward . . .

The door crackled open.

Brendan looked up, almost absent-mindedly, and winced. The form of Demogorgon was standing within the opening, staring at him rather somberly. He sat back and took a deep breath, then said, "Come in, Jana."

The man came in and walked slowly across the room, feet gliding bare centimeters from the floor. "Please don't call me that anymore," he said.

**398**

Brendan nodded. "OK. I, uh . . . I'd rather not call you Demogorgon, though."

That made the man smile. "That's no more correct than Jana was, is it? I'd like to be known as Li-jiang, from now on."

Sealock's lips twisted in a parody of a grin. "That doesn't really fit your appearance too well either."

"No." Li-jiang laughed in a light, pleasant baritone. He closed the remaining distance to Brendan and sat down at his side. The other man seemed to squirm away from him slightly, as if avoiding his touch. Li-jiang slid his arm around his shoulders and said, "I need to talk to you, Bren."

Sealock tried to force his tightening muscles to relax, but they kept getting away from him, one winding up as another loosened. He gave up and sat there, stiff, looking steadfastly at the book. "What do you want?"

Li-jiang looked up at him, at the scarred irregularities of his face. What do I tell him and how do I begin? he wondered. "I thought I'd come in here and tell you that I loved you," he said, "but I can see that's not it. . . ."

Brendan's face turned to look at him, a bland mask. "That's probably a good idea. Jana was in love with John. Demogorgon . . ." He turned away again.

"That's not so. Jana loved no one. She was trying to fool you all, and accidentally got killed in the process. This is a new person beside you."

Brendan nodded slowly once again. "If you want to become, uh, Li-jiang, well, think about it in any way that makes sense to you," he said. The man put his other arm around him, embracing the thick barrel of his chest. Brendan ruffled a hand through the sleek black hair, nuzzling him softly. "We can't do this, you know."

"Why not? Jana was no heterosexual, but she could be physically moved by some men, and Demo . . ." Li-jiang thought about the dreams that had accompanied his resurrection and felt a touch of the madness return: if only I had my old body back, I'd know how to use it now!

"It's not that." He paused, holding the man tight up against him. "It's no use. Doing this would hurt *me* too much, now that it's too late."

"I'm sorry. . . ."

"So am I. You deserve better than this. We all do." He began leafing through the book again with his free hand.

Li-jiang relaxed and slowly released his hold on him. "What are you doing?" It seemed like a good time to talk of other things: Jana and Demogorgon had both understood pain.

"I'm working on a solution to Demo's little problem."

"Is that possible? I thought he was all tangled up in the ruins of Centrum."

"He is. So was I, and here I am."

Li-jiang felt a little stab of terror, night and death threatening to return. "But . . . he's got no body to return to! I mean . . ." Will they put me back?

Brendan laughed softly. "Don't worry, we won't erase your soul. I've got something a little better in store for him than what we came up with for you." He contemplated the symbols he was marking among the pages, then said, "Look, why don't you go find some of the others to talk to, learn to find your way among people again? I think you have unfinished business with John."

Li-jiang nodded. "I do." He rose, stood gazing at Brendan for another little while, then turned and left without another word or a backward glance.

Brendan sighed and continued working. After a while he began to whistle a Parisian street song that Demogorgon had taught him long ago. Someday I'll just be a sentimental old fool, he thought.

The program swiftly took shape.

Hours later, Tem and Brendan sat before their equipment boards again, getting ready to play out a final act of their prolonged saga. The Selenite thought he understood what they were going to try but felt a need to talk it over nonetheless. Sealock's schemes seemed to grow ever more complex and so incomprehensible.

"Once again: do you really think this is going to work? I thought Centrum's problems, going off course and all, stemmed from a gradual breakdown of its equipment with the passage of aeons. How can Demo live on in there?"

"All that's true only in a limited sense. What broke down on it was the evolution and development of the Seedees. It lived off them, relied on them for correcting the deficiencies of its self-wired circuits. When they fell, it did too. Most of what was in the Mother Ship was life support for the crew, if we can call it that. Most of the ship's actual machinery along the axial core, the propulsion units and so on, are probably in pretty good shape. Once we send down some good programs, things can probably be made to work again."

Tem looked dubious. "If you say so."

"I do. The changes I've made in Bright Illimit should be enough to get the ball rolling along, then Demo can take over and organize things to his own satisfaction. He'll know what to do. Shall we get started?"

"Whenever you're ready . . ."

They plugged in, went under, and down, riding the black winds of eternity like velvet eagles on a dark, fluid tide.

The instructions that they went in on were simple, the symbolism that they led to was not. The process counter fed in through the quantum conversion scanner and began tabbing across the bare tag ends of data that it was able to touch, inspecting, identifying, looking for the one thread that would allow it to begin untying the snarled knot that it faced. The hunting went on and on until all the candidates were identified. Any remaining consciousness in Centrum or its subroutines would have helped, but there was nothing left. The place was grave-silent. The machine paused, watching its timer count away, considering its options, then it fell down all the trails at once, following the delicate spoor down an endless series of branching trails, coming ever closer to some kind of center, like a nut caught in a swift whirlpool. The great drain approached.

Far below, the dark sea of Iris waited. It was, as it had been, a flat, black, dead surface, quiet, tideless, engulfing a moonless, starless sky. The data were puddled into a formless mass. Though there was nothing present to look upward, no

**401**

living thing to see, still the scenery was there. Ghost clouds formed above, faint luminescences that swirled and moved, presaging some unknown event to come. The clouds took on form, bringing order to the void, little silvery masses in which some kind of grainy structure could be seen. Streamers of vague light reached out from each cloud, wafting across the sky in webworks of ever increasing complexity until the skies were linked together. On the surface of the sea, patterns of restive wavelets began to form. Energy accumulated as the Searcher came in on its guidepath.

A spot of dim, golden light appeared in the heavens and waxed, watching its own reflection in the mirror surface of the sea. Agitation on the water disturbed it, throwing off majestic scintillae that conspired to drown out the heavens. The golden spot continued to brighten, growing ever larger behind the silver clouds, discoloring them, peeling them back layer after layer, reversing the gauzework process that had enveloped this world so long ago. The aeons reversed themselves, and the tension became a palpable thing.

The sky broke open. The heavens around the golden spot, now a molten pool of brassy, burnished metal, were riven by a diamond flash of light, soundless, hazy rays flashing briefly away in all directions. A beam reached down, slowly, like cold fire streaming toward the surface of the dark sea. It stretched out, with agonizing slowness approaching the ebony waters, now thrashing about beneath the lash of an infinite energy. It touched.

The sea contracted suddenly, drawing the darkness inward from all directions, pulling the cosmic-event horizon in upon itself to form a dimensionless point, filling its surround with a heavy wash of gray static, a flannel screen upon which all images could then be drawn. The beam vanished, leaving the black spot alone in all of creation.

It waited, gathering its strength, and considered what it might do. The internal timers found themselves and began to tick away of their own accord. Given a structure, the program counters began to process their work, sort through the data in their channels, seeing what might be done to resume their

**402**

long-forgotten tasks. GAM-and-Redux awoke and began looking for a host to parasite itself upon, and succor.

The black spot contracted itself to that unimaginable density beyond which it could not go, and then it exploded. The gray world fragmented, glassy shards roaring away to the far reaches of space, colliding with a faint, melodious tinkling, smashing into ever smaller pieces, filling the universe with light and life. Riding the bow shock of a fleeting electromagnetic wave, all the entities that had ever been came alive, awakening, and fled outward in a great host to populate a multitude of worlds.

He awoke, dark eyes opening on the dim, swirling canvas of an interior existence, and in a soft, wondering voice whispered, I still live. . . .

Achmet Aziz el-Tabari.

I can hear you, Brendan. Thank you for calling me. I miss you.

I know. I too.

Can you still not say it?

No. I'm sorry. Believe me.

I do.

Do you understand what has happened?

I think so. What am I going to do?

Whatever you want. Fly. Live. Be happy.

You almost said it, didn't you?

Yes. Almost. Are you ready?

Yes.

Then: hold out your hands to me.

What is happening? I'm frightened.

Don't be, little one. I am passing over control to you. The world is yours, to do with as you please. You are to be the God at last.

At last?

To the end. Good-bye, Demogorgon. Take care of yourself.

Good-bye, Brendan. I love you.

□ □ □

The scene evolved out of nowhere, filling itself with the necessary denizens of life. In the highest spire of the Jeweled City on the Mountain an instrumentation chamber sprang full-blown into existence, already filled with the principal actors of the play it was about to perform. Demogorgon en Arhos, King, Lord of all he surveyed, Irrefutable Commander of the Universe, sat in a chair before his subjects, surveying them with satisfaction.

People sat before their instrument boards, reading information from archaic screens, all the people of Arhos and the world that surrounded it. Chisuat Raabo read the data for him, the beauty of Piruat Nahuaa by his side. Floating off to one side of the great chamber, as if supported by some viscous, invisible fluid, were Cooloil and her eternal companion, Seven Red Anchorelles. They might have been as they always had been, but they were changed. On the conic frustum of each hard-tentacled body lay a pair of slanted, glowing red eyes, that they might see at last by the light of the outer world. They waited together, overjoyed to live again, to be together, and to have each other for all time. The adventure for them was begun again.

In one dim corner of the room, lurking before the console of a mighty computer, squatted a great, lizardlike biped called Over Three Hills, one truly dead, reborn from the contents of a mere recollection.

Demogorgon let his throne spin slowly about. Standing behind his shoulder, hands clasped behind his back, feet planted slightly apart, Brendan Sealock, GAM-and-Redux, gazed calmly out across the scene, proud of the role he had played in making it come true.

Demogorgon looked around, smiling at his handiwork. It was done. "This is it," he called out. "Begin Systems Survey."

The two Seedees—the People, they called themselves now —swung into action. They swept to their work station, jetting through the very air, and plugged into an Action Panel, anchorelles foremost. Comnet-like, information flowed into their bodies, whirling meaningfully through their oil. Pher-

**404**

omones arced outward, forming audible words for the rest. "The repair work is complete," they said in unison. "All is in readiness."

The King nodded. It was good. *Should I let it take them by surprise? What a surprise that would be! The expression on Brendan's face would be worth the cost of his immortal soul, for such it now was. No, that would be petty of me. The effect of a warning might save their lives, at no cost to the drama of the thing.*

He turned to face the GAM replica. "Contact the humans on Ocypete," he said. "Tell them that starship *Iris* is ready to move. Warn them."

"At once," said the GAM. It tilted its head back to stare into the sky. Pearlescent oceans sprang forth, penetrating the crystal dome that topped the spire, and burst outward to the very ends of creation.

Klaxons hooted and the footfalls of hurried men thudded on through endless corridors. Technicians sweated over their minute task. Computers thought and the various enslaved functions that survived from the construct of Centrum worked at keeping up their end of the charade. Energy sources were concentrated and great ducts opened in the hull of Mother Ship, drinking in the lower atmosphere of the enfolding planet that had trapped them all in its womb for so long.

Imagination played its part, circuits working on overdrive, and the reality that it was derived from hurried to catch up with the commands that drove it. Deep in its matrices of data, the reborn mind of a child spun forth the web of its dreams, and the dream stuff caught fire and burned with a terrifying flame.

Beth sat in the common room, brooding before a de-opaqued wall, staring out across the flat vistas of Ocypete and the vast expanses of the ice ocellus they had so long ago named Mare Nostrum. *Who called it that? Demogorgon? She* tried to call up a memory of that first thrilling orbit about their new world but failed. *I can't remember.* She thought about the little Arab, now, she supposed, dead within the

**405**

electrochemical depths of Iris and Centrum. She looked up at the planet, still hanging in the sky. It was unchanged, still blue and semiclear, its rings undisturbed. A strange thing, that. She knew that Brendan and Tem were up to something but didn't know what. They never explain anything to me. Reasonable, I guess. I really wouldn't understand anyway. The man was dead and his body lived on, powered by fragments of Jana. How much of him is still alive in that body? Axie talked a little about it. Most of him is in there. Only the "I" part thinks of itself as Jana.

The events of the recent past warred powerfully against five hundred years of humanism. She knew that each human being was a unique, powerfully ensouled entity, an unpredictable absolute. Every moment of her consciousness proved it as surely as if it were etched in stone. There is a me that goes beyond my leaden flesh, and, even though I will die one day and it will stop, that doesn't mean anything. Why shouldn't it be so? My love of existence and other people, all the things that go into making me an individual? She had an image of herself as a machine, all the things that she truly was recorded on an old-fashioned reel of tape, able to be transferred at will to another machine, another muddy hulk. The idea was repellent. Things that lack meaning aren't things.

She passed on to gentler yet still more troublesome ideas. She had become united with the others during the battle in Bright Illimit. They had fought together and, she knew, facing the adversity and triumphing over it had made them close. What would the future bring to them? Undoubtedly they would return to Earth, and she had no doubt the feeling could be broadened and she would be strengthened by the knowledge that intimacy could be achieved through understanding. She puzzled over the strangest void, however— Brendan, Jana, and John were somehow totally excluded from her view of a common, joyous humanity. In fact her reaction to Sealock's resurrection was one of near revulsion. She felt infinite pity for poor Demogorgon, yet it did not extend to his repopulated body. And of course her feelings toward John were vastly complicated by all that had happened between them.

She thought of John and wondered, Did I do the right thing? I know we can never be right for each other. Our ideas about love and life are just too different. We can never come together, be one, like Seven Red Anchorelles and his Cooloil. How delicious to think of it being that way. . . . An image of John floated up before her face, still handsome and dark, brooding deep within his intelligence. Strange to think of him as such a cold, remote being at times, and so filled with his own uncertainties. It wasn't just nonsense that the fullness of him ate away at the very soul of her existence during DR. He existed in such a way that she couldn't exist as well. His ideas always ran away with him. Instead of feeling his emotions he felt *about* them. I cannot imagine, still cannot comprehend, what it must be like to truly *be* such a person. But it was more than that for him. Could it be for her as well? The very existence of another person lacked the all-important criterion of meaning. She shuddered. What an awful idea! That can't be right.

There was a noise and she looked up, jumping slightly, fearful that it would be John, come to try for her yet again. What would I say?

The slim form of Demogorgon stood there naked, in his sleek nonmuscularity somehow the perfect image of a human being. There was nothing about him that bespoke his history and his current secrets. "Hello, Beth," he said. "Can I come in?"

She nodded. "Hello, Dem . . . uh . . . Jana? Yes." She felt the hated confusion welling up. How do I deal with this?

The man smiled, walking toward her, and she found herself almost mesmerized by his slow stride. "It's hard, isn't it?" he said. "Call me Li-jiang. That's the name my parents and playmates had for me when I was a little . . . girl. After the break." He laughed softly.

"OK." She felt slightly breathless. She had been thinking very depressed thoughts, and she needed a diversion. "Li-jiang. Is that your real name?"

"No. My birth certificate read Hu Hua-hung. Changing names has always been a common pastime in the Sinified Orient . . . Mao Ze-dong. Ho Chi Minh. Chiang Kai-shek.

**407**

All made up, just like the names I used. It'd be pretty coincidental to have a Chinese revolutionary leader really be named Hair Enrich-East, don't you think?" Li-jiang was grinning. "Did you know that *caesaries* means 'a head of hair' in Latin? Very inscrutable."

"Very. I can imagine it, though. It's no more fantastic than having a French national hero being named Charles de Gaulle. Did Le Gros Legume make up his cognomen too?" Beth wondered at the course of their conversation. He's putting me at my ease, she thought. He? She? Ohhh . . .

Li-jiang was sitting at her side, still smiling, eyes shining with an eerie light, something of a reflection from Iris. He was running his fingers gently across her thigh, using just the right pressure, just the right feather touch, and Beth was horrified to notice that he had the beginnings of an erection. Demo? No, Jana. This can't be happening!

She clutched at his fingers, stopping their gentle, persuasive motion. "Demo, ah . . . Li-jiang. Please. What . . ." It was hopeless. The situation was making her totally inarticulate, gagging her from within. From nowhere, images from the depths of Centrum overwhelmed her. She saw all the times that this body had knelt before Sealock, begging for some kind of human response. She saw all the times that it had been taken advantage of, used and then sent away to suffer in silence. She felt like crying for him. The memories led to other images, the old, horrible scenes from Sealock's life, the whirling miasma of impersonal sexual contacts, the life-views that took such a narrow focus, zooming in on close-ups of women's bodies, yawning moist chasms of red flesh, ready receptacles for an insensate lust. She felt sick, and said, "Please. I can't."

Li-jiang's face, still smiling slightly, flattened out, then twisted with an evident dismay. "Beth. I . . ." He turned away for a moment, then returned to stare earnestly at her, eyes projecting some overwhelming emotion. "God, Beth. Please don't turn me away. Not now."

She felt a cold remorse, some being from deep within showing her stop frames from that last falling descent through the Illimitor World, and all the things they'd learned together. She thought of Demogorgon, then of Jana, and reached out to embrace Li-jiang, shaking.

John stood in the open doorway, undetected, invisible, watching the animals mate. Think about it, he told himself, consider it carefully and let the old emotions be pushed far, far down, where they ought to be. It might be moisture that was welling up in his eyes, but nothing spilled over, and everything could be denied. Watch her recede.

Taken as an absolute, what they were doing looked foolish. From the outside, there was none of the transcendent glory, no physiological overrides to stop the mind. He watched their rubbings and listened to them gasp, saw them burst into an athletic sweat, saw their faces become unintelligent, begin to gape and stare. It should have brought on a natural revulsion, but he felt that curious emptiness begin to fill him up once again. Talk to me, a voice whispered in his brain, but there was nothing to reply with. Self-conversation facilities can fall mute.

He pressed his cheek to the cool plastic liner of the doorway and watched, never quite aware of the things that were boiling below the event-horizon of his consciousness. Beth and Li-jiang moved against each other, grappling like gentle wrestlers, stroking, breathing, whispering to each other in what looked like some kind of planned cadence. Beth wrapped her legs around the man's slim thigh and ground herself against his flesh, cooing absurdly.

John felt a silent rage well up swiftly and then recede, consciously pushed back down into his depths by a desperate, rational hand. I could hate them, he realized, astounded. I feel almost . . . betrayed. Why is that? The hatred came back up, moving fast to avoid his clutches, and he was riven by its dense, boltlike quality. It seemed that Beth was hurting him purposely, in the most effective way, by now doing what he had wanted of her. He briefly imagined himself strangling the man's dark, slender throat. Déjà vu plucked at him.

Where have I experienced this before? He cycled back into his newfound memories, taken away from the tableau of man and woman, not quite hearing the sweet, awful words that

**409**

Beth was whispering now. I was in that room, talking to Ariane, back at the beginning, she seemed so nice and straightforward, I . . . No. This isn't. I'm not remembering something from myself. Who? It came. He was Brendan, pressed flat to an outer wall of the chamber that contained them, hating and imagining for all that he was worth. Images of Ariane and John coupling in the room, invisible eyes focused on sliding, horrid genitalia, words of love and devotion whispered in the darkness, close to the traitorous wells of inhuman, uncaring ears.

He looked out of his own eyes again, watching Beth and Li-jiang make love with an uncanny joy and happiness written large enough to perceive on their bodies. I would never have minded like this before, he thought wonderingly, so why is it this difficult now? I was always in favor of a free access, everyone with everyone, within the limits of some conceptual naturality. This is bad; I . . . I love her and want her for myself. I . . . He suddenly thought about Brendan and swam back through that recurring scene that seemed to be the man's worst-ever moment.

I see, he thought. We did nothing together, that night in that room, but his mind supplied all the images that it needed to generate those emotions, to feel so bad. He loved her more desperately than I ever loved Beth, or anyone, and every moment that took her away from him was a moment of agony to be endured. Every experience that she had without him was an experience lost to him, an agony to be endured. Love leaves its own special scars, I guess. I thought Beth and I were closer than Bren and Ariane could ever have been. Her denial of me seems that much more profound. We *know* each other.

It's silly, he realized, inexcusable, but . . . human. Now what do I say? I'm sorry? To whom? Beth? Brendan? Everyone? Maybe it doesn't matter. This hurts too much.

Li-jiang's penis, slimed with ichor, withdrew from Beth's body and the two embraced fiercely, laughing. They broke apart after a while and looked into each other's faces, smiling uncontrollably, and John turned back into his room, hoping that they didn't hear the soft whisper of his feet on the floor.

**4 1 0**

□ □ □

Brendan Sealock sat alone in front of the quantum conversion scanner and its attendant communication system, working. All indications had it that the experiment had been successful, and telltale signs on the various wave fronts seemed to say that the various subunits of Centrum, Bright Illimit, and Demogorgon were up and running. Krzakwa had gone away repeatedly during the course of the labor, drawn by some mysterious magnetism that was invisible to the other. Now he seemed to have departed for good. Sealock worked on through his cranial taps, whispering into the void, trying to reestablish communications with Demo in whatever guise he might manifest now as the primary controller function in Centrum.

It was a little bit like sitting in front of an old-time radio, a desperate air traffic controller, clutching a microphone, staring out of a stone tower into a fog-locked night, calling, "Flight X51A5, this is Mystery Lake Tower. Come in, X51A5. Do you read me? For God's sake, are you there, boy? Come in!" Brendan smiled faintly at the image. He's out there somewhere.

He scanned through the channels, seeing all the activity, trying to find the one that would let him talk to the man within again. At the moment of turnover, Demo's personality had been snatched away from him, rushing off to take its place somewhere within Centrum's complexity.

A bright light grew out of the mazy world that he searched, pulsing with insistent ruddy glow, calling his attention. He tapped onto it and listened. It said, "Hello, Bren," in a strange voice, an unknown one.

"Demo?"

"This is BI GAM/Red SRA 051B:08R0:A0N7."

"Oh." Visuals came on now and the face floated in front of him: it was his own, projected in reverse of its mirror image, real and so faintly alien to him. "Can I talk to Demo?"

"The Master is engaged in Assembly setup and is currently dealing with the Interpreter SRAs. He sent me to communicate certain things to you in his stead."

Brendan felt vaguely disappointed, knowing he'd wanted

**411**

to talk to the Arab, no longer caring about why. Still, this was probably better than nothing. "What things?"

"A preliminary survey of the working propulsion equipment in *Iris* indicates that most systems are functional. The power plant converter is, of course, still functional, and proves capable of using the lower Iridean atmosphere as fuel. The photon drive grid projects above the lithosphere and should be fireable, though it is currently immersed in dense, fluid hydrogen. We intend to light off shortly."

"You're going to fire off the engines?" He had a sudden memory of the thing they'd done to Aello, visions of fiery chaos, and thought of Jana. "What if the planet explodes?"

"Then it explodes. We're prepared to take that risk. This communiqué is a friendly warning to you all; it is a chance for you to place yourselves out of harm's way."

"What are the chances of success?"

"Odds of failure are calculated at 1:2027.048."

Brendan felt himself relax. All things considered, the chances of it working were pretty good. This would be something to see indeed. "OK. We'll begin our preparations immediately."

"Very well . . ."

"Wait a minute!"

"Input Queue NMI received. Proceed."

"Why are you doing this? I thought just being in control of a Bright Illimit-dominated Centrum would be enough for him."

"Long-term survival under those circumstances would have been a chancy thing. We mean to revive the mission. Enough submodules of Centrum itself survive to make that decision imperative."

"I see." He thought about it. It was probably a wise choice; Demogorgon would be giving himself a good reason to go on existing. And fantasies grow best in the hothouse climate of real adventure. "How long do we have?"

"Depending on the condition of the Uplink command system and how much rewrite the light-off procedures take, forty-seven hours, plus or minus eighteen minutes."

Brendan could have laughed—a week ago he would have.

They would have to get *Deepstar* reassembled more or less overnight. "I'd still like to speak with Demo."

"At the moment, impossible. Call me on this wave interface after the light-off procedures are up and running. We may be able to manage it then. End transmission."

"Good-bye."

The ruby light pulsed once, then went out, and the world within Iris withdrew from his grasp.

Brendan walked across the moor by the pool, his feet drifting, lightly touching the surface, propelling himself along with a minimum of effort, immersed in the complexities of now and then. Things had changed, and with them himself, and with him the others. Are the changes great ones? Do I *really* feel different? Do they? What have we all become? Something new? I wonder. Are we really different or is this just another masque? Perhaps we are just fooling ourselves, rationalizing away any responsibility for feeling any pain, our own and that of each other. I know now that I am capable of lying to myself. I saw that facility in other people all along, and saw it in myself . . . but I thought I was different. I thought that, so long as I recognized the capacity for self-deceit in myself, it was all right to do it. The lies and fantasies were OK, just as long as I recognized them for what they were and paused every now and again to laugh at myself, to be embarrassed at my own silliness. Perhaps I *was* right, and this is just that little refreshing pause, that little sense of the "I" in me being renewed. . . . Or maybe I'm still lying to myself. Again.

He walked on, immersed in a steep practicum of rumination, considering himself, both the natural being and the thing revealed by a forced march through his own past. I always used the memories, he mused, to wash away the terrors of any current hour that had grown too dense, too strong for me to handle easily. I reviewed myself mercilessly. He snorted, mirthless laughter emerging from his nose to echo in the silent, ersatz land. I did nothing of the sort! I used my memories in a self-serving way to absolve myself of any feeling I might have had about anything. Is that bad? Perhaps

**413**

not. A human being must have a means of survival, at all costs. Perhaps my greatest flaw lay in my lack of generosity toward others. They needed their lies and it was small of me to sneer at them. How much of that was unnecessary flaw and how much grew from my own needs? Did I serve a useful function in the midst of the others? I wonder if I really needed to . . . who am I to judge and who are they to judge me? Would I be happy in an existence divorced from all human needs, left to float my own way in a solitary jungle of thought?

He stood still for a while, drifting to a slow stop. Do I really need to consider myself as relating to other people, or is this all foolishness, self-torture? Maybe I've been right all along. Perhaps I should go with my old feeling, continue as I always have until death eats me up. Another bit of snide self-derision at that. No sense letting that poetic imagery louse up a fine bit of introspection. Those sorts of conventions are the ways people begin lying to themselves, whenever they find it necessary.

He felt like remembering then, and did, wondering if all the quietness, the need to forgive and forget and move on, were just a slow healing process, a recovery from the shock of his long fall through Centrum. When I emerge, will I be what I was before? What will that be? Am I sane or mad? Does it matter?

Memory struck.

Brendan Sealock stood atop the barrier wall of the Summit Garden of Prometheus Tower, the thousand-meter-high monad that stood astride St. James, looking out across the world, his land, hair blowing in the wind, fluffing it out so that each strand found a new position. He was barefoot, clad in a pair of blue bathing trunks and a white tank top emblazoned with the scarlet logo of Blood Street Skull, the music ensemble whose partisans had been terrorizing Long Island for the last few weeks. The wind was cool and pleasant, in a summery sort of way.

From here, from this vantage point, the world should have been green and beautiful, but it was ugly. The great towers of the eastern boroughs of New York Free City stood high in the west, growing out to meet him, steel and plastic monstrosities that glittered in the morning sun, throwing back rays of light, little flashes to catch his eyes. To the north, on the Connecticut shore, the low, sprawling outriders of a lawless Boston Megalopolis glared at him, layer upon endless layer of repulsive, antique buildings. In the south, the Atlantic Ocean was steel gray, and dead. The surface winds were calm and the sea was a worthless mirror.

There was a distant, echoing rumble from the northeast, and Nantucket Cosmodrome threw up a small rocket ship, a silver speck that climbed atop a spike of smokeless flame, narrow-swept wings that rode into the sky, accelerating, dwindling, as the man-made thing went to connect with low Earth orbit and the opening tendrils of the Deep Space Transport Network.

He looked down at the earth, far below. The square height of the shiny building gave him an odd, dwindling perspective. It looked like a triangle set on its apex. Small at first, he told himself, and then ever larger. The land was green about its base, another park, looking ridiculously small from a height, a narrow ribbon of jungle, then the concrete warrens of an older town.

I think, he realized, that I could jump from here. He imagined the wind whistling in his ears, the windows flashing by, the ground approaching, specks turning into people, looking up at him, mouths open in little Ohs of horror, scattering from the point of explosive impact, flinching from a splash of blood, crying out as they were wounded by bits of flying bone. I would become a gory crater in the ground. He knew it wasn't so, of course. There was terminal velocity to consider. I'd turn into a big, messy cross in the grass, nothing spectacular. Another asshole, trying to fly, flapping his arms and screaming to the end.

He turned to go away, to return to the woman who awaited him in the garden, waiting to collect him body and soul, to carry him off as a trophy, into the hinterlands. He went, shivering.

**415**

□ □ □

In the future another Brendan considered it dispassionately and thought, At least I'm free of those things now. Resurrection gives life its own special sweetness, at least for a little while. And continued . . .

The old-time Brendan walked through the halls of Tupamaro Arcology, padding forward on the balls of his feet, snarling deep within himself. I'll find them, he thought, and he did. He came upon them in a nexus garden, crystal fountain cascading up to the ceiling at back, standing before its watery beauty, holding hands and watching the liquid rise and fall, endlessly, mindlessly. Their fingers were intertwined and their hips were pressed together, warming to the touch of other humanity, preparing for their coming act of betrayal.

Brendan shouted, "Ariane!"

The couple sprang apart, loosing their close-held grip, and spun about to stare at him. The woman smiled and waved. "Oh, hello, Bren," she said. "Come and join us. This is nice."

*"Nice?"* It was a strangled word, gagging him, catching in his throat and making him inarticulate all at once. The planned revilements, the angry accusations faded, sinking down into a night of unrationality, and only action remained. He took a few quick strides forward and seized the small, brown-haired man, a coworker of hers he'd met before, grappling him about the neck. There was a brief, startled squawk, and then the man left his feet, flew through the air, arms whirling wildly, and splashed into the fountain. He jumped up, streaming water, spluttering, and waded out. He stared at Brendan for a moment, standing in the midst of a growing puddle, and then fled in squishy shoes, disappearing from the room and from their lives.

Ariane was planted before him, glaring, her fists doubled up on her hips. "God damn it, Brendan, what the hell is wrong with you?" He was silent, and she continued. "You can't rule my every waking moment. I *have* to be with other people sometimes. I'll go crazy if I'm around you all the time!"

He was helpless before her anger. "It's just . . . I love you, Ari. I can't stand it when . . ."

**416**

"Shit," she said. "You said you *wanted* to be here. You didn't have to come."

The implications of it enraged him. Didn't *have* to? And yet you wouldn't come to me. . . . He wished the words would emerge, but fear kept his feelings imprisoned. The parasite chewed on his soul, teeth searing him deeply. He raised his hand, as if to strike her, then let it fall. "No," he said, "I didn't have to come. But . . . here I am."

She took his hand then and led him away, his senses seeming dulled, the fires banked for another little while. They went home and made love with renewed heat.

That other Brendan, riding on the Now wave front of the future, surfing into the unknown, marveled at the things he'd felt. No one, ever before, no one now, no one ever again. Is that how it will be? Is that what I want? The tortures were hard, but the intervals between were so sweet and glorious as to make it seem all worth while. Will I have the will to go on?

One last memory came to plague and inform him, restoring the missing parts to his psyche. He was on a white sand beach somewhere on the shores of the enclosed fresh-water lake that Rio de la Plata had become, perhaps to the east of Buenos Aires. He was lying on top of Vana Berenguer, the epitome of mindless, animal thrusting, and her breath was a stentorian engine beside his ear. Her orgasm came as a squirming, high-pitched outcry, then his own injected semen deep into her body and they were still. His breathing slowed, stirring the tangle of her hair less and less.

He rolled off, flopping onto his back, and gazed at the pale blue sky, blinded by sunlight. He groped about, found his sunglasses, and put them on. The world was reduced to a fine sunset level, and he looked around. Vana was sprawled at his side, eyes shut, legs apart, gelatinous liquids marking the place of his entry and exit. She was breathing slowly, deeply, lips pressed tightly together, smiling slightly, perhaps concentrating on the fading sensations of satiation, prolonging the sense of contact and pleasure.

A human shadow fell across the blanket and he looked up quickly. It was Ariane, naked and beautiful. She was grinning

**417**

slyly, her teeth showing white against a dark tan. She raised one hand and waved, a little wiggling of fingers.

Brendan felt dismay. "Ari, I . . ."

"Oh, shut up!" She jumped into his lap and kissed him, grinding herself against the wetness of his groin. He wanted to speak, to say something, anything, but she wouldn't let him. She forced him back on the blanket, worrying at his body, bringing him up into a new round of responses, almost unwilling. She squatted over his face, making him service her will, lay on her back and pulled him onto her, guiding him into her, moving under him in cadences all her own.

Vana watched them and, presently, began to stroke his back gently, rubbing the sweat around, smoothing it into a thin layer that evaporated with swift coolness.

The future crashed down on him and began the present again. Well, he told himself, I wish I'd had that kind of cavalier attitude to play with. I certainly would have been happier. Is that what I am now? Perhaps I am reduced to their level. In a way I hope so.

He walked on, seeking the things that he knew would come, going to watch scenes that would prove certain things to him once and for all.

Tem and Axie were sitting together on a couch in the CM's common room, enjoying afterglow, watching the yet uncompleted actions of the little group before them, and talking quietly of the future. The time to come was a little hard to contemplate right now, but surely something would come of it all. Perhaps the adventure of Iris and Centrum was over, perhaps not, but *Formis Fusion* would come, bringing its horde of USEC scientists, and perhaps they would be allowed to join that group, contributing the knowledge that had already been gleaned. Brendan had promised a few surprises.

"What do you think they'll do?" asked the woman.

The Selenite shrugged. "I can't imagine. We've considered that they might punish us for all the destruction that's been wrought, but I don't think so. There's no jurisdiction out

**418**

here, not yet, and there are enough competing power groups in the Solar System that I imagine that we'll be safe."

Aksinia paused and reflected for a moment. "Here *we* all are, all except Beth. It would never have occurred to me before how John and Brendan and Jana are freaks, outside the accepted norms, and how their presence is so divisive among us. I thought I was the freak. They keep pushing the limits, shredding and reassembling themselves according to the moment. And everything—everyone—is grist for their mill."

Tem watched the cavorting bodies at his feet. "I don't think I know what you mean. I am a physicist after all. I am guilty too."

"We are all guilty," she said. "Only some of us are guiltier than others. Perhaps I am being unfair. It's so difficult to think without falling into these endless paradoxes. I will not cast the first stone."

"Is that all? Should *we* try? Would it hurt anyone to try and draw him in, make him a part of the group at last? We know that's what he wants."

"Do we? The only way we can tell is to not help him. Until he makes some effort at a rapprochement on his own."

"But he is my friend. Maybe . . ."

The door crackled open and they fell silent. Brendan came in and drifted down on the couch beside them, bouncing lightly. Tem looked at him apprehensively and then glanced across the room. Vana, Harmon, and Ariane were there, locked into a slowly moving, three-cornered embrace. How would the man react? There was no way to predict his response, but he was frowning already, staring at the three naked bodies. Krzakwa tensed himself against possible violence.

Brendan stared at them, absorbing the scene. It was, he thought, typically foolish-looking. It was unaesthetic, but he could imagine how the participants felt quite easily. Vana had her head buried between Ariane's legs and she was, herself, sucking on the man. Harmon had positioned himself poorly and so was forced to work on Berenguer with the fingers of one hand. Brendan's frown deepened. So it doesn't bother

**419**

me anymore. So what? All it means is that I don't care anymore. Why not? I guess I don't care about that either. I don't care about any of these people; I probably never have. Funny how I could mistake selfishness for love. . . . Was it that? Yes, on both our parts. The only person on this ship who was ever capable of real love was Demogorgon, and he was *really* crazy! It's probably just as well . . . or am I fooling myself there too? If so, I should accept it as being a necessary thing to me. A little voice from deep inside argued against that tack, but he ignored it. There were more important things to worry about now. He could fret and whine about the absurdities of his immortal soul some other time, when he was bored and had nothing better to do.

He turned to Tem and smiled. "I finally managed to get in touch with Demogorgon," he said.

Krzakwa breathed a sigh of relief. "Yes? How is he?"

"Hard to tell. I didn't get to talk to him directly, but he delegated a section of Bright Illimit to communicate with us. He seems to be doing fairly well."

"So what will be happening next?"

Brendan grinned broadly and a bit of the old satanity lit up his features. "A lot. He's planning to fire up the Mother Ship's photon drive."

Tem felt an electric tension growing in him, a stern jolt of horror that made him sit slowly upright, releasing Axie's hand. *"What?"* he cried, aghast. "Oh, Jesus!"

Sealock stood up, laughing at him. The old self returns, he thought, and welcome back to reality!

Things proceeded swiftly then.

The technicians among them swept into a nightmare matrix of action, pushing the others aside as they went about the tasks that would have to be accomplished so quickly. Tem and Brendan worked side by side once again, a team for just another little while, joined by the computer skills of Ariane and the limited technical competence that was Harmon's. Lijiang worked with them, contributing Jana's knowledge that had been carried over into Demogorgon's body.

*Polaris* was torn asunder, never to rise again, quickly reduced to a pile of reusable components. The colony was gutted. Domes were collapsed, cut apart, the CM was brought forth to stand once again beneath the everlasting darkness that Iris so easily dominated. The beambuilder machines went to work, resurrecting the matrix of girders that had once been the core of a ship. The Hyloxso matrices were recharged from the waters of their pool, the reactor was gingerly transferred back to its spot, and the ion drill, an engine once again, was slid back into its nacelle.

*Deepstar* was reborn, sitting on its four spindly legs upon the smudged and scraped ice, all its components restored as if they had never been touched. The colony site would never look as it had when they first arrived. It was a ruined space, littered with broken and useless throw-offs, dirty and, in its way, depressing. Where the domes had been there were porous-looking, circular discolorations of the ice.

They finished, exhausted, but it was done in plenty of time. In the end, there was more time to think.

Beth waited with the others, sitting in reclining chairs in the common room, finally content to let the imagery come in through Shipnet. John sat near her, seeming to seek her attention from time to time, but she ignored him. Some things were best left unsaid, some concepts left alone, by all of them now.

She glanced furtively at him and he caught her eye. "It's all right," he said. She turned away with evident difficulty.

The magnified image of Iris against a sky washed clean of stars splashed over her, and her attention was blissfully stolen by this familiar sight. She wondered if they shouldn't have left the little moon world by now, fled as far as they could from the Iridean system in the time that remained, but Brendan had insisted on staying. "This is going to be the greatest thing you ever saw," he told her, seeming childlike and excited, very much like a father she'd lost so long ago. "Even if we get killed, which I doubt, it'd be well worth seeing." So they stayed.

Li-jiang had sided with him in the decision. The Jana part of her, ever dominant, waited with keenly expressed anticipation. Perhaps the Demogorgon part held her horror at a world's destruction at bay. In any event, her mind was quiet. Suddenly, it happened.

Iris hung silent in the sky for one moment more, and then it changed. The atmosphere around the north pole began to well upward slowly, bringing muddy clouds from the depths to brighten the once blue mantle. Eddies formed about the area, giant hurricanes that whirled ever outward, carrying clouds in their wake. A spiral pattern formed about the north pole, a blossoming flower that grew until it covered the northern hemisphere. It paused then, hanging fire for a few minutes, and swept on until the entire world was a boiling nightmare. The clouds twisted and roiled like smoke, coiling patterns within patterns that formed and disappeared within a minute.

The air over the pole seemed to bulge, and a great plume of gas sprang up, pushing outward into the dark sky, highlighted by the rays of the distant sun. A dim glow formed at its base, a glow that brightened steadily, swiftly. "It's working!" whispered Sealock in a voice that was yet loud enough to fill the entire room. No one else felt they would be allowed to speak. The sound of breathing was loud and irregular.

The glow suddenly became an incandescent flare, blinding to eyes that had become adapted to the dimmer light, and Beth cried out, trying to turn her eyes away, unable to do so. The light blotted out everything else, and a dense beam of energy leaped up from the planet, hurling itself away into interstellar space. Someone seemed to cheer, a deep voice. Krzakwa? It didn't matter, now.

A world was on the move, pushing itself into the depths once again.

Deep within the immense confines of the Mother Ship, far within Iris, things were beginning to happen. With the torchfire of the photon drive lit off, pushing with a still small acceleration, the multiple throats of the intake mast began to open wider. A whirlpool formed in the southern hemisphere as the reaction chambers drank down vaster amounts of hydrogen, converting them to unimaginable energies along the

**422**

axial core. Just forward of Centrum's blue sphere, the control moment gyros, long still, began to spin again, counter to the direction of the planetary rotation. The world slowed fractionally and the rigid body of the lithosphere cracked like eggshell, shards buoyed aloft by the ringing tsunamis that crisscrossed the lowest stratum of the already boiling atmosphere. The gyros spun up, keening a wild, silent song, spinning ever faster, and then they tipped away from the equatorial plane . . .

Slowly, and at first imperceptibly, Iris was imbued with a will to go. Holding its fiery beacon aloft, the blue-white world seemed to shrug. The great clouds arrayed in waves swung across the globe faster now, and in close rank, as she began her turn. The emission beam of the drive described a slow arc against the background of the fixed stars. The gyros tumbled back to their neutral position and the turn stopped. Iris' axis of thrust was now pointed in its direction of travel.

The intake throats opened still wider, swallowing gigatons of atmosphere, and the deceleration began to increase. The planet slowed in its course, things unimaginable transpiring within, while the humans on Ocypete watched its developing splendor. The heavens were ablaze, bathing their minds in an eldritch, violet glow.

Common sense was violated at once. The moons did not fly off wildly into space, but their orbits began to stretch into more and more eccentric ellipses. They corkscrewed away from Iris' equatorial plane, their apirideons pointing toward the apex of the world's diminishing motion. The world in their minds shrank imperceptibly. As its velocity was slowly canceled, Iris' relationship with the sun changed as well, dying down from its original hyperbola through parabola and ellipse to the precise, curved line that drove a chord through the tiny circle that was Mercury's orbit. And so, no different than a rubber ball dropped from a ten-story window, Iris began to fall.

The gyros tipped again, reorienting the thrust axis, and then it began to accelerate down, full-throat into the gravity well of Sol. Precisely controlled, as unnoticeable as the hour hand of a clock, the stars began to shift. Whipped about their

**423**

lord, Ocypete, Podarge, and Aello assumed even stranger orbits, following a high-order rosette as they began to precess. And, with the passage of time, they settled into ever lengthening ellipses, their apirideons tipping farther and farther into the northern hemisphere. The exhaust plume of Mother Ship grew ever brighter and the temperature began to rise.

Somewhat more slowly, the badly disturbed ring particles held close to Iris' bosom followed suit, and the dazzling elastic band, no longer a thin line, began to stretch out and disperse.

Brendan and Li-jiang sat in the kitchen module of *Deepstar,* whipping up one of an endless series of the small snacks and quick meals that had sustained them during the day and a half since it had begun. The long hours of observation were taxing them, leaving them increasingly tired. Gathering in this experience, the two of them tended not to sleep, whereas once the initial excitement had died down the others had returned to more or less normal sleep patterns. They munched on thick, creamy yogurt loaded with fruit and unnameable crunchy particles. Suddenly the ship lurched, and a deep, groaning rumble filled the room, a palpable presence from the world outside. A gyro started up above their heads. Li-jiang shook her head and wiped at the yogurt that had dribbled unto her chest. "Another one," she said.

Brendan nodded abstractedly, gazing out the window at Ocypete's massively altered landscape. The hard radiation scattered from the photon beam had raised the ambient temperature to such a point that the highlands that composed much of the surface were subliming away and the inrushing pressure of air, for such the combination of noble gases, nitrogen, and CO could be called, was filling with white mist, undoubtedly methane vapor. "We should expect quakes," he said. "This place is undergoing a lot of stress."

"Too right. How much longer can we delay a lift-off?"

"Not much longer. I'd like to stay, but . . . we've got to get out of here in a few more hours. The peripheral particle cone of the exhaust is going to strike us by tomorrow noon at the latest." He laughed. "The fireworks'd be pretty to watch but painful to endure." The ship rocked slowly again and the plain outside crackled, electrostatic discharges released as the still supercold water ice was stressed.

Temujin came up into the room looking worried and shaky. Moonquakes were serious business in the underground cities of Luna. "Bren? We're getting some kind of an attention-getting signal over the QCS."

Brendan's face brightened. "Good. This is what we've been waiting for." He leaped down into the common room, reached out, grabbed a handful of leads, and, walking over to the nearby gang-tap, plugged into Shipnet, whole once again.

The voices started. . . .

Brendan?

It was a soft, gentle whisper, the old voice made real once more, calling to him out of a gray and misty sea.

Demogorgon? Are you all right?

Yes, my friend. I've never been better. I wanted to thank you for all that you've given me, at last. . . .

I'm glad you like it. What're you up to?

A lot of things. You'd be surprised.

I'm sure I would. What are you planning? That's what I meant.

I called to tell you about it. I've got to do a number of things to get the ship back on its original mission. There's a great deal to be done. . . . I'm going to dive Iris to within about five million kilometers of the chromosphere, burn off as much of this garbage as I can, and see if I can explode off all the rest. I'll use a phase boost and head for a globular cluster about six thousand parsecs from here. XGC5152, it's called.

Why there?

Pieces of the Centrum records indicate that's where the last functioning Seedee colony was emplaced. I want to see if there's anything left, maybe learn from what has developed over the course of a couple of billion years. From little acorns

**425**

. . . Maybe I could pick up another crew. I could use a few physical hands.

Sounds like a good idea to me. Listen, what's going to happen to the moons? Things're getting pretty hot up here.

That brought a ghostly chuckle.

I wondered if you'd ask. You'll like this one: this ship has some pretty sophisticated technology; things like the old SF tractor beams are available, working from a limited sort of gravity control that the Starseeders worked out when they discovered QTD, way back when. It's useless for spacecraft propulsion, but it can be used to do a lot of work when you've got a really big planet to use for a fulcrum. As soon as you get out of the way I'm going to bounce the moons. You'd better move quickly, though; there's not much time left.

I know. Where are you sending them?

There was a girlish giggle.

I've worked it all out: I'm going to send those cocksuckers billiarding through the Solar System! Once around Jupiter and through the belt, splitting them apart. I'm going to inter-act Aello with Phobos and drop her into a loose elliptical orbit around Mars. Instant economy. Then I'm going to let Podarge smash right into Venus. Instant Earth. Like it?

Yeah. There's only a small contingent of scientists on Venus, so it shouldn't be a big problem. How fast'll it hit?

18 kps. No big explosion. Podarge'll break up before impact and come down as an asteroid shower. Lots of steam. Earth will have a lot of work to do, still, but if they act quickly, get the preliminaries done in under a generation, people could be living on the exposed surface in less than two centuries. Maybe less, if they hurry.

What about Ocypete?

That's yours, pal, I'm going to drop it into a "Toro" orbit, right where it'll do the most good. I think you and John could find some use for a trillion ceus' worth of inner-system water. . . .

John and I?

Think about it. The others don't need you. I saw what was going to happen, back when I took the survivors through Bright Illimit that last time. You did a good job with that

GAM. They won't need either of you, but you may need each other. Promise me you'll at least consider the idea.

I already have. You could be right.

I know I am. You'll be feeling like your old self again in a few days, I think. The shock must be wearing off pretty quickly.

Yes. I wish I had you back, though.

Hey, that's nice to hear. If I were still alive, you'd have me blubbering all over you. Listen, I've got one last little present to give you. Latch this data . . .

It squealed suddenly into his head at nearly a million-kbaud rate. Brendan Sealock convulsed and fell to the floor, hemorrhaging from his nose and ears, body beginning to twitch into the opening phases of a grand mal seizure.

*Formis Fusion* had been dropping along a swift hyperbola toward Iris when the photon drive lit off. The new planet had been only a few days away and now . . . this. The crew and the scientists they had brought watched, thunderstruck, as the planet began to move. How could such a thing possibly happen? They called back to USEC headquarters on Ganymede, looking for directives, fearfully awaiting new orders. The command came back swiftly: Proceed with the mission. Go in there and take over. Now. They accelerated into Iris' path, entering into an interaction that they did not understand. The planet swelled before them, a boiling, flaming demon, no longer the gentle water carrier. They looked for her harpies and were horrified to discover that their positions were so far from the predicted place. What was happening? They looked at the glowing exhaust plume, at the dirigible infrastar, and consulted the capabilities of their spacecraft. A converted high-energy freighter, the ship had five-g legs. They fired up the engines, hoping that it was not too late. . . .

An hour and more passed and Brendan was sitting up in his bed, recovering, sipping a cup of camomile tea heavily laced with sugar. John sat in a chair beside him, watching him drink. "How are you feeling?" he asked.

"Better, I think. I've got a real skull-pounder of a fucking awful headache, though."

"Do you want anything else?"

"No, thanks."

"What happened?"

"One of Demo's brighter little ideas. He popped me with a massive data flow and sent it in at a machine-style flow rate. I'm surprised that the GAM let it happen. He must be running some kind of override to make it cooperate with the in-flight procedures that are outside its danger parameters."

"Was he trying to kill you?"

Brendan smiled wanly. "No. He just doesn't understand, yet, the full meaning of what's happened to him. A data flow rate like that one wouldn't faze him a bit. . . ."

John nodded slowly. "When are we leaving?"

"In a little bit. Listen, I've got some things I wanted to talk to you about. . . ."

Krzakwa popped into the room, gliding across the floor with a puzzled, concerned expression on his face. "Bren? We're picking up some kind of modulated radio signal from the space near Iris' outer atmosphere. . . ."

"Something from Demo?" Sealock was rising to his feet, staring wistfully at the planet, squinting into the glare of its bright exhaust.

"No. I don't know what it is. It's on the standard distress frequency, but the static from the drive is overwhelming it almost completely."

"Standard distress frequency?" He thought about that and then was horrified. "Holy Fuck!" He located a tap and inserted it. "You don't suppose . . ." The flash overloaded his visual cortex.

Outside, the others cried out and, when he opened his mind again to dancing shadows, he could see the billowing ball of a thermonuclear explosion blossoming out from Iris. At least in the fifty-megaton range, it left a great crimson pockmark in the planet's gaseous outer integument as it faded.

"Sweet Jesus," murmured Temujin Krzakwa.

**428**

"Yeah," said Sealock, his mouth dry. "Say good-bye to our friends from USEC."

"Stupid bastards," said Cornwell, and was surprised at himself.

Sealock turned to grin in his direction. "Yeah? There's a lot of that going around lately. . . . Come on, we've got to get this shit can on the road."

They went below, calling the others to action.

*Deepstar* squatted for a while in the ground-hugging mists of Ocypete, and it began. Opaque wisps of mist were drifting about, slowly rising toward the level of the CM. A view of the bottom part of the craft showed that the struts and nozzle mounting were hidden by the stuff. And the sky was slowly brightening, a twilight that masked the dimmest stars. Ocypete was breathing, outgassing the atmosphere that had once been hers, and more. She would soon have a substantial atmosphere instead of this thin muck. Dissolution would happen rapidly as methane, ammonia, and finally carbon dioxide evaporated. The pressure would rise over two, then three, bar, and the features on its face would be wiped out by clouds and haze. As it was, and would be, the little world could never again be the same. Already the stars were going out.

Tendrils of methane fog crept up the sides of the ship like some immense living force, striving to hold it down, engulf it, and hold it to its bosom forever. Moments were passing. The people inside the mechanism activated it.

New gases swirled out from the base of the ship, driving the mist before them, creating an island of stark clarity. Venting hydrogen, *Deepstar* teetered slowly, gently, then began to climb. As it rose, entering new regions of obscurity, Bernoullian eddies of vapor swept across and around the thousand complex surfaces of the ship, finally to be captured in the fountain of descending gas pressure to stretch and disappear. Safely aloft, the Hyloxso engines were lit off—a bulbous spike of bright flame appeared, red, then yellow, then a translucent white clarity that was defined only by its flickering outlines. Below, the mistscape had turned to jealous, hateful chaos.

**429**

The mists waited things out, then flowed back in to claim the spot that humans had vacated. All was quiet for a moment, the worlds swirling beneath the violet light of Mother Ship's flame.

A bright spark appeared in the sky, throwing new shadows. *Deepstar* fled from Iris on the flare of its heavy-ion engine, a dim, tiny light drifting slowly away into a deepening night.

We'll meet again, the world beneath them sighed on newborn winds, in another year.

When they were gone, five million safe kilometers away, a tall, periscope-like mast slowly rose from the dark sea of Iris. It looked around carefully, then began sighting in, first Aello, then Podarge, then Ocypete. An invisible beam of power flashed, carrying the deepest insight of Quantum Transformational Dynamics. Three jolts and the three moons, soared away, punted from the toe of a cosmic boot. Iris drove inward, still accelerating. At the precise moment when the proper velocity had been reached, the drive shut down and darkness closed in. The ship, enclosed in a still substantial world, fell on.

Shorn of its moonlets and ring, the world seemed infinitely forlorn and blank. For a long time, a year, Iris simply fell along the mathematically complex but nearly straight path that Demogorgon had chosen. Finally she came within ten million kilometers of Jupiter, into the sway of the much larger world, and her course altered, narrowing its incoming tangent to the sun to within finely tuned parameters. It was going well.

By this time the swirling bands that mottled Iris' cloud banks were a strangely entangled mess compared to the familiar bands and zones of Jove. The temperature rose, and the solar wind began to rip handfuls of world away. Newly ionized particles began to stream outward at a slightly different angle from the barely visible haze that trailed directly behind. Iris was becoming a comet, the greatest comet that ever could be.

Eventually it was visible from Earth, from the few dark regions where light pollution didn't blind the night sky. A second-magnitude star, not yet large enough to present a

**430**

disk, and growing to make a belt buckle for Ophiuchus. When it was lost again in the twilight glow, it was first magnitude, and slightly elongated. Then, from the vantage point of Earth, it was lost behind the mask of day.

The lengthening teardrop of Iris proper continued to fall. More than three times her original size now, sixty thousand kilometers in diameter, the world was larger than Uranus, though as solids vaporized and her atmosphere bubbled out to nothingness her density had become an insubstantial 0.3 $gm/cm^2$. Indeed, were it not for the high-albedo clouds which hid the depths of her atmosphere from the searching heat of Sol, she would already have been ninety percent gone. As it was, much of the hydrogen was still present, though ineffectively held by gravity. It would only be a matter of time before the small atoms found the trajectory that, in their wild oscillations, would allow them to leak into the void.

Iris was slowly developing into the traditional shape of a comet, lengthening at the point of her teardrop into a broad tail of streaming gas. At the height of her acceleration she had come to have a more or less regular flow pattern, flowering out from her leading hemisphere and spreading, to disappear in the dark halo of her nightside. Now, all pattern vanished and she was a featureless raindrop of milk, falling crazily toward the light.

The orbit of Mars passed unheeded. The sun waxed slowly brighter, with its promise of freedom and the Grand Design, the mission of ages, reborn. Iris fell . . .

As spring came once again to the northern hemisphere of Earth, billions waited in curiosity as the diffuse spot of light that was the approaching Iris climbed out of the morning twilight. Even before it could be seen in near darkness, the bright stain had spread over most of Scorpio's chelae, covering perhaps five times Luna's half degree. From this perspective, it was still only a slightly elongated circle of haze with a bright center. From night to night its progress through the stars could be seen, and, briefly, the demon eye of Antares was swallowed and disgorged. Soon the central spot alone was brighter by far than Venus, also visible in the early morning sky.

From the heart of the CFE, Ennis Cornwell watched as Iris reached out and, like her goddess namesake, stretched a bright white rainbow across the night sky. Radiating from a central sphere brighter than the full moon, hazy only at its outer edge, the comet sent out a huge tail, itself hugely bright and spreading to cover almost a fifth of the sky.

When he was a young man, this was the way he'd expected Halley's comet to look, waiting for its apparition in 2062. When it actually came, he could barely make it out against the haze-ridden sky, and really saw it only on the entertainment nets.

Now *this* was a comet.

And his son was riding it home!

A year and more had gone by, and now *Deepstar* orbited above Ocypete once again. Iris had gone past the sun, shedding all her mighty airs, and the drive had gone on again. Trailed by a bright, violet flame, the Mother Ship had driven off into the night sky, riding outward toward the stars and a world far away.

John and Brendan were in the common room of the CM, looking through a deopaqued wall at the fog-shrouded, half-molten world below them. The sun had taken over when the photon beam's nimbus no longer remained to heat the little moon. They were alone in the ship. During the long flight, contacts had been made and negotiations had proceeded. Expensive lawyers and diplomats were hired, judges bribed, and governments bought. A threat had been made by certain members of the Comnet Design Board; Maggie Lewis and Cass Mitchell had broadcast a joint statement, harsh and unforgiving in its tone. Do it, or else. . . .

Finally they had made rendezvous with a cruiser of the Contract Police, a ship that bore the guarantees for a Writ of Pardonment. The others had gone aboard, a unified group, never looking back. Cornwell understood that they lived in a giant palace somewhere, wealthy beyond imagination; he didn't know where and found that he didn't care.

**432**

"Well," he said, "there's our money. What shall we do with it all?"

Sealock leaned forward toward him and grinned. "I know, and I think you do too."

Cornwell nodded. "Maybe you and I can do business after all."

Brendan stirred suddenly and said, "There's a lot of money bubbling away down there. Money enough to build something really great. . . ."

"And so?"

"I never did tell anybody what was in that big data squeal, Demogorgon's last gift. . . ."

"I noticed that. I figured you had your reasons, as always."

Brendan nodded. "Well, it was the Starseeder technology."

John's eyebrows rose a trifle, a study in controlled inexpressiveness. "So. All of it?"

"Propulsion. Long-term life support. Genetic engineering. Suspended-animation techniques. The whole works."

"How much do you suppose it'd cost to build a good-sized starship?" They were sublime now, talking through the shadows of a too long past.

Brendan nodded toward Ocypete. "Not more than that."

John grinned appreciatively, wondering where all the old, horrid emotions had gone. He felt bland but wonderful. It had all been worth while, then. "Maybe it could be a lot less. This starship doesn't have to be *too* big. . . ."

"True."

"Who should we take along?"

"Does it matter?"

"No, I guess not." John was thinking, It certainly doesn't. We all loved each other and, in the end, it was as useless as anything could ever be.

Brendan's face turned serious again. "Why take anyone? Why not just us?"

John smiled and shook his head. "That doesn't sound like a very good idea."

"No, I guess not," Brendan said. "We'll think of something."

**433**

"Right." John started to turn away, then stopped. Well, he thought, if I put this off again, it's not going to get done. I *have* to. . . . "Bren?"

The other man looked up from a developing reverie.

Cornwell hesitated again, then said, "I know you've always mistrusted my, well, what I like to think of as my sincerity, but . . . Hell. Will you engage in Downlink Rapport with me?"

Sealock looked vaguely uncertain for a moment, not quite taken aback. "After all we've been through? You don't let go of things easily, do you?" He smiled then. "All right."

Feeling a small jolt of surprise, Cornwell thought, *All right?* But . . . Shit. Am I ready for this? I'd better be. . . . He thought about Beth and said, "At least you seem to know who you are."

Brendan turned away to look out at the bright clouds of Ocypete again. "We never quite learn, do we? You know, I feel that I've changed some—maybe I haven't. I could say a great deal about the changes that I think should have taken place in you, but I won't. Maybe that's the only evidence I have that those changes have taken place at all."

John nodded slowly. "Perhaps. And you can give me the only evidence that I know is true enough to accept. . . ." They were silent for a moment, then he added: "In any case —the world goes on."

Brendan turned and fixed him with an emotionless stare. "If you never lie again, you'll never speak truer words than those."

Five years later Temujin Krzakwa lay on his back on a padded seat in a shuttlecraft, awaiting lift-off from Baikonur Cosmodrome. A sickly sweat bathed his face and desperation twisted with cold fingers inside him. He watched the countdown clock on the bulkhead move inexorably toward zero, and he thought about what had happened.

It was an unpleasant thing to run away like this, but it seemed the only way. They had him *imprisoned.* Sometimes he thought back to his youth on the Moon and remembered how he'd longed to get away from that congenital entrapment, escape to the lovely freedom that was Earth. Freedom! It had

**434**

a bitter taste to him now, and he could remember the excitement with which he'd fled Lewislab eight years ago, on his way to a rendezvous with the Triton colonists.

Why has it come to this again? he wondered. No answer? Then why had he slowly oozed out of the solidarity that the others had found in the great château by the Dzungarian Gates? They lived lives of contentment and only wanted him to be happy. . . .

His lips twisted with an almost uncontrollable rage. He damped the feelings down and exhaled heavily. Contentment? Jesus, what's *keeping* this thing on the ground? He looked up at the clock again and felt a sudden, scalding nausea. The progression of numbers had been replaced by a flashing red bar. Emergency hold.

He sat forward and looked out the porthole of this venerable Russian spacecraft. There was a handsomely designed sportsGEM racing across the parched concrete toward him in a cloud of dust, pursued by the flashing blue lights of spaceport security. The police caught up with the intruder, quite nearby now, and forced it to a stop. The hovercar's door popped open and a little figure jumped out. It began running toward the ship. The police pursued the runner on foot and soon had the tiny figure pinned to the ground. When they were gone, the shuttle lifted off only a little behind schedule.

Comforted by the roaring engines and the inertial pressure on his back, Temujin began to relax. But he thought, I'm sorry, Axie; I just couldn't take it. You were just another childhood to me: you put me back on the Moon.

Tears tried to well up in his eyes, but he suppressed them successfully.

The armored inner airlock door of interstellar exploration vehicle *Deepstar 1.5* slid back into its interhull recess and Temujin Krzakwa looked into the brightly lit space that held Brendan Sealock and John Cornwell.

In their mid-forties now, the two had changed only a little, taking on just the faintest patina of middle age. Cornwell was a little thinner. His face seemed to foreshadow a dour gauntness to come, and a few permanent lines had appeared around his mouth. Sealock seemed the same at first glance, but a very small amount of subcutaneous fat had appeared under his skin and it made his face a little softer. The contours seemed to have smoothed. . . . Tem supposed he must look to them now like some giant bag of ambulatory cellulite. The image amused him.

Sealock held out his hand and said, "Welcome back, asshole. I knew you'd show up."

"Did you really?"

"No. But I always hoped I'd have an opportunity to say that to you."

Tem turned to face Cornwell. "What about you? Do you have anything sarcastic saved up?"

He shook his head. "I'm afraid not. I'm glad you're here."

"So am I." As they walked up the corridor toward the control room, Tem said, "It was too much."

Brendan turned to look at him curiously, read familiar signs, and nodded. "Relationships like that, ones with expectations, usually are."

And John said, "Maybe that's why we're here. I guess this *is* what I was looking for, after all. Maybe there are worse things than being alive. . . ." There was a program in the machine now, an interesting one.

Assembly. End. Go.

About the Authors

William Barton is the information systems manager for Health Sciences Consortium, a nonprofit medical/educational publisher. A member of the British Interplanetary Society, he is also a computer programming consultant and freelance writer. He is the author of two previous science fiction novels, *Hunting on Kunderer* and *A Plague of All Cowards*, and has written for such diverse publications as *Final Frontier* and *80 Micro*. He lives in North Carolina with his son, Matthew.

Michael Capobianco is a founding partner and C.E.O. of Not-Polyoptics, a software company specializing in orphan computers. An amateur astronomer and eclipse chaser, he is a member of the International Occultation Timing Society. The satellites of the outer Solar System as revealed by the *Voyager* spacecraft continue to fascinate him. He has just finished his first solo novel, *Burster,* to be published by Bantam Spectra in the summer of 1990. He lives in Northern Virginia with his wife, Lise.

Mr. Barton and Mr. Capobianco are presently at work on their next collaboration, *Fellow Traveler*.

BOOKMARK

*The text of this book was set in Baskerville, composed by Berryville Graphics Digital Composition, Berryville, Virginia. The display types are Elan Black and Elan Book, set by Zimmering Zinn & Madison, New York. The typography and binding design are by Paul Randall Mize.*